The Kingdom Come Series

Book Two

The Kingdom Come Series

Book Two

Penance

by

Brandy Ange

Printed in the United States of America

First Printing, 2021

ISBN 978-1-947992-03-0 (paperback)

Marturia Publications

www.brandyange.me

For Distribution Inquiries:
Ingramspark
Global Headquarters
Ingram Content Group
One Ingram Blvd.
La Vergne, TN 37086

For Sandie Ange

I wish I wrote faster

Acknowledgements

I would like to thank all of my friends and family who patiently endured conversation after conversation filled with stress and anxiety about this books. I would also like to shower a massive amount of thanks to those who sacrificed their time to give me feedback and a second pair of eyes, Jo Beth Elliott, Debbie Broyles, and Marcia Eatmon. A special shout out to Mollee Holloman for some of the most inspiring coffee dates of my life, full of fresh insights and new perspectivies. My eternal heartfelt gratitude goes out to three specific teachers, professors, and role models I looked up to and who not only encouraged my writing, but who helped me to develop as a person, Beth Kraft, Bob Ebert, and Rafael Rodriguez, I couldn't have done any of this without you. I would also like to thank Phil Thomas for all of his artistic contributions as well as brainstorming conversations, which helped me to develop the world and shape the story. Finally, a special shout out to Marshall Rushe, thank you for your support, and welcome to the cast!

Praise and glory and wisdom

and thanks and honor and power

and strength be to our God

for ever and ever. Amen!

Revelation 12:7

Books by Brandy Ange:

Choose

Or Be Chosen

"Those who escape Hell
however never talk about it
and nothing much bothers them after that."
-Charles Bukowski

Achaia woke up wiping glitter out of her eyes. "What the-?" She had forgotten about letting Yellaina and Amelia do her makeup the night before. They had taken her out for a girls' night to celebrate her seventeenth birthday. She rolled over and heard the crunch of hairspray in her hair, her curls no longer malleable, but stiff and rigid.

As she stood, she risked a glance in the mirror; she jumped back, immediately regretting that decision. Her eyeliner had smudged down under her eyes, and her mascara had run, transforming her into a ginger raccoon. A glittery, ginger raccoon. Her hair stuck out in every direction including, unfortunately, straight up. No demon she saw during her visit to Hell a couple months before could compare to the grizzly sight before her.

Achaia grabbed her towel from the hook on the back of her door and opened it to proceed into the hallway. "OH SH—," her dad screamed, nearly jumping out of his skin at the sight of her. "I mean—morning, sweetheart."

"Nice try, dad," Achaia said still holding a hand to her chest and leaning against her door for support, after jumping back herself.

"So, you got in late. How was ladies' night?" he asked leaning against the wall.

"I don't know how you're doing it." Achaia stared at her father in disbelief. "I can't stand here just *knowing* what I look like. How are you actually *looking* at me? I think I'd scare the crap out of Lucifer right now." Achaia paused; her dad just looked at her blankly. "Let me take a shower and I'll tell you all about it after."

"Deal," her dad said releasing his breath and looking away quickly with relief. He regained his composure slightly with an apologetic wince back at her before walking to the living room.

After three shampoo treatments, four face scrubbing pads, and one very torn up loofah, Achaia emerged from the bathroom looking and feeling more like herself again. "Oh, my

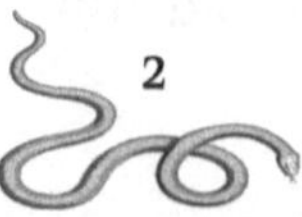

go...sh," Achaia caught herself, collapsing onto the sofa in her comfiest pj pants and tank top. Her hair was tossed up into a wet messy bun, which dripped cool water down her neck. "I can breathe again! Like, through my pores!"

"Glad to hear it, and not see it," her dad said coming over with two mugs of hot chocolate with extra whipped cream on Achaia's.

"Mmm, thank you," she said taking the cup from his hand. The weather had started to warm with spring, but the air still had a bitter chill to it some days. "Washing off the blood and guts from a hoard of demons was easier than getting all the mascara out of my eyelashes. If they force that crap on me again, I'm demanding it not be waterproof."

"Definitely how you should dress for battle. Your enemies will flee before you." Shael laughed.

It was nice to hear her father laugh, but Achaia scowled. "Ha. Ha. Ha," she said sarcastically, rolling her eyes.

Shael sat next to her. "I mean great job being terrifying, Hun. I can't teach you that kind of shock-factor. That just comes naturally!"

"Were you just sitting around, thinking of these, while I was in the shower?" Achaia cocked an eyebrow.

Shael smiled. "Maybe… So, tell me about your night." He relaxed, leaning back into the couch next to her, still chuckling to himself.

"Well, we grabbed dinner at a place downtown before the show. It was so good! Of course, Yellaina told them it was my birthday so they did the whole bring-me-dessert-and-sing thing."

Shael smiled. It had been a long time since Achaia had felt this normal or seen her dad this relaxed. After Lucifer had taken him and held him prisoner for months in a frozen circle of Hell, they had both been a little on edge. It had taken weeks for Achaia to be able to sleep through an entire night. She had only been able to rescue her father with the help of her friends and they barely made it out alive. She still had nightmares. She'd never ask, but she wondered if her father did, too. Most of their references to the event were done casually in passing, as if that would somehow make it feel normal, and like it wasn't a big deal. Ironically it was the normal conversations like this that felt unusual.

"How was the show? What did you see again?"

"We saw STOMP. They drum on trash cans and stuff; it was awesome!" Achaia air drummed a little beat on the air.

"Nice, then what?" Shael asked, setting his empty cocoa mug on the coffee table.

"Then Yellaina really wanted to go dancing. She said the show made her want to 'get up and move.'" Achaia made air quotes with her fingers. Yellaina was her girly-friend. She'd never had one before; girly-girls had always annoyed her. But Yellaina was so kind that her girliness was just endearing.

"Where did you go?" Shael asked looking more apprehensive. Her father had always needed to be protective of Achaia, and letting out the leash was a struggle for him.

"I don't know what it was called, some small little club down a back alley, with a bouncer that reminded me of Bale, and dudes offering us drugs at the entrance."

Shael's eyes grew wide, before he cocked his head in disbelief.

Achaia rolled her eyes. "I don't know, dad, it was just a little place that played live jazz music. Emile and Olivier actually met us there. Emile loves jazz. I guess he goes there a lot. The servers already knew his order." Emile was an old soul; Olivier was his younger brother and Achaia's best friend. They had bonded over a shared love of classic comic books.

"Well it sounds like you had a great time." Shael smiled, looking at Achaia's hot cocoa. "As soon as you finish that we'll start training."

"I think I'm going to need something a little stronger," Achaia said sighing, still not fully awake.

"I'm not letting you have whisky in your cocoa," Shael said, shaking his head.

Achaia laughed. "I meant coffee!"

"I'm not letting you put whisky in that either…" Shael smiled at his own dad joke, and Achaia rolled her eyes. "Okay, well, you go get dressed, and I'll brew some."

"Deal." Achaia took what was left of her hot chocolate to her room to change. "What are we doing today?" She called from her room, as she dug through a box looking for yoga pants. Achaia and her father had moved too often to ever bother with fully unpacking.

"More defense, and then a lot of intel," Shael said. Achaia could hear him taking out the French press.

"When are we going to start offense?" The question came

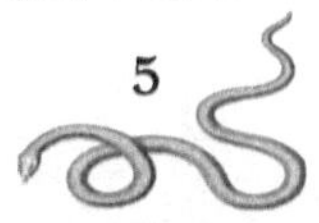

out a little whinier than Achaia liked. She pulled a sports bra on over her head, and got her arm caught in the neck instead of the arm hole. She had thought training with her father was going to be exciting; her father was, after all, the most legendary and highly skilled fighter the Nephilim had ever known. After their fall from heaven, though, the angels had held him responsible and exiled him to live as a human. But he was still a father, and Achaia felt like he was playing it safe with her training. As if maybe, if he didn't teach her how to fight, she would never need to. Achaia was gifted in her own right, though, literally. Achaia's spiritual gift from God was an inherent ability, but she still needed to learn how to make the most effective use of it.

"Whenever I feel like you could live long enough in a fight to be able to use it," Shael said pulling mugs out of the cabinet.

Achaia let out an angsty moan, as she picked up a shirt out of a pile of maybe-potentially-clean clothes.

Noland stood alone in his bare room, staring out of the single window as he talked on the phone. It was dark, as he had neglected to turn on the light, relying on the small amount of natural light making its way in. "Okay, thanks for the call." Noland hung up the phone, and tossed it onto his bed.

He'd spent the last few weeks developing his theory that not everything was right with the council. They had been cold and distant since everything that had happened with Achaia. Even though he had claimed his seat on the Council of Elders, as the

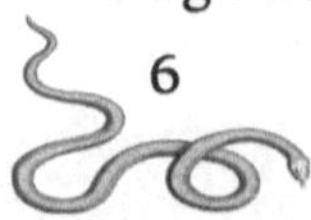

first born of his generation, they had been less than forthcoming with any real plans or news about what exactly was going on. They just insisted that he focus on his job as a Guardian, a sort of bodyguard, to Achaia. Considering the fact that they didn't particularly like or trust Achaia, that was a red flag.

The terrorist attacks hadn't stopped with the bombings he and his friends had witnessed in Moscow during their stay at the safe house there. Noland himself had actually been blown up by one of the bombs, and he had the scars on his torso to prove it. He had only been saved by the grace of God, and his gift of being able to handle fire. In the month or so that had passed, safe houses all over the world had experienced near-misses. The only thing Noland was able to get out of the council, though, was that Lucifer must be behind it all. Noland didn't buy it.

Pulling Achaia out of public school had been Noland's idea. Things were still a little awkward between them since Achaia found out that Noland had kept to himself the knowledge that they were soul mates. He could understand her concern. He was trying to give her some space to process it all. It must be strange for her, being raised as a human, to recognize something truly mandated for angels. Humans had the free will to choose. Achaia, being half-human, had the freewill to choose, while Noland didn't; he was bound to her.

He was a little concerned that it was taking so long for her to come around to the idea. He was hoping she would have warmed up to him again before her birthday. But he hadn't wanted to ruin her night by showing up if she didn't want him there.

He looked again at his phone. Bale had tried to get more information on all the attacks, but the council was giving him the cold shoulder as well. Noland had told Bale all of his suspicions, and Bale was in agreement that something shady was going on.

At one point, Noland had tried talking to Emile's father, but he insisted that Noland was being paranoid, and that he needed to just drop it. Noland wished his parents were still alive to talk to about all of this. He especially wished his mother were there to explain women… Sometimes it sucked being the only one whose parents had died, the only Nephilim anyway. Nephilim didn't usually die, and until Noland's parents were killed, they hadn't even realized it was possible.

Noland realized he was pacing and stopped He looked down at the rug that ran alongside his bed; it now had a path worn into it from the last few weeks of this kind of behavior.

"This is ridiculous." Noland shook his hair out of his face, and pulled it back into a ponytail. He knew he should probably get it cut, but that had fallen pretty low on his list of priorities with everything going on. He grabbed a light coat, so he wouldn't stand out in just a t-shirt. Spring had stayed cold this year. Though April had just turned to May, there were still some pretty cool days, especially in New York. It was like even the climate knew things were heading south in the spiritual realm.

Noland opened his door to leave and found Emile standing there, about to knock. "Hey."

"What's up?" Noland asked.

"Just seeing if you were going to show your face today," Emile smiled.

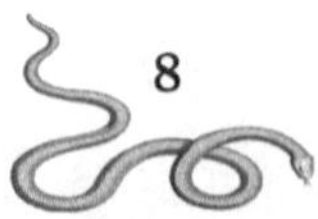

Noland had been unintentionally isolating himself, while he searched for proof of foul play on the council's part. That was probably why he was going a bit stir crazy.

"Yeah, I was just going to go check on Achaia. I want to at least say happy birthday."

"About time!" Emile said, relieved.

"What?"

"You've been avoiding her for weeks," Emile stated flatly.

"I didn't think she wanted to see me," Noland justified.

"Did you ever consider that maybe she is thinking the same thing about you?" Emile's lips stretched thin as his eyebrows raised, looking at Noland as if he really expected him to be more intelligent.

"I—," Noland stopped. "Well, no."

"I'm going to break my rule this once, because you guys need all the help you can get." Emile was able to feel other peoples' emotions, but he had a rule about not sharing the feelings of people he actually knew with other people they actually knew, something about respecting privacy and whatnot. Emile pushed Noland back into his room and gestured for him to sit on his bed. Emile looked pale and thin. Noland knew that with all the attacks and mass panic that he must be feeling more stress than ever and was probably exhausted. But Emile never complained. He didn't need to for Noland to see the wear on him in the dark circles under his eyes.

"Okay, help." Noland waved his hand palm up, for Emile to proceed with his expertise.

"Alright. She doesn't hate you. She was a little ticked that

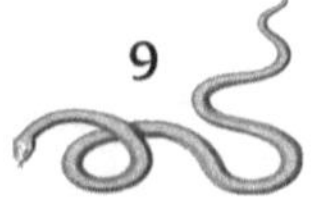

you didn't tell her you knew that you were mates, but she was mostly shocked and a little embarrassed. She felt crazy guilty about going after her father and basically manipulating us into following after her. Things didn't go so well down there, which was a bit traumatizing, and that made her feel even guiltier. If anything, she has been giving you space because she probably thinks you're angry at her or hate her for all of that. You avoiding her just gives her more reason to think that is true. Now grow up. You guys seriously need to learn to talk to each other and stop assuming you know what is going on in the other one's head, because unlike me, you suck at it."

Noland sat dead still with wide eyes. "Is that all?"

Emile took a deep breath. "You guys may be mates, but you still have a long way to go in getting to know each other." Emile paused. "Okay, that's it."

"Okay, sweet." Noland stood up. "Good talk, man." He clapped Emile on the shoulder.

"So, you're going to talk to her."

"Yeah, I'm going to grow up on the way over, too." Noland smiled.

"Finally! I was wondering when that was going to happen!" Emile laughed.

"You're right, I am terrible at feelings." Noland shrugged. "It doesn't help that girls experience them in rapid succession, and in abundance…" Noland was used to leading but trying to be someone's partner was completely new to him.

"Well, I hate to break it to you, but you've got a long road ahead of you; this is nothing. Just wait until you accidentally

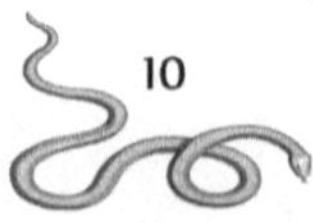

insinuate that she looks fat in battle gear."

Noland looked at Emile, horrified. "Is that something you really think I'd do?"

"Not intentionally, but let's be real, you're not really great with girls."

"I'm a Nephilim. I never thought I needed to be! How was I supposed to know my mate would be part-human, and have a choice?" Noland stopped, thinking about what all that actually meant. Hopelessness washed over him. "What do I do?"

Emile smiled, "Flirt."

Any remaining hope fled. Noland sighed. This was going to be ugly.

Achaia and her dad stayed on the roof until both of them were completely exhausted, but only her dad was willing to admit to it. "Break for lunch?" Shael suggested.

"Sure," Achaia said pulling her hair out of the ponytail that was barely holding it up. "I'm kind of in the mood for grilled cheese and soup."

"When are you not?" Shael laughed. "Well, we are actually fresh out of soup, since you ate it all. So why don't you take a shower, and I'll run to the store and get some more."

Achaia smiled guiltily. She did have a thing for soup and crispy grilled cheese. "Okay," she said throwing her hair back up into a tighter ponytail. "But grab some roasted red pepper and tomato."

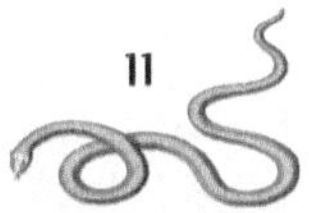

"Will do."

Achaia headed straight to the bathroom once back inside the apartment. She quickly stepped out of her sweat drenched clothes and thought that she might take a bath instead; she could already feel her muscles growing sore. She remembered that she had some bath beads still packed in a box in her room and wrapped herself in a towel to retrieve them. As she crossed the hall there was a knock on the door.

I bet he left without his keys and locked himself out. She laughed at the idea as she opened the door. "Forget something?" Her smile fell. Noland stood in the doorway his face going from shocked to amused. "Oh my go-sh." Achaia said reaching to cover more of herself with the towel.

"Expecting someone different?" Noland joked, walking inside.

"What are you...? Get out! Can't you see it's a bad time?" Achaia fumed, any pleasant opinions of him fleeing her mind.

"I see a lot of things, none of them bad." Noland's face flushed, he looked surprised at himself. "That came out—"

Achaia felt her face warm. *Are you serious!* She thought, and grabbed her dad's raincoat off of the rack to cover herself.

"It's not like I haven't seen you in less," Noland pointed out, digging himself deeper. Achaia remembered the time he saved her from hypothermia when their plane had crashed in a blizzard. At the moment, it didn't make her feel any more positively about him, though.

"Okay, that's it. You need to leave." Achaia could feel her face growing red.

"I just wanted to make sure you made it home okay last night. Since everything seems fine, I'll go," Noland said, but didn't move for the door.

"Well done. Your Guardian duty is fulfilled." Achaia tapped her foot impatiently.

Noland's face fell flat. His smile disappeared, and he looked almost hurt. He shook his head and looked at the floor. "Kaya," he said softly. He was the only one who called her that, and she secretly loved it. He looked like he was trying to find words. "Actually, I wanted to wish you a happy birthday, and give you this." He handed her a package, which she took and held in a way that covered more of her chest. "And see if maybe we could talk."

Achaia felt her wall of sarcasm falter. "Maybe some time when I'm clothed?" Apparently, it was a strong wall... Noland seemed to understand that she didn't mean it cruelly. He also seemed to just remember that she wasn't, in fact, dressed.

"Oh, right..." he blushed. "You don't look fat in that towel."

"What?" Achaia stepped back in surprise and glared at him with a look aimed to warn him to tread carefully.

"I said you *don't*."

"But why?"

"Because you're not fat."

"No, why would you say that? Or feel the need to specify?"

"Because Emile—" Noland sighed, "nevermind."

"Emile what? Thought I look fat?"

"N—" Noland stopped. "Would you be mad at him

instead of me, if I said yes?" Noland smiled weakly, cocking an eyebrow.

"Probably not." Achaia said, trying not to laugh.

"Then, no. No, he didn't." Noland said smiling and shaking his head.

"Okay—" Achaia looked down at her feet. After an awkward moment she sighed and looked everywhere around the room except at Noland saying, "yeah, I'm still not wearing any clothes. So…" Only then did her eyes land on him.

"Right. Um, text me when you're free. Maybe we can go to the Farmacy and…"

"Yep, sounds good." Achaia smiled awkwardly, shooing him toward the door.

"Okay, bye," Noland said walking out the door quickly. She shut it behind him, pausing to try and process what all just happened.

"That was just so much awkward," she said to herself, turning to go back to her bath.

As the bath water ran, Achaia sat on the edge of the tub and unwrapped the package. It was a copy of Charles Dickens' *Great Expectations*.

"Okay?" Achaia cocked her head, and opened the cover. Inside was an inscription jotted in ink, and Noland's old school handwriting; it was as neat and as intentional as him. She didn't know anyone else who wrote like that.

Kaya, here's to picking you first.

Happy birthday,

~ Noland

Achaia felt her hands fall to her lap holding the book. Her eyes scanned the room as if it would be written on the walls- what she should think, how she should feel, and how she should respond.

She sat the book up on the back of the toilet and stared at it through her entire bath trying to figure out what he could possibly mean.

Dealings with demons were easier to navigate than the perils of dating.

Shael returned with the groceries, and poured the soup into bowls to microwave as he started on the grilled cheeses.

Achaia came out of the bathroom wrapped in a towel and clutching a book.

"Getting in a little R and R?" He cocked an eyebrow as he read the cover. "Since when do you read Dickens?"

"I don't. Noland came by and gave it to me for my birthday." She looked a little perplexed.

"Doesn't he know you're more of a comic book girl?" Shael asked, flipping the sandwiches in the pan. He wasn't sure why, but this gift annoyed him. "Now may be a good time for

15

some fatherly advice; never date a guy who tries to change you, or tells you in various ways that he doesn't think you're smart."

Achaia rolled her eyes. "I don't think that is what he is trying to say. I mean, I think it's supposed to mean something, but I don't get it— like an inside joke I forgot…" Achaia stared at the book in her hands.

"Did he say anything when he dropped it off?" Shael asked, tossing the grilled cheeses onto plates and pulling the soup out of the microwave.

"Um, well, it was just an awkward conversation, but he didn't say anything about the book." Achaia's face turned pink. Shael was trying really hard not to hate this Noland kid. To be fair, he didn't actually know the guy. Shael didn't like that he never really came around. Olivier practically lived at their apartment. Shael wished Olivier was Achaia's soul mate, but he had to assume that God knew better than he did.

"Well, I'm sure you'll figure it out." Shael set lunch on the counter, and Achaia sat down.

"Okay, so, afternoon training is intel. You eat, and I'll talk." Shael took a bite out of his grilled cheese, realizing how hungry he was. "Before you study your enemy's weaknesses, you should have a full understanding and respect for their strengths. The last thing you want to do is overestimate their flaws and get cocky."

Achaia nodded as she sipped her soup. Shael smiled. It was during moments like this in their training that he regretted not telling her the truth sooner. He could have raised her like this, talking battle strategy over dinner, and weapons over breakfast.

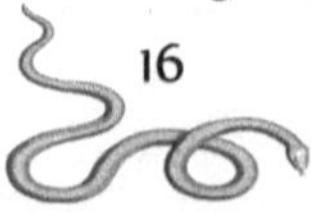

She was his daughter up one side and down the other.

A balloon of pride inflated in his chest when he saw how eager she always was to learn. She worked hard, and always gave training her everything. Shael wondered if that was only because she truly understood the life or death importance of it now, or if she would always have been this thirsty for what he had to teach her.

"So, what are Lucifer's strengths?"

Shael sighed. "I think the list of things that aren't his strengths would be shorter. He is a very skilled fighter, a strategist, a master manipulator, a liar, a natural leader, and more charismatic than Hitler."

"And I'm an Irish-Israeli redhead. I should have him quaking in his boots." Achaia shrugged casually, but Shael could see in her eyes that her casual air was a cover. He didn't need to tell her to take this seriously. She'd already experienced a hint of Luc's terror.

Shael smirked. "Let's start with manipulation. That's usually his preferred method. If he can get you on his side, or to do his dirty work for him, he prefers to put off a fight. Not that he isn't capable, but he is like a sadistic cat who likes to play with his food before he eats it."

Achaia grimaced. "I guess in this instance my stubbornness might actually be an asset? Who knew!"

Shael smiled. "I'm actually kind of glad you inherited that trait from me. I've always really loved that about you. Initially I wondered if that was your spiritual gift."

Achaia laughed.

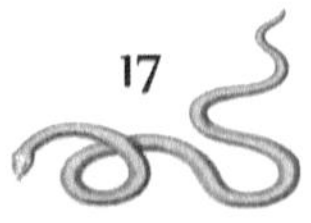

Penance

Once again, Shael regretted the years he had wasted in secrets.

Achaia and Olivier rounded the corner, and opened the door to the Farmacy. "Oh thank God," Achaia said, taking a deep breath through her nose, making her stomach growl.

"Hey Achaia!" The guy behind the counter wore a vest over a dress shirt and an old grey ascot cap. He was twirling a glass in his hand before making someone an egg crème. "Hey Olivier!"

"Hey Marshal," Achaia said, leaning up against the counter.

"What up man?" Olivier reached out a hand to perform a not-so-secret handshake over the counter.

"Not much, you guys want dinner or dessert?" Marshall set the egg crème he had finished in front of a girl at the bar.

"Both," Achaia and Olivier said together.

"Awesome, let's get the food going, and I'll grab your desserts later. You hangin' out for a while?"

"As always," Olivier said, taking up a menu.

Achaia read over his shoulder. "Yeah, I'm going to be boring and stick to my usual."

"Grumble Grumble," Marshal nodded.

"What is it with you and soup and grilled cheese?" Olivier smiled at her.

"Comfort food, hello!" Achaia said laughing.

"Speaking of grilled cheese, how on earth have I neglected this beauty all these years?" Olivier said staring at an item on the menu. "I'll try the Triple Lutz, and a cherry soda."

"Done and done." Marshal shot a finger pistol at them and winked.

Olivier led the way over to a table by the shelves lining the wall opposite from the counter and sat down. Achaia sat across from him, rolling up the sleeves of her sweatshirt. It was warm inside.

"Your hair looks really good today, by the way. Very..." Olivier scrunched his face up searching for the right word, "bouncy."

Achaia chortled. Olivier had the best facial expressions and always talked with his hands. "Thanks, Yellaina gave me some oil stuff... actually I have no clue what it is." She shrugged and looked down at her curls, which were more defined, and softer without all the usual frizz. "She and Amelia have been giving me *extracurricular* lessons." Achaia said making eyebrows at Olivier to signify that these were apparently very important lessons, indeed.

"In grooming?" Olivier chuckled.

"In 'girling'," Achaia said sarcastically, correcting him. "According to Amelia, half the art of intimidation, and ruling over your enemies, is mascara."

"Well, granted I don't know much about mascara, and I don't always agree with my sister, I never disagree with her verbally because I am too scared of her. So, in this instance, I'm going to say she is *probably* right." Olivier leaned back in his chair. "She's like the scariest person I know."

"Here you go guys," Marshall came over carrying armfuls of food, and set the plates down in front of them. "Want to go ahead and tell me what you want for dessert?"

"I'll take the American Dream, please." Olivier smiled down at his triple decker cheese and pesto sandwich. "Hello, gorgeous," he said, winking at it.

"You enjoy your American Dream," Achaia said, smiling over at him, "I'm going to have 99 Problems."

Olivier looked up with wide eyes. "Digestion is going to be one of them!"

Marshal laughed at them and walked away.

"I don't get it, where do you put it all?" Olivier said looking under the table.

"Those double training sessions with my dad and Noland." Achaia huffed a sigh. "Neither of them trusts the other to train me properly. My dad seriously wishes that you and I were the ones who were mated." Achaia laughed.

"Are fings beddar wiff Nolam?" Olivier asked with his mouth full.

"Better? Yeah. Great? Hardly. Confusing? Definitely." Achaia shrugged as she took a slurp of her tomato bisque.

"Confusing, as in he is a handsome and mysterious hunk of man candy who makes you doubt yourself? Or?"

Achaia snorted as she struggled to swallow her soup as opposed to having it come out of her nose. "Soup is hot, and I don't want to smell tomatoes for a week. Next time wait until

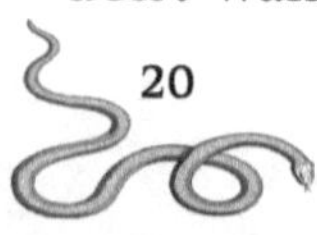

after I swallow," she laughed, coughing.

"Deal," Olivier smirked.

"Confusing as in he gave me this book for my birthday, and I think it is supposed to mean something, or have some kind of significance… but I have no clue what it is."

"That reminds me of this episode in *Gilmore Girls* when Logan gives Rory a rocket…" Olivier stopped, looking embarrassed by his extensive knowledge of *Gilmore Girls*. "I digress. Which book is it?" Olivier cocked his head in interest trying to move on as quickly as possible. He put a chip in his mouth to keep it busy lest it run away without him again.

Achaia smirked in surprise "You know *Gilmore Girls*? I've never even seen *Gilmore Girls*, and I'm a girl."

"I love that show!" Marshal said from behind the counter, not bothering to pretend he wasn't eavesdropping. He looked at Olivier, "I got your back, man! Besides Lorelai is hott!"

Olivier shoved more food in his mouth and rolled his eyes. Achaia choked back a laugh and nodded at Marshall as if that made it excusable.

"The book was *Great Expectations*," Achaia said, returning to her and Olivier's conversation.

"Maybe that's what he has for you?" Olivier laughed. "Or maybe he just wishes you read more classic lit, instead of… OH MY GOSH! I don't know how I forgot! Have you read that Thor comic I gave you?"

Achaia smacked the table top, a little too loudly, "Yes! It was so good! My favorite so far. I can't believe I didn't think I was a Thor fan."

"Right!" Olivier said, eyes wide with excitement. "I had to correct that judgement error ASAP." He shook his head at her in mock disapproval.

"Maybe my dad is right," Achaia laughed. "You and I make so much more sense."

Olivier smiled and nodded. "Yes, but we are practically the same person. So, in a relationship, one of us would be superfluous." Olivier chuckled. "That, and the point of mates is to cover your areas of weakness and help you to grow as a person."

"Yeah, yeah, yeah. Thanks, Doctor Phil." Achaia smiled as she dipped her grilled cheese in her soup.

2

The Perils of Dating

"Again." Noland clapped his hands and wiped his hair out of his face. It was slipping out of his golden man bun and curling around his temples with sweat. They were in the training room and gym at the New York safe house, where Noland, Emile, Olivier, Amelia and Yellaina all lived under the care, supervision, and training of Yellaina's father Jacob. "You don't need to see me. You need to learn to *feel* where I am behind you."

"That sounds so wrong," Achaia said, spinning around to face him. Their sparring sessions had moved from attacks and blocking, to full-on fancy footwork and blind attacks. Achaia shook her head, out of breath after having been at it for over an hour. She was thankful at least that Noland was teaching her some offense, where her father was making her earn it. In that sense, it helped to be training two and three times a day.

"You need to be hyper-aware of all of your surroundings, able to predict all of the most probable attacks and strikes. But do so without being overconfident, or your opponent may yet surprise you." Noland ignored Achaia's remark. He was all business today.

"So, know everything, but pretend I don't? You're talking in circles. How can anyone do any of this?" Achaia gripped a dagger in her right hand, and brass knuckles in her left. But, her weapon of choice was her snake whip Akakios. Noland had given him to her when he had first begun her training. Akakios was special in that he almost had a mind of his own, and at times, seemed to be alive. He had chosen her, really. Noland, however, was determined to make sure she was comfortable with every weapon, and didn't rely too heavily on her comfort zone.

"Again." Noland said, pivoting on his left foot, and grabbing her around the neck in a headlock.

Achaia spun, escaping his grip before he was able to tighten his arm. She brought her left hand down between his shoulder blades and was swiping down with her dagger just as he turned, arcing his sword. Achaia spun away fast, her waist-length braid flying out behind her, just barely avoiding being sliced through her torso. The end of her braid hit Noland hard in the face. He spit her hair out of his mouth.

"You know we should get you a hair tie with razor blades; your hair could be its own weapon." He stuck his tongue out and pulled a hair out of his mouth. "That being said, if your hair were in a bun, or shorter, I would have gotten you that time."

Achaia smiled and shook her head.

"You know what. You need to get more comfortable with anticipating another person's movements. You're too independent. Fighting is like dancing. Only, if you're a beat off in fighting you don't just look stupid, you're dead."

"Was that your way of asking me to dance?" Achaia joked.

Noland's cheeks flushed. "You can critique my flirting when I can no longer critique your fighting."

"Wait! You're flirting?" Achaia widened her eyes in mock surprise.

"No. No, I'm not flirting. I am trying to train you. Now be serious and come here." He grabbed her waist and pulled her into him, hard. Unprepared, Achaia tripped a little over her feet, catching herself on his shoulder.

"Watch it there, Grace," Noland smirked.

"Oh, shut up," Achaia said, looking down at her feet, as Noland lead her around in a slow circle.

"Don't look at your feet. You look at your opponent. When face to face, always keep your eye on your opponent."

"But right now, wouldn't you be my partner?" Achaia said, trying to be difficult.

"*Always*," Noland said looking her in the eye. His eyes had settled back down into their forest green, his face was shiny with sweat, and his cheeks slightly flushed.

Achaia, taken aback at his bluntness and change of tone, just stared.

Noland leaned forward, his face drawing slowly closer to hers. He smelled sweeter than usual. It occurred to her that that meant she knew his *usual* scent. He kept his eyes on hers, and she knew he was giving her a chance to back away if she wanted to; she just wasn't sure if she wanted to. Part of her was curious, part of her was captivated, and the other part was…

"Hey guys!"

Noland jerked back away from her, releasing his grip and ending the dance.

"Olly," Achaia said, and hoped Olivier thought her cheeks were flushed from training.

"Sorry, did I just walk in on one of those near-kiss moments? Dang it! I hate those! It's like you get all excited and worked up, and then major let down!"

"Well, luckily that is totally not at all what was maybe happening. Noland was actually just criticizing my footwork—"

"Not one of the flirtation techniques we discussed," Emile said, following Olivier through the door.

Achaia sighed. Sometimes, she noted to herself, it was not ideal for all of your close friends to be intimately familiar with the peculiar nature of your maybe, maybe-not relationship status. She appreciated them wanting to be helpful, but she also wanted to be left alone for her and Noland to figure things out on their own.

"You guys talk flirtation techniques?" Amelia said, trailing Emile.

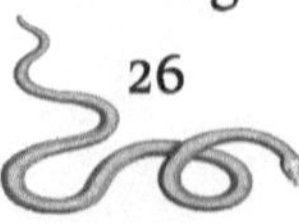

Noland looked up at the ceiling as if praying for patience, or to disappear. His cheeks were a little brighter, too. Achaia could feel heat emanating from him.

"Well, you have to admit, this is a weird scenario," Olivier said, smiling at Achaia and Noland sympathetically. "Nephilim don't generally have to woo their lovers—"

"You just *had* to use the word '*lovers*'…" Achaia said disdainfully, cringing. She could feel her cheeks burning and was too embarrassed to even look in Noland's direction. "I'm sure you guys mean well," she started.

"But could you just *stop talking*?" Noland finished, sharply.

"Finishing each other's sentences? Now *that* is good." Emile said, smiling.

"We were just coming to see if you guys wanted some dinner; Yellaina is almost done cooking." Olivier moved on, prompted by the look on Achaia's face.

"Is it Russian?" Noland asked.

"Probably," Amelia answered.

"Then, no," Noland said bluntly.

"Come on man, she is a good cook!" Olivier said, a tad on the defensive side.

"I know she is, but I don't want anything Russian for a very long time."

Achaia winced, knowing that he didn't want any reminders of their time in Russia, which was mostly her fault.

"I'm just sick of it, that's all," he said more softly. Glancing over at Achaia he added, "I'm just going to go out and grab

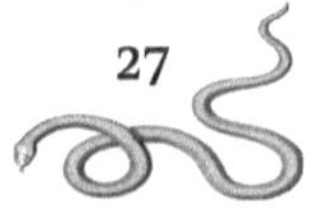

something."

Achaia wondered if that were an invitation for any of them to join him, or for her specifically to join him, but was so uncertain of either that she just stayed silent.

In fact, everyone remained silent, apparently wondering the same thing.

"Well, I'll see you all later, I guess." Noland looked at each of them as if they were acting strangely, and shook his head at them as he walked out of the room.

Once the door closed behind him, Olivier blurted, "Holy awkward moment, Batman!" He stared at Achaia with a silent laugh in his eyes. "I totally have crap timing! I am so sorry!"

Achaia, unable not to, burst out laughing. "Seriously, I don't even know what you walked in on. Don't worry about it."

"Poor guy," Emile said staring at the door Noland had exited. "He's just got no game."

Amelia laughed.

Achaia felt a little miserable, and wondered if she was supposed to go after Noland or not. She decided to text him later, to finally set up a time for them to talk.

Noland walked into his room realizing the bareness of his walls. He'd never noticed it before, so it had never bothered him. But he'd just come from Yellaina's room, which stood in a stark contrast to his blank slate. She hadn't been in; she was probably out with Olivier. They made it look so easy…

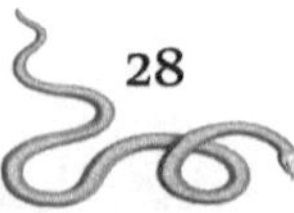

He paced his room for a few minutes before deciding that a shower would be a more productive use of his time. The stone floor of his room froze his feet. The Cathedral was one of the oldest buildings in the city. Humans didn't realize how old it really was. It had always been a place of refuge for Nephilim who had nowhere else to go. It was meant to be a temporary fix, so all of the rooms were incredibly plain. Nephilim on assignment usually only stayed a few days max while they looked for more long-term living arrangements. Jacob, though, had thought it the best place to store the Nephilim youth while they trained.

The rooms were the size of a closet. Each of them contained a single-sized bed, a nightstand with a single candle on it (Yellaina's had a tasseled lamp), and a small wardrobe (Yellaina's was overflowing). Unfortunately, part of its charm was that it also lacked rugs. Yellaina had, of course, taken the liberty of decorating hers with lush thick ones. Noland lacked the motivation or ability to decorate with confidence. So, Yellaina had bought him a rug for either a birthday or Christmas that was the only bit of decoration in his room. And he had worn it through pacing.

One thing Noland was grateful for was that they did manage to have their own bathrooms; if you could call them that. The bathroom was a dimly lit sub-closet with a toilet, minimalist sink, and a shower head. So that whenever you took a shower the entire room was soaked. For this reason, you could never take a change of clothes in with you, and you'd better leave your dirty ones outside as well lest they get soaked. Another fun fact was there was no door to separate the bathroom from the rest of the room; this made showers nice and drafty, to insure pneumonia in the winter, at least for any normal human.

Noland waited for the water to heat before he stepped into the bathroom, which took about five whole minutes. The floor steamed from the hot water colliding with the cold stone and eased Noland's sore feet. He stood under the hot water letting it cascade through his hair and down his back and chest. The steam cleared his head and helped him to think.

Achaia had finally texted him two days after the most awkward moment his friends had ever subjected him to. He was torn between relief and wanting to vomit. They had decided to meet up at six and go for a walk across the Manhattan Bridge. Noland lathered shampoo through his hair, and thought, not for the first time, that he was long overdue for a haircut. His curls wrapped around his fingers as he scrubbed his scalp, and rinsed the suds out of his hair.

He washed his arms. He was still finding new scars on them from the tunnel fight out of Hell. His own skin was unfamiliar to him. He wondered if he was angry at Achaia for leading them there. No, he didn't think so. It was more like he regretted that she, or any of them, had to experience what they had. Did he feel *responsible*? Noland really wasn't good with feelings. He didn't even know what he was feeling half the time. How was he supposed to understand what anyone else was thinking? It made processing trauma that much harder. He really couldn't pinpoint what he thought or felt about it all. It was easier to just not think about it.

Noland shut off the water and wrapped a towel around

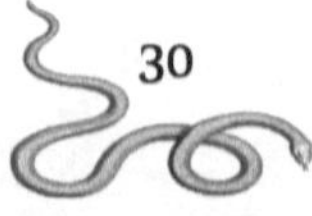

his waist. Wet, his hair stuck to his upper back, his curls fighting against the weight of the water, to bounce back up to the base of his neck. He dressed, sponged off his hair, and tossed it up in a wet, messy man-bun.

Noland looked in the mirror. He had never really given much thought to how he looked, but there was a shadow of facial hair along his jaw that made him look older. He didn't have time to shave, now. He grabbed a black zip-up hoodie and put it over his navy blue shirt and jeans. Then he took it off. Was there a rule about that? Navy blue and black…

Noland opened the door and walked down the hall to Yellaina's room again and knocked. She opened the door, and Noland saw Olivier behind her, sitting on the bed. "I hope I'm not interrupting anything."

"Not at all," Yellaina said, smiling innocently.

"I'm meeting Achaia in an hour, and I need help." Noland looked at his feet, trying really hard to keep the skin of his face its normal color.

"I have waited my entire life for this moment!" Yellaina jumped once and clapped.

"She never says that about me." Olivier complained in mock dejection.

"This is going to be fun!" Yellaina ignored him and took off leading the way to Noland's room. Noland followed, with Olivier bringing up the rear.

Yellaina walked in and looked at the hoodie on the bed. She looked up at Noland as if asking him if he were actually considering wearing it. Noland shrugged. She looked appalled.

"So," Yellaina smiled, regaining her composure, "is this a date?"

Noland's face drained of color. "I don't know. I asked if we could get together and talk, but I didn't really use the word *date* when I asked. I just told her to text me when she was free."

"Oh my gosh, why do guys never specify?" Yellaina muttered. "You need to be clear about your intentions. Now, Achaia is probably not sure what to wear!"

Noland rolled his eyes. "Clothes would be perfect." He said, sarcastically. "Is it really that big of a deal?"

"For a girl, yes. A girl could say 'yes' to hanging out, but would have said 'no', if she knew it were a date. Its nerve-racking not knowing exactly what you've agreed to." Yellaina looked through his wardrobe and pulled out a ripped up grey t-shirt that had been very nice once, and a leather jacket.

"That shirt is destroyed. I just never threw it out after that night hunting."

"It looks intentional. It's *chic*." Yellaina thrust it out toward him, and he took it. He pulled off the shirt he was wearing and exchanged it for the grey one torn at the neck line, and the seams on the arms. He put the leather jacket on over it and looked at Yellaina for approval.

Yellaina looked down at his bare feet.

"Wear these, dude." Olivier pulled out his black boots. "Just wash them up a bit first, there's some blood on the toe of this one," Olivier said, inspecting the boots with a cocked eyebrow.

Achaia was digging through all the boxes in her bedroom. She knew she had something other than t-shirts and jeans somewhere. It wasn't yet warm enough for a dress. But that would be too much anyway. He just said he wanted to talk—*this isn't a date*, Achaia thought repeatedly to herself. *Is it?*

It seemed like everything she owned was either what she wore every day, or was overkill. In the end she settled for a pair of jeans, which were darker than all her favorite light wash pairs, and an emerald green sweater that she hadn't worn in a year. She threw on a brown leather coat that was warm, but not thick and puffy like her white coat.

She looked in the mirror and marveled again at how much she was starting to look like her mother. She pulled up the leg of her jeans and strapped on a holster for some throwing knives. She stood up straight and looked herself over again. Her hair was cooperating today, falling in ringlets down to her lower back. She had put on some mascara and a bit of brown eye shadow to just accentuate her eyes a little more than usual. The overall effect was just enough to make her look a few years older.

It had been a beautiful sunny day so far, but Achaia wasn't sure how late they would be outside, so she dressed on the warmer side. She grabbed her wallet and her metro card and put both into her jacket pocket. "Okay, I'm off," she said walking out into the living room.

"To where? With who?" her dad asked sitting on the sofa in the living room.

"I'm meeting Noland to go on a walk."

The color drained out of his face. "Is this a date?"

"What?"

"I mean you look nicer than usual…" Shael sat up stick straight, scrutinizing her. "Is that make up?" Shael squinted, leaning forward. "Oh God! You're wearing makeup." He stood up and started pacing in front of the sofa. "Lord, give me strength," he prayed aloud. "I always knew this day would come, but I just thought I'd have more time… I didn't even think you actually liked the guy!" He looked at her hopefully, for her to confirm that she didn't 'actually like the guy'. "I hoped your human side would keep you safe from the whole 'knowing' thing. Shi—," Shael thrust his head into his hands.

"Dad!" Achaia yelled.

Shael stopped and looked at her. "You know what I'm capable of. I will exhaust myself on him if he tries anything with you. You tell him… No. I'll tell him… Is he picking you up?"

"No, with my apparent gift of foresight, I spared him this awkward moment, and suggested I meet him there." Achaia's face was warm, and she was sure her cheeks were pink.

"Well, if he tries anything, remember yesterday's training." The day before, Shael had taught her how to dislocate an assailant's shoulder using their own momentum. He had also accidentally mentioned how to kill someone with a proper blow to the throat. She didn't ask which lesson he was referring to.

"Okay, dad." Achaia smiled and stood on her toes to kiss her father on the cheek.

"Pressure points are important— I'm not okay with this," he said as she walked toward the door.

"Dad, it's going to be fine." Achaia smiled as she reached

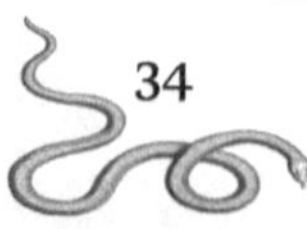

for the doorknob, Akakios glittering on her wrist.

"I trust that you have more than your whip on you," he said.

"Of course. You'd be surprised what all you can hide under a pair of skinny jeans." Achaia smiled.

"Now, that's my girl! As long as you're only referring to weapons…" Shael winked.

Achaia walked the couple blocks from the A train to Manhattan Bridge. She crossed half the highway to the sidewalk in the middle, where the walking path of the bridge started. She liked coming here with Olivier; they would walk the bridge and read all the random graffiti along the path.

Noland was waiting for her, leaning against the railing, looking like a supermodel. He hadn't seen her yet, but she watched as girls, grown women, and even a few guys checked him out as they passed by. Achaia felt a knot tie itself in her stomach, and her hands felt like they had started shaking in her pockets.

Noland looked up then and saw her. He smiled. She liked his smile. It was bright white, but not perfectly straight. It gave him character and reminded her that he wasn't entirely perfect, which actually made him a little more perfect. As she closed the gap between them, she smiled. "Hey."

"Hey," he said looking down at her. He turned and started walking down the path. "Thanks for coming."

"No problem." Achaia fidgeted with her hands in her

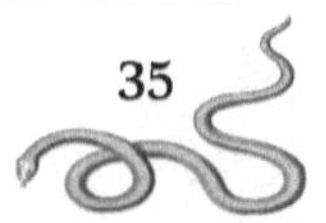

pockets, at a complete loss for what else to say or do. She had never felt more out of her element.

"So, Emile tells me on almost a daily basis, that I'm an idiot when it comes to you." Noland smiled down at her. "Unfortunately, I think he's right. So, I wanted to clarify some things, if that's okay."

Achaia took his smile as a good sign, and tried to relax. "Well, if you've been an idiot, then so have I. I'm glad we're finally doing this."

"Me too," Noland chuckled in his chest. "I suck at talking about my feelings, so I'm just going to jump right in. I'm not mad at you, if that's what you think; I don't know. I never was."

Achaia noticed that though Noland's legs were much longer than hers, he walked at a pace that was comfortable for her. It was a little thing, but she noticed, and she appreciated it.

"I understand why you did what you did, for your dad, but you didn't seem to be happy with me, before we left to save him, so I assumed you wanted some space to process the whole," he lowered his voice, "being mates thing." He shrugged and she could tell how awkward this must be for him. "After everything that happened in the tunnels, I should never have just assumed anything about what you were thinking— I'm sorry. I haven't been avoiding you or ignoring you. I just was trying to give you space, if that was what you wanted. But I think I was just too scared to ask what you wanted or needed."

Achaia smiled up at him. "I can understand that. I am terrifying." He responded by lightly elbowing her.

"It is though," his face went serious. "It's terrifying

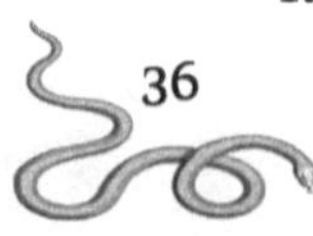

knowing that I am eternally bound to you, and never knowing if you'll ever feel the same way about me." He avoided meeting her eye when she looked up at him, startled by his raw honesty. "I have a whole new respect for humans, and their pursuit of requited love." He laughed half-heartedly, trying to lighten the mood.

Achaia *felt* her eyebrows raise, more than she *told* them to. She tried to control her facial expression, but she felt her cheeks flush. She hadn't been expecting that and didn't know what to say. What came out of her mouth was, "I wasn't mad at you either." *Okay then, just bypass that whole comment why don't you*, she chided herself.

Noland glanced down at her.

Achaia sighed before continuing, "I was afraid that you were angry at me. And I was—okay I was a little mad at you at first, for not telling me. But after walking through Hell, I didn't care about that anymore. It was just a lot to process, on top of having my dad back, and having so much to learn, and to fear. I think it—," Achaia reminded herself that Noland had just been raw and honest with her. She owed him as much if they were ever going to actually understand each other without Emile as a middle man. "It—," Achaia huffed out a breath. "It feels dangerous to care too much about anyone right now, when that could be used against me."

Noland stopped, and grabbed her elbow, turning her to face him. "Loving someone requires a lot of vulnerability, but it doesn't make you weak. I mean yeah, it gives you one more thing to lose, but it gives you more to fight for."

Achaia looked down at the ground.

"I know it is a lot for you to understand. And I know that you think that God *made me* have feelings for you." Noland lifted her chin, so she was looking him in the eye. "Achaia, I liked you, before I knew I loved you. I chose you before I *knew*. So, if you doubt my feelings for you, and think that my feelings aren't my own, then don't."

The heat in Achaia's face amplified, and she knew her cheeks had to be blood red.

"I know that you aren't really there yet," he dropped his hand from her face. "But I'm willing to wait. Not just because I have to, but because it would be an honor to pursue you."

There's that old soul. Achaia tried not to smile. Instead she looked down at her feet again. "God, you make me so nervous." She laughed, and Noland laughed.

"I'm sorry, I'm not trying to. Are you embarrassed? Don't be!" He smiled.

Achaia peeked back up at him. "I know. It's just who you are. The way you carry yourself, the way you make eye contact with people is very off-putting. I mean not in like a bad way; it's just intense. And your eyes are like crazy. Who has eyes that green?"

"Was that a form of compliment?" Noland laughed and leaned back against the railing.

"Shut up!" Achaia hit him lightly on the arm.

He grabbed her arm and pulled her against him, keeping hold of her hand.

"I'm working on it," she smiled, blushing again. She

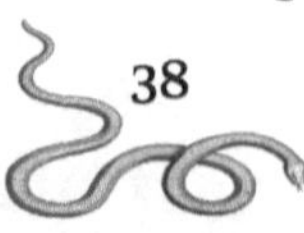

couldn't look at his face for more than a few seconds without getting shaky. Every nerve in her body was tingling.

"You're doing great," he joked, smiling.

Achaia laughed. It felt strange to be this honest, and this close to Noland. None of it really felt real. She felt like she was watching her life through a sort of filter. Like it was more of a movie than reality. She felt distant from herself, so out of her natural element of keeping everyone at arm's length.

"You're so beautiful," Noland said softly. "The first time I saw you, I thought you looked like a porcelain doll, but I've since learned you're significantly less breakable. You are the strongest person I've ever met. And you did it all without being raised like us."

Achaia felt herself lean more heavily against him, as if her legs were having a hard time holding her up on their own. But her eyes finally looked up into his. "The first time I saw you, I didn't realize I was staring at you." She laughed, trying to release some of the nerves building up in her stomach like a horde of butterflies.

Noland chuckled, and put his hand back under her chin. Achaia looked up at him, as he leaned down. She questioned whether or not she should back away, if she was ready for this. What would happen if she let him kiss her? Would everything be different?

But then, she was knocked hard to the side. Noland had pushed her down and was standing with his back to her, holding a blade he hadn't been clutching a moment before. Achaia realized that the blade wasn't his; he had caught it.

It was a strange *xiphos*, made of what looked like diemerillium that hadn't been taken care of. The green was muted and foggy, instead of the crystal-clear, beautiful metal the Nephilim used. It belonged to a demon standing up the path about ten yards away. *Why would a demon be carrying an angelic blade?*

Achaia got back to her feet and stood next to Noland. His hand was bleeding, where he had caught the blade out of the air. Achaia stared at the demon with loathing. He reminded her of the uruk hai in the *Lord of the Rings* movies. The demon was tall, and broad with muscle. He had long dark hair that was matted together in primal dreads. His skin was a leathery, dark gray-brown.

Noland looked down at the blade in his hand as Achaia looked up at all the massive rafters supporting the arc of the bridge. Strangely, there were no other pedestrians on the path. Achaia had been too distracted to notice that that seemed 'off'.

"You have staggeringly bad timing," Noland said, lowering the *xiphos*.

"Noland," Achaia said gesturing up with her eyes.

Noland followed her glance then leveled the demon who had thrown the xiphos with a glare. "You're not just a random horde of demons, are you?"

"We've been sent to deliver a message," the demon growled.

"Then out with it; I'd like to get back to my evening," Noland spat.

Achaia respected the amount of sarcastic venom he

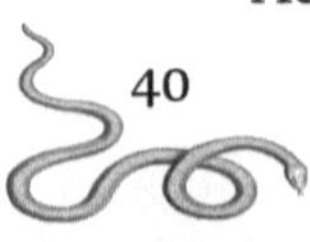

managed to cram into the sentence.

"The message isn't for you; it's for *her*." The demon nodded his head toward Achaia.

"Yeah, I gathered that." Noland cocked his head to the side. "If you're trying to say that you'll only tell her privately, not a chance."

"So, spit it out," Achaia added. "You're wasting our time."

"You don't have much of it left," the demon said, turning his attention to Achaia.

"Is that so?" Achaia crossed her arms, grabbing hold of the whip on her wrist.

"He is coming for you. You will spend sleepless nights, waiting. Every sound you hear, you will think it is time. When he comes for you, you will be too weary to fight. You will welcome the relief of knowing it's over. You will see him as a merciful captor."

"Really? You actually think that is how this is going to happen? Just goes to show Luc doesn't know me very well." Achaia unleashed her whip. The demon took a step back. "Let me tell you what is actually going to happen. I'm going to continue my pleasant evening. I'm going to go home and sleep like a baby and have freaking awesome dreams. I'm going to hear sounds for what they are, and dismiss the ones that aren't important, because Luc doesn't get to mess up my life after I fought so damn hard to be able to live it. He is a pathetic, sore loser who can suck it."

Achaia heard Noland huff a laugh behind her.

"If you think you're intimidating, after what we battled

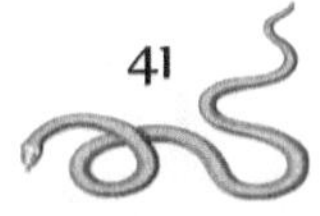

in the tunnels, you look like *Teletubbies*," she added for good measure. Granted demons probably didn't know what *Teletubbies* were, she hoped that didn't diminish too much from the effect.

Noland put a hand on her back as if to say "that's enough."

"You ready?" he asked.

"I get that guy," Achaia said gesturing to the uruk-hai-looking demon.

"Alright." Noland cut left behind her and flung himself up into the rafters, running up them, toward the demons that were hovering above. Achaia lashed out with her whip catching hold of one of the steel suspension cables and ran, using the resistance to launch herself into the air and kick the demon hard in the face.

He was hardly shaken. It was times like these Achaia wished she weighed a little more. She recalled her whip back to her and wrapped it around his throat. She hauled herself up his back and pulled the whip tight.

The demon elbowed at her, catching her once in the gut, and knocking the wind out of her, but she held tight. Another demon dropped down from above and grabbed at her from behind. Achaia looked up, catching a glimpse of Noland fighting two demons at once on the rafters. Achaia snapped her head back, hitting the demon in the face. It grunted. Achaia hopped back, kicking the demon behind her in the stomach as she spun. He lurched forward as he gasped. She wrapped the extra length of her whip around the second demon's neck while it was hunched, and prayed this worked.

She ran around them and leaped onto the railing and over the chain link. The force of her body weight pulled them up,

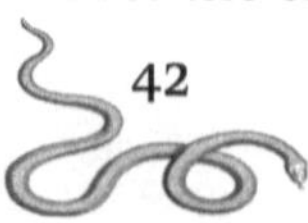

but not off their feet. Their heads slammed together. She heard one of their necks snap. The first demon still stood choking, so she rappelled down the chain link, pulling and tugging as hard as she could, until she heard the second snap.

She grabbed hold of the links, and climbed back over onto the path. Noland was dispatching his last demon. "Heads up!" he called, as the demon's head fell in front of her. The body fell to its knees, then over onto the ground. Achaia stepped back as it landed on top of its head.

"Well done with the literal!" Achaia smiled as Noland leapt down.

"You, too." He smiled. "So, I was thinking: ice cream or coffee?" Noland took her hand and started walking back down the path.

"Coffee sounds good," Achaia said squeezing his hand in hers, thinking that if this was her normal life, it wasn't half bad.

"So what's a *Teletubby*?"

Achaia and Noland entered a coffee shop Achaia had never been to. They sat at a small table for two looking out at the street. Noland had a draft latte, and Achaia hugged her plain black dark roast in her hands.

"I mean, we knew he was going to move against you," Noland was saying quietly, leaning in across the table so that only Achaia could hear him. The coffee shop wasn't exactly crowded, but they were far from alone.

"I'm not surprised. In fact, it seems too predictable. I've been training with you and my dad. I'm not really sure what else I could be doing, but I still don't feel ready," Achaia said, looking down into her coffee. "And what was with the announcement? He sure has a flair for the dramatic."

"I don't really think there is anything you could do to feel entirely prepared." Noland took a sip of his latte. "We aren't going to get any support from the council. They don't trust you or your dad."

"They *hate* us; you can just say it. They hate us." Achaia took a sip of her coffee.

"But Bale is in, whatever he can do when the time comes."

"That means a lot since he hated me at first, and calls me the death angel."

"You grow on people," Noland said, smiling. He reached across the table and took Achaia's hand. Achaia let him.

She smiled at him weakly, torn between feeling happy and afraid. "I'm scared," she said in almost a whisper.

"I'd be more worried about you if you weren't. Being confident is different than being cocky. You've improved so much in these last few weeks, but there is always room for growth. There's a difference in having confidence in your ability to hold your ground and being cocky enough to think you can go against him head to head and win."

"Yeah, no. I don't know enough about him, yet. I feel like my dad has been telling me all this stuff, but it's like the tip of the iceberg. I feel like I know all these facts *about* him, but until I actually know him, it's never going to be enough."

"'Know your opponent and you will never lose; know yourself and you will always win,'" Noland smiled sadly over his glass.

"Wow," Achaia said, staring at him impressed. "That was deep."

"I can't take credit; that was Sun Tzu."

"*The Art of War*?"

Noland nodded. "I think you've been so focused on how to beat *him* that you haven't considered what he is thinking, or what he is fearing about trying to defeat *you*."

"You think he has any fears when he thinks about me?" Achaia laughed without humor.

"I think he has put a lot of time and energy into going after you and your dad. He wouldn't be so determined if there wasn't something about the two of you that terrified him. Something about you, Achaia, disturbs him. *What is it*?" Noland asked, keeping his voice low.

Achaia sat back in her chair, completely at a loss. One of her hands sat wrapped around her forgotten mug as she stared at the edge of the table. That thought had never crossed her mind. "I have no idea."

3

Summons

"The willingness to show up changes us.
It makes us a little braver each time."
-Brené Brown

Olivier walked up to Emile's door and was getting ready to
knock when it opened, and Amelia appeared.

"Oh, thank God. Maybe you can reach him and tell him
he isn't a father."

"That we know of," Olivier amended.

"What?" Emile looked up at him then. He had been
wearing a path in the stone floor of his bedroom.

"I don't know. What's happening?" Olivier asked plopping
himself on the bed. "I just came up to tell you guys dinner is

ready."

"Tell him he isn't Noland's father, and he needs to stop acting so stupid," Amelia said.

"Stop acting stupid, so Amelia can wipe that look off her face. You know that look always sets me on edge. Don't set me on edge," Olivier said pleadingly.

"It's been two hours and he isn't back yet, and we haven't heard from him," Emile said. He had stopped pacing, but he was still visibly anxious.

"So? When Yellaina and I go out, we're gone for hours all the time," Olivier shrugged.

"But that's different. Noland is so bad with girls, and Achaia has a choice."

"Let them figure it out. Who knows," Amelia shrugged, "maybe it's going really well and we've all underestimated Noland's ability to be charming."

"Noland, charming?" Olivier cocked an eyebrow. "That's like saying you think your drill sergeant is sweet."

"It is not," Amelia swatted at Olivier's arm as she walked out the door into the hall. "Come on, I'm starving. Anyway, what I was trying to tell you is that the council wants to call us all in to get full individual reports of what happened with Achaia. They want to see if our stories all line up."

"Wait, if we haven't gotten a summons yet, how do you know this?" Emile asked, now giving her his full attention.

"Bale told me." Amelia shrugged. "He thought we might appreciate a heads up."

"You still talk to Bale?" Olivier asked, stopping in his

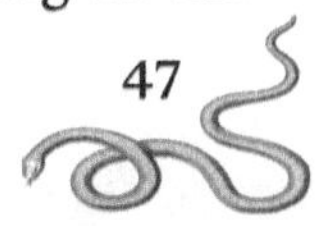

tracks. Emile stopped right beside him.

Amelia turned around to look at them both. "Noland does, too." She settled them both with a look that told them it wasn't a big deal.

Olivier didn't buy it.

"Noland has a reason to," Emile said. "And why didn't Bale just tell Noland since they're such good pen pals?" Emile looked suspicious.

"That's a fair point." Olivier crossed his arms, mirroring Emile's stance. "Exactly how many times have you talked to Bale since we left Russia? Is this a common occurrence?" Olivier asked.

"You're both ridiculous," Amelia said, setting her feet apart and putting a hand on her hip.

Oh no, Olivier thought.

"Who I talk to, is none of your business. I can talk to who I want when I want, however I want."

"Woah! Oh God, there's a '*however*'. Need to know info only, please!" Olivier cringed away. "If you're talking to him in a *how* fashion, please don't share!" Olivier put his hands over his ears but could still hear Emile when he yelled.

"He is way too old for you! He is the keeper of the Russian safe house for God's sake! The next time I see that pervert, I'm going to—,"

"First of all, I never said it was anything like that," Amelia yelled back. "You can't just threaten the only Nephilim on Earth who isn't fallen! He hasn't even done anything wrong."

"If he is chatting up my little sister, that is several levels of

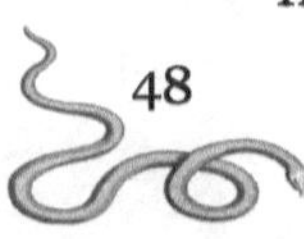

wrong!" Emile yelled back.

"Please, you're what? A few minutes older than me?" Amelia scoffed.

"HEY!"

Amelia turned, and Olivier and Emile leaned around her on either side to see Yellaina standing at the end of the hallway.

"First of all, dinner is getting cold. Secondly, the evening Bible study is in session downstairs, and I think they are learning a little more than they bargained for." Yellaina pivoted on her foot and strutted back toward the kitchen.

"We aren't finished here," Emile pointed sharply at Amelia, and followed Yellaina toward food.

"Yeah, not done here," Olivier added, making a not-convincing serious face at his sister as he passed her.

"Oh, shut up," she punched him hard in the arm.

The four of them entered the kitchen, where Yellaina had set plates around the kitchen island. They perched themselves on barstools, and looked down at their plates.

"What is it?" Amelia asked.

"It's eggplant parmesan," Yellaina smiled. "I thought I'd mix it up and try some Italian. Where's Noland?"

"Still out with Ach—," Olivier started but was cut off.

"Did you know that your best friend is talking to a guy that is *an eternity* older than her?" Emile asked, looking at Yellaina accusingly.

Amelia rolled her eyes.

"Bale?" Yellaiana asked. "Yeah, he's gorgeous."

"So, you approve of this behavior?" Emile looked livid.

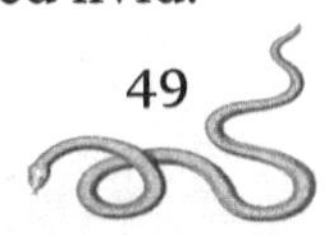

"Of course I do, I mean when you *know*…"

Amelia's face went scarlet.

"KNOW?" Emile slammed his fork down on the island.

"You haven't told them yet, have you?" Yellaina looked at Amelia with a deep apology in her eyes. Olivier stared at his sister in disbelief.

Amelia was staring intently at her lap. "He told me he knew when you guys went after Achaia, and after you got back it never really felt like a good time to bring it up."

"Never a good time? It's been *months!*" Emile said leaning forward on the counter. Olivier had never seen Emile this aggressive.

"Well if it makes you feel any better, he wasn't creepy about it, and I haven't felt anything yet, and neither has he. It's just a knowing."

"He is literally an eternity older than you!" Olivier pointed out.

Amelia glared at him. "And in a few hundred years, what difference is that going to make?" Amelia rolled her eyes. "The only reason we even think of it as being weird is because we grew up here. The generations from heaven wouldn't even blink an eye." She looked back and forth between Olivier and Emile.

Olivier couldn't wrap his mind around it. Bale was literally a figment from their history lessons, and he was mated to his sister…

"This is why I didn't want to tell you," Amelia stood up and left the kitchen.

"Now, look at what you've done. Well played." Yellaina

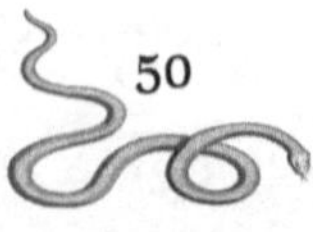

looked scornfully at Emile.

"Yeah," Olivier said, hoping it wasn't too late to change sides.

"Oh, shut up, it's not like you helped," Yellaina said grabbing her plate and Amelia's and leaving the room.

"How bad did we just screw up?" Olivier asked, once both girls were gone.

"They'll get over it. But—," Emile looked flabbergasted.

"Right?" Olivier widened his eyes and raised his eyebrows. "Freaking weird!"

"Yeah," Emile said nodding. "You can't really argue with God; he knows what he's doing. But I can't wrap my mind around this one."

"Is it weird?" Olivier asked, after a moment. He was looking at Emile, studying his face.

"I thought we just established that it was?"

"No, I mean being the only one left without a mate?"

Emile blinked, and looked down. "I guess I hadn't realized that I was." Emile picked up his fork, looking thoughtful. Olivier looked away, not sure if he had just struck a chord.

Olivier and Emile ate the rest of their dinner in silence.

Achaia sat on her bed with Yellaina and Amelia. Yellaina lay on her stomach, flipping through a magazine with a cup of tea sitting next to her. Amelia was sitting cross-legged, polishing a dagger. Achaia leaned against her headboard with her legs out in front of her, two cups of coffee sitting on a tray between her and Amelia.

"I can't even imagine Emile reacting that way, but I guess you are his twin… was anyone going to be good enough for you?" Achaia laughed.

Amelia shrugged. "I'm just flabbergasted why anyone else thinks they have a say in the matter. It is between me, God, and Bale."

"It is weird, though. I didn't get the feeling Bale liked us very much. Well, I mean, especially me, being the Angel of Death and all." Achaia cocked her head to the side. "But what is this summons?"

"It's basically a debriefing. They've been putting it off, I think, because tensions were high when you got back. I think they were wanting to let things settle. I think they just want to get as much information as possible, see what we know."

"Is it going to be like an interrogation like before?" Achaia felt her stomach drop.

"I don't think so. They will probably want to get us alone, and see if our stories all match," Amelia said, dropping the dagger down on the bed covers. It was shiny, and shimmering, like a creek running over the duvet. Achaia stared at it, never tired of how crystal clear and beautiful diemerilium was.

"They think we are lying?" Achaia asked.

Yellaina shut her magazine and sat up on her knees. "It's protocol, all pretty standard really, save for that they have waited so long."

There was a knock on the door. Achaia looked up. Noland

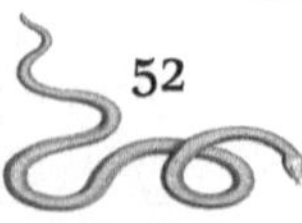

was standing in the doorway. "Hey," he said, without smiling.

"What's up?" Achaia said, scooting closer to Amelia to make room for Noland to sit.

He walked over and sat facing Achaia, then turned to face the others. "I got the call today. We're being summoned to the council to give individual reports. They want us to come in the day after tomorrow, so we leave in the morning."

"How long will we be gone?" Achaia asked.

Noland looked down at his hands for a moment before looking up at her. "You aren't being summoned. You made your stance pretty clear that you weren't going to be exactly cooperative with the council. I guess, in their minds, you've forfeited the right to have a voice. Joash thinks he can learn all he needs to, from us."

"So, I'm not invited. I can't go?" Achaia said flatly.

"They were pretty curt about that point. And I think keeping as much distance between you and the council wouldn't be a bad idea for now. Until all of this blows over, and they hear us out for what we have to say. Maybe once they hear the whole story, they will realize that you aren't a threat to them?" Noland tried for a half smile, but it was a lousy attempt. Achaia could tell that he wanted to comfort her, but he didn't have a lot of hope himself.

"But you're my Guardian. How long are they going to keep you away from me? Can they do that?" Achaia asked, her frustration showing itself in her voice.

"We will see you guys later. We better go pack," Yellaina said with a weak smile at Achaia. "I'm sure we'll be back in no time." As she stood and went for the door, she leaned over and kissed the top of Achaia's head.

"See you later, I guess," Achaia said, waving as Amelia followed Yellaina out.

"Your father has kept you safe for a long time. I'm sure he can handle a weekend." Noland grabbed hold of Achaia's hands in her lap. "I'll see if I can go first, and come straight home after. I won't be gone long."

"I know this is supposed to be standard procedure, but what do you think they are looking for?" Achaia shifted, the coffee cups teetering dangerously until she settled.

"With the way things are going now, I'm sure any information about what is going on in Hell, and anything Luc might be planning, will help us figure out how we can protect humanity better. This is a good thing. If we can all get on the same page and put our heads together, maybe we can predict what Luc is trying to do with all these terrorist attacks. I feel like we are all holding different pieces to a puzzle. If we can just put aside all the animosity and put the puzzle together, maybe we can—"

"Stop him?"

"My hopes aren't that high," Noland shrugged. "I still think there's more going on than the council wants to share, and I can't help but think that Luc wouldn't have been able to do all he's done without help. While I'm there, I plan on keeping my eyes open. Emile is going to be trying to target members with emotions that don't fit the situation. There's got to be a leak somewhere. If we can figure that out, too—"

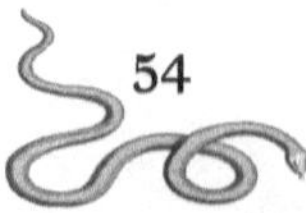

"Well, we aren't at a lack for moving parts. What can I do? Give me something to do while you're gone." Achaia sat up straighter.

Noland looked thoughtful.

"I know I'm just your Charge, but I want to do more. I want to help." Achaia squeezed Noland's hands.

"You can stay alive," Noland smiled.

"More than that." Achaia cocked her head to the side with a look that told Noland to do better.

"I don't know," Noland frowned. "That might be hard enough."

Noland and Achaia had spent the afternoon sitting in her room talking. The conversation had moved from talk about the council to the two of them sharing stories about growing up. Most of them were pretty funny, but some of them not at all. Noland listened as Achaia explained the differences between Marvel and DC comics, and why she liked DC more. Achaia listened as Noland told her about being forced to learn music as a kid, but how he had actually learned to love guitar. He preferred acoustic. He told her how nothing helped him relax quite like music, when he was stressed.

Noland felt relaxed. It was nice to talk about things besides demons and death and trying to stay alive. It was nice to remember there was life; there was more than just destruction. There were little things, that when put together, built a foundation for more, for a future.

After a few hours, Achaia started yawning. Her head was laid on Noland's shoulder, and Shael had started coming around in ten-minute intervals to poke his head in the door.

"I should let you get some rest. You've been training really hard lately." Noland sat up and looked down at Achaia's disappointed face. His heart flared up as he thought of her being disappointed at his departure.

"And you have to pack," Achaia frowned.

"Yep." Noland stood. As he did, he looked down and saw the book he had given Achaia on her nightstand. There was a bookmark sticking out, about a quarter of the way through the book. "Are you enjoying it?" he asked smiling.

"Ish?" Achaia laughed. "It's not my usual reading material. They talk weird."

"Well that's not really why I got it for you, it was more for the inside joke. But I'm glad you're reading it." Noland laughed.

"Oh yeah," Achaia nodded, but Noland could tell that she hadn't gotten his meaning.

"You don't remember do you?"

"Remember?" Achaia looked incredibly guilty.

"It's okay if you don't. It was my attempt at a thoughtful gift. I'm not really great at the gift giving thing," Noland laughed at himself. He thought this would have usually been an awkward conversation, but he and Achaia had, over the last week, gotten much more comfortable around each other. "I just thought of my favorite memory with you, and then got something that reminded me of it. Apparently, it didn't remind you of it."

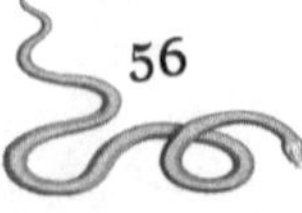

"That's so sweet," Achaia smiled at him. "I'm sorry I didn't get it. What is your favorite memory of me?"

"When we were on the train to Russia, and—"

"We were actually getting along after everyone else was asleep." Achaia looked at the floor, as if playing the scene back in her mind. Then she looked up at him with a huge smile. "You said you would pick me first in gym class."

"Or any other scenario," Noland said pulling her into a hug.

Achaia squeezed him around his torso and buried her head in his chest. Noland kissed the top of her head long and slow.

"Stay safe for me," he whispered.

"I'll do what I can, but you know me." Achaia pulled back and winked at him.

Noland looked down, studying her face. He hated the thought of leaving. He ran his fingers through the hair falling into her face, and tucked it back, wrapping his fingers around the back of her head, and leaning down. His nose brushed against hers and he could feel her breath brush his skin.

"Just leaving?" Shael said from the doorway, and Noland stood up, rigidly straight.

"Yes, sir," Noland said, smiling guiltily down at Achaia.

She squeezed his arm as he walked out of the room. "Have a safe trip," Achaia said reaching up and hugging him around the neck. Noland tried to relax into it but couldn't. He was acutely aware of the death glare Shael was shooting him from just behind Achaia, because Noland was wincing back. The mental image of Shael single handedly annihilating the Assyrian army came unwelcomely to mind.

"You're going on a trip? That's great! For how long? Forever?" Shael smiled.

"Dad," Achaia said reproachfully, turning to glare at him. She had the same scowl as her father. Their coloring might be different, but their facial expressions were nearly identical. Noland tried not to smile.

"We've been summoned by the council to give account of the events back in March," Noland said, looking only at Shael as he spoke.

"And they don't want to hear from me or Achaia?" Shael's arrogance deflated, and he just looked annoyed. "When are they going to learn? Sometimes you have to… Never mind." Shael shrugged. "I'm not really surprised. I knew they were stupid, but man are they missing out on hearing from me. I know more than anyone about what Luc is thinking, planning, and doing, but because of their pride, or maybe it's fear, they aren't requesting an audience with me?" Shael huffed a humorless laugh. "Idiots."

Noland straightened his back. "Sir, would you be willing to meet with me, when we return?"

Shael cocked an eyebrow at him. The resemblance between family members always intrigued Noland. He was too young to care to notice such things before his parents died, but he often wondered, now, who he resembled when he talked, when he joked, when he scowled.

"I would very much like to speak with you, about a number of things," Noland raised his eyebrows, as if to reaffirm

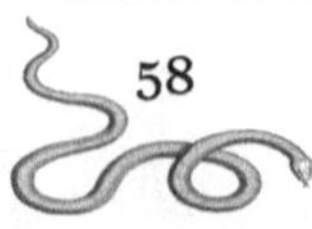

that he was serious.

"You know," Shael smiled crookedly. "There's a number of things I would like to discuss with you as well."

Noland felt a turn of nausea in his stomach at the thought of all that Shael meant. "Of course."

"Right, well, have a good trip." Shael smiled widely, opening the door and practically shoving Noland out through it.

"See you when you get back!" Achaia shouted around her father's shoulder.

"Bye, Kaya," Noland yelled as the door closed. Noland shook his head and shook out his tense limbs. "He does *not* like me very much."

Emile sat next to Noland on the plane. Yellaina and Olivier were near the front, sitting together and laughing. Amelia sat next to the window with air pods in. Noland was incredibly anxious.

"I mean, Shael has a chip on his shoulder, which is understandable, but he has a point. If the council is looking for information about Luc, he is the one to talk to. He was with him for months. It's just that they firmly believe that he is on Luc's side. Maybe after hearing our accounts, they will consider the possibility that he isn't," Emile offered.

"Do we really know that he isn't?" Noland asked. "I mean, not to play Devil's advocate, literally." Noland cocked his head to the side. "I mean, I don't believe he is working with Luc, or that he wants what Luc wants, but do we *know*. No, we don't."

"Fair point," Emile shrugged. "I mean we haven't really spent a lot of time with him, and none of us have exactly asked him to tell us his side of the story."

"I did," Noland said bluntly.

Emile sat up shocked. "You what?"

"I asked him if he would be willing to get together when we get back." Emile could feel Noland's nervousness.

"That was bold. Human or not, that man has done—" Emile swallowed, "He intimidates the fool out of me." Emile looked at Noland with all the respect in the world. "He was the greatest mercenary the world has ever known, and you're dating his only daughter. That has to be terrifying."

"Yeah, that part isn't exactly a blast," Noland nodded. "So, the council," Noland changed the subject, and Emile could feel his shift to determination.

"What do you want me to do?" Emile asked. "What's the plan?"

"I'm going to need you to drink a lot of espresso, because I need you to spend as much time, with as many people as possible. The council is bound to feel curious, afraid, maybe a little disappointed in us or angry. They may feel grateful for information, maybe even hopeful that we know something that might help."

"Right," Emile nodded. "So, what exactly am I going to be looking for?"

"I don't know. Just anything that seems to not make sense, maybe," Noland stopped.

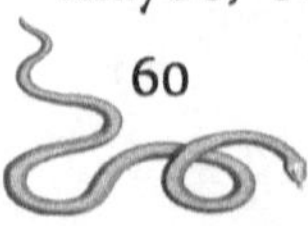

"What?" Emile asked.

"Look for anyone who feels indifferent."

"Indifferent?"

"Yeah, because to them, it doesn't matter what news we bring back. If they are in league with Luc, we can't possibly say anything they don't already know. At the most we may be annoying to them. Look for people who are annoyed, or indifferent."

Bale sat in the library, surrounded by dusty shelves and dilapidated furniture. He sat next to the fire, with a scroll on his lap. Few people had the handwritten copies of the scriptures; Bale himself only had a few. This was a gift to humanity. Many Nephilim never bothered themselves with what the scriptures said, but Bale had always been curious.

The scroll he read now was the Revelation of John. A number of humans had been endowed with knowledge from the Lord. John had been given a glimpse into something even the angels weren't all privy to. Bale couldn't comprehend the arrogance of the Nephilim, and their lack of pursuit of the topic.

Since the first time Bale had seen Achaia, he had a darkness growing in the back of his mind, a sinking feeling in his heart, which would not allow him to rest. Something was coming. Initially he had thought it was Achaia herself, but he didn't think so now. Since the young Nephilim had all left, he had thrown himself into two things: his studies and investigating the council in whatever capacity he could. He agreed with Noland;

something was amiss in the council. There were more than a few council members Bale didn't trust. Investigating them was difficult without help, since they gave him a wide berth.

Every once in a while, Bale would find out something, but all his investigating had produced so far were a bunch of tiny insignificant-seeming facts that he couldn't stitch together to mean anything. Truth be told, Bale didn't really trust any of the first-generation Nephilim on Earth; they were all fallen. Young though they were, Bale was learning to trust the later generations more; they were not fallen for their own sins, but their parents'. Perhaps their character was stronger.

Parts of the scroll Bale held had been destroyed, so he had purchased a Bible at the bookstore a few blocks away. He compared what the Russian translation said to what he gleaned from the original texts, filling in the scroll's gaps with the translated version.

There were a few passages that truly concerned him. He flipped the page and rolled down the scroll, his hands beginning to shake as he read. "Oh my God." He put the scroll down, praying. "Oh my God."

Bale stood, dropping the scroll and the book down in his seat, and took off to his office. He needed to prepare.

Noland and the others sat in a sort of waiting room outside of Joash's office. Noland was slouched, with his head leaning back against the wall. He hadn't rested at all on the plane,

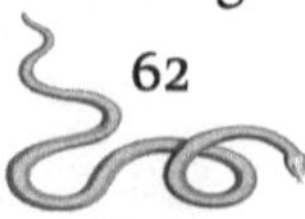

and he was exhausted from overthinking.

Yellaina sat on his left, and Emile on his right. Olivier and Amelia on either side of them. He was flanked by the people he trusted more than anyone else, and yet, he couldn't help dreading what was about to happen.

The door to Joash's office opened. A few council members came through, Joash, followed by a man named Osalath, and a woman called Dina. Noland stood. "Sir, I would like to volunteer to go first."

"First?" Joash sneered. "I think not."

"But—," Noland started.

"You'll be going simultaneously."

"Together?" Emile asked.

"Separately," Joash sneered. "No chance to change your story based on anyone else's slip ups." Joash's face was a stone mask of dislike.

Dina shot him a look out of the side of her eye. Noland was sure she found his behavior and his decision odd. "What cause would they have to lie?" she asked. Noland gave her brownie points for being so direct with him, when few council members would dare. Then again, if Noland was correct, Dina wasn't first generation. She was maybe second or third, old and wise, but not fallen on her own accord.

"What cause indeed?" Joash responded, twisting her question to make it seem like they were all questioning the group's allegiance.

"No reason, because we aren't lying. You'll see for yourself." Noland fixed Joash with a steady look that wasn't itself

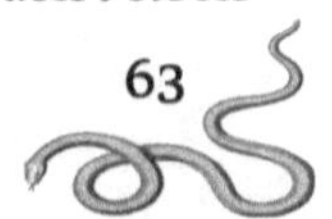

obstinate, but assertive none the less. "I'm hopeful that this can be a useful exercise to help us figure out what information is pertinent in forming a plan to combat Luc. The global situation is deteriorating. You need what we know to figure out how to stop this. And you'll need our cooperation, so I suggest you change your attitude, really quick." Noland stood maybe an inch taller than Joash, and he was glad of it just then.

"Watch your tone and the way you speak to your elders, Noland bat Nathaniel."

"I will if you do," Noland cocked a smile. "I'm your elder, too. Don't forget it."

"You'll be coming with me Amsel." Joash shot him a murderous look, as Dina and Osalath stood staring at them.

"Do you think that will be the most productive interview? Perhaps Noland should go with Osalath," Dina said assertively.

Joash glowered at her. "Amsel comes with me." He straightened out his face, in an attempt to look diplomatic and powerful again, which Noland didn't buy.

"Rosanov, you'll go with Dina. The DuBois will go with Osaloth."

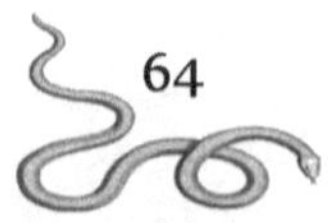

4

Penance

"The difference between treason and
patriotism is only a matter of dates."
-Alexandre Dumas,
The Count of Monte Christo

Yellaina sat down in a comfortable office with Dina. It was painted a light gray-purple and had comfortable chairs in a light cream color. There were live plants on plant stands and on the tables and desk. Yellaina thought for a second she wouldn't mind an office job in the council if the offices looked like this.

"Yellaina Rosanov, I am Dina Xenakis." Dina smiled at her as she took a seat next to Yellaina in the other cream-colored chair, instead of behind the desk.

"You are Greek, then?" Yellaina asked excitedly,

temporarily forgetting the weight of the situation.

"My mother surfaced in Greece shortly before giving birth to me," Dina nodded.

"Then you are second generation?" Yellaina's eyes widened.

"So are you," Dina smiled with humor.

"Well, I mean, yes. In the sense that my mom and dad are fallen, but you were born like right after it happened."

"Correct, and to be specific I was actually the first Nephilim to be born on Earth. I am the Elder of the second generation."

"Wow!" Yellaina felt like she was sitting in the presence of royalty. Dina wasn't necessarily tall, but she carried herself as if she were. She had long dark brown hair, and hazel eyes. She had flawless olive skin, and a face that should have been immortalized in a marble bust. She looked like a Greek goddess.

"We should probably begin. Starting with the day that you met Achaia bat Shael. Can you tell me everything that you remember, sparing no detail? Anything may be significant in the grand scheme of things. Please be as thorough in your report as possible." Dina smiled encouragingly at Yellaina and took a clipboard with a notepad and pen off her desk.

"Okay, but before I begin, I should warn you. I'm quite a talker, so this might take a while." Yellaina smiled.

"It's okay, I have a pitcher of water on the bureau and all the time in the world."

Amelia sat between her brothers in front of Osalath's desk. It was a sparsely decorated room and smelled like man. She slouched back in her chair and waited for someone else to be the first to talk.

"I want to hear each of your accounts of the events that transpired. However, for the sake of efficiency, why don't we select a mouthpiece for the events that you were all present for. The other two can interject when they remember, perhaps, any pertinent details that were left out."

"I'll speak," Emile said immediately.

"Do either of you object?" Osalath asked.

Amelia and Olivier both shrugged. Amelia had seen Emile and Noland talking on the plane, and she didn't know what kind of plan they had come up with, but she would go along with it. She trusted them both, sometimes more than she trusted herself.

Emile began, and Olivier filled in the parts that he had witnessed, when he and Achaia had been alone, or when he was at her apartment and seen Shael or Naphtali.

Amelia hadn't been super excited to welcome yet another person into her life that would cause her pain, whether Achaia meant to or not. Amelia had kept her distance in the beginning, and didn't have anything to add as Emile talked. Then, she was unconscious in the cabin, after the plane crash in the Alps, and didn't have anything to add. Then, she had kept mostly to her and Emile's cabin on the train. It struck her how little part she had played up to this point. The world was going to Hell all around them, and she had barely done anything. She'd been terribly busy distancing herself but had done very little else.

Emile finally arrived at the part where the guys had left to go after Achaia. Finally, it was up to her to fill in what had happened while they were fighting their way down to Hell. Emile paused in his tale and looked at her.

"After they left…" Amelia hated talking to people she hadn't met before, especially sharing information that she considered personal. To be honest, she didn't really have any practice in it, so she was just figuring out how much she hated it.

"Start at the beginning," Joash ordered, sitting behind his desk, before Noland even had a chance to sit.

Noland cocked an eyebrow and nodded, appreciating Joash's efficiency and directness. "You promise not to interrupt, even if you don't like what I have to say?" Noland said, crossing his ankle over his knee, and leaning back. He wouldn't let Joash feel like he was intimidating him.

Joash gestured with an upturned palm for Noland to proceed with his blessing.

Noland went into his tale, closely studying Joash's facial responses as he did, paying almost more attention to Joash than to his own retelling of the events that had transpired. He could tell that Joash was trying to be more controlled than usual. Joash was aware that Noland was watching him, and Noland was aware that Joash was tearing his story apart in search for something that wasn't there- treason.

For hours the two sat face to face in a show down. Noland finished his report with a sore, dry throat, and Joash looked like he had a headache. But what was even more disturbing was that, despite looking exhausted, Joash looked happy.

Yellaina walked out into the hallway expecting to see everyone looking exhausted from waiting for her. She and Dina had talked a lot, but all in all, Yellaina had thought the debriefing went well. However, the only one sitting in the hall was Noland.

"Hey," she said, and he stood.

"How'd it go?" Noland asked.

"Good, I think. Dina is nice." Yellaina suddenly felt less casual, looking at Noland's expression. "What's wrong?"

"Joash just seemed way too happy."

"That's not good. Why?" Yellaina turned and looked at the man's office door, half expecting him to come out of it and bust them talking about him.

"He isn't there; he went to confer with some council members. I told the truth, but I wouldn't put it past him to twist it. At some point I must have given him just enough for him to think he could."

"The more we have to interact with this man, the more I hate him. He has all the charm of a rattlesnake. How did he get voted team captain?" Yellaina fumed.

"Intimidation and bravado." Noland shrugged. "The Nephilim were vulnerable and scared. They voted the person

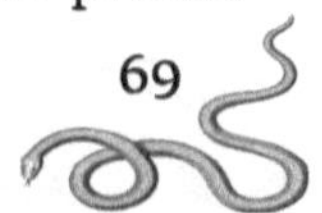

who talked the best game, and he is super full of it."

"Oh, he is full of something, alright," Yellaina could feel her cheeks flushing. "What is taking them so long?"

"Well, there are three of them who need to talk, and Olivier had a lot of alone time with Achaia that the rest of us couldn't report on. In that room, they have the whole story pieced together, all the parts are covered. That's bound to take a while."

"Want to go find some food then?" Yellaina realized she hadn't eaten since breakfast and it was after two.

"Might as well." Noland gestured for her to lead the way down the hall.

When all was said and done, Emile sat before Osalath's desk exhausted and feeling like half the day was gone. "So, what now?" Emile asked.

"A portion of the council will confer, and then we will bring you back this evening, and we can all discuss next steps," Osalath said simply. "I suggest you get some rest this afternoon. Get some food, and just relax. We will be in touch when we're ready for you all to come back."

Emile shrugged. "Easy enough." He stood, followed by Amelia and Olivier. "I guess we will see you later."

Osalath nodded, and stood, still looking at the notes that he had taken.

Emile led the way out of the room into the empty hallway.

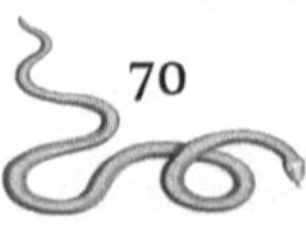

They grabbed food on the way back to the hotel and found Noland and Yellaina in the girls' room.

"Hey man, Osalath said they are going to call us back tonight after they relay our stories to the others. Then we can all sit and figure out what to do."

"You believe that?" Noland sighed. Emile could feel his frustration. "Joash is going to twist everything and manipulate everyone into doing whatever *he* wants to do, just like always. If you still think they are going to let us be a part of any decisions, Osalath has greatly exaggerated."

"I don't know. I think Dina would side with us." Yellaina looked at Emile and his siblings with hope in her eyes. She and Noland were at opposite ends of the emotional spectrum on this subject.

"In any case, my mandate from God comes a little higher than where Joash wants me and when," Noland said putting his coat on.

"What do you mean?" Emile asked. "Where are you going?"

"I promised Achaia I would come back as soon as possible. I don't think there are actually going to be any real plans made tonight that we will actually get to be a part of, so I think I'll skip that little meeting. You can fill me in later. I need to get home."

"I don't know. I think you should wait. Leave tonight after the meeting with us," Yellaina begged. "Joash is already looking for ways to discredit you."

"You guys will be at the meeting; I don't think you'll let that happen. Too many people there will know the truth. I'm a

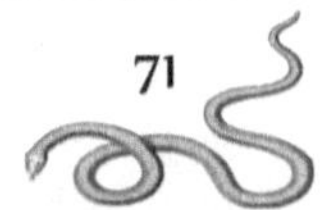

Guardian first. And I've got a job to do."

"Let him do what he wants. He's right. We'll be there," Amelia said shrugging.

"Yeah, we've got his back." Olivier agreed.

Olivier was surprised when they entered the auditorium to find it full. "I thought this was just going to be a meeting with the heads of each generation, the elders," he whispered to Emile.

Emile didn't respond but held his head up high and walked confidently into the room. There were five chairs set in the middle, where a few months before Achaia had sat alone.

Olivier took a seat between Emile and Yellaina; Amelia sat on the other side of their brother.

"You're one short," Joash said from his place on the dais. "Where is Noland ben Nathaniel?"

"Fulfilling his Guardian duty. He had to return to his Charge."

"Achaia bat Shael." Joash nearly spit her name. Olivier felt like punching him in the jaw, but he didn't think that would benefit their cause.

"We will have to proceed without him. Trust that I can relay all the necessary information once we've concluded," Emile said, sitting up straight.

"Just so," Joash sneered. "After reviewing the information you all have supplied, the council has determined to issue a state of crisis. Much has been compromised at the hands of Noland

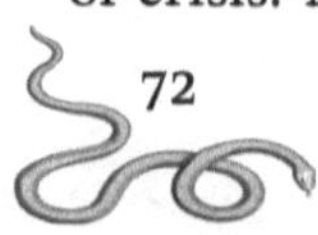

72

Amsel: the protocols, the hierarchy, the teachings, and secret training practices of our people. It is not our custom to train our Charges to defend themselves, or reveal the secrets of the spiritual world, and we certainly do not furnish them with weapons. For these reasons, as well as many more, Noland Amsel is hereby sentenced to exile."

"What the Hell!" Yellaina yelled.

"That's language I've never heard her use before," Olivier whispered over to Emile as Yelliana stood to her feet.

Olivier felt her rage in his own chest. He could hardly believe what he had just heard, and because his brain couldn't process the information, he couldn't react to it.

"No one has ever had a Nephilim for a Charge before. Certainly, under the circumstances, it would be appropriate to make an exception. Or at the very least a reasonable punishment, but exile!"

"What would be appropriate is for you to remain silent, and take your seat Miss Rosanov," Joash said, not altogether unkindly. "You need not be concerned for yourselves of course. The error was entirely that of Noland Amsel, and he alone will pay for his folly. We do not exile underage Nephilim. You were all either innocent or following his orders. As such, we will be keeping a closer eye on you, in his absence, and, where necessary, reforming your teaching where it has been negatively influenced."

"Reforming?" Emile asked, under his breath. Olivier didn't like the sound of it either.

"Miss Rosanov, as you played little to no part in any of this, you are free to return home. Olivier DuBois, as you are still very young, you will remain here, and continue your studies under the guidance of your parents, and when they leave, you will return with them to France. Emile DuBois, you will take Noland's seat, as the next oldest Nephilim of your generation. Amelia DuBois, we have an assignment for you, and you will be placed in the safe house in Chile, to study under its caretaker."

"You're splitting us all up?" Emile asked outraged.

"You are Nephilim. Your job isn't to get comfortable and *hang out* with your friends. Your job is to go where you're told and do what you're told. Do you understand?" Joash said contemptuously, losing his temper. Apparently, he didn't like being questioned in front of the council. A fire was growing in Olivier's stomach. He wanted to punch something, preferably Joash's face, repeatedly, and in quick succession.

"This is ridiculous." Yellaina was on her feet again. "Achaia's protection was Charged by *God*. Noland follows His orders, not just yours. And what would any of you have done if you had been in our shoes? Hunted by demons, not just coming across them. Noland and the rest of us did what we had to do. He was doing his job!"

"No, Miss Rosanov, he wasn't. With the way you are disrespecting us here today, the way you speak—, we might almost question your allegiance, no doubt further proof of his influence." Joash was losing his patience.

"Sit down, Yellaina," Olivier said urgently under his breath, grabbing her hand and tugging it.

"No," she sneered at him, shaking him off. "You don't have to *question* my allegiance," Yellaina said, in a tone Olivier

had never heard her use before. It had more venom than a king cobra. "I am loyal first to God, and then to Noland. Not to *you*." Yellaina leaned forward and stared Joash in the eye as she spit the last word.

The council was in uproar. Council members were shouting, booing, and talking with one another. Joash put his hand up to try to silence the crowd. "You are lucky we do not exile young Nephilim."

"Were you not listening?" Yellaina said, walking up to the edge of the dais and looking up at the elders sitting there. "If Noland has no place here, then neither do I."

"Yellaina." Olivier's voice caught in his throat, but he was on his feet.

Yellaina turned around and walked back over to him. Again, the room was filled with shouts of outrage. "Come with me," Yellaina said, catching Olivier's hands in hers.

Olivier was speechless. Hundreds of thoughts were swirling around in his head, and he couldn't pick out a single one to voice. As if from the recesses of the chaos of his mind he heard his own voice say, "I can't."

The look of betrayal on Yellaina's face pierced through Olivier's chest and left parts he didn't realize he had, hollow inside of him. "Goodbye, Olivier," she whispered, leaning to kiss him on the cheek. Then she left the room and was gone. Olivier stood staring after her, still waiting to process what all was happening.

Penance

Achaia had woken up with a craving for doughnuts. Shael, in an uncharacteristically good mood since Noland had left a couple days before had suggested they experiment with making their own. Achaia had looked up a recipe online that looked to be at their non-existent to beginner level of cooking that used oil, canned biscuit dough, and cinnamon sugar. It sounded easy enough. They had oil and cinnamon sugar, but her dad had run out to the store for the biscuits.

Of course, now it had been almost an hour since they had begun the project and they were both starving. He texted her when he was on his way back and told her to start heating the oil and get ready to go.

Achaia poured a generous amount of oil in the pan and turned the burner on. Her stomach growled.

The oil had started getting really hot when there was a knock on the door. Achaia turned around and saw her father's keys hanging on the hook by the door. She skipped over to open it. "Forget something?" It wasn't her dad at the door, but four men. She made a mental note to start asking, "Who is it?"

The first man was standing in front of the other three. He had a scar that ran the length of his face and continued down his neck into his shirt. The eye it covered was swollen and red, but she could tell it was a scar, and that the wound had already healed. His teeth when he smiled were yellow with black stains between them. His breath smelled like tacos, really pungent tacos.

The three men behind him were equally gruesome. One had dark hair and looked Latino. One of the other men had blond hair and skin so pale Achaia swore she could see his veins. The fourth man was black and wore a suit. He had muscles the size of states, and a busted lip that looked like it had been torn off and was still bleeding. The sight of them made Achaia's stomach turn.

"Achaia Cohen, you've been summoned," the guy with the scarred face said.

"I'm guessing it wasn't the council who sent you." She backed away slowly at first, then turned to run. The men followed with incredible speed and agility for men their size.

Achaia hurdled the counter and landed like a cat in front of the stove. She grabbed the hot frying pan and turned just as Scar-face was coming over the counter at her. She swung the pan like a baseball bat, hitting him across the temple as two of the others came around either side of the counter. The hot oil from the pan sloshed out, splashing the Muscle-master right in his eyes. The thick coating flowed down to his bleeding lips. He covered his face with his hands and screamed out in pain at the same moment Scar-face fell to the floor.

The pasty blond guy grabbed her from behind. His arms squeezed tightly around her, making it hard for her to breathe. He clamped something around her wrists, cuffs of some sort. Achaia felt one of her ribs crack and she threw her head back, breaking Pasty's nose.

In the split second his grip loosened, she turned on him, grabbing him by the back of the neck, realizing that though she was cuffed, the cuffs weren't connected to each other by chain. She slammed his face down onto the hot burner and he screamed

out, thrashing around with his arms. He knocked Achaia's arm making her lose her grip on him and stood. She was amazed by how easy it was for him to dislodge her grip. As he did, parts of his flesh stuck to the burner. What was left of his face dripped with blood and pus. Achaia realized that the men were definitely human, not demons. She looked down at the corroded looking green metal the cuffs were made of, like really old diemerilium that hadn't been taken care of.

The fourth man, the Latino, shoved burnt Pasty aside and came at Achaia head on. She hadn't realized before how small he'd been compared to the others. Unfortunately, he was also much faster. He moved swiftly and silently, throwing punches and kicking.

Achaia kept running through all her defensive maneuvers in her head. But for some reason, though she was strong, she wasn't *angel strong*. Her eyes weren't on fire, and she wasn't fighting effortlessly. She raised her fist to block a punch and realized that it must have been the effect of the jade colored cuff.

She had to try hard to block each of his attacks. She found herself with her back against the living room window and looked down to the street below to see her father walking casually into their building. She had only lost focus for a second when the Latino man grabbed hold of her neck and squeezed.

No matter how hard she hit him, he felt like a brick wall. The other three men had joined him, punching her in the ribs and the face. She felt blood spray from her mouth as she opened it to yell for her father, but nothing else came out.

The Latino man started slamming her head against the

window. She could feel herself losing consciousness. As if from a distance, she heard the glass behind her head breaking from the impact of her skull. She kicked out and swung punches, but her body had no strength left in it. Then everything went black.

Diaspora

"You have enemies? Good.
That means you've stood up for something,
sometime in your life."
-Sir Winston Churchill

Shael hated himself as soon as he rounded the stairwell and saw the door was open. He dropped the can of biscuits, which exploded, and ran into the apartment. Everything was in chaos. Furniture had been broken, the kitchen was a smoking disaster, and the window looking out onto the fire escape had a spider webbing crack the size of a human skull, with blood dripping down. He ran over to it and saw some of Achaia's hair stuck in the crevices.

All the physical violence that Shael had inflicted during

his centuries on the earth paled in comparison to how he was flogging himself internally for leaving Achaia alone. He should have called Naphtali…

Shael called himself the cruelest names for the lowest of humanity, then sank to the floor. He stayed there, stunned and full of self-loathing.

A little over halfway home, Noland's stomach dropped. The flight was actually pretty smooth, so it wasn't because of turbulence. Noland took a few deep breaths, trying to calm his increasing pulse, when the sense of déjà vu clicked. It was the same feeling he had felt in Moscow, right before he had followed Achaia into Hell.

Noland felt sick to his stomach with panic. He was stuck on a plane for a few more hours at least. There was nothing he could do. Then another thought occurred to him. Joash had seemed happy. Had the summons merely been a diversion, to free Achaia up and make her vulnerable? But Shael was with her; he would protect her. Unless… maybe it wasn't the council; maybe it was Luc. Noland's mind was racing.

The rest of the flight was sheer agony. By the time the plane landed, and Noland turned his phone back on, he had three missed calls from Yellaina, and two from Emile. After trying to call Achaia a few times, with no answer, Noland called Yellaina back first.

"Noland," her voice was strained, and at that irritating pitch of urgency girls get sometimes, where it becomes shrill and nearly inarticulate. But this was Yellaina, so she still spoke clearly, "where are you?"

"Just landed. I have a bad feeling in the pit of my stomach. I think Achaia might be in danger. I'm heading straight to her place. She isn't answering her phone."

"Noland, listen to me," Yellaina said, uncharacteristically unconcerned with Noland's anxiety. "Joash had you exiled."

Noland felt like he had run into an invisible brick wall, one that hit him really hard in the chest. After a few seconds he realized that he had stopped breathing.

"Did you hear me?" Yellaina asked, "are you there?"

"I'm here," Noland said flatly. He didn't know what else to say. He was dumfounded. He knew that Joash wasn't his biggest fan, but to manipulate the story to the point of having Noland exiled? "Is Emile with you?"

"No."

Something about Yellaina's voice was off. "I left."

"Left?" Noland asked.

"The council. I left the council. They gave Emile your seat. They are sending Amelia to Chile, and Olivier to France. They were splitting us up. I told Joash to shove it, and I left. I'm at the airport now waiting for the next flight to New York."

"Call me as soon as you get here. I have to make another call."

Yellaina agreed and hung up the phone. Noland dialed Achaia again, still with no answer. He boarded the subway. If it

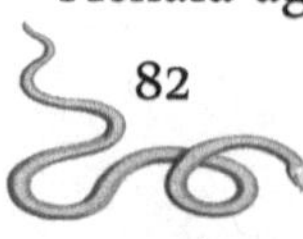

weren't four o'clock in the afternoon he would just fly, but the sky was clear, and there was no way he wouldn't have been seen. Noland unclenched his jaw, which was starting to hurt, and typed out a text on his phone.

IT'S HAPPENED

N.

When Amelia walked back into the hotel room, she was unsurprised to see Yellaina's things were gone.

She tried calling, but it went to voicemail. "Hey, just wanted to make sure you're okay. I'm assuming you're on your way back to New York. I'm proud of you, girl. I couldn't do what you did, but it was awesome. Just call me back when you get this. I leave for Chile in the morning. Emile can work from anywhere, so he is coming with me. We'll talk to you later."

"She's probably already on a plane," Olivier said sounding wounded. He plopped down on the foot of her bed. Emile was pacing back and forth in front of the windows on the other side of the room looking frazzled. He had kept his cool in the council meeting, but now he was free to decompress, and he seemed to be letting it all go.

"Why didn't you go with her?" Amelia asked, turning her attention back to Oliver. She knew her little brother loved Yellaina more than life.

"I flaked. This is all I've ever known; it's my family. Yeah,

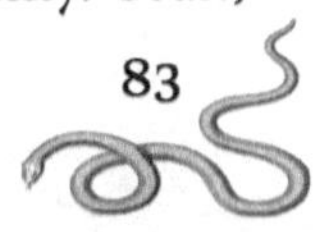

it's a little messed up, but we can't fix it by leaving." The room was dark. The sun had set, and the only light in the room was coming from a small lamp on the nightstand. The room was covered in a dark brown wallpaper. The bleak surroundings weren't lightening the mood of the place. Amelia back tracked to the door and turned on the overhead lights. They didn't help.

Amelia could see both sides. Obviously, she would always be loyal to Noland, but she hadn't left either. Partially because she was too stubborn to give the council what they wanted, and partially because she agreed with Olivier. If things were ever going to change, all the decent Nephilim couldn't leave.

"Noland still hasn't called me back. Do you think he is still on the plane?" Emile said, changing the trajectory of his pacing, and relocating to the foot of the beds.

"Shouldn't be. He took the jet. He should have been there like an hour ago," Olivier said, tossing his clothes into his bag.

"I'm going to try him again." Emile looked pale. The strain on his face made him look older, somehow.

Amelia sat down on the bed and watched her brothers. Her slightly older brother was pacing and calling his best friend in a panic, and her younger brother was packing to go back to France with their parents. Her best friend was gone, and her mentor exiled. How on Earth had it all come to this? Her disbelief was settling into something else brewing in her gut. Unlike Emile, it wasn't panic. It was something much more akin to rage. The council couldn't get away with this. She would find out why they were being divided, and if she could take Joash down in the process, all the better.

"Shael?" Noland had gotten to the apartment to find the door wide open and Shael crumpled up on the floor comatose.

Shael didn't move. He just sat, staring. Noland darted past him into the apartment. The place was a mess, and there was a lingering smell of burning flesh. Noland sprinted down the hall, "Achaia?" He checked her room, the bathroom, her dad's room. He ran back to the kitchen trying to piece together what had happened. There were at least two men, large, human, by the smell of their flesh.

Noland turned off the stove. He could see where they had come over the counter, the frying pan on the floor from where she had fought back. The fight moved to the living room. Then Noland looked up and saw the glass. The window had a spider webbing crack in it the size of a girl's head, Achaia's head. It was smeared with blood. There were glass fragments on the floor all around it.

"It was Luc. Wasn't it?" Noland said without turning to look Achaia's father in the eye. "I knew he was mad, that he'd come for her. But..." *The council couldn't have done this*, Noland thought.

"I should have been here," Shael said, in barely a whisper. Noland felt his sentiment more than he heard it. He was thinking exactly the same thing.

Penance

Yellaina stood in the hopelessly long security line at the airport. She was tapping her fingers on her passport and ticket, and her foot on the floor. She felt like she should be running 900 miles an hour, and yet, she was stuck just standing there in an agonizingly slow-moving line. As the man in front of her moved forward, she kicked her duffle bag forward.

"Yellaina!"

Yellaina turned. Dina was waving at her from the arched entrance, being stared at by half the people in the room. Yellaina shook her head, intimating that she wasn't about to give up her spot in line. Dina looked at her in such a way as to make Yellaina simultaneously miss her mother and also feel a little scared as to what would happen if she didn't go and talk to her.

Groaning, she picked up her duffle bag, and repeated her excuses as she moved to the back of the line, and back to the entrance.

"What are you doing here?" Yellaina asked, trying not to sound as annoyed as she felt. Crankiness didn't even begin to describe her current mood.

"I think the more important question is, what are *you* doing here?" Dina said looking stern.

"I think I've already made my point perfectly clear. Or were you not in the meeting?"

"Oh, I was there, but that doesn't mean I'm going to let you keep making a mistake that can still be undone." People were cutting around them like water around rock, trying to get through security to make their flights on time.

"A mistake? To quit a society of people who are corrupt—"

"Yes." Dina said bluntly.

Yellaina couldn't possibly fathom what Dina must be thinking. "And why would that be a mistake?"

"Refund your ticket and come get an espresso with me."

"My friend is in trouble. I have to get home."

"And how are you going to help?" Dina looked at Yellaina apologetically. "I don't mean to sound harsh, but I think you could be of far greater help here."

Yellaina couldn't hide her surprise. "How is that?"

"How 'bout that coffee? Step back with me and look at the bigger picture. Clarity often comes with distance." Dina smiled.

Noland sat in horrifically awkward silence with Shael for a span of fifteen minutes that felt like five thousand.

"We're going to need allies," Noland said half to himself.

"Could you call in some of your council buddies, or do they all hate us?" Shael asked.

"Well, seeing as how they exiled me today—"

"They what?" Shael looked up temporarily distracted.

"Yeah, I am exiled for the role I played in rescuing you." Noland said this without any bitterness. It might have even had a note of humor in it. "You think that timing is suspicious?" Noland asked, speaking his mind.

Shael shook his head in a non-committal way. "Did you all get exiled?"

"I think it was just me. I mean, I am the head of my

generation, Achaia's guardian, and her soul mate. I was probably like enemy number one on Joash's list." Noland looked around once more at the chaos around them. "Really, I should have known it was coming. Bale said it would."

"Bale?" Shael said the name with surprise. "You keep in touch with him?"

"Yeah," Noland said slowly, wondering if maybe that was better left unmentioned. Bale and Shael weren't exactly best friends. He was saved by his phone ringing. He had forgotten to call Emile back. "Hey," he answered.

"What's wrong?" Emile asked abruptly. Even an ocean away, he knew when something was up.

"She's gone." Noland said. "Luc took her. Or maybe it was the council. I don't know. I wouldn't think the council could do something like this, but then again…"

"What? Tell me everything."

Noland could hear Amelia asking what happened in the background.

"We're still— That's all I know."

"We'll come home," Emile said hastily.

"Why?" Noland didn't mean to sound harsh. "She's not here. Wherever she is, she's not here." Noland stopped, and Emile gave him a minute to just breathe. "No, you do what you've got to do, and I'll be in touch whenever we figure out more. I'll keep you posted. Where will you be?"

"I'm going to Chile with Amelia. Olivier is going back to France with *maman* and our father."

"Okay." Noland hung up the phone. He couldn't deal with

anything other than what was happening in this room.

"So, you don't have any weapons on you, do you?" Shael asked.

"Not many, no," Noland answered. "I traveled light."

"And you can't step foot back in the New York safe house. I obviously can't. I've only got about a duffle bags worth, which isn't enough."

"Enough for what? It would take an army to take on Hell. Our weapons are not going to do much damage against the council. We don't even know who we're fighting." Noland heard the incredulity in his voice, but he didn't care to concern himself with delicacy just now. He thought back to the tunnels of Hell and what it had taken for them to escape. If Luc had Achaia, he was sure to have amped up his security. And if the council had her, Noland didn't think he could wage war on the Nephilim. He still considered them to be his people. They were all the family he had.

"As you said, we need allies. Our list grows thin, but there is one person very well placed." Shael was starting to come around and sound more coherent. His eyes were looking clearer and more alert, more himself. Noland felt something like relief, looking at him. He was exiled, yes. But he wasn't alone.

"Bale," Noland said, naming the one Nephilim on Earth who was neither fallen, nor bound to Earth by birth.

"You could call him, in any case, and see if he is willing to help. If he distrusts the council… If he could just…"

"I'll call him. But, don't set your hopes too high. I'm not sure what he'd be able to do. You should call Naphtali." Shael nodded. Noland checked his phone battery, nearly dead. He took a deep breath and tried to slow and steady his thoughts. He would piece together every loose end, and potential resource he had to figure out what had happened to Achaia, and to find her.

Yellaina sat across from Dina at a small café table with her duffle bag sitting on her feet.

Dina took a deep breath, wrapped her hands around her mug, and leveled Yellaina with a steady gaze. "Look, I understand where you're coming from. But I don't think you should leave. I'll cut straight to it. There's a war coming, Yellaina. Tensions are mounting every day. The council is more divided than ever. Charges are dropping left and right, Guardians are going missing... The Nephilim are anxious, more so than ever. When this war is finally declared, we're going to need you."

Yellaina knew Dina was being serious, but she couldn't understand how on Earth Dina expected her to fit into this. "Why me? I can't fight. I'm untrained. I'm worthless in battle; in fact I'm more of a liability." Yellaina thought back, painfully, to the day the boys left her and Amelia behind to go after Achaia. She had never felt more like a burden and less like an asset in her life.

"Not all wars are won with swords, Yellaina." Dina leaned forward lowering her voice conspiratorially. "Diplomacy is vital. The council is more divided than ever. Miscommunication and secrets abound. People might not always like what you have to

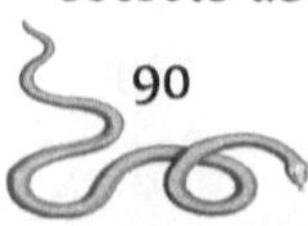

say, but one thing is certain, when you speak, they listen. And, you can speak to *all of them*." Dina's eyes were glittery with something like mischief.

"I don't understand." Yellaina wasn't sure if she just wasn't following or if there was some crucial information missing that explained how a seventeen-year-old, untrained, half-Cherubim half-Nephilim girl was somehow essential to winning a civil war.

"The Lord scattered men and confused their speech when he saw what they were capable of, when they were all on the same page." Dina smiled. "Joash can only directly communicate with a third of the Nephilim population, because of his arrogance and insistence that he shouldn't have to learn their language, they should learn his." Dina smiled. "With unity comes power. Thousands of Nephilim have been ostracized for centuries. Not everyone believes as the council does. If we are going to win this war, we are going to need numbers. Unity, getting everyone on the same page… That's something *you* can give us."

"So, let me get this straight. I declare my utter loathing for the council, and you think I want to become a recruiter for it?" Yellaina couldn't believe what she was hearing.

"Not for the council, not for Joash. For the rest of us. For the Nephilim. For those of us without a mouthpiece who sit silently in our seats disagreeing with him but feel powerless to pursue change." Dina looked like she was absolutely desperate for Yellaina to understand. "You can speak in a way that makes people listen. They *hear* you. Challenge them. Help us to understand we're not alone, and that change is possible. You can piece together the *remnant*."

"You want me to be the mouthpiece of a revolution." Yellaina finally understood. It wasn't the council that was corrupt; it was the loudest members of it. She could make a difference here. "To call out the cancer, and unify the Nephilim?"

Dina nodded. "We're not all like Joash; the council isn't all bad. It just needs some clarity, and some pruning."

"I don't really know how to do this, but I'll try to help. What did you have in mind?"

"Start in Chile with your friends. Don't go back to back to America. Go to all the safe houses that don't hold seats in the council. Band them together. Find out any news that you can. Information is everything. Knowledge is power." Dina leaned back and took a sip of her coffee, eyeing Yellaina over the brim of her mug.

Yellaina stared down in her cup, mind racing, head spinning, heart pounding. Could she really make a difference? Was this really something she could do? She thought of Noland and Achaia. She wasn't really sure what was happening, or if there was anything she could do to help them. She'd sat on the bench last time. But this, this was her domain, her *gift*. With the ability to speak every language she could purify the council, and ready the Nephilim for the real battle- the biggest one they would ever fight.

Yellaina had spent the night with Dina, thinking things through and clearing her head. Early the next morning she

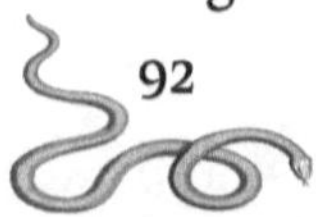

knocked on Amelia's hotel room door and waited for her to open it.

"I thought you would have been back in New York by now!" Amelia stepped aside, and Yellaina walked into the room, dropping her bag at the foot of the first bed.

"That was the plan, but Dina found me at the airport and convinced me to stay and go with you guys to Chile."

"Does Noland know you're coming with us?" Amelia asked. Emile was sitting on the foot of his sister's bed, and she stood beside him, squeezing his shoulders comfortingly."

"No, actually I need to call him back. When he got to New York he said he had a bad feeling about Achaia. I need to check in and see if everything is alright." Yellaina pulled her phone out of her pocket to make the call, but stopped at the look on Emile and Amelia's faces. "What?"

"It's not alright," Emile said.

"I thought you knew," Amelia added.

"Knew what?" Yellaina felt a weight building at the bottom of her stomach, and her heart felt like someone was gripping it tightly.

"Achaia is gone."

The weight in her stomach dropped. If she hadn't been sitting, she would have been forced to.

"When you say 'gone'?" Yellaina couldn't breathe.

"We don't know," Emile started. "Noland wasn't really in a place to talk. He just said that Achaia had been taken."

"Taken." Yellaina exhaled relief. Not everyone was as precise in their language as she wished. She had been terrified that "gone" had meant *dead*. Taken, taken they could work with. But maybe that was her fatal optimism. "By who? Luc?"

"We don't know," Emile said.

The door opened and Olivier walked in. Yellaina felt a lump rise in her throat.

"I thought you left," he said, his voice low and even.

"I was going to."

"But, you didn't." Olivier's eyes searched hers, hopeful. She couldn't tell him, here, that she hadn't come back for *him*.

"I didn't know about Achaia." Yellaina looked away from him, but not before he looked down to the floor. "What are we going to do? What's the plan?"

"What can we do?" Emile asked, but with a tone that implied there wasn't anything to be done. "We're not equipped for a rescue attempt."

"We saved Shael," Yellaina started. In the back of her mind, she was acutely aware that she hadn't played a big role in the "we".

"No, we didn't." Emile said harshly. "We barely made it out alive. And the only reason Shael came back with us is because Iesou showed up. If anything, it just proved to us we can't take Luc on."

Yellaina opened her mouth to respond, but Emile went on before she could say a word.

"What do we really know about him? The original generation are the only ones who had really ever known him, and they don't talk about him. Everything the Earth-Bound generations teach us is hearsay. We know more about him than

94

they do, because we are the first ones to see him in centuries," Emile said looking at Olivier. When he looked back at Yellaina his voice softened. "You don't know what you don't know," Emile added compassionately. "You weren't there."

Yellaina felt a fire spark in the back of her brain; instantly angry she said, "I wasn't there because *you* wouldn't allow it. I know it was dangerous- but we can't sit back and do nothing!"

"I'm not suggesting we do nothing," Emile said calmly, which made Yellaina even angrier. "I'm saying, if we rush into something we're unprepared for, like last time, we could end up making matters worse. You have no clue how lucky we were."

"So, what? We just leave her there, while he is doing God-knows-what to her, while we piddle around trying to come up with a battle strategy?"

"That is exactly how war works, Yellaina. You can't just rush into a battle you're not prepared for. That is how battles are lost. Casualties happen. That's not saying I am comfortable with the idea that Achaia is going through any number of things, while we have to figure out how to rescue her, but you do have to acknowledge the facts. The facts are, we don't even know for sure that Luc took her. If he did, we have no clue where he is holding her, or where to start looking. We don't know how to get to where we don't know where to go, and we also are walking on thin ice with the council. If we don't go to Chile and Olivier doesn't go to France, they may cut off all of our resources and weapons, and we will be completely powerless to save Achaia, wherever she is, with whoever took her." Emile took a deep breath.

Yellaina could feel her face turning red with frustration.

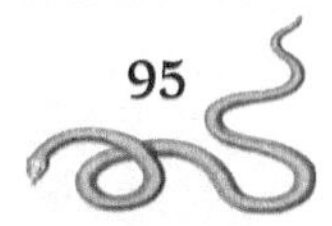

"We can't just sit here."

"Don't make the mistake of assuming I don't care, and I'm not compassionate to whatever it is Achaia may be going through right now. It is because I care about her, that I want to make sure we don't screw this up. If he knows we're coming, and he feels threatened enough to punish her for it, I won't be able to live with that. Will you?" Emile looked tired, as if all his energy had been drained from his body, leaving him an empty shell.

Yet, the challenge made Yellaina want to slap him, and vomit all at the same time. She knew he was right. But it also didn't feel right to sit in the hotel room and prepare to just fly to Chile like nothing was happening.

Olivier took a step nearer to her and put a hand on her shoulder. "At least you guys can still go and make some sort of difference. I have to go back to France. I feel like all of this madness just happened and I'm being sent to my room, grounded."

Yellaina reached up and squeezed his hand. She knew this must be hard for him. Out of all of them, he was the one being left alone.

"I mean she's my best friend, and what am I doing?" Olivier sat down hard on the end of the bed, making it bounce. His shoulder leaned against her back.

"I'm calling Noland. We need more information. We've got nothing…" Amelia said, pulling out her phone and calling him on speaker.

6

Day One

"Whatever happens to you has been waiting
to happen since the beginning of time."
-Marcus Aurelius

Noland had his phone in his hand getting ready to call Bale. He had spent the night helping Shael fix the door so that the neighbors wouldn't peep inside and ask questions. He had also helped him clean the apartment and try to get rid of the burnt flesh smell with sprays and candles. There was no getting rid of the broken window, though. As they cleaned, they had traced and retraced steps as best they could to try and figure out what had happened. Noland had originally thought there had been more than one attacker, but after studying the details all night,

Shael seemed pretty set on four.

When his phone rang, he and Shael were sitting, exhausted, at the kitchen counter with cups of steaming coffee in their hands. He answered his phone immediately.

"Hey." It was Amelia.

"Hey." Noland felt numb. Whether from physical exhaustion or being emotionally spent, he didn't know. It was probably a combination of the two.

"We were wondering if you could tell us anything else. Please, we're going crazy over here. Yellaina is here, too. She came back," Amelia explained sounding anxious.

"Am I on speaker?" Noland asked, looking over at Shael; he looked as weary as Noland felt.

"Yes," Emile, Olivier, Amelia, and Yellaina said together.

"Okay. Well, we've been studying the apartment all night, and it looks like possibly four human men took her. She put up a hell of a fight," Noland looked at Shael, who despite everything gave a slight proud nod.

"Humans?" Amelia said surprised. "Are you sure?"

"Based on the smell of their flesh, and the color of their blood, yes." Shael said, coming over. "There's no sign of any angels or demons."

"Mr. Cohen," Emile said. "Hello, sir."

"Hey," Shael said into the phone.

"Mr. Cohen," Olivier said. "Next time, a little less gory detail." Olivier was the only one who had spent enough time at Achaia's house, and with her father to speak to him so casually.

"You better get used to it," Shael said sounding serious.

"This war is just getting started."

There was silence on the other end. Noland looked at Shael and met his eye. Finally, Yellaina spoke. "Is there anything we can do? Please give us something to do."

"Naphtali is asking around to see if any of his contacts saw or know anything. Are you going to Chile, too?" Noland asked.

"Yeah," Yellaina and Amelia answered.

"Do that. I'll keep you posted if he contacts us, or if we figure out anything else."

"What about you?" Amelia asked.

"Yeah, you can't go home. Where are you staying?" Yellaina asked, sounding like the group mom, as she often did.

"With Shael, for now." Noland looked at Shael. They hadn't actually hashed out the details, but he thought it was implied.

"Do you have anything? Weapons? Supplies?" Yellaina's mommy-instinct was in full gear.

"Nope." Noland swallowed. "I was actually going to call Bale. It's a long shot, but he is the only one with the resources, who doesn't care what the council thinks, who might help us."

"Let me call him first," Amelia said. "I can talk to him."

"You're going to get us a better response, are you?" Shael said not unkindly, but without confidence.

"I'm his mate, so yes." Amelia said with her usual attitude that rises when challenged.

Shael looked shocked, but pleased. "Well then, thank you."

Bale sat in the dining room with a pastry and a cup of black coffee, looking at the windows that had been blown in during the bombings. They had been repaired and replaced, but sometimes when it was quiet and he was alone, he could see it all over again, clear as day in his mind. He shook the thought away and sipped his coffee, thinking about Noland. He had called late the night before and confirmed what Bale had predicted a month before. The council had exiled him.

Bale had a sinking feeling that this was the beginning of everything. The council was picking off anyone who challenged them, or spit in the face of their authority. They had been colder to Bale, and more distant than ever since Achaia and her friends had been sent to him. And Achaia…

Bale thought about her more than he cared to admit. She had come shrouded in shadow like an omen of death, to him. And death had followed her. Or, had she come because death was upon them? He had been so sure that she was the Angel of Death, here to begin the end of days. She had chosen the sign of the serpent, without even knowing what signs were. It called to her, perhaps. Lucifer had taken the shape of the serpent in the garden, the betrayal that started The Fall for everyone. Then again, it was also a serpent raised in the desert who saved the lives of the Lord's people. Maybe things were not always as they appeared. Maybe she was the serpent sent to undo the threat of the first.

Bale abandoned his coffee. It had gone cold as he mused. As he pushed it away, his phone rang. When he saw Amelia's name he answered immediately.

"Bale," her voice sounded worried.

"What is it? What's happened?" Amelia was strong. She never sounded worried. She bore everything with a stoic dignity, or at least an angsty sarcasm.

"Something has happened, and I need a favor."

"I'm listening."

"Achaia is gone. She's been taken, and Noland has been exiled."

"I knew about Noland but when did—"

"Noland found her apartment ransacked when he got home. He has nowhere else to go. He has no supplies no resources. He is completely cut off from the council. He is staying with Shael, but that apartment has been compromised."

"That is no favor at all. He is always welcome here," Bale said simply.

"That's not the whole favor…" Amelia's voice was hesitant.

Bale cocked his head in curiosity. "What else?"

Amelia paused. He could hear her take a breath, "Shael comes with him."

Achaia opened her eyes to a dim light reflecting off ice. Her head throbbed under the intensity of the dark. She blinked and squinted, unable to make out any of the shapes surrounding her, willing her eyes to focus. Feeling her head, she scratched at her scalp where it hurt. Something crusty chipped off in her fingers. Blood. The blood was not only dried, but frozen. It ran all through her hair in brown icicles like dreads. Her vision began to focus. *How much blood was there?* As her mind began to process her surroundings, she realized she was shaking, slumped against the wall. A frozen *ice* wall.

No. She thought, sitting up straight. *No.*

Noland hadn't ridden coach in a long time, not since he had taken a vacation with his mom and dad that wasn't council sanctioned. They had flown to Uruguay to visit an old Charge of his father's whom he had maintained a friendship with after his assignment was over. His father wasn't a typical Nephilim. Noland wondered if that ever upset the council. He had been too young to really notice. He had been ten at the time and was excited to be able to go with them for once, even if it wasn't on a mission.

Noland looked out of the window. He was seated at the wing. It was a clear day, and the flight attendants were making their way down the aisle, serving drinks and taking lunch orders. Shael was sitting next to him on the aisle.

"So, Amelia and Bale, eh?" Shael asked, taking a sip of his coffee.

"I guess so," Noland confirmed, looking at his water shaking in his cup on the tray table in front of him.

"Nephilim are being mated a lot younger than they used to be," Shael mused.

Noland looked over at him. His face was serious as he

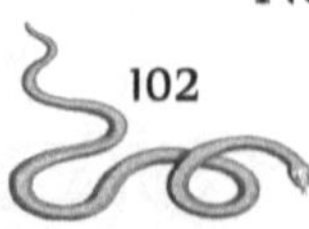

stared into his black coffee. "You think that's significant?" Noland asked, sincerely.

"Yes, I do." Shael looked over at him, studying his eyes. Noland wasn't sure what he was looking for. It wasn't quite a challenge, but almost like Shael was testing him. "I think it means we're running out of time."

"Mates can share abilities, and the situation has been going downhill as of late." Noland said quietly.

"He's preparing His troops for battle."

"For this war that's starting," Noland nodded.

"For *The* War, that's *started*," Shael corrected. He scratched his chin and looked, if possible, even more exhausted.

Yellaina stood outside of the airport, throwing her hair up into a messy bun. Her mascara was burning her eyes, and she knew it had been way too long since she had washed her face. Emile was hailing a cab, or trying to. Amelia was checking her phone, again, to see if there was any word from anyone about anything. Which, there wasn't.

Amelia was usually the stoic one, but Yellaina didn't need Emile's gifts to sense that her best friend was stressing.

Emile, finally successful, was putting their luggage into a cab. Yellaina followed Amelia into the back seat. She stared out of the window, numb, as they passed brightly colored, run down looking houses on the outskirts of town. They were heading toward the coast from the looks of it. "Welcome to Chile," she said dully to herself.

The houses grew scarcer, and the vegetation wilder. Hours later, they pulled into a sand drive for a seemingly little shack. It dangled precariously over the edge of a cliff with thin pilings at wonky angles holding it in place. There were plants all around, so that Yellaina couldn't see over the cliff, but she could hear the ocean.

A pretty latte colored girl with long black braids came out to meet them. She had eyebrows that were thick and perfectly sculpted that made Yellaina a little envious, and metal beads in her hair that made her look like a warrior princess. She had multiple piercings in both of her ears, and despite the warm weather, was dressed in all black, a leather apron and some bulky gloves.

"*Hola*," She said, walking over to them, and taking her glove off of her right hand to shake Amelia's hand who was first out of the cab. "You must be Amelia?"

"*Si*," Amelia confirmed shaking the girl's hand back. Emile walked around the cab from the passenger side and reached his hand out as well.

"And you must be Emile?" She smiled a quirky crooked white smile. Her teeth were an endearing sort of crooked, that also made her look a tiny bit like a super friendly vampire since a sharpish tooth on each side stuck forward a little.

"I'm sorry, my father wanted to be here to welcome you, but he is stuck in a taco."

"That sounds delicious," Emile said, a little delirious from lack of sleep and too much stress.

The girl looked at him confused.

Yellaina slid out of the back seat to join them. "A taco, in Chile, is a traffic jam."

Amelia frowned. "That doesn't sound as good."

"Yeah, no. I'm still imagining, like a giant taco." Emile smiled gazing into nothing but his imagination shaping out the gigantic taco with his hands.

"I'm sorry, we were only expecting the DuBois twins." The girl said stepping toward Yellaina to introduce herself.

"I'm Yellaina Rosanov." Yellaina shook her hand.

"I am Veronica. I can show you to where you will be staying while we wait for my father." She turned to go into the house and shouted, "Vito! Vidal!" She turned back to face them. "You'll find our safe house is," Veronica paused, "underutilized. We never see visitors. So, you'll have to excuse your sleeping quarters."

The house, as they entered it, smelled like wood, spices, and sea salt. Two boys came running up a set of steps and stopped short when they reached the top and saw their guests.

"My brothers," Veronica said gesturing to the boys who were also, obviously, twins. They looked to be about fifteen, and only had one noticeable difference between them. One had a dark freckle on the top of his left cheek, just under his eye, and the other did not. "Vito." The freckle-less boy waved. "And Vidal." The boy with the freckle nodded. She turned and in rapid, horrible Spanish told her brothers that they would be giving their beds up for the girls, and told them to show the ladies to their room. They didn't look pleased at the idea but obeyed.

"You can follow them," Veronica said tuning back around. Yellaina was already moving forward.

"You understood?" Veronica asked Yellaina, smiling.

"Barely." Yellaina smiled. "I'm a polyglot, but I still have a hard time with Chilean Spanish."

"That is because we often just make it up as we go." Veronica laughed.

The initial sting of the ice had subdued into a chilled numbness. Achaia's jaw was beginning to hurt from clenching her chattering teeth, and her shoulders and upper back were sore from shivering so violently. Her lips were so chapped they burned as they cracked and bled. She could taste the blood when she licked them. She had chewed her bottom lip raw, anxiously waiting for something, anything, to happen next. The waiting was more agonizing than the hyperthermia.

Achaia strained her ears for any sound. A distant set of footsteps echoed down what sounded like a tunnel. They were coming closer… The steps grew louder as they approached, each one ringing. It raised the hair on the back of Achaia's neck. She sat frozen, waiting to see if they would pass by, when they suddenly stopped. With the sound of cracking ice, her cell door slid open. Light poured in from the hall beyond, creating the silhouette of a figure before her. She blinked and squinted, willing her eyes to see. In the doorway, black hair in an intentional mess, his bright blue eyes sparkling at her, stood Luc.

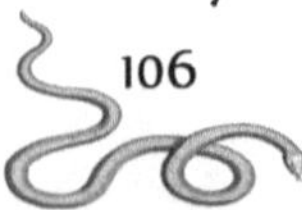

"Hello Love." He smiled, his lips shimmering like melting ice. Though they were visibly cracked beneath the surface, they were smooth and didn't look alive enough to bleed. He looked like a beautiful moving ice sculpture. "Did you miss me?"

Achaia thought it prudent to remain silent and see where he took the conversation. She was in no position to be sarcastic but was too angry to reasonably believe that anything else would come out of her mouth, if she opened it.

"Walk with me?" Luc asked, holding out a thick piece of fur like it was a coat.

Curious, and freezing, Achaia stood. Luc wrapped the fur around her shoulders and kept a hand on the one furthest from him, tucking her under his arm.

"This isn't exactly how I wanted this done, mind you." He winced, as if that were about as close to an apology as he could get. "I've been dying to get you alone, since I met you."

Achaia cocked an eyebrow and leaned away from him as they walked, giving him a sharp side-eye.

Creeper much? she thought, uncomfortably.

"Relax darling," he smiled. "I've simply been anxious to speak with you, without anyone else trying to put in their two, unnecessary, cents." He turned them down a tunnel to the right. It was narrower and darker, a deep blue. His voice skated across the ice as he spoke, gliding at times, and echoing back off of it in an audible Lutz. "I know you must have heard plenty about me, all from people who hate me. And I hardly made a good first impression the last time we met. So, I thought it was only fair for you to hear both sides…" he paused, turning to face her. Achaia looked up at him through knitted eyebrows. "You need all the information, the whole story, before you can truly decide for yourself, which side you're on. This is after all the most important decision you'll ever make."

Achaia took a step back but couldn't deny that she was intrigued at the opportunity to hear Luc's side of what all had happened. He had known her father longer than anyone, and they had been close. He hadn't always been the figurehead of evil… He had been *holy*, once.

"In here, if you please." He ushered her through a doorway into a small room with what looked like a projector, though it didn't look like any projector she'd ever seen before.

Achaia only guessed at what it was based on the fact that it was projecting a stream of light onto the opposite wall. However, in place of the usual reel of footage, there was a series of wires that appeared to be made of smoke and ash. She swore that if she tried to grab a hold of one, her fingers would pass straight through them.

"If you're willing, I would like to show you some things." Luc gestured for her to take a seat on a fur covered chair chiseled from the icy floor.

Achaia figured in order to keep him happy, until she figured out what was going on, it was probably best to agree. "What kind of things?" she asked, finally speaking. Her voice was raspy and hoarse from disuse.

Luc took a seat behind the projector where the floating smoke wires swirled in the air. "My memories."

Noland and Shael were led to the library, which was collecting dust again since Achaia and Amelia had cleaned it. They sat in front of the fire waiting for Bale. After fifteen or so minutes, he arrived followed by the housekeeper. "I've arranged for a late dinner; would you like a drink while we wait? Coffee, *sbiten*, tea?"

Noland declined. He wasn't feeling very thirsty, mostly just anxious, and exhausted.

"Vodka?" Shael asked.

Noland looked over, surprised. Bale simply shrugged and mumbled something to the housekeeper, in Russian. She went away to presumably fetch their drinks.

Bale joined them, taking up an armchair in front of the fire. "Where to begin?"

"Let's start with what we know." Noland suggested, leaning forward, elbows on his knees. Bale sat back and crossed his legs. Shael leaned against the arm of his chair, absentmindedly stroking his facial hair. "Achaia was forcibly removed from your apartment," he continued, looking at Shael, "after putting up what looked like a hell of a fight."

"The assailants were presumably human," Shael added, for Bale's benefit.

"All of this happened while I was summoned away by the council, and the exact day the council exiled me for my part in what happened in March— and probably everything leading up to it since January." Noland shrugged.

"Who represented you during your trial?" Bale asked.

"What trial?" Noland asked confused.

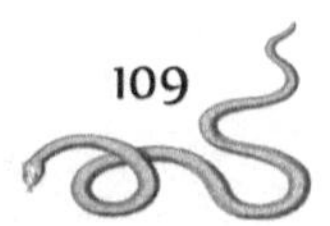

Bale and Shael looked at each other. "Even I got a trial," Shael said, looking skeptical.

"Nope, no trial. We were called in to report on the events surrounding your rescue." Noland looked back and forth between the two older Nephilim.

"Did they interview you together or separately?" Bale asked.

"They interviewed the DuBois together, Yellaina on her own, and me on my own. Wanted to make sure our stories matched," Noland explained.

"Why not split up the DuBois if that was the case?" Shael asked.

Noland shrugged. He hadn't thought about it before.

"Who interviewed who?" Bale continued. "And more specifically, who interviewed you?"

"A Nephilim named Dina interviewed Yellaina. I don't remember the guy's name who interviewed the DuBois, Osa-something but he seemed levelheaded. I was interviewed by Joash."

"And who else?" Shael asked.

Noland cocked his eyebrow, "No one else, just Joash."

"So, conveniently, no one else was in the room to hear your testimony and report it to the council."

"The others only had one interviewer too, so I guess I didn't think about it."

"And they didn't want to interview Achaia?" Bale asked sounding suspicious.

The housekeeper entered the room with a rolling cart,

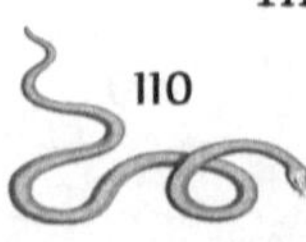

with beverages. She handed Bale something steaming in a mug, *sbiten* Noland guessed, Shael a shot of vodka, and Noland a hot mug of tea. Noland hated Russian tea.

"Oh, no thank you, I'm not thirsty," Noland said, holding up a hand, to politely refuse the disgusting drink.

"Take it and hold it. It'll help you relax. There's something comforting about a hot mug for a shaking hand." Bale looked down at Noland's hands, which were in fact shaking. He waited for the housekeeper to leave before continuing. "It was illegal for Joash to exile you without trial. How did the council respond?"

"I don't know, I wasn't there. Yellaina called to tell me. I wanted to get back to check on Achaia. I didn't like leaving her alone."

Shael cleared his throat.

"You know what I mean," Noland added apologetically. "I didn't like leaving my post," he amended.

"Understandably, look what happened," Bale added sympathetically.

Just then the nurse who had tended them after the terrorist bombings burst through the door yelling something in Russian. Bale stood up and gestured with his hand for her to calm down. They were talking too quickly for Noland to get much, but he was pretty sure she wasn't excited about them being there. She kept going on in shrill angry tones, until Bale shouted one curt word with finality. She fell silent. Bale's face was angry when he gestured for her to leave the room.

"It seems my staff is unsettled by the prospect of harboring fugitives." Bale smiled and retook his seat. "However, I am not of the council. I don't care what it declares or wants. I serve a higher

master."

"Amelia?" Noland asked, nodding solemnly.

Bale looked at him startled. "I was referring to God."

Veronica gave them a tour of the safe house campus. It was the smallest safe house Emile had ever seen. The garden shack-sized house that they saw from the driveway was little more than an entry hall. The house was built in levels scaling the side of the cliff.

The second level down had a small open kitchen and living area with two sofas facing a wall of windows looking out over the ocean. There were sliding glass doors that went out onto a large balcony with an outdoor dining set, and some lounge chairs. Down another level were the bedrooms, three bedrooms. One belonged to Veronica, which was where Emile was to sleep. One belonged to the twins, with a bunk bed in it, where Yellaina and Amelia would sleep, and the other belonged to Veronica's parents.

Down another set of steps was the bottom level which housed the weapons and training room. It was terrifyingly small, and Emile was wondering how they actually trained in there, when Veronica said, "We don't actually train in here. This is pretty much just an armory. We do most of our training outside. No one else lives around here for miles, so we train on the beach most days. Here, I'll show you."

Veronica opened up a solid wooden door that led them

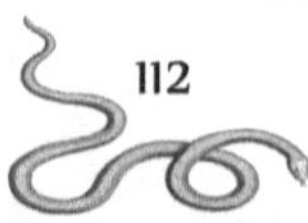

out onto a small stone patio, off of which there were stairs leading to a path. The dusty path was surrounded by thick overgrown vegetation, so that they couldn't see anything else until it opened out onto the beach. The salt air filled Emile's lungs, and for a second he forgot how stressed he was. The water was crystal clear and beautiful. The cliffs were like towers surrounding them, so that they had their own private stretch of beach. At the other end of the beach, surrounded by a few sparse trees were two small huts.

"What are those?" Yellaina asked.

Emile looked at Veronica. Her skin was luminescent in the sun, and her dark eyes shown as she smiled. "One is my forge, and the other is a storage hut."

"Forge?" Amelia asked.

"My gift is craftsmanship. I make weapons. All the weapons you saw in the armory were made by my father and me. We forge most of the weapons the council uses."

"Impressive," Emile smiled.

Veronica smiled back at him, a blush of pink spreading across her high, angular cheekbones. "Oh," she said, looking over his shoulder. "Here he is."

Emile turned around to see a short broad-shouldered man, with the same black hair and eyes as his daughter, but who carried a lot more muscle.

"Papa, come meet our company!" Veronica yelled running down the beach to meet her father. He jogged back with her and extended his hand first to Emile.

"*Hola*, my daughter tells me you are the new head of your

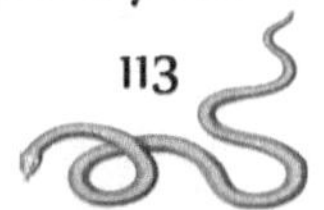

generation. Forgive me for being tardy. I had some business a couple of towns over."

Emile frowned. He didn't take pride in his new position the way Veronica's father obviously thought he should. In fact, he felt like a traitor. Granted, if he didn't take it, it would be Amelia, and Emile knew that she didn't have any interest in dealing politically with the council. If she passed up the opportunity, too, Emile wasn't sure who was next in line, or if they could be trusted. So, here he was, shaking Veronica's father's hand, and trying to look happier than he felt, politics, and whatnot.

Veronica's father was a man of complex emotions. On the outside he was professional, diplomatic. But under the surface, something didn't fit. Emile was having a hard time reading exactly what it was he was feeling. It was almost like a language barrier, but with emotions. Emile had never encountered someone so well masked, even from him.

"My name is Martinus, but you can call me Martis, and I believe my wife, Alexandra is preparing dinner for us."

"Tacos?" Amelia asked.

Yellaina looked at her amused.

"The traffic jam made them sound good," Amelia shrugged.

"Actually, I believe she is making *bistec a lo pobre*."

Emile looked at Yellaina. She smiled at him as they walked back toward the house. "Poor man's steak," she whispered to him and Amelia as they followed Martis and Veronica back to the house.

Back in her cell, Achaia pondered over the scenes Luc had shown her from his life. They weren't much in and of themselves. He had told her they would get to "the good stuff" later. Tonight, if it was night. She had no way of knowing what time of day it was. She was trying to figure out if she could believe whatever he showed her, or if the memories were somehow tampered with.

They had played out on the wall like a home movie, flashes of what Achaia assumed was Heaven, but they were blurry. Luc explained that he had been imprisoned, himself, for so long, that he couldn't truly recall what Heaven looked like.

The memories were indistinct. They were more like depictions of the *feeling* of home, than of any actual place, or event. From what Achaia could gather, if the memories were true, was that Heaven was beautiful, absolutely, perfectly, wonderful. If she had ever called it home, she would miss it, too.

Once the awe of the ability to watch someone else's memories wore off, and she was able to tear her eyes away, Achaia had started watching Luc. At first, she had stolen glances, trying to see if he thought he was tricking her. But then, she had been surprised to find that he wasn't watching her at all. In fact, it was like he had forgotten she was even there.

He was captivated by the images, by being able to see his memories again with his eyes, and not just his mind. His face had looked unguarded and haunted. Most of the time Achaia had spent with Luc, it was as if he was playing a part, wearing a mask and portraying a persona. But watching him look back at Heaven, he looked like a child who had run away from home, and who desperately wanted to go back. If Achaia didn't hate him so much, her heart would have broken for him.

Day Two

"Some memories never leave your bones.
Like salt in the sea, they become
part of you and you carry them."
-Unknown

Noland woke up in what had been his room in the Russian safe house. Only this time he wouldn't walk next door to Emile's room to see if he was awake yet. When he walked into the dining room, his friends weren't there already grabbing at pastries and coffee, chatting away.

No, this time, Noland walked through the halls in silence. And when he entered the dining room, it was Shael already there, looking as if he had never left his seat from dinner the night before.

In his hand, Shael held a mug of coffee, and was staring at the wall of windows.

"Morning," Noland said, taking a seat on the opposite side from Shael.

"Which one did she dive out of?" Shael asked, without tearing his gaze away from the windows.

Noland could still see the incident clearly, like it was burned into the back of his eyelids- the day the Moscow safe house was bombed. He pointed to the one on the far left. Shael's eyes followed his gesture, and he smiled faintly. "There isn't much Achaia can't do. In fact, I believe she can do anything she sets her mind to," Noland said, remembering the day the smoke had billowed through those windows and Achaia had fearlessly pursued the cries of the people in need.

"She's got gumption, my girl. Gets that from her mother."

"She's gotten a fair share from you—" Noland stopped short, unsure if his comment was appropriate.

"Like what?" Shael asked, finally turning to look at him. He took a slow sip of coffee.

"A mind of her own, for starters. A healthy suspicion of those in authority, and a forgetfulness when it comes to the definition of the word 'retreat.'" Noland smiled, and reached for a croissant and jam.

Bale entered the room, pristinely dressed in a full suit, his everyday wear. "I've had a thought," he announced.

"Just one?" Shael asked sarcastically.

Bale ignored him. "We aren't one hundred percent sure if the council or Luc took your daughter. But, when it comes to

holding a prisoner who doesn't want to be held, what is the one place they have in common, that hasn't been used in centuries, that they might hope is willfully forgotten?"

Shael's face turned white.

"What is it? Where is it?" Noland asked, looking back and forth between them, confused.

"The council doesn't teach young Nephilim of its existence. You've likely never heard of it," Bale explained, pouring himself a cup of coffee.

"But what is it?" Noland asked again.

"We don't speak the name," Shael said, still staring at Bale. "You really believe it's possible?"

Bale looked compassionately at Shael, "We can ask Naphtali to look into it, but what does that gut of yours tell you?"

Shael swallowed and pushed his coffee away. "Probable."

"Still clueless over here. Can you at least describe it in vague terms?" Noland said, losing patience.

"There was a prison the Nephilim built together during the war on Heaven: strong enough to hold angels, awful enough to torture them, isolated enough to make it extremely difficult to find, nigh, impossible."

"Sounds like a great place to keep someone you don't want found," Noland nodded.

"It was abandoned in shame, after the repentance. The Nephilim never spoke of it again. For Luc, it was worse than his own prison, and a dreadful reminder of what he had done, had, and lost. It fell into disuse," Bale finished.

"Then why don't you speak the name? What power is

there in the name of something forgotten?" Noland asked.

"Remembrance," Shael said.

"To remember is powerful. And some things are so dark, they are better left forgotten." Bale seemed to think better of his coffee and pushed his away, too. "When Yahweh remembers, He acts," He added under his breath as if to himself.

"Well if remembrance has power, then let's remember," Noland said simply, setting aside his half-eaten pastry like he meant business.

Yellaina sat down at the counter for breakfast and was grateful to see cereal and milk as options. Her stomach was still processing the beef, eggs, and fries from the night before. She poured herself a bowl of Cheerios and searched the drawers for a spoon.

"*Buenos días,*" Veronica said joining her in the kitchen, where she dug a pan out of a cabinet and started frying eggs.

"*Buenos días.*"

"So," Veronica leaned against the counter across from Yellaina, "you are a polyglot? That must come in handy."

"*Sí,*" Yellaina smiled.

"And your friends, what are their gifts? If you don't mind me asking." Veronica had a way of making you feel comfortable, like you could let your guard down. Still, Yellaina didn't think it was her business to share, so she winced and shrugged apologetically.

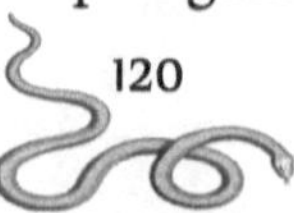

"I understand," Veronica smiled, and tapped the counter before turning back to her frying eggs. She had a sort of abundance of energy that you could feel. She poured her eggs onto a plate and returned to the counter. Yellaina watched the way she moved, graceful, succinct. "Honestly, it is just nice to meet Nephilim my own age. We are a little secluded out here."

"Well, your English is really good," Yellaina said, genuinely impressed.

"Well, my tutor, while she lived, was from England. The council wouldn't send us anyone, so my father trained us in combat, and hired a tutor from the safe house in Edinburgh. Her family had worked for the Nephilim for generations. She taught my brothers and me the histories and languages. Though, I don't think her knowledge of demonic tongues was what it ought to have been. And aside from that there is Netflix."

Yellaina laughed. "Well, I can help you with the demonic. I don't think that one's on there," she offered.

"I would love that. Not much use for it out here; we don't get a lot of demonic activity. But," Veronica lowered her voice, "I am hoping I won't be here too much longer."

Yellaina looked out the wall of windows to the blue ocean, and white beach, "Why would you ever want to leave?" she sighed.

"Don't get me wrong. I love making weapons for the council, but I would actually like to use them some day. I want to train to be a Guardian."

Yellaina smiled halfheartedly, and looked down at her cereal, completely unable to relate.

"What about you?" Veronica asked.

Yellaina didn't even have to think about it. "I want to be a healer."

"You strike me as a lover, not a fighter." Veronica smiled. "That suits you."

"I'd like to repair damage, not make more. I know Guardians and the political positions are necessary, but healing... I just feel like that's what this world really needs." Yellaina, took another bite of her cereal and chewed, and Veronica smiled at her over her eggs.

"*Bon matin*," Emile said coming into the kitchen.

"Wrong language, bro," Amelia said following him.

Veronica laughed. "When you're done with breakfast, my father is waiting for you in the weapons room."

Emile nodded and grabbed a banana, "I'm done."

Amelia followed suit, and Yellaina took a few last large bites of cereal before she hastily joined them in the parade down the two flights of steps, abandoning her bowl on the counter.

As they entered the weapons room, they found Martinus in a pair of athletic shorts that made him look too young to have a daughter Veronica's age. "Ready for your brief?" he asked smiling at them, and gesturing to the door outside. "I thought I could fill you in over a jog."

"It's too early for cardio," Amelia moaned so that only Yellaina could hear.

"Sounds good," Emile said, ready to show up and prove he could at least try to fill Noland's shoes.

Amelia and Yellaina soon fell behind, but Yellaina could

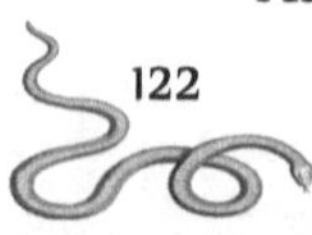

hear snippets. Charges dropping left and right, weapons going missing, Guardians going radio silent. It sure sounded like the world was going to pot. Then she heard the words 'serial killer' and 'weapons dealer', and she pushed harder to catch up. Emile was mostly doing a lot of nodding; he had probably been filled in on most of this back in Rome, but it was news to Yellaina. Amelia, beside her, looked bored and miserable.

Cardio was actually the only kind of exercise Yellaina really enjoyed, granted running in sand was an unwelcome new kind of experience. But she did like a challenge, *sometimes*. She wasn't Achaia; she didn't live for them. When they reached the edge of the cliff on the far end of the beach, they stopped for a break and a stretch. Yellaina took off her shoes and dumped the sand out of them.

"So, you don't think demons are behind it?" Emile asked, stretching out his legs.

Martinus glanced at Veronica, and said, "We've never found any demonic evidence. In fact, everything looks really human. Not sure why the council sent you down here. It's not really our jurisdiction. I mostly got involved out of boredom, more of a hobby really, human law enforcement..."

"They just wanted to get rid of us," Amelia mumbled under her breath to Yellaina.

Yellaina pulled her leg up behind her for a deeper stretch, and nodded her agreement.

"Figures they'd send us somewhere with nothing to do. 'We don't exile underage Nephilim...'" Amelia mocked. "Like Hell."

"Still, if you need any assistance with the investigation, we would love to help," Emile offered.

Martinus, smiled, nodded, and then gestured for them to jog back. Emile kept up with him no problem, but Yellaina was extremely impressed that Martinus was in such good shape at his age. Her own father kept to teaching these days. She couldn't remember the last time he really joined a fight. It was all politics and tutelage nowadays. Nephilim didn't age like humans, but the ones bound to Earth felt it in a way that was unknown to them in Heaven, where they hadn't aged at all.

"Well at least investigating a serial killer doesn't sound boring. Totally not our job, but it's something to do," Amelia said, only now starting to sound short of breath. "Also, I hate sand."

"Me too," Yellaina weezed at her side.

Achaia had no idea how long she had been in her cell. She wasn't sure if a night had passed, or just a few hours, or if it had been days. All she knew was that her eyes burned from being too cold to sleep, and that she couldn't keep herself from yawning every few minutes. She wished she could; every time she opened her mouth, her lips would split painfully making her taste blood. Likewise, her hands were cracked and scratchy. Her shoulders itched, and her legs felt like they were being stabbed with pins and needles. This was her longest stint in Hell so far, if that was where she found herself. She wasn't sure what this place was, but it lacked the hustle and bustle of the circles that she had walked

through before.

The door to her cell cracked open and Luc was there, cloaked in midnight blue, with black skinny jeans underneath, and a silver button-down tunic. His hair was intentionally messy, and his cheeks glistened like melting ice. "Hello, Love. Are you ready for another memory?"

"I suppose." Achaia stood. She couldn't think of anything better to say, or do. Anything was better than sitting alone and silent in her cell. At least with Luc she knew how quickly or slowly time was passing. She felt completely disoriented. "I have a question for you," Achaia ventured, as they walked the corridors back to the projection room.

"I'm willing to hear it," Luc smiled.

Achaia took a real look at him, and it struck her. Satan, the Devil, wasn't myth; he wasn't just a legend. He was real. He was next to her. He had form and feeling. He was beautiful. But, how much of it was real? "When you show me your memories, are they as they happened, or as you remember them?"

"They are as I remember experiencing them," he said, his voice level.

"And can you tamper with them?" Achaia cocked her eyebrow at him.

"Always the mistrustful maiden," Luc said halfheartedly. It wasn't as though he could expect her to trust him. "No. I can't change them. There is no editing that takes place between my memory and the projection of it that you see. Otherwise, I might have filled in the gaps from our last session, and they would have been clear and not out of focus."

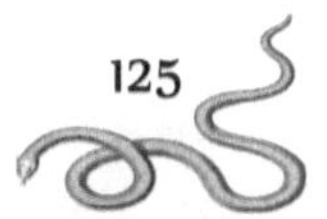

"So, you don't even remember Heaven, not clearly anyway?"

Luc thought for a moment. "I remember how Heaven made me *feel*. I don't remember exactly what it looked like. That was a long time ago, and the aesthetic isn't what my mind held onto." Luc's voice and demeanor were becoming more guarded, but Achaia pressed on as they entered the projection room.

"How did it make you feel?" Achaia dropped the skepticism from her gaze, and allowed herself to look as she was, genuinely curious.

Luc looked caught off guard by her inquiring gaze. She felt a new sort of openness between them. He looked as though it pained him to search his memory to put words to his emotions. Finally, looking at the floor, and refusing to meet her eye, he said softly, "It made me feel small."

Achaia studied his face, his clear white skin, the sculpt of his cheeks, nose and chin, the depth of the blue of his eyes— He was truly a masterpiece, a study of beauty and masculinity, the perfect marriage of the two… She dropped her own eyes, then, as she processed.

Luc had caught her staring, and smiled to himself as he said, "Have a seat." He offered her a fur blanket to curl up in. It didn't help much, but it was better than nothing.

Luc readied himself, and Achaia watched him carefully, reserving judgement, trying to keep an open mind in order to find out the real unbiased truth. "Where are we going today?" she asked.

"A garden." Luc looked sideways at her, without smiling.

Somehow, now that his face was growing familiar to her, it was harder not to look at it. Something seemed different about him. He wasn't his usual charismatic snarky self. It was almost like he was letting his walls down, giving her a peek behind the veil. But she couldn't be sure that it wasn't an act. So, she sat back and stared at the wall, ready for who-knew-what to play out before her eyes.

"So, if this prison place you won't tell me the name of is still usable, and not completely derelict, how do we find it?" Noland asked.

Shael respected the kid's drive, but Shael himself wasn't feeling too hasty about revisiting his old haunt.

"How did you take prisoners there before?"

"We didn't," Shael said simply, hating this conversation, and having to think about days long forgotten.

"Then how—"

"We didn't take them. We sent them."

"Okay, how?" Shael could tell Noland was getting frustrated.

"Okay, stop. Let me just go back and explain this to you. Don't get ahead of yourself."

Noland clenched his jaw and nodded in a way that told Shael to "get on with it then."

Bale hid a smile, but not effectively. Shael noticed, and felt one coming on himself. Noland had guts, and despite himself, the kid was growing on him. If nothing else, Noland really loved and respected his daughter, and what else could a father ask for.

"You've grown up extraordinarily accustomed to the *physical* world. But what we are dealing with here is of the deepest *spiritual* nature. Spiritual war is what?" Shael asked.

"Spiritual," Noland said, nodding as if he knew this, but was trying to look at it with fresh eyes.

"Exactly. It isn't *physical*."

Noland's eyes grazed the room without taking in its sights as he tried to comprehend.

"You can't take someone to a spiritual prison. You send them there. You can't go. It's not so much a *place,* as it is a *state*."

"So how have you seen it?" Noland asked, confused.

"Because that was our punishment," Shael said quietly, staring at the table.

"When you lost…" Noland finished. "You were sentenced to what you had used to make others suffer."

Bale nodded superiorly, and Shael wanted to punch him. "Anyway," Shael continued, "you're sent there, and 'mind over matter', for lack of a better explanation, creates your reality. It is more of an experience. You don't know what to believe, so whatever your mind creates becomes real. Since you fear the place is awful, your own imagination becomes your greatest enemy. You create your own prison with all your worst nightmares, which only teach you to dread and create darker nightmares and greater evils… You also watch your worst memories on a loop until they are exaggerated to something even worse, a lie that you grow to believe about yourself, or someone else…"

Noland looked like he was going to be sick. "So, how do you get out?"

Shael was silent.

"How?" Noland repeated.

"No one has ever broken themselves out. Prisoners have only ever been released, or perished."

"Perished? As in, they died?" Noland asked.

"Perished as in, they feared they ceased to exist in some way, or that they never had at all, and so they ceased. Or they feared death, so it came for them, in the most brutal fashions possible."

"I get the picture," Noland said looking down.

"And, you really believe she's there?" Noland looked, now, at Bale.

Shael desperately wanted him to say "no", to give him one more sliver of hope. To talk about other scenarios, but—

"I am almost positive. It seems the most likely place, whichever side took her. If you want to get rid of someone, that's where I'd take them," Shael admitted.

Noland felt a knot growing in the pit of his stomach. "What is Achaia's greatest fear?" he asked.

Shael looked at him and sighed, "I don't know. Your guess is as good as mine."

The sight on the wall was almost enough to warm Achaia. She had never seen a more beautiful landscape. When Luc had said garden, Achaia had imagined a flower bed, or some bushes, but what she saw before her was paradise. "Where is this?" Achaia asked.

"Eden," Luc said, looking at the scene longingly. "We had watched him work, knew he was creating something completely new, and I wanted to go down and see it."

From what Achaia could gather, she was lying on the ground, looking up at the trees and sky. There was a gentle breeze blowing the grasses back and forth, and the flowers were unlike anything she had ever seen. Each one was perfect, without any splits in their petals, or browning on their leaves. It was almost like an edited photograph, but so much more real. "I can see why."

As she watched, creatures came and went in total harmony and peace. Lions licked the heads of lambs, like house cats grooming each other. Then, a man and woman appeared. They were completely naked, but they were perfect and beautiful.

Luc's face hardened.

"Who are they? Adam and Eve?" Achaia asked.

Luc nodded.

As the scene played out, Achaia watched as the man and woman took the fruit and bit into it. Then they became embarrassed, and ashamed, and ran from each other. The memory ended.

"I don't understand, what happened?" Achaia asked.

Luc took a deep breath and let it out. "I wanted to see what my Lord had created. I had heard of a tree which bore fruit that could make One like him, and a garden..." Luc stated this

as though these were just facts, easily recalled. Then he paused. "When I got to the garden, I saw the true pinnacle of his creation." His eyes were troubled.

"Adam and Eve?"

"He had made them in *His* image. He hadn't even made *us* in His image but, He made them…" Luc swallowed, but couldn't choke down his rage, or was it pain? Whatever it was it was still evident all over his face. "I wanted to be more like Him. I sought the tree to be more like *Him*." He sounded like a child who was desperately confused and disappointed in trying to make his father proud. He paused, regained his composure, and then continued. "Of course, one doesn't simply eat a fruit like that, without making sure it is safe, so…"

"You tricked Adam and Eve into eating it, first."

Luc winked at her, and smirked. "What had they done to earn His honor? Why should He bestow on *them*, His image?" Not that it was right, but it made sense to Achaia. "You were jealous?" She tried to speak without judgement. She just wanted to understand. "You had everything in Heaven with Him, and you were jealous of humans?"

"Everything?" Luc looked more than incredulous. He looked offended that Achaia didn't comprehend. He came toward her quickly. She flinched away, and he almost looked hurt. Achaia felt a pang of guilt at the look in his eyes.

Luc slowed as he came and sat close to her. He looked deeply into her eyes, desperate for her to understand, "I had obligation that sprung from allegiance. Humanity didn't just get His image, they got *freedom*."

When Emile and the others got back to the house, Veronica's twin brothers Vito and Vidal were running out to meet them.

They were yelling something frantically in Spanish, and Yellaina looked stunned at Emile and Amelia. "What is it?" Emile asked her quietly.

Before she could respond, Martis spoke. "It looks like your timing is most opportune. It appears there has been another murder. I will take you with me, but you must stay in the van until I tell you to come in." Martinus turned and went into the house.

Emile looked to Veronica, who was feeling a mixture of dread and excitement. Her adrenaline had kicked in.

"My father doubles as a detective so that he can gain access to crime scenes and keep an eye on things in the mortal world. He works in homicide. Now that I have taken over most of the weapon making, the council doesn't keep my father busy."

"Your safe house is very unconventionally run," Emile said perplexed. He had never been to a safe house so far from demonic activity, that was so close to exposure to the human population. "I don't understand—"

"My father stopped receiving invitations from the council a couple centuries ago. In my lifetime, he has also stopped receiving instruction or commands. All we receive is weapons orders. We hadn't heard from an actual councilman in years, until they told us they were sending you. Weapons orders and pick up dates are submitted by a secretary. We thought, 'maybe, they are bringing us back into the fold' sending you to us?" Veronica shrugged, but she felt hopeful. "Maybe they have finally remembered us."

Emile followed her with the others back into the house. *Why had the council abandoned one of their own safe houses? Were there other safe houses sentenced to static? Why wouldn't there be more?* The more Emile thought of what he'd experienced of Joash, the less it surprised him.

Achaia walked back through the corridors next to Luc, who was uncharacteristically quiet. "Are you going to show me what happened next? What happened after they ate the fruit?"

Luc didn't look at her as he answered. "They were cursed, as was I."

"Cursed how?" Achaia asked. She felt an odd urge to touch his arm consolingly, but held back.

"They were banished from Eden, and their lives made bitter and difficult. But they still had freedom, and thanks to me, knowledge." He sounded bothered, as though he had somehow helped them. "I was cursed, brought low and humbled, forever unable to reach what I most desired."

"To be like God," Achaia said, knowingly.

Luc looked down at her, and for the first time, behind his eyes, she saw how worn down and exhausted he was, striving for what was always just out of reach.

"Then what happened?" Achaia couldn't help her curiosity.

"War." Luc said the word as if it was a bitter memory.

Maybe he regrets what he's done. Maybe he would do things differently if he could go back? Achaia looked away from him. They were back at her cell door. She handed back the fur blanket that Luc had given her in the projection room.

"You keep it," Luc said gently. He reached up as if to wipe some hair out of her face, but caught himself, smiling bashfully as he lowered his hand.

Achaia hardly knew what to think or feel as her cell door closed behind her, when she realized that if he had reached for her face, she wouldn't have backed away. *Was it so bad to want to be like his father?* But that was only the beginning. Much had happened since the garden. Lucifer had done truly terrible things. What was his excuse for those? She couldn't possibly be— how was it that his side of the story made so much sense? If she was honest with herself, she could relate more to Lucifer than she could with Joash… But Luc was evil, she reminded herself.

She remembered the look in his eyes. Someone who was meant to be the embodiment of evil couldn't possibly be that sad. Was he unguarded, and showing her kindness? Or was it all a manipulation? Achaia hugged the blanket around herself and slumped down onto the floor, more confused than ever. He was either very good at manipulating people, or… She was terrified of the alternative, that what she'd been told about Lucifer was all wrong, a biased opinion or lie about a guy who was just

misunderstood, a victim. How hard was the council pushing her away, and what had she done to deserve it? Right now, she didn't think that on the inside Luc looked that different from her.

Olivier sat in the back row of his first council meeting without his friends. The shadows fell heavy here, while the center of the room was illuminated. The council was deliberating, and his parents were sitting with Joash on the dais.

How did things get so messed up? How am I here, left alone, being baby sat, while Emile and Amelia get to go to Chile, and Noland is excommunicated? Olivier looked up to Noland more than Emile, more than his own parents. Meanwhile, Achaia, his best friend, was God-only-knew where, and no one was out there looking for her. *No one in this room gives a damn, and I am just sitting here.* Olivier scanned the room, angrily, filled with nervous energy- the feeling of standing on the edge of a cliff and being told to jump, but discovering that you have no wings. He thought of Shael and how helpless he must feel to help his daughter. He looked down and noticed that his hands were shaking in his lap. He balled them into fists and felt his nails cut into his palms. No, Shael would never feel helpless. He was the greatest warrior heaven had ever produced…

Olivier hated this feeling. More than stress or anxiety, more than worry or fear, more than hopeless, he felt, worthless. His brother and sister still had a purpose, a mission. Yellaina was taking her life into her own hands, and here he sat, in the back,

being quiet: an obedient *child*.

As the Council all reentered, and started finding their seats, Olivier stood. He looked first at the door, where council members were trickling in. Then he looked down the rows to the front. He shifted his gaze to his parents, on the dais, and almost rebelliously, he started down the stairs. His mother noticed him and looked confused. Olivier kept her eye, almost as if to make her watch as he took a seat on the front row. She looked away from him, to his father, who didn't turn to look at him, and the meeting recommenced.

Joash stood before them all, like a king, with his lords and ladies behind him backing him up. Olivier wasn't sure how much his parents really aligned with Joash; truth be told he hadn't really ever talked to them about politics, but he had hardly talked to them at all in years. Nephilim just weren't that attached, or maybe that was just what he was taught to believe. He looked at Achaia and Shael, and there was a bond there…

"Brothers and sisters, we meet again under such conditions as to make us wary. The world has become tumultuous, but we are not of the world. Sent here to aid humanity, we must remember that we are not a part of it, but separate. Their concerns are not our concerns. We will help where we are able, and assigned, but this is not our war."

Not our war? Olivier thought. *It's not like we can just pack up and leave!*

"Our information leads us to believe that these terrorist attacks are by humans towards humans. The proximity to some of our safe houses is coincidence. Our safe houses just happen

to be in major cities that appear to be targeted. However, now is not the time to let down our guard! More than ever we need to defend our Charges and protect them from the spiritual forces of darkness. The dominion of evil ever moves against us," Joash paused for dramatic effect.

Olivier rolled his eyes. *Coincidence? That's likely. And, of course evil moves against us. Tell us something we don't know.*

"Let us focus our energies on our own war!" Joash paused again, and a few older Nephilim grunted their agreement. "Let us remain vigilant and unified. Whatever *spiritual* force moves, we will hear of it. Whatever war is waged, we will end it!" Joash raised his arms as if to rally the troops. Shouts rose around the stadium.

I'm sorry was that supposed to be inspiring? Olivier shifted, unimpressed, in his seat, staring at Joash as if he expected him to continue. When he didn't, Olivier cleared his throat.

Silence fell like an eclipse of sound. Joash stared at him. His mother swallowed. Olivier stood. "Yeah, but that doesn't really answer the question."

Not a whisper was spoken amongst the crowd.

"What question?" Joash feigned patience, but loathing filled his eyes as he cocked his head at Olivier.

Olivier met him head on, summoning his inner Noland, with a glare that would make Achaia proud. "Are these the end times? Is this the final war?"

Murmurs broke out in the crowd, and Joash's jaw clenched. Joash raised his hands to hush the crowd. When the talking ceased, Joash spoke in a reasonable tone. "We have been living in the last days for centuries. Every generation looks for signs and foretellings that it is the end. The Lord himself states that no one will know the day or hour."

"But you could take a guess and say it's coming, can't you?"

"This young generation of Nephilim seem to be under the delusion that when things get hard, that means things are over."

"That's not what I'm saying at all," Olivier stepped forward. "What I'm saying is, they're just getting started."

"This is a council meeting, son, for a council on which you hold no seat. I have been patient enough, but you will hold your tongue in our proceedings, or you will be disinvited." Joash's face was red in anger. "Who knows, maybe you will even learn something?" Joash added like a jab.

Oh, you bet I will, Olivier smirked and nodded at Joash as he sat back down.

As the council filed out, Olivier beelined it for the door. He didn't feel like dealing with his parents right now. He would catch them later. It was going to be a long train ride back to France.

As he made it to the hall, he felt a tight grip on his arm, and someone was yanking him backwards through a door. The door shut, and Olivier turned to see Dina standing staring at him like she couldn't believe him. "When is your generation going to learn to keep your mouth shut, and fly under the radar?"

"What?"

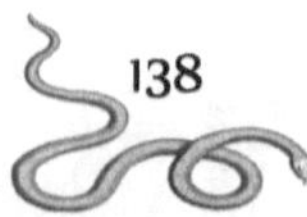

"You want to be the eyes and ears in a council meeting and report to your friends what is really going on here. You probably shouldn't call so much attention to yourself and get yourself kicked out of meetings." Her cheeks were pink, and she was shaking her head and pacing. "I didn't pull all the strings I had to get you to stay here, so you could ruin everything!"

"Strings?" Olivier was having a really hard time following.

Dina looked at him, annoyed, like he was an idiot. "Sit."

Olivier obeyed, and took the chair that was in front of her desk. Dina took her chair and leaned forward on her elbows. Her desk was covered in piles of paperwork, and discarded mugs of half-finished coffee.

"I feel like we should start over?" Olivier offered, in question-like suggestion. "Hey, how's it going?"

"Well, until you went off in there." Dina said curtly. Olivier stared back at her clueless.

Dina took a deep steadying breath. "Have you ever played chess?"

"Not really, but I've played D&D."

"I don't know what that means." Dina shook her head. "In any case, in order to play a successful game, it is all about having the right pieces in the right places. You follow?"

"Not really." Olivier was nothing if not mostly honest. "I get that you are the one who had me kept here but I don't understand why."

"Noland is obviously a powerful player. The head of his generation, confident and willing to speak out against the council."

Olivier nodded.

"Joash wanted him out of the way. Thing is, so did I," Dina grinned. "That one was easy to persuade. So, with my support, Joash was more than happy to go against protocol and exile Noland without trial."

"Wait, you supported that!" Olivier couldn't believe his ears.

"I did, and I'll tell you why when your ears stop blowing smoke."

Olivier huffed a breath and leaned back in his chair, trying hard not to check out of the conversation, though he really wasn't sure how she could redeem herself now.

"As long as Noland was a seat holder and a Guardian, he was always going to be under the thumb and eye of the council. What he really needed was freedom. Joash dismisses him. Noland was only a threat if he had the ear of the council and the resources of a Guardian. Now, he is presumably weaponless, and without connections. As far as Joash is concerned he is an eighteen-year-old boy now trying to make it in the world as a human. However, I made sure that Joash sent you all to Bale back in March, and from what Yellaina reported, Bale took you in. So, I effectively introduced you to your only possible ally who isn't affiliated with the council. You're welcome by the way."

Olivier cocked an eyebrow and stared at Dina. "You've been playing this game a while—"

"You bet I have." Dina smiled. "I have a gift for foresight. It's not like I can see the future, but there are certain things I just know are going to happen. I am as sure about them as I am that

the sun rises every day, and gravity works."

"Go on," Olivier leaned forward on his knees, intrigued. He hadn't been sure at first, but Dina was looking like his kind of person.

"I met Yellaina at the airport because I couldn't allow her to exile herself. She has a role to play still." Likewise, your brother and sister are exactly where they need to be, as are you. Now, in order to play your role, I'm going to need you to mind your 'p's and 'q's and be a good boy. Can you do that?" Dina leveled him with a challenging look.

"Contrary to popular belief," Olivier smiled, "I actually can."

8

In Dreams We Wake

"In the garden of memory, in the palace of dreams...
That is where you and I shall meet."
-Lewis Carroll,
Alice Through the Looking-Glass

Emile and the others waited for Martis to give them the okay.

"Your dad lets you visit crime scenes?" Yellaina asked the twins.

"Lets us? More like makes us," Vito said. "We went to our first when we were six."

Amelia looked at Emile, and he could feel her surprise and discomfort. He agreed. Six seemed a little young for murder scenes. But he supposed that first-generation Nephilim, having never been young, would have a hard time grasping what was age appropriate and what wasn't. Perhaps he and his siblings were lucky to grow up in a city, surrounded by humans to gauge such things by.

Martis walked out of the house with what looked like his crime scene photographer, and some other police. He nodded at them to go in through the back door.

"Okay, don't touch anything, or in any way disturb the crime scene. My guess is we have about ten minutes before the coroner comes," Veronica said, shuffling them around the back of the house.

Emile went in first with Veronica. They entered in through a kitchen. It was immaculate. The counter tops literally sparkled. Everything was in its place as if the house were being shot for a magazine. Through the kitchen was an archway that led into a living room. The pristine kitchen made the next sight that much more startling. Everything was bathed in blood, the walls, furniture. It even dripped from the ceiling; pools of it were spreading over the floor.

"Woah, this gives new meaning to blood bath," Vidal said looking at the consistent spray of blood coming from the ceiling fan. A drop hit Veronica in the face, and Emile without thinking, moved to wipe it from her cheek. She looked at him, a little taken aback by the gesture.

"What happened here?" Yellaina said, sounding like she was trying not to vomit. Emile could almost feel her heart beating hard in his own chest. She was by far the most upset at the sight. She didn't usually go out into the field back home.

"*Dios*," Veronica said, looking behind a sofa.

"What is it?" Emile went to her side and looked to see two small children butchered on the floor, as if they had been trying to hide. The father was by the front door, likely the first to be struck down, and his wife was in the middle of the room.

"Well this certainly is *a negative* turn of events," Vito said rounding the sofa to see the children as well. Emile was struck more disturbingly by the lack of emotional response coming from the twins. The level of emotion he sensed from them was akin to them watching a movie or playing a video game. As if they didn't register that this was a real family, that those children were probably terrified in their last moments, and no more than three and five years old. Emile supposed their lack of compassion and empathy was probably a negative consequence of their early exposure, and the normalization of murder in their lives.

"O come now, *be positive.* If we can find some clues, we can catch who did this," Vidal responded, studying the mother's wounds.

"Seriously?" Veronica stood up, and Emile could feel her annoyance.

"What?" Amelia asked, though she was perturbed by their nonchalance, too.

"They are talking in blood type puns." Veronica rolled her eyes and glared at her brothers.

Vito grinned. "*O negative* Nancy, don't be-"

"On the contrary," Vidal cut him off, smiling at Veronica, "*be negative* all you want! But fear not! *A positive* turn of events is sure to arrive!"

"Really guys, not the time," Veronica snarled. "You're

seriously disturbed."

Emile felt Yellaina's horror and saw it written across her face in a look she shared with Amelia.

"Okay we'll stop. Are you *AB* now?" Vito laughed, leaning over the father.

"Actually, I think I'm *AB negative*, but I'm not *positive*." Vidal studied the blood splatter on the walls.

"Well, you wouldn't be, obviously." Vito tossed Vidal a camera to take photos of the splatter. They smirked at each other, clearly unperturbed by the scene or how upsetting their behavior was to everyone else in the room.

Emotionally stunted, Emile decided.

Veronica threw her hands up in the air, and huffed a sigh, clearly giving up on her brothers.

"Actually, Nephilim have their own blood type. It is poisonous to humans, corrupts their veins," Yellaina put in.

Vito and Vidal looked at each other in amazement and said together, "We like this one."

"She's full of fun facts." Vidal winked at Yellaiana, and she recoiled, rolling her eyes, and saying, "I'll wait outside. I just can't…"

"For shame," Vidal said, going back to his work. "From the looks of it, I would say the murder weapon doesn't match the rest of the murders. This is more brutal than the usual MO."

"I would say a blade for the father and the kids," Vito added.

"Too big to be a knife," Veronica said, studying the wounds on the children, "machete?"

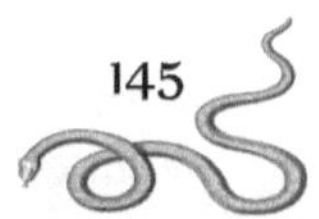

"Axe?" Emile said, leaning over the youngest. "Look how deep it penetrated." Over the blood, he could still smell baby bath soap. He felt his chest tighten.

"Maybe," Veronica looked up at him.

"The mother is lying on her wounds, so we can't say for sure. But I think the blood on the ceiling is probably hers. The walls, I would say a blade makes sense, but the ceiling—I can't tell without seeing her front, but maybe more of a slinging weapon?" Amelia looked at Emile.

"Like a mace?" Emile asked doubtfully.

"I was thinking more like flagrum," Amelia said, squatting low to see as much of the mother's wounds as possible.

"That would certainly account for the splatter, but do humans even use those anymore?" Veronica said joining her on the floor.

"I think we need to stop assuming these attacks are human," Emile said, taking in the room. "When something this brutal happens, something more sinister is usually at work."

The group made for the back door as they heard voices approaching the front. "Veronica," Emile said, watching through the back door window as the coroners collected the bodies.

"Yeah?"

"I'm going to need you to fill me in on every detail of all these murders."

Shael, Bale, and Noland sat in the safe house library. They

had poured over every history text Bale owned that so much as mentioned the war. "That's it." Shael slammed his last book shut with a cloud of dust.

"There's got to be more. You were there; you have to remember something." Noland sounded desperate, and Shael felt it to his core.

"How did it come into being? Who created it? It had to come from somewhere. Surely whoever created it, would know its weaknesses," Bale said sounding annoyingly logical. But he was right.

"Only two beings in creation could have created it, and God wouldn't have," Shael said. "The only other would be—" Shael smiled. "I haven't seen him in centuries. Bale, do you by any chance know where I could find Martinus ben Yahweh?"

"Actually, *I* do," Noland said, looking surprised. "That is who Emile was sent to in Chile."

Achaia didn't think it would matter if Luc had gifted her a thousand furs, her bones would still quake with cold. She could see how being a Nephilim and unable to just curl up and freeze to death was Luc's curse. She was sure that if she had been more than half human, she would have died by now. *How is it possible to be this cold?*

It seemed that all the moisture in her body had frozen and cracked. This was reflected in her skin, which had bloody crevices that spiderwebbed across her hands, up to her shoulders;

they stung and itched. She slumped against the wall of her cell, shivering so badly her body was sore all over, and her jaw ached from clenching her teeth. She distracted herself with a daydream. She reminisced about warmth, trying to remember what it even felt like. The sun on her skin? No. She remembered it only as someone could recall something they had never experienced themselves, but only read about in books, or seen in movies.

Achaia sighed and tried again. She tried to remember burning her mouth on hot pizza or with fresh coffee. Nothing. She knew it had happened, but it was almost like it had happened to someone else, and she had only heard about it. The feeling long gone. It was merely a fact, or story, rather than a memory. She was beginning to understand how it must be for Luc. Her time here had been so limited, and already she was beginning to forget; his time had been nearly infinite.

Achaia pulled the fur closer, and tried to engage her other senses. She smelled it. It smelled cold, like blue or white. She shook her head. *Great, now I'm losing my mind*, she thought. Exhaustion was making her illogical. Letting the fur fall to expose her arms, Achaia dug into her forearm with her nails, leaving half-moon indentions where blood pooled. She could feel *that*, though the numbness of her flesh dulled the would-be pain.

The blood reminded her she was alive. It also reminded her of the scars covering her, that she had forgotten had become a part of her landscape, along with her freckles- Scars from where shadows had clung to her and scratched, in the forest, after their plane crashed in the Alps in a blizzard. They were only thin little white lines now... Noland had swooped in and carried her to

148

safety. Noland who kept her safe, kept her *warm.*

Achaia tried again. She thought of Noland starting a fire in the cabin, flying next to her, and holding her hand, radiating heat through her entire body. Noland sliding over to her in her sleep and enveloping her in warmth. The peace, safety and warmth she had felt. The memories were there, but she couldn't feel them. She whimpered and kicked out at the wall. She felt the pain shoot up her leg from her bare foot.

Achaia curled in on herself, trying to conserve her own body heat. She kept thinking about Noland. Where was he now? What was he doing, thinking, feeling? Was he trying to find her? Was anyone coming for her? Darkness gradually took her, and she fell asleep, thinking again about Noland holding her safe and warm.

Noland ran back to his room to pack a bag. He and Shael were leaving for Chile within the hour. Bale was buying their tickets and arranging for a car to take them to the airport. Noland opened his bedroom door and stopped short; there was a lump of something, or someone under his covers. Noland pulled a dagger from his belt and paced forward silently. Then he saw the red curls spilling over his pillow and lowered his weapon. "Achaia?"

Achaia stirred and opened her eyes, looking up at him. "Hey," she smiled. "Where are we?" She looked around. "Moscow?"

"Yeah, we're at Bale's, how are you here?" Noland asked, closing the space between them and sitting on the bed next to her, stroking her hair. Her skin was blistered and cracked, and her lips were blue. "Come here." He laid a hand on her cheeks and focused on warming her.

"Hmmm," she smiled and closed her eyes. "This is a good dream. I couldn't remember what warmth felt like. I was thinking of you, about how warm you are."

"Achaia, you're not dreaming. You're here," Noland said, squeezing her tightly.

"Until I wake up."

Noland decided to play along with her delirium. "Where will you be when you wake up? Hell? Is that why you're cold?" Noland asked, moving his hands to her arms.

"I don't know. It is like Hell. But then it isn't." She was mumbling, delirious and exhausted.

"Was anyone there with you?" Noland asked, watching the color start to come back to her face.

"Just Luc," She was falling back asleep.

"Listen to me Achaia, you're not dreaming. You're here. Can you please sit up?" Noland begged.

"I'm not here. I'm only dreaming. I'll have to wake up soon. I don't want to wake up. Please don't make me wake up." Tears were streaming out of her closed eyes.

"Achaia, please just wait here." Noland ran to get Shael as fast as he could through the halls. "She's here!" he yelled when he got to Shael's room.

"What?" Shael looked at him in utter confusion.

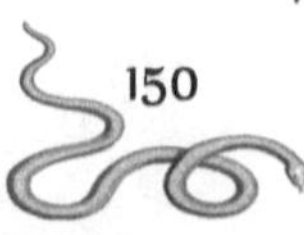

"Achaia, she is here! She's in my room!" Without another word, Shael was on his heels as they ran back to Noland's room. The door still stood ajar.

The room was empty. Achaia was gone.

"I swear, she was right there. I came back to pack my bag, and she was curled up in my bed, sleeping." Noland was confused.

"You're sure you weren't hallucinating? Neither one of us has slept much lately." Shael put a hand on his shoulder, the first fatherly gesture he'd ever offered him.

"No." Noland turned to Shael, desperate to be believed. He went over to the bed and pulled back the covers, as if Achaia could be hiding under them. Then he saw it resting on his pillowcase, a long, curled length of red hair. "Look!" He held it up and showed it to Shael.

"She was *here*," Shael's voice was faint, and broken. A look crossed his face that broke Noland's heart. It wasn't hope, but anguish. "Did she say anything?"

"A lot," Noland confirmed. "Let's get Bale, and call Naphtali."

Olivier decided to join Dina at her game. He came up with a plan of his own, and after bouncing ideas back and forth and getting direction from Dina, he was ready to go deep undercover. He felt like Batman, living the ultimate double life, and he was ready to put on his Bruce Wayne face. Olivier knocked on the door and listened for a reply.

"Enter."

Olivier opened the door and was a little gratified to see the shocked and annoyed face that met him. Joash sat at his desk, and when he saw Olivier, he leaned back, clasping his hands across his belly. Olivier thought briefly of all the mob movies he'd ever seen, then decided he needed to stop comparing his reality to tv, at least for the next ten minutes. Then he could be Bond, James Bond.

"Yes?"

"I wanted a moment to speak with you, brother Joash."

Joash looked skeptical but gestured to the seat across from him, and Olivier took it.

"What is it?" Joash asked, shortly.

"I wanted to personally apologize for this morning. I've been thinking about it and, with all due respect to Jacob, I've realized that most of what I know has come from Noland. Him being recently exiled and all, I can't help but think, my education has been a little limited. Jacob is a great Nephilim, but perhaps his hands have been a bit full with the older kids, and I've been a little overlooked. I want to learn, sir." Joash grinned smugly. "And I'd like to learn correctly," Olivier added for good measure. He thought he might be laying it on a bit thick, but Joash was proud and he would eat what you fed him if it was what he wanted to hear, according to Dina.

Joash smiled, showing that his pride and ego were, in fact, his greatest weaknesses. "So, you come to me, for a mentor?"

"I like to shoot high, so if I fail, I still land pretty far up."

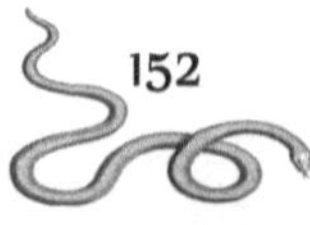

Olivier smiled.

"At least someone of this young generation is starting to show some sense. I'd begun to fear you were all irrational radicals."

"I've received the histories from Jacob, and gone through all my tutelage; but what my teachings lack, is where we stand in these modern times. What are we doing, and where can I fit into that plan? I want you to know, I am ashamed to say, my speech from this morning came from a place of anxiety. Which, I have come to realize, came about due to a lack of understanding. I think if I knew more about where we stand, and what our goals and missions are as a whole, I would feel a greater sense of purpose which would prevent future attacks of stupidity."

Joash laughed and leaned forward. "A solid plan. I am happy to see someone of your age so self-aware. A rare quality. You get that from your father. A *great* Nephilim."

"I believe times of introspection to be excessively prudent. That is, if one is to grow into one's greatest self." Olivier smiled. He patted himself on the back inwardly for sounding so mature. Little did Joash know, it was because he was channeling his inner Noland.

Joash nodded. "So, where do you see yourself fitting into this plan?" Joash asked.

"Well, in the long term, I think I'd like to work for the council. As exciting as the life of a guardian sounds, I just don't know if it is for me. I'd like to do something more grandiose. A healer or historian, I think, would be too monotonous; and besides, I want to move forward, not back." Olivier saw a light spark in Joash's eyes, and he knew he'd hit the spot.

"So, you want to become a council member?" Joash leaned back again, and looked a bit like a dragon, arrogant in his security, and reckless in the divulging of his tender underbelly.

"I think that is the path that would best suit my goals." Olivier nodded.

"Well then, how about an internship? You can shadow myself."

Olivier smiled. "You mean it?" Olivier asked with childlike excitement.

Joash smiled. "Don't sound so excited. You'll mostly be fetching coffee and taking the minutes in meetings."

Olivier smiled even wider, "Sounds like a perfect starting point." Taking notes in all of Joash's private meetings sounded like the perfect starting off point, indeed.

"At least our suspicions are confirmed." Bale sighed, not taking any true comfort in this fact. He had ardently been hoping he was wrong.

"So how quickly can we get to Chile?" Shael asked. "I need to speak with Martinus immediately, convince him to help us."

"That won't be easy, convincing him to go against not only the council but Lucifer himself. However, you must try. I have booked your flight to leave this evening. I suggest you try to take food and rest while you can." Bale sighed again, as if it was

becoming a habit. His anxiety over the situation had only grown with the confirmation that it was, indeed, Lucifer who had taken Achaia.

Noland, who had looked dazed, and in his head, spoke, "What does he want with her? I mean, is this payback? What?" Noland looked haggard for someone so young, the cares of a generation resting on his shoulders, even though he had been exiled. He seemed to forget he was no longer a leader. Just a boy, he couldn't stop being an adult. First generation Nephilim never got to be kids, but this boy should have had a chance.

"I think it must be punishment, for me. Revenge," Shael said, full of self-loathing.

"I'm not so sure," Bale countered, remembering the first time he had seen Achaia. "The first time I saw Achaia, I knew she was powerful. More powerful than she knows, and I think you have been too close to the picture to see the full of it," he directed to Shael. "I could feel death dance around her. An unsettling amount of power for one so young. I thought perhaps it was because she was half human. The power of angels with the free will of humanity, I thought her an abomination. Now I am less certain."

Shael had flinched at the word abomination, but otherwise guarded his expression.

"I agree," Naphtali added, on speaker phone. "Achaia has been getting a lot of unwanted attention from nearly every spiritual being she has come in contact with. She is like a magnet for it."

"So, what are you both thinking, now?" Shael asked,

anxious for clarity.

"I think she is a great weapon. A free agent, with the power we've all longed for at some point, and the freedom to choose." Bale leaned forward. "If *I* felt it the first time I met her, what do you think *Luc* felt? What do you think Luc desired?"

"He wants to use her," Noland said, something behind his tired eyes waking up.

"I wouldn't stop there. Think of Luc's character. He takes things selfishly, without thought of what should be, or who…" Naphtali added.

"If you're implying what I think you are, I'm going to vomit," Noland said, following Bale's implied meaning.

"I'm going to *kill* him." Shael said at the same time, practically steaming from the ears.

Hours passed in intermittent speculation and light snacking. A smorgasbord lay before them on the table, but no one's heart was in the eating.

"As long as Achaia's darkest fear isn't falling in love with Lucifer, she should be safe," Naphtali said, still on the phone. "At least for a time." Noland could hear all the background noise, of Naphtali traveling to get inconspicuously to them. He had been in Singapore when they called him with the news.

"He would try to manipulate her first. He wants to be wanted. He would give her the chance to join him willingly first." Shael agreed.

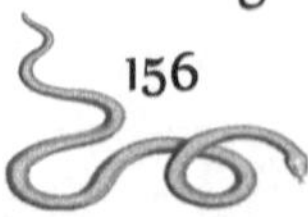

"What if her greatest fear is that she is like him?" Noland asked, not really wanting anyone to answer. He wished he knew what her greatest fears were, aside from cockroaches. They hadn't exactly gotten around to those conversations.

The tv playing in the corner snowed for a second, and the news cut in with the alarm of an important announcement. Bale turned in horror to the images on the screen.

"*Oh my God*," Noland said.

Shael was silent.

"What?" Naphtali asked, unable to see what they were talking about.

A nuclear bomb had been unleashed on China, a retaliation unleashed on America. World War III was being declared.

The three of them stared at the screen in horror.

Bale regained his senses first. "World war three has just been declared, Naphtali. Obviously, for more reasons than one, we can't allow Luc to wield Achaia. We have to get her back. We have even less time than we thought, it seems. I'm afraid, you will not be able to get here fast enough using human methods," Bale said bringing them back to their own pressing matters.

"We?" Noland said, sounding hopeful.

"I am with you." Bale stood a little straighter, as if at attention. "The final war has begun."

9

Day Three

"Experience is a brutal teacher
but you learn. My god, do you learn."
-C.S. Lewis

Achaia woke up feeling as if she had actually gotten some sleep. She groaned. *Tell me I'm not getting used to this place.* Then she remembered her dream, Noland and his warmth. She took a deep breath and sighed. Then she stiffened. She breathed deeply again. When she had smelled it before, the fur hadn't smelled like anything but chill. She sniffed it again. It still didn't. She smelled herself. She smelled, like Noland. *How?*

"Rise and shine, beautiful girl." Luc's voice came from the other side of the opening door. "Are you ready for your next lesson?"

Achaia regained her composure quickly and stood. She wrapped the fur snuggly around herself and followed him.

"Today is a big day," he informed her, uncharacteristically cheerful.

"How's that?" she asked, indifferent, still preoccupied by her dream.

"We are celebrating with my most crucial memory yet."

"What are we celebrating?" Achaia asked, hesitantly.

"I'll tell you after." Luc grinned, as he opened the door to the projection room.

Achaia took her usual seat, and Luc took up the smoke to reveal his history.

The wall turned dark with black clouds. There were streaks of light, like lightening. "A storm?" Achaia asked.

"A war," Luc said, sounding reverent.

Achaia realized that the lightening was actually the clash of blade on blade, as angels dueled. They moved like vapor, hard to see, unless you focused. They were everywhere all at once, mixing and melding against each other, and causing explosions of electricity and fire as they collided. It was both terrifying and beautiful.

Thunder shook the very air around them, and Achaia felt it quake in her chest like a heart attack. She sucked in her breath, horrified. She'd never felt warfare like this. It made her escape from Hell look like a child's play date.

She couldn't see earthly bodies like they wore now. She couldn't follow rational bodily movement with her eyes, so she

never knew where the next blow would be struck, or where each fighter was. It seemed like when and where she least expected it, there was lightning followed by the thunder. Her breathing was heavy and erratic. She couldn't figure out where to focus her eyes.

"Can you see them?" Luc asked.

"No," Achaia said, frantically searching the projection.

"Here," Luc came to stand behind her, against her back. Gently, almost sensually he placed his hands on her temples down to her jaw, and her eyes were opened.

She could see them, the heavenly beings. They were brilliant, beautiful, and terrible all at the same time. Their warfare looked like dancing, all grace and glory. With terrible power they clashed and writhed. It would have been lovely had it not been so broken. She felt the collapse of a dream, like when you're working on a painting, and the rinse cup spills across your wet paint, turning your spring day to black. Or when you're trying to build a gingerbread house for your dad, and with one false move, it crumbles. It was all majesty, but not as it should have been. It was a shattered image of power. It was a tainted perfection- these beautiful angelic beings, acting against purity and bliss for the cause of destruction. It was repugnant.

"I can see them," she said breathlessly.

"I knew you would," Luc said, his hand sliding down her neck as it relaxed to rest on her shoulder.

Achaia shivered as a chill went down her spine and a pang of nausea shimmied through her stomach. She flinched away from him, and the projection stopped.

Achaia turned around. Luc had a strange look in his eye.

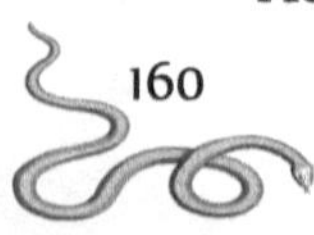

"You liked it didn't you?"

Achaia wasn't sure if he was referring to the touch, or the image he had shown her, but the answer to both was the same, "No."

Luc looked shocked for only a second before he guarded his look. "I have to say I'm surprised."

Achaia had never felt more offended or disgusted in her life. "Why would you ever think *I* would *like* that?"

"You've never been more open to me," Luc said stepping forward toward her, closing the small space between them, and slipping his hand around her waist. She could feel him against her, and she lurched away feeling more afraid than she ever had, and more and more like having to throw up.

Luc, unfortunately, only looked amused. "Let me explain something to you." He grabbed her wrist hard, and pulled her into him again. His face was inches from hers. "The longer you're here, the more your nature will become like mine. The more you will become like me." His voice was like venom. His eyes were vivid blue. He pulled her to him, his lips against her ear. "Before long, you will beg for me." She yanked away again.

She couldn't speak. It took everything in her to keep breathing without throwing up or screaming. She had to keep herself in control of herself. "That will never happen." She spat.

"You've already thought of it; I see the way you've looked at me, the way your eyes linger over me. You will be my queen." Luc sounded so assured.

Achaia felt sick at the thought of how she had looked at him, had studied him, had shown curiosity, but not in the way he

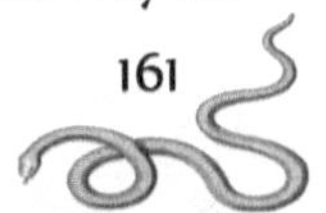

suggested, not for that reason. Then her brain caught up to the word *queen*.

He stepped toward her then, and added in a low tone, husky with breath, "and the two will become one flesh." He reached around her waist again. Achaia was stunned. "You are like me. And with your power added unto my own, *we won't lose*."

Achaia's mind spasmed at the way he said *we*. "Lose what?" she asked, backing away from him toward the door. He released his grip on her, but slowly, and she slid out of his hand which caressed her on the way.

"The final battle," Luc smiled. She couldn't believe she'd thought his eyes were beautiful.

"The final battle?" Achaia repeated breathlessly, leaning against the door.

"That's what we're celebrating, Love." He smiled, stepping closer to her again. "It has begun."

Shael and Noland had been entranced by the news. Their flight, and every other had been canceled. The whole world seemed to be in a frantic hustle toward lock-down. Shael wasn't exactly comfortable being stuck in Moscow with bombs being deployed. So far, they had all been detonated in transit, and no country had taken a hit. But it was only a matter of time, and the tension was thicker than cement.

Bale was in his office trying to arrange a plan for them to

get to Chile. Shael wished, now more than ever, that he still had his wings. There was no way Noland could carry his extra weight any distance.

"Maybe you should start without me. I'll get there eventually and meet you," Shael said, adding to a conversation he had started in his head, that Noland had not actually been a part of aloud.

Noland looked startled. "No."

"Excuse me?" Shael asked, more out surprise than anger.

"I'm not going anywhere without you. In this current climate, we don't need to be separated. Not to mention, what am I supposed to do? Knock on Martinus' door and say, 'Hi, I'm Noland, exiled friend of Emile. Mind if I crash here a few days? Oh, by the way, mind sharing your top-secret plans to what is probably your biggest regret? That'd be great. Thanks.' You're the one who knows him, and knows what questions to ask him. I don't know if he is trustworthy, or how much information to share…"

"Okay, okay!" Shael put up a hand. "We stick together." Shael remembered that Noland was only eighteen. He was still just a boy. The world was literally coming to a slow end, and he had no parents. Shael felt a deep respect then for Noland and the way that he had been carrying himself in spite of his circumstances.

They fell back into a tense silence, staring at the tv. Attacks were taking place worldwide. There were a few countries that didn't seem to know which side they were on, and were attacking everyone, isolating themselves and insuring their inevitable demise. Shael felt sympathy for their human panic. As if on cue, thick dark clouds had rolled in, shutting out the sun outside the windows. A mist of rain splattered across them, turning their view to a collage of grey. Creation knew what was coming, and it was bracing itself for impact.

"Whatever happens next," Shael said with a strong voice. Noland looked up at him. "I'm proud of you." Shael looked Noland in the eye, man to man.

Noland was saved having to respond by Bale entering the room.

"It's not ideal. It will take way too long, but so far, it is the only way I can find to get you to Chile. You'll take the car, with my driver. You'll drive to Sierra Leone, where Naphtali will meet you. He thinks he can come up with a jet he is willing to commandeer from the council to get you to Brazil, under the pretense of aiding a safe house there. You'll be on your own then to get to Chile, but at least we can get you onto the right continent.

"We'll take it," Shael said. "Thank you."

"Keep me informed. I have a lot to do here, what with all hell breaking lose, but if things escalate, call me. I'll be there." Bale reached out and shook Shael's hand, then Noland's.

Noland and Shael had their bags ready and followed Bale down to the street where a well-dressed man waited next to a black Hyundai Solaris. The streets were pandemonium. Shael took the front passenger seat and Noland slid into the back.

"How long is this drive going to be?" Noland asked.

"Without sleep? If we rotate drivers and don't stop, four

and a half days," Shael said feeling the weight in his stomach.

"Wait," Bale said knocking on Noland's back window. The cook was there holding a basket and a canvas tote bag. "Some provisions for the road."

"*Spasibo*," Noland said to the cook. He placed the parcels in the seat next to him with the duffle bag of weapons that Bale had packed for them. "*Spasibo*," he said again to Bale.

Bale nodded and the driver took off.

"I think I can shave some time off once we get out of the city," he said in his thick Russian accent.

"That would be greatly appreciated," Shael said. "Let me know when you get tired, and I'll take the next driving shift.

Emile had been pouring over case files for hours, taking note of every similarity and difference. Amelia took notes as he rambled thoughts and findings aloud. He could feel her weariness. "What do you make of it all?" he asked. They sat alone, down the beach from the house, at the firepit outside the forge shack where Veronica was inside hammering something metal into obedience. Emile didn't know why, but he liked being near wherever she was, listening to her work.

"I think you're right. I think someone has gone through a lot of trouble trying to make this look human, but why the change in MO? Why such an obviously dated weapon choice?" Amelia smoothed down the notebook page she had been scribbling on as it caught in the wind.

"Maybe they forgot it was old?" A voice came out of the trees behind them. Amelia jumped. Emile felt her spike of alarm along with his own and turned.

"Can we help you?" he asked, sounding a little barbed.

"I hope so," the man said. "My name is Eran, and that was my Charge that was bludgeoned with her family." Eran was a slim, toned Nephilim with skin kissed by the Philippine sun. His dark eyes were calculating as he took each of them in.

"Her family. So, the mother was your Charge?" Amelia asked.

"Yes," Eran looked sad. "I failed her and her family. I want to find who did this."

"So do we," Emile said. "Do you agree that this wasn't a human murder?"

Eran bristled. "I could have protected her against a simple human claim on her life. Yes, this was of a spiritual nature." He let out a breath as if to calm himself. Emile could feel him struggling to be patient.

"Who was she? Why was she a target?" Emile asked, looking at Amelia to be sure she was writing.

"Camila was a part of the peace talks. And as I'm assuming you heard, they did not go well without her."

"Heard?" Emile looked at Amelia. They had been so secluded from news, and had their heads buried so far into these cases, they had scarcely come up for air.

"World War III was declared today." Eran looked incredulous that they had not paid closer attention to world affairs.

Emile felt a weight like a stone bomb his stomach. It knocked the breath out of him. He and Amelia stared at each other in disbelief.

"It's happening," she whispered.

"It is," Eran seemed less surprised. "I do not think these things are unrelated. Charges have been targeted and dropped at an alarming rate. It is not that we Guardians are inept. These are strategic attacks, not the work of clumsy demons."

Emile looked to his sister, then back to Eran, dropping his voice to a conspiratorial low. "You think *someone else* is behind it?" The breeze rustled the leaves of the surrounding vegetation like creation wanted in on the whispered conspiracy.

"I've had my suspicions for a while. But anyone who speaks out has been silenced." Eran, too, lowered his voice, and took a seat on a log opposite them. "Who is in the shack?" he asked, nodding toward the work shed, before going on.

"My mate," Emile said without thinking. He felt Amelia's surprise, and realized he felt none for himself. It was just true.

"So, she can be trusted?" Eran asked.

"I believe so," Emile said, but kept his voice low all the same. The ocean waves provided yet more cover for their conversation, though there was no one around that they could see.

"She can," Veronica's voice came from the window above. She was leaning out, smiling down at them.

"Care to join us, then?" Emile asked.

She winked at him and disappeared. A moment later she was sitting next to them on the beach, covered in soot, and

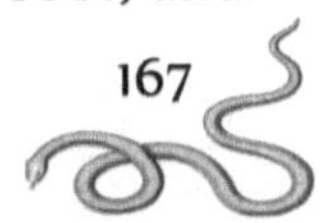

wiping her hands on her leather apron, her dark braids reflecting pieces of the sun, like amber.

"Our friend, and the head of our generation, Noland Amsel, was exiled for speaking out last week," Emile said, restarting their conversation.

"I heard about that. The job passed down to you, did it not?"

"Yes," Emile said, trying not to sound resentful.

"That is a valuable seat you hold. I am fallen, but pretty low on the totem," Eran explained.

"So, what are you thinking?" Amelia asked. "We are trying to piece together the puzzle, but half the pieces are hidden, and the other half aren't exactly shared with *children*." She spoke the last word with disgust. Emile felt her frustration. Veronica, on the other hand felt excited. Emile knew she was probably looking forward to getting in on some action rather than just making the weapons everyone else got to use.

"Children though you are, if anything is going to change, your generation will bring it about."

Emile could feel that Eran wasn't nearly as confident in their generation as he wished he was, which would have frustrated Emile, if he had not thought of how Noland would have used it as an opportunity to prove himself. His doubt was understandable. What had they done so far to earn respect or trust?

"How loyal are you, to your father?" Eran asked Veronica, point blank.

Emile felt her startle, though her face remained stoic.

"Why do you ask?" She didn't answer, but Emile knew she loved her father deeply.

"Because I don't trust him. I don't see him doing his job, and many murders have happened on his watch, most of them charges. Is he despondent or inept?" Eran asked, not without sympathy.

"Neither!" Veronica answered. Emile could feel her fire, but she held herself composed very well, he thought. In this moment she reminded him of Noland. Figures he'd wind up with a girl just like his best friend. "We are without resources and information. The council gives us nothing. They have shut us out almost entirely. I assure you we were not informed these humans were charges, or my father would have sent aid."

Eran looked confused. "We have been hit hard here, and the council cares not?"

"The council doesn't care, or the council wants you left in the dark and voiceless?" Amelia asked. The breeze kicked up a whirlwind of sand, as they all looked at each other and felt the conclusion speak for itself.

Olivier sat in a corner chair, not at the oval conference table with the council leaders. He'd been there for an hour taking notes about boring business, for instance, budget line items like the cost of jet fuel, safe houses requesting their cars to be fixed, or food allowances increased as young Nephilim boys reached puberty.

They talked about their numbers. Guardians had decreased, either to career moves to other departments, or silence. From what Olivier could tell, nothing much was being done to investigate those who had gone silent. What if those guardians were in serious trouble? Noland's parents had been proof that they weren't completely invincible. However, Joash preferred to think of them as AWOL.

"Moving on," Joash moaned. "Imports."

"Are we on track for the Chilean delivery?" An old Nephilim who showed his age, much like Joash, asked from the other end of the table. From what Olivier gathered, he balanced the books. "We've already paid for a shipment, but we have yet to receive it," he said.

"They are in production," a woman said. "Apparently the daughter has taken over production. She has her father's gift, I am assured." She sounded confident. "She just hasn't learned his speed, I suppose." She added, sounding more bored.

"Have them put a rush on it. I don't like paying for things before they are delivered. I don't know how that slipped through the cracks," Joash ordered, sounding displeased.

"Speaking of Chile, I gather there has been another charge lost, the entire family slaughtered," a younger-looking Nephilim chimed in.

Olivier's ears perked up.

"We're not there, yet," Joash snapped. He pressed on with more mundane matters, until finally saying that that was all they could possibly do today, and leaving all important matters unaddressed. Olivier couldn't believe it, when, without question,

the other leaders of the council simply stood up without argument and began to file out of the room.

"Sir," Olivier started when they had all gone, and he was left alone with Joash.

"Yes?" Joash heaved in an annoyed sigh. "You never came back around to the Charge loss in Chile," Olivier said, making a point of looking studiously over his notes. "Did that need to be addressed sooner rather than later?" He asked trying to sound as naive as possible.

"It can't be undone. The charge has been lost already. That makes it not as important as items that are still moving forward. A team will eventually be sent out to investigate, but as long as the safe house keeper is doing his job, it isn't an issue we need worry about, here. It's called delegating. As a leader you'll need to learn how to facilitate rather than taking on every petty task."

With an effort, Olivier tried to keep his face passive as he nodded and remained silent.

"If you have no more questions, you're dismissed for the day." Joash said rubbing his temple with his left hand.

"Thank you, sir," Olivier said, slipping quietly out of the room without a lot of show of leaving. He closed the door behind him, and immediately headed first for food, and then to Dina's office.

"What do you make of it? Anything interesting?" Olivier asked. "I wish I knew exactly what I was listening for."

"That's the thing with espionage. Sometimes it's the unimportant that is significant. For example, this shipment that

was paid for before arrival, what is it for? Who authorized the payment, and why?" Dina looked at Olivier.

"I don't know. They didn't get into it," Olivier said.

"I think we start there," Dina said, putting the notes down on her desk.

The phone on Dina's desk beeped, and there was a frantic voice coming through on it. "Dina, are you there?"

"Yes," Dina picked up the phone. Though Olivier could hear the shrill and excited tone on the other end, he couldn't make out the words. Dina's face went white. She opened her computer and started typing quickly across its keys. "Oh my God." She hung up the phone.

"What is it? What's happened?" Olivier asked.

"America and China have just declared war."

Olivier, unable to think properly said, "That's huge."

"That," Dina said, still in shock, "is the beginning of World War III."

Olivier stared at her, unable to process or speak.

"Our schedule just bumped up into overdrive. We don't have nearly as much time as I thought."

The driver, who Noland had found was called Nikolay had made it about 12 hours before Shael insisted they switch and the driver take a break. The sun was coming up over Poland with all the quiet of the early morning. Nikolay was fast asleep in the back, and Noland and Shael had gone half an hour without

talking. Noland was in a dreamlike state. The monotony of the road, and the surrealness of their situation washed over him a state of almost numbness.

It wasn't numbness though, because inside he was screaming. He had to get to Achaia. He fought to control the torrent of thoughts racing through his brain, lest he blow the car up in his rage. He had to stave off the images of what Luc might be doing to Achaia at each given moment.

Without saying anything about it, and even though it was still quite a cool start to the spring in this part of Europe, Shael had turned on the air conditioning. That had been the first indication that Noland was not as in control of himself as he looked on the outside.

"We should eat something," Noland said, playing his role as copilot by digging through the provisions Bale's cook had prepared them. He handed Shael a *vatrushka* and started tearing one apart himself, nibbling absentmindedly at the cheese Danish. Shael was flying down the road pushing one hundred miles per hour, and still their progress seemed agonizingly slow.

"We'll have to stop for gas soon," Shael said, staring at the gauges in the dashboard with loathing.

Stop, they did. Noland woke Nikolay to see if he needed the restroom. They made the stop count, stocking up on coffees and water before getting back into the car until they ran out of gas again. That happened halfway through Germany. Since Noland was familiar with the language of the road signs, he volunteered to drive the next shift.

He felt a little less restless being behind the wheel, in

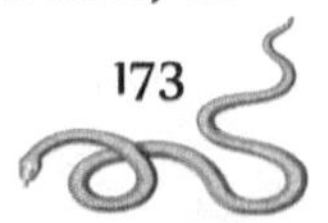

control of at least the speed of the car. The good thing about the world being in chaos was that police seemed to be preoccupied and had more on their minds than traffic violators. They were making better time than anticipated.

Luc hadn't been as gallant when he had thrown her back into her cell as he had been the day before. When the door closed behind her, she promptly vomited in the corner.

"You're not sick are you? That sucks," a voice said behind her.

Achaia shot up stick straight. "Who are you? And what are you doing in my cell?"

"I'm Jude. And my guess is, same as you?" He shrugged. He looked to be a little older than Achaia, and had dark skin, the color of rye chips in snack mix. Achaia liked those best. His eyes, though, were a Caspian Sea kind of blue. They made her wonder what it would be like to surf. His hair was waist length and shaped into clean thin dreads, slightly sun-bleached. They must have taken a long time to form.

"Satan wants to make you his wife?" Achaia asked.

Jude's eyebrows shot up in surprise. "Not the same, then." He nodded curtly, his lips pulled thin in a 'this is awkward' stance. "So, should I call you-?"

"Achaia," she said, nodding at him in a belated welcome.

"Achaia, *not* Mistress of Evil. Got it." He snapped and shot a finger pistol at her. "How long have you been here?"

"I don't know, a few days? A week? Months? You kind of lose track when you can't see the sun."

"I get that." Jude nodded, taking a seat on her fur.

"No offense, you seem like a super cool guy," Achaia started.

"I feel a 'but' coming." Jude looked at her encouragingly.

"Shouldn't you be freaking out or something if you just got here?"

"Ah, right. 'Woe is me! What am I going to do! Where am I? What is this place? Somebody, save me, please!'" he whined sarcastically.

Achaia cocked an eyebrow at him.

"Not my first stint," Jude said casually.

"You've been here before?" Achaia asked amazed.

Jude nodded.

"And you, left?" Achaia continued.

Jude nodded again.

"How did you get out?" Achaia asked, taking a few steps closer to him.

"I guess my dad decided enough was enough."

"Your dad?" Achaia asked, perplexed.

"I guess you call him—"

"Luc?"

Jude laughed. "You're ballsy. Most refer to him as Lucifer, Prince of Darkness, or The Coming Damnation. Depends on what circle of Hell they are from…"

"I'm not that respectful," Achaia said with disdain in her tone.

"Word of advice?" Jude offered, sizing her up, but not unkindly.

Achaia nodded for him to go on.

"That's probably what he *likes* about you."

Achaia gagged again. "So, what did you do for him to lock you away?"

"Which time?" Jude asked, as if this were an old story.

"How many times has he locked you up in here?"

"I lost count after twelve." Jude shrugged. "I think the guy just gets lonely. Then when he realizes I'm not the son he wanted, and I'm not going to be much fun, he lets me go. Or in his words, he banishes me from his sight, at least, until he wants company again." Jude waved his hand as if to say 'and so on and so forth'.

"That's awful. I should no longer be surprised by his repugnance, but there you have it." Achaia sat next to Jude on the fur.

"How old are you? You can't possibly look your age. Your vocabulary is too good."

"My father was a professor for a little while. I'm seventeen. And you?"

"I'm nineteen."

"So, who is your dad?" Jude asked.

"Shael ben Yahweh."

Jude's eyes went wide. "So, I take it that is the second reason you're here?" Jude laughed without sympathy. Everything about him was casual.

"Probably. My dad and I kind of pissed your dad off recently."

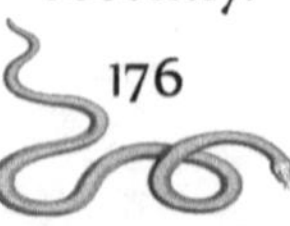

"I heard about that. Your mom was human, right?"

Achaia sometimes forgot this was a novelty amongst Nephilim. "Yeah," she sighed.

"Mine too," Jude said smiling. "I thought I was the only one until I heard about you. I thought it was too good to be true." His smile grew wide.

"Wait, you're *hybrid*?" Achaia asked surprised.

"Yeah, my mom was a witch doctor in Uganda. She died giving birth to me though, and I was adopted by Americans."

Achaia stared at him with wide eyes. After a moment she said, "I'm sorry, I just don't know what to say to that."

"How about, 'congratulations'?" Jude laughed, and Achaia followed suit. "You know speaking of moms, maybe that's what I should start calling you." Jude joked. Achaia grimaced and punched him playfully in the arm.

Day Six

"She wore fire like a crown
and when the devil glanced her way,
you can be sure he winked."
-JM Wonderland

Jude brought light with him everywhere he went, including Hell, if that is where they were. Achaia enjoyed not only having someone to talk to, but *Jude* to talk to. He was unfailingly optimistic and cheerful in spite of their circumstances. Achaia felt his outlook and personality revive her spirits and give her a fresh sense of hope. She found it funny, how much some casual conversation could help in not-so-casual circumstances.

Some people might consider being held captive against your will in a prison colder than Antarctica in minimal clothing, more than a dilemma, a full-blown crisis. But not Jude. This was just a small detour to him. After being locked up and released enough times, he had learned not to consider his imprisonment of a permanent nature, and the occurrence had lost its direness ages ago.

Achaia knew her imprisonment wasn't the same. But the mindset helped ease her mind. She had heard that misery loved company, but in this case, company had drastically reduced her misery. Luc seemed to be giving her the silent treatment. Either that, or he was waiting for Achaia to have a change of heart. Whatever the case, he hadn't come for her in what she guessed to be about two days.

Achaia and Jude were playing a round of *never have I ever* when the door opened. It wasn't Lucifer, but a behemoth of a demon, whose face stood higher than the doorway, and couldn't be seen. "Come," it said.

"Who?" Achaia asked.

"Both." The demon was a non-man of few words.

Jude stood first and held a hand for Achaia, helping her to her feet.

"Where are we going?" Achaia whispered as they followed the giant demon down ice tunnels Achaia had not yet taken.

"My father's idea of a night out." Jude didn't sound enthusiastic. "You'd think, as old as the guy is, he'd learn what works and what doesn't. But alas, he's the same old, same old."

By the time he finished speaking, the tunnel opened up into an arena. In the center was a massive cage, the bars going up to the arched ceiling.

"He doesn't want us to…"

Jude put a comforting hand on her back. "No, he wants us to watch," Jude said lowly in her ear. He kept his hand on her back, and she could feel a tiny hint of warmth from it.

When they sat on the bleachers surrounding the cage, Jude sat up against her, and put his hand on her knee. His arms were so long, his forearm rested up her thigh, not in a romantic way, but in a way that made Achaia feel less scared and alone. Where their legs leaned against each other, warmth began to spread.

Lucifer arrived, dressed to the nines for the occasion. He reminded Achaia of a ring master in the circus, but from the Victorian era.

"Lady, gentleman, and those of nefarious origins," Luc started, speaking from his diaphragm so that his voice carried but didn't sound like yelling. The crowd of demons' voices trailed away to quiet. "Tonight, I give you a gift!"

The demons cheered.

"True entertainment!"

They roared.

The gigantic demon that had led Achaia and Jude into the atrium reappeared, dragging something, no, *someone* into the arena. Achaia realized with horror that it was a beaten and bruised Nephilim. She had the almond eyes of a fallen who'd landed in Asia, and fair skin like porcelain. Achaia thought she looked like a once mighty samurai, but she had definitely already taken a beating. Her cheek was bruised, and her left eye swollen. Scratches covered her face, but her eyes still held honor, and

defiance.

The demon threw her into the cage. She tried to brush it off, and stand with dignity, but she was limping, and obviously worse for wear.

"How did they?"

Jude took his hand off her knee and grasped her hand, squeezing it gently.

Achaia fell silent, a horrible feeling filling her stomach. It was like watching an accident in slow motion. You knew it was going to be awful, and that there was no chance of it not ending badly, but you couldn't stop it, and you couldn't tear your eyes away.

Dina sat at her desk, holding her head in her hands. She'd had the headache for days now. There was no sign of it stopping, not until the madness was over. She was waiting for Olivier. She had played her part well so far, and was trusted. She really shouldn't second guess herself, but she always did, which led to an ever increasing amount of stress and anxiety when she was around anyone else. It was easy to trust yourself, but the more people you let in on a plan, the higher the probability things can go wrong.

Olivier came in and shut the door. "I brought this for you," he said setting a cup on her desk, and handing her a handful of pills.

"How did you know?" Dina asked. "You have your

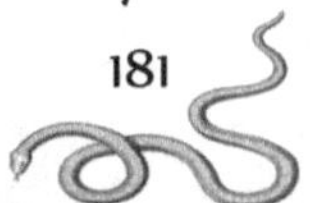

brother's gift," she smiled. She breathed deep the mint tea, and took the pain pills for her head.

"Not really, you just always have a headache these days. I read somewhere that mint is supposed to help. Either that or Yellaina probably mentioned it, repeatedly. She's into healing."

"Have you talked to her?" Dina asked.

"No." Olivier was getting better at guarding his expressions from what he was truly feeling, but Dina knew that he couldn't be happy. "Do you have a mate?" he asked finally, looking curious.

Dina sighed. "Yes."

"Where is he? What does he do?" Olivier asked. They hadn't done much small talk or actually gotten to know each other. It was pretty much mission impossible, but perhaps the hyper focus was taking its toll on both of them.

Dina took the tea, cupping the warm mug in her hands and breathing in the mint, and leaned back in her chair. "Harlem. He was one of the first to disappear. Nephilim hate looking back, because it forces us to admit weakness and gives birth to regret, so it is the ever pursuit of forward. But I believe there is something to be learned from the past, if we take the time to reflect."

"What happened? Was he found?" Olivier asked, hesitantly.

"No, he wasn't," Dina said sadly, "because no one looked."

Olivier looked appalled, then. "Not even you?"

"I was following orders. By the time I regretted that decision, the trail had gone cold. Hence our current course."

"I'm sorry," Olivier said, and looked like he truly meant it.

"Take my advice," Dina said, fiddling with the tag of the

tea bag hanging from the side of the cup. "Don't wait. Talk to her."

Olivier didn't say anything, but he nodded.

"Everyone assumes I've forgotten, because they have." Dina went on, almost bitterly, "but I would have chosen my mate, even if God hadn't dictated it. Harlem was everything but God to me."

"You still have hope?" Olivier asked.

"I try not to, but I'll fight until it runs out," Dina said, taking her first sip of tea, then setting the cup down. "Now, business—"

Noland and Shael had made it to Sierra Leone, and Nikolay was driving them down a dirt road surrounded by lush green vegetation. The dust from the road kicked a cloud up behind them. The top of a house peeked up over the treetops around a curve in front of them. A large house with a wide, open field in front of it. A small jet sat partially obscured beside the house.

Nikolay parked the car in front of the entrance, and a Nephilim came out to meet them. "Hello!"

Noland was happy to find that they spoke English here. Driving through what felt like half of creation to get here, there had been several times he had wished Yellaina were with them. Between himself, Shael, and Nikolay though, they had made it. He got out of the car and took a few tentative steps, feeling very much like he had sea legs. After being cooped up in a car for days, walking almost felt unnatural.

"Will you come in, and be refreshed?" Shael moved forward unexpectedly, and the Nephilim opened his arms to him. Noland felt oddly shocked, at the display of affection.

"Brima!"

The Nephilim smiled wide, and hugged Shael tightly. "It has been a long time!"

Shael took him by the shoulders and looked him over, "It is so good to see you!"

"You as well!" Brima said smiling. "Come inside, wash, eat, sleep. We will leave once darkness covers us." Brima lead them up a dirt path to the house.

Noland didn't know if it was his age and seclusion that led to the odd way Brima spoke, or if it was his Sierra Leonean English. In any case, Noland followed him inside.

The house had all the comforts of home without being overly done. It was a simply and sparsely furnished house. Entering it, Noland felt a wave of weariness wash over him. Shael and Brima fell immediately into conversation as Brima started boiling water for tea. Noland found the shower on his own, and entered into it like a zombie, just standing under the cold water at first. Steam rose off his skin, creating a dense cloud in the bathroom. Eventually he shook the water out of his face, and began to wash.

When he came back out into the open living room and kitchen, he found the tea was ready, chamomile. He wasn't a huge fan, but he knew it would help him sleep, and he knew he

needed to be rested. Shael and Brima were still talking. Nikolay was already asleep on the sofa.

Noland sat, sipping his tea, zoned out, until he realized Brima's voice was being directed at him.

"I'm sorry?" Noland said, looking up from his cup. He was pretty sure he was sleeping while awake. He had never been this tired in his life.

"I said, you have the heat of the sun," Brima smiled at him.

"Yes," Noland said.

"Is that your only gift?" Brima asked politely.

"No," Noland said, not meaning to be rude, but being too tired for conversation.

Brima seemed to read his exhaustion on his face, "Come." He led Noland to a spare room with two small beds inside. "Here."

Noland went to the nearest one and sat down. "Thank you," he mumbled, setting his tea on the nightstand and lying down. He was asleep before his head hit the pillow.

Eran insisted that their meetings remain secret. Despite Veronica's assurances, he still didn't trust her father. They had discovered that many of the murder victims had also been charges. Their guardians had left and been reassigned since. Unlike them, Eran wasn't so hasty to give up. Camilla had been his first loss, and Emile thought he was taking it pretty well, but he wasn't like most Nephilim who shake it off, and go in for their next assignment.

"Like Camilla, these humans were hunted," he was saying. "They weren't even made to look like accidents, or natural. Lucifer usually likes to cast the blame on humanity, but these killings are too blatant, too similar. It raises suspicion. It just isn't his style."

"And I don't know many demons who use weapons against humans," Amelia agreed.

"So, we really think this is, what I think it sounds like?" Veronica looked like a disillusioned child.

Yellaina who had joined their group looked at her sympathetically. "We've had a few months to warm ourselves up to the idea."

"You really believe the council is issuing these attacks?" Veronica looked at Emile.

He could feel her dread, and anxiety. He sighed as he looked into her frightened eyes. "Yes, or a rogue angel." He said it simply, but it was anything but. "It really appears like the only possible scenario. This has to be the work of Nephilim. Who else? It's not humans; it's not demons; it definitely wouldn't be God."

"I can't believe it." Veronica shook her head. She looked a bit like a child who had just found out their superhero was a villain. The thought of superheroes made Emile think of Olivier. He missed his brother. He wished he had come with them. Nephilim weren't supposed to be as sentimental as humans. It appeared though that each generation born of earth took on more and more human characteristics, because Emile was very attached to his siblings. He couldn't imagine what he would do if anything happened to them, and he preferred to keep them close.

"Try," Eran said, not without kindness. "Now we have to figure out what to do next."

"I guess find out exactly which Nephilim is behind it. If the council is calling the shots, they are probably keeping the number of people who know about this mission small. If we find out who all is involved, gather evidence, and take it to the full council, I'm sure they will be outraged. They can put an end to this," Emile said.

"Still putting your trust in the bureaucracy?" Eran said with surprise.

"We can't do this alone," Emile said reasonably. "Who else can we trust?"

"Not them. They never listen. They never learn."

"Maybe they just don't understand," Yellaina said optimistically.

Eran looked at her questioningly. Emile could feel something like hope blossoming in her chest.

"And how do you propose we get them to hear us out?"

"We need numbers, right? Not just chairmen. What if we find them, the outliers, like your dad." Yellaina looked at Veronica. "What if I found them, and I made them understand. We could outnumber the council with the numbers of Nephilim who are actually out in the field, seeing what is happening, not protected by their council walls."

"How are we supposed to get them all together? And even if we did, how are we supposed to make them understand?" Eran sounded doubtful, and Emile could feel him growing tired

and frustrated.

"I can," Yellaina said with confidence. "I can do it. I just need help finding them."

"Well," Emile said looking at Eran.

"Well?" Eran asked.

"Can you help with that?" Amelia asked exasperated.

"I suppose I could go back, and look into it. But if I go back, I'll be reassigned, God knows where."

"Maybe that's good," Yellaina said. "If we spread out, we can cover more ground. We just need to pick a time and place big enough to bring everyone together, whoever will come."

"Wait, we're getting ahead of ourselves. We need more evidence. What are we even supposed to tell them? That we have suspicions?" Emile said.

"You're right. We need proof," Veronica said.

"Ronnie!" Martinus' voice came from down the beach.

"Go!" Veronica looked at Eran.

He slipped away into the bushes behind the forge.

Veronica stood just as Martinus came into view. "What are you doing?" He sounded angry. "*Mija*, you know we have orders to fill. Why aren't you working?"

"Sorry papa, I was just taking a break." Veronica, feeling guilty, went back to the forge.

"What are we doing here?" Martinus asked.

Emile pulled out a file, "studying the cases."

"And what are you finding?" Emile felt something interesting then. Martinus was feeling anxious. Emile wasn't sure why this struck him as strange, maybe he was desperate for them

to find something, or maybe he was afraid that they would, where he hadn't. Something inside Emile told him to guard himself.

"Not much," Emile shrugged nonchalantly. Amelia glanced at him for a millisecond, as did Yellaina. They recovered themselves, though, and followed his lead. He was grateful.

"Shame," Martinus said. "Well, I have to get to work, my human job." He nodded, and headed back down the beach.

Amelia fixed Emile with a look. "You don't think we should tell Martinus what we think about the council?"

"Yeah, he has been shut out. He is bound to agree with us." Yellaina added.

Emile watched Martinus walk back down the beach, and felt his *relief*. Emile shook his head, "I don't think we can trust him."

Achaia was waiting for a demon to enter the cage with the Nephilim woman, but when he had finished speaking, Luc shed his cloak to reveal fighting gear, and entered the cage himself. Achaia gasped and squeezed Jude's hand back, hard.

Two demons came to the cage door carrying a chest of weapons. Luc leaned over it thoughtfully before choosing a scythe and machete.

He crossed to the far corner and gestured for the woman to make her choice. She drew up a katana and a tanto. She held her head high and walked to the other corner.

"What is happening?" Achaia asked, more in disbelief

than for actual explanation.

"First tournament?" the demon sitting on her other side asked conversationally.

Achaia and Jude looked at each other, then at the demon. He was as gnarled looking as an old tree and looked like something out of a wicked fairy tale story, dark and menacing. "Yes," Achaia said.

"Ah, well, the rules are, third blood wins, fourth blood forfeits. First to draw the third blood on their opponent wins."

"Oh," Achaia said relieved. "I thought it was a fight to the death."

The demon laughed cruelly. "Who said it wasn't?"

"Fourth blood forfeits. What does that mean?" Jude asked.

"Just what it sounds like. If you keep fighting after your third blood, and you've already won, you're a blood thirsty bastard, and you forfeit. We're not savages." The demon spat, as if the thought were offensive.

Achaia and Jude exchanged a look, as if to say 'could have fooled us'.

Achaia held onto hope as the match started. The woman was obviously a skilled fighter. Her fighting style was beautiful, like dancing. Luc's was harsher and more sporadic. As much as his fighting wasn't as beautiful to watch, Achaia couldn't help but notice, he expelled significantly less energy, while the woman was using up a lot. Her movements were fluid, but there were a lot of them, as she spun and kicked, and slashed out at him. Luc almost lazily side stepped and blocked her blows, as if bored. The

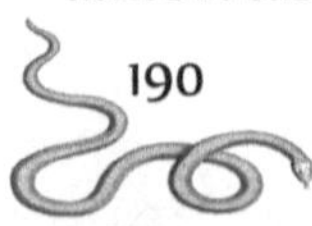

demons howled.

Achaia watched them, as if studying. She hadn't ever had the leisure to simply watch two skilled fighters actually fight, rather than spar. The woman's weapons shone and reflected the light from the ice, the diemerilium casting green prism-like reflections. Luc's weapons on the other hand were a duller green, and looked weathered perhaps, as if they hadn't been cleaned and maintained properly.

Then the woman spun through the air, blades spinning around her, and Luc didn't move fast enough. She nicked his arm.

The demons booed and hissed, but Luc just smiled sadistically as if he'd been waiting for this. Achaia didn't like that he seemed to be enjoying himself. She briefly thought of his face watching the scenes from Heaven. He had been a completely different person. She'd fallen for it; but this, this is who he truly was. She hated herself for ever thinking there might have been a gentleness to him; even if there was, it didn't change the fact that he was a monster.

He retaliated in his first assault. Achaia had never seen anyone but Olivier move that fast. The woman, also seemed caught off guard, and just barely defended the blows, clumsily stepping backward. She was backed against the cage, and kicked up and off the wall to summersault over Luc, to the open part of the cage. She was agile and graceful. Luc reached up in an arch with the scythe, and the woman's head landed on the opposite side of the cage from her body, with two terrible thuds.

It had happened so fast, Achaia felt like the air had been

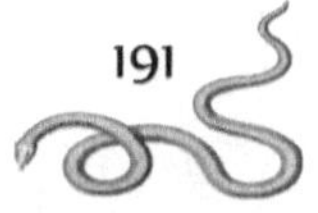

punched out of her chest. The demons were on their feet cheering. Achaia sat frozen in place. Jude wrapped his arm around her. She was staring at Luc, unable to tear her eyes away. The woman's blood was sprayed across his face.

He tossed his weapons to one of the demons with the trunk and said something to the other, who turned and looked at her, and nodded.

Luc left the arena, with the cocky and arrogant walk of a champion. Achaia was finding it hard to breathe. She stared at the unmoving body of the woman. "Look away," Jude whispered in her ear. Achaia hadn't realized until that moment that she pictured death as something that happened more slowly. It had come so quick, so sudden.

"Come with me," the demon Luc had spoken to said, appearing in front of her.

Achaia finally tore her gaze away to look at the demon speaking to her.

"He wants you to come and dress his wounds."

Achaia cocked an eyebrow in disbelief, but thought to herself, that she shouldn't be at all surprised.

"I can help," Jude said standing with her.

"That would be a first," the demon scoffed. "I think not. Take him back to his cell," the demon commanded of the demon who had been sitting next to them, explaining the rules.

Achaia was led to a room with a large bed covered in furs. Everything else was ice. There was a sort of table coming out from the wall, on which sat a tray with medical supplies. After

a minute, Luc entered the room, shirtless. He had a gash on his arm that looked worse than she had thought from the stands.

He leaned against the table next to her. "What did you think?" he asked, smiling at her.

I didn't know ice could bleed, she thought. "You fight well," she said, thinking it unwise to piss him off just now.

"I hoped you'd be impressed." He touched her cheek with the back of his knuckles. There was something about the way that he looked at her that made her feel exposed. She didn't like it.

Achaia flinched away, and grabbed a rag from the tray of supplies. "You want me to clean that for you?"

Luc didn't answer but turned around so that the wounded arm faced her. He leaned against the table, and Achaia noticed how surprisingly muscular he was. His pale toned skin looked like a roman marble sculpture, pure, unblemished, and perfect, that is, save for the ice fissures beneath the skin's surface.

With the supplies, there was a bottle of alcohol that hadn't frozen. She poured it on the rag and started to wipe the blood away. Thinking that that tactic was taking too long, Achaia took the bottle and poured it over the gash. Luc flinched. Achaia couldn't help it; she smiled.

Luc turned to face her, his hip leaning against the table now. She unintentionally noticed how low riding his pants were before looking back up at him. He was smiling at her. "You like causing me pain, don't you?"

Achaia didn't answer. She kept working on the wound.

"I could let you, you know."

Achaia didn't like the tone of his voice, bordering on longing.

"As a wedding gift."

Achaia slammed the bottle down on the table, the crack of glass on ice, loud to her ears. She held her tongue and said nothing.

"Don't worry," Luc laughed. "I can be patient."

"You disgust me," Achaia let slip.

"Matches have been made with worse starts."

"Murders too," Achaia quipped.

Luc threw his head back and laughed. "True."

Achaia grabbed the gauze.

Luc laid his hand on hers, stopping her. "Have you ever done stitches?"

"No," Achaia said, pulling her hand back.

Luc grabbed a needle and threaded it for her. He handed it to her and smiled. "There's a first time for everything."

Again, the tone of his voice made her want to vomit. She took the needle and, with shaking hands, raised it to his arm. She punctured the skin, and Luc didn't flinch. She began sewing him back together. Her stitches weren't neat or even. She was pretty sure it would leave a scar. She had no clue how to do it correctly, like a doctor. So, she pretended she was mending a hole in a pair of jeans. It didn't have to be pretty. It just had to keep them together.

"You'll learn to love me," Luc said lowly. "Your nature will begin to change soon. You'll become like me, you'll see. It won't be long now. You won't be miserable forever. You're already more

like me than you want to admit."

The horrible part was, Luc thought this was comforting. Achaia shivered.

"How do you like Jude?" Luc asked.

Achaia sighed, unable to relax. No conversation topic was surely safe footing with Luc. "He's nice," she said simply.

"You can see my disappointment." Luc rolled his eyes.

Achaia scoffed.

"You don't have that defect." Luc said it as if it were a compliment. "Perhaps one day you can give me a worthier son." He brushed her arm, too gently. Achaia stepped back.

"I have to vomit." She looked at him, in total disbelief. "Can I please go back to my cell?"

Luc looked almost wounded, but also a little annoyed. "Actually, I have an exercise that might speed up the process to end your misery. Luc grabbed her by the arm, gripping hard. It would leave bruises, and dragged her out of the room.

Shael entered the room while sweet golden afternoon light poured in from the window. Noland was sleeping like the dead on one of the small beds. Shael sat on the other and looked at him. He was beginning to feel lucky that God had picked Noland. He couldn't imagine anyone being more attentive or devoted than this boy was proving to be. In fact, he thought, morosely, he was grateful. He would be dying soon. Soon, in Nephilim terms. When he was gone, who would take care of

Achaia? The end times were beginning to come to a boil; Shael was sick to his stomach at the thought of leaving his daughter to face them alone. He was happy that Noland had found her, that she had formed friendships and alliances with his friends. All in God's timing he thought, sleepily.

Shael laid down, and let sleep take him. When he woke up it was dark outside, and Brima was standing in the door calling for them to ready themselves for flight. In his half-awake state, Shael thought like he did in the old days, of his wings. In an instant, though, he remembered himself and that he no longer had them. The only flying he did nowadays was on planes, claustrophobic things that they were.

Noland looked surprisingly alert, the adrenaline of a young boy roused by purpose. Shael remembered that feeling, too. When did this happen? Shael thought. When did he become a reminiscent old man? Perhaps it was seeing Brima again and talking about the old days. Shael felt it in his bones now, how old he was getting. Way older than any human ever had the right to be, and that is what he was now, wasn't it? He couldn't let himself forget.

Shadows

> "I don't think people have demons,
> I think they have themselves and things
> they aren't ready to be honest about yet."
> -King Longton

Achaia sat chained to a throne in a room the size of a walk-in closet, the ice walls so thick they were a deep cerulean blue instead of white. There was very little light reflecting off the surface, so that the pale ivory skin of Luc's face looked like a ghost in the dark. Luc was locking the last chain saying, "this might not look like much of a gift, but I promise it will help you embrace who you really are, by helping you to *see* yourself."

"What are you talking about?" Achaia pulled back on the chains, but they were strong. The room was dark, but she saw the green glimmer and realized that the chains were made of diemerilium, the strong angelic metal holding her prisoner in Hell. This struck her as ironic. "What are you going to do to me?" Her heart was beating hard and fast, and as much as she hated to admit it, for the first time since she found herself, wherever they were, she was afraid.

"*I'm* not going to do anything," Luc said softly. "But I believe you're familiar with this particular breed?"

As he spoke, the shadows swooped in, filling the room. Achaia tensed. The last time she had seen these demons, they had nearly torn her to shreds, and then she had been free of restraints. They had also whispered darkness into her mind. "No, don't do this," Achaia pleaded for the first time, forgetting the façade of strength. "Please," she begged.

Luc shhhed her. "You need to remember perspective, Love." He leaned down and kissed her on the cheek, dangerously close to her mouth, before turning and bolting the door shut behind him. The shadows hovered for only a moment before they descended. Even Jude, who was on the other side of the prison, could hear her scream.

Naphtali had been on the plane when they boarded, looking just as tired as Noland had felt that morning. After what seemed like an agonizing eternity of a flight and a road trip from Hades, Brima was delivering them into a driveway of a little house on the precipice of a cliff.

Noland got out of the car and stretched as he took in his surroundings. Lush vegetation grew about the place so that it was pretty well hidden from the road, easy to pass by it if you didn't know exactly where you were going. Noland wondered if Brima's spiritual gift was GPS. He knocked on the door, but there was no answer.

"Let's check down this way," Naphtali said finding a little path and some steps around the back of the house. They made their way down to the beach and heard voices. Noland saw a small group of people down at the far end, where there were two small shacks against the wild looking forest. As far as safe houses went, this one looked like paradise.

The Nephilim started off down the beach and had made it about halfway before they, or at least two of them, were recognized.

"Noland?" He heard Emile's voice. "Noland!" Emile was running toward him. As they met, they embraced, laughing with relief. It was good to be reunited. Noland hadn't realized the extent to which he had missed his brother.

Yellaina and Amelia weren't far behind him. Yellaina didn't stop running until she collided into him. He diverted her momentum, spinning her around in a hug as she laughed.

"How are you here?" Amelia asked happily, clearly shocked.

They sat down by the shacks, where there was a fire pit and some benches on the beach, and filled each other in on the news. No one was pleased to hear the update that there had been little progress and even worse news, the confirmation of where

Achaia was.

Noland was interested, but not as much as he usually would have been, to hear about the murders and the theory that the council was behind them. Brima was not at all pleased by these theories, but he admitted that they weren't completely unrealistic.

"Some Nephilim have grown restless. We are not the great people we once were," he said.

"So, not to sound ungrateful, but what are you doing here?" Emile asked.

"That's the thing. Martinus, the safe house director, where is he? We need to talk to him." Noland said.

"He's at work," Emile answered.

"Work? Isn't this his job?" Naphtali asked.

"He has a human job as a detective. The council cut back his resources and stopped sending him anything but orders for weapons."

"Weapons," Shael said interestedly. "Yes, he is a great craftsman; they would use him as their—"

"Actually, his daughter Veronica fills the orders, since he is preoccupied," Emile informed them.

Shael cocked an eyebrow. "He has a daughter?"

"Yes," Emile smiled. "Actually, she is very gifted."

"Is she now?" Noland asked under his breath so that only Emile could hear him. Emile blushed.

"I'd like to meet her," Shael said. "Is she here?"

"Yes, she is working," Emile said, standing. They entered the forge and crowded the room. The room would have felt

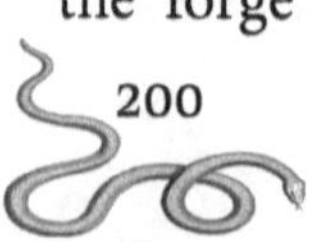

crowded with four people let alone double. It was hot in the shack, like sauna hot.

Veronica stopped her work and lifted her protective mask, rubbing her arm across her face to wipe away the sweat. "Hello?"

"Ronnie, these are my friends, Noland, Shael, and Naphtali, and their friend Brima."

"The exiles?" Veronica looked shocked, and a little off-put.

Noland felt butterflies in his stomach. He hadn't actually tried communicating with anyone connected with the council since his exile. He had almost forgotten what it really meant. "Yes," he answered though, simply. Veronica would have been beautiful without all the soot on her face, Noland thought. She looked part warrior princess, part medieval times blacksmith. He was happy for Emile. "We don't mean to impose; we just need to see your father. Do you know when he will be home?"

Veronica looked at Emile for a second before responding, going on his trust of them, it appeared. She answered, "He should be home in a couple of hours. Can I get you anything to eat or drink?"

Shael smiled diplomatically, "That would be most welcome."

Veronica smiled weakly, looked again at Emile, and cut through the crowd to lead them back to the house.

Olivier thought that Dina's headaches might be contagious. He didn't typically have one, but he was beginning to come home with one every day after leaving her office. He was staying at his parents' flat in Rome. They were gone most of the time. His room was small, but it at least had a window looking out over the nearer buildings. He took out his phone, and with butterflies in his stomach dialed Yellaina's number. He quickly calculated the time difference in his head before calling. It would still be early afternoon there.

He had been making excuses in his head. She'd still be asleep. She'd probably be busy. If she wanted to talk to him, she'd call. He hit the button and listened for the ring. She picked up just before it would have gone to voicemail, and it caught him off guard for a second. "Olly?"

"Yellaina." He said her name like it was a secret he shared only with himself. Her voice sounded familiar and foreign at the same time. It marveled him how it was the same, but it felt like forever since he had heard it.

She was quiet, but he could hear her breathing and knew she was still there. "I miss you," she finally said.

Olivier breathed a sigh of relief. "I miss you, too."

Before he could say anymore, she spouted off "Noland is here."

Olivier felt like he ran into a wall. "What?"

"Noland and Shael are here. Please don't tell anyone."

Olivier felt like he'd been smacked in the face. Why would he tell anyone? This wasn't the conversation he wanted to have with her. He swallowed. "Okay."

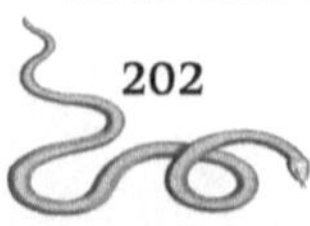

"They think they know where Achaia is," she said excitedly.

Olivier had never felt so separate in his life. Everyone he cared about was there; they weren't scattered to the wind, just him. And they were working together to find and save his best friend, and he wasn't doing anything on that front. Olivier all of a sudden felt stiff and nauseous.

"Olly, are you there?" Yellaina's voice called after him.

Olivier wasn't there. He wasn't. He was here, alone. Without knowing exactly why, or deciding to, he hung up the phone. He felt tired, and numb, and sick, and done. He tried his best to shut it down, this downward spiral he could feel coming on. He knew he shouldn't have called.

Achaia was shaking when Luc finally unlocked her chains. She might have even been whimpering. She wasn't aware really of what she was or wasn't doing. She wasn't even aware that Luc was taking her back to her cell or depositing her into it.

"Achaia!" Jude rushed to her as the door clanged shut. "What did he do to you?"

Achaia could hear that Jude was talking to her, but the words weren't registering to her. She couldn't think that anything that was happening right now was very much important. It was a blur compared to what was happening inside her head. The visions she had seen, the shadows had shown her the truth. It was her fault her mother was dead. It was her fault her father was broken and human, that he was dying. Her parents' demise was all her doing.

"Achaia, God, you're bleeding." Jude was patting her face and her arms with something soft. What was blood? Hers wasn't important. Abomination blood, that's what it was. She had brought the end times. It all started going downhill with her. She brought this on everyone. The angel of death. What kind of angel was death, when death was a demon? A demon that stole away loved ones… Death was a demon, and she was death. She delivered it to everyone she met.

Yellaina put the phone down. She tried not to feel shell shocked. They must have lost signal. "The call dropped," she said, looking up at Noland. "I am so glad you're here." She smiled brightly. It was true. It felt like their family was coming back together. Together they could solve any problem or combat any evil. As long as they were together it was all going to be okay. Except they weren't all together. Olivier and Achaia were missing.

In their place they had Shael and Veronica. Yellaina was trying to like Veronica, but she wasn't the same. Granted, she and Achaia were both powerhouse girls who could go out and get what they wanted. They were like a light and dark version of the same person, but then again, they were so different. Veronica was the obedient daughter, and Achaia was the rebel. Though she worked with it all day long, Veronica lacked Achaia's fire. Maybe that's what it was. Veronica reminded Yellaina of Achaia, but

didn't deliver the best parts. She would always fall short. It wasn't fair of course. Veronica was her own person. Missing Achaia was Yellaina's problem.

"What's going on up there?" Noland said affectionately tapping Yellaina's temple. "You've got your pensive face on."

"Just Achaia," Yellaina said. "And these murders, and our family, and Olivier—"

Noland smiled sympathetically and nodded. He pulled her into a side hug, a kissed the top of her head. That was her favorite thing about Noland. He didn't always feel the need to say something. He just sat with you and let you feel what you were feeling. Yellaina felt such a calming peace knowing that he was there with her. Like her big brother, he just made her feel safer. No— peace? No— *anchored*.

A commotion roused their attention as Vito and Vidal entered, horsing around and wrestling each other in their pursuit of the fridge. They stopped short when they saw Noland. They looked at each other, and then back at Noland.

"Your mate?" they asked Yellaina in Spanish.

"No," she told them who Noland was, then told Noland who they were.

"*Hola*," Noland said pathetically. Yellaina loved when he tried to speak languages he didn't know.

"What's up?" Vito asked.

"You speak English?" Noland rolled his eyes.

"Yep," Vidal laughed.

"They remind me of Olivier, but it's like having two of him." Noland smiled.

Yellaina sighed. She missed Olivier, more than she was willing to say out loud. There was an intensity to her missing him that was excessive maybe, or pathetic, if she said it out loud. People didn't talk that way anymore. If she were to describe it accurately, her language would be that of the old poets.

Noland was telling the boys that he was waiting for their father.

"Oh, he is home. He is outside," Vito said, turning and pointing back at the door.

Noland immediately stood up to leave. Yellaina followed him.

Noland had fetched Shael and Naphtali, and together with Yellaina they had gone down to the beach, led by the boys Vito and Vidal, to find their father. Martinus was walking back down the beach toward them. "Hello," he said with no small amount of surprise as he got closer and saw who was with his sons.

"Martinus," Shael said, taking in the sight of him. Unlike Shael, Martinus hadn't aged much. He still looked the same to him.

"Shael, what are you doing here, and who is this?" he asked looking at Noland.

"Noland ben Nathaniel." Noland answered for himself.

"I need to speak with you, perhaps in private."

"Whatever it is that would bring you out of hiding to

speak with me, must indeed be important. And you bring a Seraphim in tow."

Shael was a little surprised by the comment, since he hadn't truly been in hiding in months. Naphtali just nodded an acknowledgement.

"Shall we walk, then? Boys, go back to the house. You should be training."

Vito and Vidal rolled their eyes and jogged back to the house. Martinus looked at Yellaina, as if waiting for Shael to send her away. Yellaina took the hint, and sighed as she went off. Shael knew she was eager to be in on the conversation, but Shael was sure Noland would fill her in.

"I'm sure you've heard my daughter has been taken by Lucifer."

"Actually no. I believe I heard she was missing. But I didn't realize her whereabouts had been confirmed."

"That is a more recent development," Shael said cautiously, unwilling to say too much just yet. He was still feeling him out.

"So, you have a family?"

Martinus swallowed uncomfortably. Shael wondered if he took the question as a threat. What must he think of him? "Yes, a daughter, Veronica, and the twins," Martinus said factually.

"And you're a safe house director." Shael couldn't keep the surprise and skepticism out of his voice.

"You may well be surprised." Martinus stopped walking and looked at him then.

Shael honestly couldn't believe it. Noland stood silently just observing them. He was a smart boy. "Honestly, I don't understand it. Lucifer, stuck in Hell, I was always held at arms length and then shunned, and you are given charge of a safe house?" Shael looked at him suspiciously. "The three of us paved the road to Hell, and you are glorified in this new world."

Martinus laughed, but his face was guarded. "Hardly glorified. The council scarcely remembers I exist unless they need something from me. But I don't hold a seat on the council, nor am I invited to take part in their sessions. I am basically exiled myself. They just find me too useful to banish, I suppose."

This struck Shael as true. They continued to walk. "So, you may have guessed by now where Achaia is being held."

"Seeing as how you have risked exposure to come to me, I have guessed. What I haven't guessed is what you expect me to do."

"You aren't an idiot Martinus. You must have calculated the danger and the risk. I know you would have planned a way out, in case you were ever locked in your own prison," Shael said. "I know you. You always have a contingency plan."

Martinus laughed again and nodded. "True, true. But what we didn't anticipate is how long it would go without use. How we would forget about it. I may not look it, but I am old Shael; I feel it in my mind. I don't remember every block I built any more than you remember every word you wrote in those books of yours."

"You kept tabs on me then?" Shael asked cocking an eyebrow.

"Contingency… I like to know where the moving parts are." Martinus smiled.

"For someone who likes to keep tabs, you seem strangely out of the loop. I haven't been in hiding for some time. I have openly been living in New York."

Martinus only showed his surprise for a moment.

"Yes, well, as I said. The council has grown cold and distant. I don't have the resources I once did." He sounded bitter. Shael understood that slight. He had received it himself on several occasions.

"You're the only one who can help me get her back." Shael stopped walking again, turning the conversation back to what was really important. "If it were your daughter, what would you do?"

Martinus stopped, no need to think of what he would do. "Kill anyone who stood between us."

"Don't bring it to that," Shael said coolly.

"I will help you," Martinus said, compliant. He smiled, "We both know I don't stand a chance against you. I was always a creator. You were always the destroyer."

Olivier sat in Dina's office waiting for her. When she came in she smiled.

"No headache today?" Olivier asked, unaccustomed to seeing her so happy.

She shook her head. "No, it's still there, but I have finally figured out who authorized the payment before the weapons delivery."

"Awesome! Who?" Olivier asked.

"Who isn't as important as why." Dina smiled even wider.

"Okay," Olivier said playing along, "Why?"

"Joash told them to," Dina said.

"But wait. He acted pissed, and like he didn't understand why…"

"Because it was supposed to be a secret," Dina said. "Joash is moving parts behind the scenes. And he doesn't want anyone to know he is doing it, which means…"

"It isn't council sanctioned, hopefully." Olivier brightened, as well.

"Which means," Dina smiled, "things might not be as bad off as we feared. More Nephilim may be for us than against us."

Olivier smiled. "That's awesome, so now what do we do?"

"We talk to the weapons dealer to see if they know what these weapons were commissioned for. What kind of weapons. And you know who the dealer is?"

"Since I know they are from Chile, I'm guessing you're going to tell me it's near the safe house my brother is stationed at." Olivier prompted.

"You are getting the hang of this, only it isn't close. It is the safe house your brother is sanctioned at, and the daughter that is making the weapons is your brother's mate." Dina looked as if she'd won the lottery, but Olivier felt like he'd been smacked in the face. His brother had found his mate, and no one had told him. Olivier tried to keep his feelings in check. That wasn't important right now. "I think you should request a visit to your brother and sister and investigate."

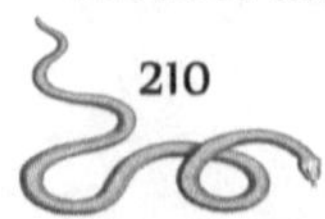

"Go undercover to visit my own family?" Olivier asked, shocked.

"No," Dina said looking abashed. "Well I mean, yes, as far as Joash is concerned, and the Chilaen safe house, but of course you can tell Yellaina and your brother. Just remember the more people we get involved, the higher the risk this won't work. Make sure you only tell those you truly trust. And we don't know your brother's mate or where her loyalties lie. If you get there, and think he might tell her, be wise, not loyal."

The sun was setting when Veronica brought hammocks out to the shack for Noland and Shael. Martinus had had the twins clear it out enough for the men to hang hammocks to sleep. He had said he would let them stay in the house if he wasn't so afraid of what the council would do if they found he was harboring exiles.

Shael thought he might also be afraid of what Luc would do if his spies reported that he was helping Shael. He could understand his unease. Shael had also, always, intimidated him. Even though Shael was weak and human, Martinus still seemed wary of him. Brima and Naphtali had left to attend to some heavenly mandates, but assured them that they would check in, and if needed, would return.

Shael had hung his hammock and was sitting in it, trying to get a pillow to stay up under his head comfortably. Noland finished hanging his and took off his shoes to climb in.

"Seeing you with Emile reminds me a lot of me and Luc, in ages past." Shael looked over at Noland, who looked up surprised.

"Really?" Noland slid back into his hammock and reclined with his hands in his lap. He was young, strong, and wide awake.

Shael felt older than ever, and tired; he nodded. "Not in personality. Just with the way you're closer than brothers. You can read each other."

Noland looked down at his hands before looking back up at Shael. "I've never really stopped to think about what Luc was like before the fall. Not really. Is he vastly different, or can you still read him?"

Shael thought about it for a moment in silence. "Better than ever." Shael let his eyes drift over to the door as he thought about what life had been like in Heaven with Luc, and what it had been like in Hell. "I guess when you've gone a long time without seeing someone, before you see them again, you see them with fresh eyes. You see them from a distance, not from the middle of the life you share. In so doing, you glimpse their core. You can differentiate between the constant and their many phases. When you see what it is about them that endures through the *experience* of life, all the other characteristics or qualities are stripped away by trials and heartbreak. You see what they are really made of. Then, they're more exposed than ever. The centuries may have changed him, but fundamentally, he's the same old Luc. I'll always be able to read him. He is terribly simple. The one thing he always lacked was complexity."

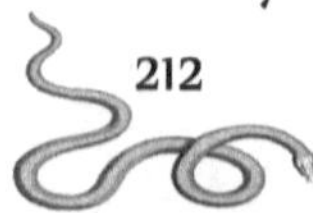

Noland was looking at him thoughtfully. "Do you think he'll hurt her?"

Shael looked Noland straight in the eye. He could see that Noland's concern, though different, was just as great as his own for Achaia. "Yes," he said bluntly. "But the one he really wants to hurt is me. Second to God, it's always been me."

"But didn't he love you?" Noland asked.

Shael could tell he was thinking of his comparison of Noland and Emile to himself and Luc.

"I think the only way you could ever hate someone as much as he hates me and God, is to have once loved them. Hate that grows from love burns with the remnant passion of it. Any other kind of hate could fizzle out, but hate from former love can burn forever."

Noland looked deeply pensive for a while, long enough that Shael thought the conversation was over, and shifted to lay down.

"Do you still love him?" Noland asked, not looking at him, but reclining staring at the ceiling.

"You're thinking of Emile?" Shael asked. Noland remained silent and didn't answer. Shael thought for a moment. "If Emile had hunted Achaia down and murdered her right in front of you, you would only have two options," Shael said flatly. "To admit that he was no longer the brother you knew and loved, or that you had never really known him to begin with."

Shael looked at Noland, and could practically hear the gears turning in his mind. "So, you love the man that never really existed, or you mourn him as gone forever," Noland said, not in question.

"Only after wondering how you could have ever been so blind," Shael added softly. He had never talked about Lucifer like this with anyone. Granted, none of the other Nephilim had ever needed to ask. They had their own complicated feelings toward Luc. Still, none of the younger generations had ever bothered to ask. Shael had seldom tried to unpack the burden he carried when it came to Luc. He just bore it without wondering if it could ever be lightened by talking about it.

"Love is blind," Noland said, factually as if this would make Shael feel better. "We see what we like, and convince ourselves the rest doesn't matter, or isn't true."

Shael nodded.

"Do you miss him?" Noland asked, even quieter, as the sun disappeared behind the waves outside the window. This was whisper hour, where the rest of the world turned to quiet.

Shael thought for a long moment about his brother, who Luc had been before the Fall, before his garden deception, before humanity had taught him jealousy or bitterness. It had been paradise. "Like you'd miss your lungs."

12

Wars Waged Within

"No one can tell what goes on in between the person
you were and the person you become. No one can
chart that blue and lonely section of hell. There are no
maps of the change. You just come out the other side.
Or you don't."
-Stephen King, The Stand

Achaia sat against the wall, blankly staring at the wall opposite her. All the while, Jude sat staring at her. From the outside she looked comatose, like there was nothing going on. He had mopped the blood up from her face, neck and arms. She hadn't flinched, because she no longer felt the pain.

Inside, though, Achaia was on fire, burning herself from within. She argued with herself, trying to convince herself that the visions the shadows had shown her weren't true. But every argument she made, her own brain fought against her, coming up with any shred of evidence it could to prove the contrary, and clinging to it for dear life, playing every scene of anger or hatred toward her on a loop. Everyone who had ever told her something about herself she had always considered false- she was now choking down the memories, deeply considering whether they were actually true. Abomination. Angel of Death. Mistake. Rash. Irrational. Mean. Ignorant. Immature. Foolish…

Achaia felt powerless. If she couldn't make herself worthwhile, if she was so bad, the world was better off without her. All she did was screw up everything she ever tried. Selfishly wanting to rescue her father, she had drawn Noland, Olivier, and Emile into trauma and almost death. What if they had died because she was unable to listen to reason? She only cared about herself and what she wanted. She wasn't a good friend. They deserved better, especially Noland. He didn't deserve to be bound to something as disgusting as her.

Jude tried again. "What's going on in that head of yours?" He scooted closer to her, brushing her face gently with the back of his hand, along her temple. His blue eyes filled with a deep concern that Achaia couldn't process.

She sighed deeply, but didn't answer. She could hear him, but was trapped in her mind, unable to stop the thoughts long enough to reply, too exhausted by the exertion of her mind to be able to speak. She couldn't tell him what she was really thinking. He would try to argue, to tell her that she was wrong. She didn't want to hear that. Something inside her needed to cling to despair for some reason. It wrecked her, but it was easier than fighting it.

"If you can hear me, I need you to listen." Jude's voice

was soft. "I'm here. I'm right here. I'm not leaving you. You're not alone."

Achaia argued in her head. She'd never been so alone in her life. He couldn't join her in her head.

"I don't know what he did to you, so I can't try to make you feel better. But I'm going to remind you what I've learned about you so far." Jude leaned against the wall next to her, his shoulder resting against hers. He fiddled with his fingers in his lap. "You're funny. You keep your composure, even when someone has watched you vomit your brains out. You're feisty. You don't take crap from people. You're a ball buster. You've never busted mine, thank God, but I can just tell," he smiled.

Jude looked over at her. "I think you're a fighter Achaia. So that's what you need to do. You need to fight." Jude's voice cracked.

Achaia remembered fighting. It was the one thing she couldn't come up with any evidence proving she was bad at it.

"Don't give up. Don't give in." Frustration took him over.

Achaia didn't know how many hours or days had passed of him trying to comfort her, when she wasn't worth it.

"GOD!" Jude screamed angrily, standing up, turning around and slamming his fist into the wall. Red slashed across the surface of the ice. Achaia looked up at him then.

He looked down at her, breathing heavily. "I hate him for whatever he did to you. I don't know if you're sad or feel broken, or what you are," he said, staring her down in the eye. "But I need you to not be broken. What you need to be, is angry."

Jude squatted down in front of her and took her face in his large calloused hands, staring her in the eye. His eyes were like blue fire, hot with frustration. "My little warrior, I need you to get pissed."

Achaia blinked, for a moment thinking, *I can do that.*

Noland went for a long run on the beach the next morning. The sun hadn't come up until he turned to run back. He hadn't slept well. Trying to sleep in a hammock had only been half the problem. His mind had kept going back and forth between meditating on what Shael had said about Luc, and what Luc might be doing to Achaia. Finally, he'd decided he needed to move. He needed to feel like he was going somewhere or doing something. He needed to feel progress, instead of drowning in static.

As he got back to the shack, he saw smoke coming up from the forge, and a fire lit in the windows. He walked up to the open door and saw Veronica working on trying to get a good fire going.

"I can help with that," Noland offered. She turned to look at him. She didn't startle easily he noticed.

Noland cocked an eyebrow at the fire, and it roared to life.

Veronica looked at it and smiled at him, "*Gracias.*"

"No problem." Noland leaned against a rustic wooden work bench. He looked around at the weapons in progress. "This

isn't diemerilium is it?" The green was dull, not the deep green of the emerald.

"No, it's new, and better," Veronica said. "We've been using pyrite."

"Pyrite?" Noland said to himself. "When did the council start using these?" Noland asked.

"They haven't yet. I'm still trying to finish the order. It's harder to forge though. It doesn't bond as easily with the diamond and steel. My fires aren't holy, and it isn't the same, not hot enough." Veronica looked at the fire that Noland had started. "But yours are." She smiled.

Noland picked up a dagger. It was still a little rough, not polished or finished yet. He ran his finger along the blade. Blood pooled on the surface in the wake. "It's sharp." His finger stung.

"Yeah, be careful," Veronica said, looking down at his figure.

He picked up some of the other weapons, taking in the artistry on the handles. "I guess this is another reason the order is taking so long? This is stunning." Noland picked up a longsword with a large bird carved into the handle with wings spread wide, the feathers detailed and embellished with gold, and the blade like pitch polished to shimmer.

"The *Alicanto*," Veronica smiled. "That one was a passion project. I was experimenting with different gems. That was the first one to turn out well."

"What is this one?"

"Onyx, for confidence, perseverance and protection."

Sure enough, the blade was much darker than the handle.

Noland swung it. It was weighted steady in his hand, and almost seemed to go before him as if it anticipated his movements. "Exquisite. You are surely gifted."

"Keep it," Veronica smiled. "It suits you."

"How so?" Noland looked at her.

"Do you not know the legend of the *Alicanto*?"

Noland shook his head.

"The *Alicanto* is a creature of luck. He eats silver and gold, and shimmers like the sun and moon. If you follow him, he'll lead you to riches untold. But," Veronica smiled mischievously, "if he catches you following him, he'll lead you off a cliff."

"You think that suits me?" Noland asked.

"Only time will tell." Veronica said, hammering the sword she was just beginning to shape. "But I'm inclined to believe so. From what Emile tells me, I think the council has made a grave mistake in underestimating you, and you caught them following."

"But I'm not leading them anywhere," Noland laughed.

"Aren't you?" Veronica looked at him, and pushed her mask up. Then she cocked her head to the side, as if she'd heard something. Noland was straining his ears to listen when the door burst open. A group of demons stood in the doorway, and hesitated only a moment before they charged in.

Noland looked to Veronica, who tossed aside the unfinished sword and grabbed at the poker. "Here," Noland reached out a hand. She placed the end of the poker in it, and he heated it to glimmering. In her other hand, Veronica held her hammer. She held them both out to her sides, ready for battle. Noland turned arcing his sword to cut down the first demon

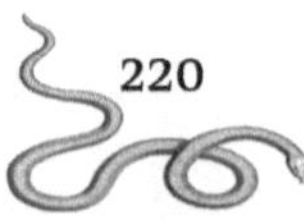

with ease, but there were more behind him.

The ones that got past him were met by Veronica's blows. She hammered in their skulls, brains splattering her anvil. She stabbed the burning end of the poker into the throat of an oncoming beast, and Noland could hear the sizzle of the demon's flesh cauterizing even as it choked.

Noland beheaded the next demon to come in the door and waited for another. None came. He looked back at Veronica. "You okay?"

Save for a gash on her arm, she was fine. Noland walked outside and looked down the beach where the demon tracks had come from.

Shael emerged from the shack, dagger in hand. "You too?"

Noland nodded.

They followed the tracks at a run, back toward the house.

Noland heard a scream that sounded like Yellaina, and picked up his pace. As they got there, Noland saw Emile dispatching the last of the intruders.

"It would appear that Lucifer knows you're here," Martinus said, cleaning his blade.

Yellaina looked mildly shaken, and Amelia was kicking over the corpse of a demon at her feet; he'd gotten close.

Shael clenched his jaw, looking inconvenienced. "Sooner, rather than later would be good; if you could give me whatever information you can about your creation."

Martinus fixed Shael with an incredulous look.

"What creation?" Vito asked, looking back and forth

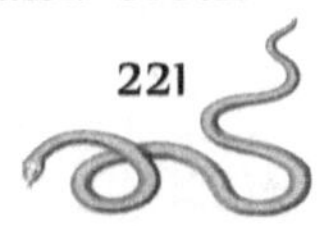

between the two men.

"What is going on here?" Veronica asked.

"My mate," Noland spoke up, after a moment of tense silence. "She was taken by Lucifer. She is being held hostage in a prison your father built. We are trying to break her out."

Veronica stared at her father. "What kind of prison?"

Martinus looked at her as if he was going to be sick. "A regretful one." He looked at Shael. "You and I should take a trip." He looked at the room around them. "I don't know why they aren't turning to ashes, but clean this up," he said to his sons.

Vito and Vidal looked like they'd been told to clean their room or take out the trash. Shael and Martinus left through the front door, and Noland heard the car start and drive away.

"You wanted some action," Amelia smiled at Veronica. "Wish granted."

Veronica shook her head smiling. "We should clean up our mess," she said looking at Noland.

The two of them walked back down the beach to the forge. "Your mate, tell me about her."

Noland smiled. "If you think I'm fiery, you haven't seen anything yet." He chuckled as he thought a little more. "She's a fighter, tiny but absolutely fierce. If I know anything, Lucifer has his hands full with her."

"That's quite a deal of confidence," Veronica said smiling.

"I am worried, but when I really think about it, I find comfort in knowing her, and knowing she can hold her own. I'm only worried because I know she has goodness and restraint, and Lucifer does not."

Veronica nodded. "Her name is Achaia, right?"

Noland nodded. "I mean she's a hellion for me, and she likes me. I can only imagine how much trouble she'll give *him*. But that worries me, too. I don't want her to waken his anger."

"Well it sounds like, if he wakes her anger, he is in for his own world of trouble," Veronica offered in form of comfort. "What is her gift?"

Noland smiled. "Fighting."

"Fighting?" Veronica looked at him, prodding.

Noland's smile left his face. "You're Emile's mate. Does that make you trustworthy?"

Veronica stopped walking and looked at Noland straight on, unflinching. "I am Veronica. That makes me trustworthy."

Noland smiled and nodded a small apology. "According to Bale, Achaia is a death angel. Her gift is killing things."

Veronica kept his eye, but hers widened a little in surprise. The look lasted only a millisecond, before she controlled herself. "I see." She started walking down the beach again. "Yet, if she is against Lucifer, she has chosen God?"

"She's not pledged herself to anyone."

"Ah," Veronica looked nervous. "But you think she will choose God?"

"It's difficult to say. I hope she will, but the council is doing everything possible to turn her off to that idea." Noland had never worded it that way before, but saying it aloud, it clicked in a new way in his head. Perhaps that was their intention. He would ponder more on that later.

"But God is not the council," Veronica offered.

"Yes, but she is still learning that."

"She sounds fierce." Veronica smiled. "I'm sure she will pull through or die with honor," Veronica said, as if they were both happy endings. Noland didn't want to think about Achaia dying. He wasn't sure if she would perish as a human, or as an angel. One might find her in hell forever if she died without allegiance, and the other might find her as if she'd never existed at all. Seeing the look on his face, Veronica put a hand on his arm, wordlessly. They had reached the forge. "What do we do with them?"

Noland looked over to the bonfire pit. Veronica nodded.

Olivier boarded the plane with his baggage and his reservations. He wasn't entirely sure why he wasn't stoked to be joining his family. He'd felt isolated for weeks. But now that he was on his way to Chile, he wasn't sure that was going to bridge the gap. He had been waiting for the chance to ask to see his brother and sister. But when in the council meeting yesterday the late weapons order came up again, he volunteered his services to see what was taking so long and go to motivate them to hurry up.

The jet took off shortly after he boarded. Plane travel was shut down across the world, leaving people stranded in countries they had dared to visit before the war started. Everyone was panicked. Every passenger was a potential terrorist, or sleeper agent. The paranoia had taken grasp of the rationale of every country on the planet. But the council had power. They

had money, better technology, and divine intervention. They operated above the human authorities, and in total secret. God had always seen to that- well, that, and their own spiritual abilities and influence.

Olivier shut his eyes, and when he opened them again, they were landing in Chile. He thanked the pilot and carried his bag off the plane. A car was waiting for him. It was a nice one, with a driver. He thought about how many Nephilim must have been seduced by the perks of being "in" with the council. This would have been cool to Olivier when he was younger. Now, it was a mere convenience. He needed to get to his family, and this car was taking him there. Period.

He sat silently in the back seat, not speaking to the driver, as he drove him through the streets closing the distance between him and Yellaina. He hadn't called again or told her he was coming. He wasn't sure why. Anyone looking at him would have thought he was older. The way he carried himself, his demeanor had changed so much under Dina's tutelage, as to make him almost unrecognizable.

Too soon, the car was pulling into a driveway, and the driver was opening his door. Yellaina and two boys, who were obviously twins, were following Amelia out of the house. "Olly?" Amelia said, excitedly. She had never sounded or looked so happy.

Olivier couldn't bring himself to smile. But he hugged her back as she grabbed him. Over her shoulder he made eye contact with Yellaina, who looked stunned.

As Amelia pulled away smiling, Yellaina stepped forward.

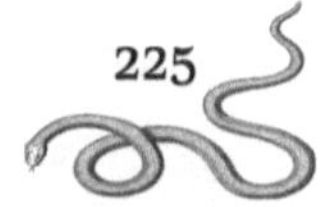

"Why wouldn't you tell me you were coming?" she demanded angrily. Amelia and the twins looked shocked and awkward. They looked at each other, and then Amelia gestured for them to come with her, and they disappeared down a path behind the house. The driver ignored all of them and got back in the car and pulled away. He had better places to be, like, anywhere else.

"I don't know," Olivier answered honestly.

"What's gotten into you?" Yellaina asked, looking at him as if he were a stranger.

"I don't know," he answered again, honestly.

"Why did you come then?" Yellaina asked, frustrated.

"Work. I need to see the smithy," Olivier said factually.

Yellaina looked exasperated. "So, that's it?"

Olivier shrugged.

Yellaina yelled in frustration stomping her foot. "What is this? What is happening to us? You look like a zombie. Feel something!"

Olivier stepped back, surprised. He'd never seen her like this. "What do you mean feel something?" Olivier asked, now feeling frustrated. She had left him, and then come back only to leave him again to go off to another country with his brother and sister. She'd left him.

"Say something! You're just standing there!" Yellaina's face was flushed.

"We're having a conversation, or a semblance of one. I'm talking only slightly less than you are," Olivier said pointedly.

Yellaina's face flushed.

"I don't know what else you want from me," Olivier said,

fed up.

"Me neither." Yellaina spat, looking at him with total disbelief. After one more glare, she stormed off into the house.

"Which way is the smithy?" he called after her. She pointed down the path the others had walked down before slamming the door in his face.

Olivier huffed his bag over his shoulder and started walking.

Martinus drove them to a cliff and started climbing. Shael followed, slightly frustrated. He was human and didn't have his previous endurance. Nor did he have the same ability to survive a fall from this height. When they had reached the top, Martinus sat on the edge, and looked out at the sea, breathing hard.

Shael sat next to him.

"Do you ever struggle to remember?" Martinus asked.

"What, specifically?" Shael asked.

"Life before now? The old days. How we became how we are." Martinus' face was stone still.

"My problem is more like, I wish I could forget, but I remember in excruciating detail." Shael said, watching the waves crash beneath them.

"Oh, that our minds were reversed," Martinus sighed. "I come here when I want to remember. It is easier to think where it is quiet. Three kids doesn't make that easy to come by."

Shael nodded.

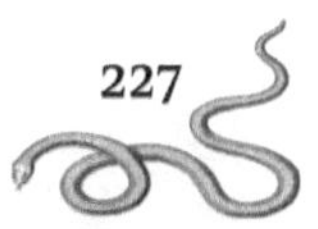

"I want to help you," Martinus said. "But I think that first you may need to help me."

"To remember?" Shael asked.

"Among other things," Martinus swallowed and looked at him.

"What do you mean?" Shael looked at him curiously.

Martinus sighed. "I've done things Shael, so many things. Sometimes the weight of them is suffocating. A time may come when they catch up with me. You can relate, can't you?"

Shael made no move to respond.

"How did you disappear? How could you possibly hide in a world so full of eyes?"

"You want to go into hiding?" Shael asked surprised. "Why?"

Martinus looked uncomfortable. "It may someday be necessary."

"I wouldn't wish it on you or your children. It is a life of constantly looking over your shoulder and moving. You'll never rest again," Shael said bleakly.

Martinus nodded sadly. "Now, help me remember. Talk to me of things you can't forget."

Shael began to talk to him of heaven right before the fall, of the gruesome battle that followed, of what they did to those who opposed them, for God's sake. He spoke of their misaligned loyalty, and beliefs, the intimacy of their tortures…

"I remember fearing retribution," Martinus said, his eyes unfocused, looking at things long past in his mind's eye, not at what was before him. "There was a day I remember I realized we

were lost, that we would become forsaken. I was afraid. That was the first time I had ever felt *fear*." Martinus was lost in thought.

"What did you do when you became afraid?" Shael asked, trying to pry deeper.

"That's it," Martinus said. "That's what I would have done. I would have locked it away."

"Locked it away where?" Shael asked.

"Where no one could get to it, but me. Because no one knew it was there."

"I don't understand."

"What is the last thing you'd feel in that place we built with fear and despair?"

"Hope," Shael said.

"Exactly. You unlock your freedom with hope. But no one would feel hope when they believe there is no form of escape. The one who dares to hope will find freedom."

"That tells me nothing. How can I get her out!?" Shael's voice was rising involuntarily.

Martinus looked sad, "You can't."

"Damn it," Shael slammed his fists into the ground.

"Only she can," Martinus said.

Achaia sat silently next to Jude, watching their third duel that week. Lucifer once again butchered his opponent. Achaia still hadn't spoken a word. She listened to Jude, hanging onto his voice, his words. She carried them with her into the den of shadows. She drank in everything around her, and was intentional in deciding what was real, and what wasn't. She built up a fortress in her mind, and walled herself in, seeing the shadows for what they were, half-truths twisted into lies.

Her eyes were the only windows. She had begun analyzing Luc's movements, when he was fighting, and when he wasn't. She listened to him talk. His belief that she was broken had his guard down. He felt like he had won. Sometimes, though, he would grow frustrated at her silence. His tantrums revealed to her more than he knew, when he thought she was gone. Her visits with the shadows had grown shorter and less frequent. Luc was sometimes afraid he had gone too far, that he had broken her mind more than he had intended. At least that is what he said the last time he grew weary of her silence.

He came for her again after his victory. He took her again to his room, to mend his wounds. She tended him in robotic silence.

"I miss you," he said softly, looking at her sadly. He thought that he had tortured her into insanity. She wanted him to think so. In order for that to remain the case, she had to keep it up even around Jude.

Jude- whose anger had only grown with each day of her brokenness. The truth was, despite the torture, Achaia was still there, deep inside. But she had to crawl into herself if she was going to survive. Every thought she had seemed distant. Her days went by almost in a haze. She rarely came to the surface to see what was going on around her. But she surfaced for the shadows. She talked with them. She had to talk to someone. She

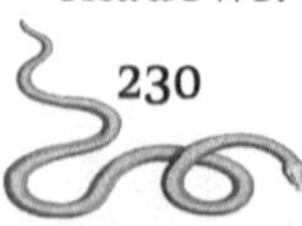

listened to them, and she argued with them, and with herself. The darkness was there, too, on the inside. She hadn't built her walls up fast enough. The darkness was trapped inside. Everyday, it threatened to suffocate her. But Jude's voice could be heard, telling her to remember, to be angry, to fight.

Achaia was fighting. It just didn't look like she was. Some things were harder to fight than others. Demons were easy, your own thoughts and beliefs, not so much. Her body was sluggish, and even more pale than usual. But in her mind, she was vigorous in her hunt, hunting down everything she hated about herself, and killing it. That's what she was good at. All she needed was more time.

Once she killed all her weaknesses and the lies she believed, she would be a force to be reckoned with. Yellaina had once told her she was like a bomb. The more Luc tried to break her and convince her she was weak, the more Achaia used his attempts to fuel her hate and righteous anger. Instead of a cold despair, he was stoking a fire in her. One day at a time, she just had to keep fighting, fighting to build a fire big enough to fight the shadows in her mind, to shut out the darkness and fill her with light and warmth.

"You are but a shell of what you once were," Luc said sadly, studying her. "It appears as if my ice has finally quenched your fire. I have destroyed what I loved best about you."

Achaia flinched at the word *love*. Luc noticed.

"Perhaps this is the effect of the demons, your changing nature." Luc looked pensive. "It can't be that what I loved best about you was your humanity." Something in Luc's eyes told her that was a deeply disturbing thought to him. That he had *loved* her *humanity*. That in that way, he could possibly be more like his father than he thought.

Her *nature*, Achaia thought, her changing nature; she could feel it. It was slowed down by her humanity, but she wasn't immune to her chameleon Nephilim nature. The demonic energy only helped her hatred. But her humanity helped her to stay in control of it. She wasn't a mindless thing that took joy in killing and pillaging. She had motive and thought. Was her composition changing to include not only angel and human, but human, angel and demon? What would that mean?

"Maybe a few days alone with Jude will bring you back to me," Luc said sadly. "I do not bring it out of you." He brushed his fingers tenderly along her face, and leaned in to kiss her temple. His lips were cold, as was the gesture, cold and distant.

Luc took her back to her cell and locked her inside. Jude came and received her from him, and helped her over to the furs on the floor. He sat her down and sat up against her. She could feel his warmth.

Once Luc had left, Jude spoke to her. "Please don't leave me alone here."

Achaia felt the words in her head. She knew what it was like to feel alone. Distantly she thought, she didn't want that for him.

"Achaia, please come back to me." Achaia thought then of Noland. That's who she wanted to go home to, to his warmth, to his voice. Jude put his hand along her leg, grabbing hold of her knee and squeezing. Achaia wished he was Noland. But she didn't

want him to be afraid or hurt either. He seemed like a really nice guy. Without meaning to, Achaia reached up and grabbed his hand.

Jude looked at her surprised.

"I'm still here," she said, her voice weak and raspy.

At nightfall, Noland and the others were still camped out by the firepit waiting for what little remains were left to burn down completely. The night air was chilly on their skin, but not on his. Yellaina had even pulled on a coat. She sat across the fire from Olivier. He hadn't seen the two of them talk to each other since Olivier had gotten there. Olivier had arrived as they were piling the last of the corpses on the firepit. Noland noticed something was off about him. He wasn't his usual self. He seemed heavier.

Veronica and Emile sat huddled together, whispering to each other and smiling. Amelia was silently staring into the fire. Noland wondered what she was thinking. She was the mystery of the group, uncommonly good at keeping people at a distance, even when she didn't mean to. It was a habit.

Vito and Vidal were joking around, throwing sticks and things into the fire, and poking at limbs hanging out of the pit, pushing them in as room allowed.

Noland had a thought, then. "Does anyone, per chance, have a guitar?"

Vito and Vidal looked up at him. Amelia smiled. Veronica

asked, "Oh, do you play?"

"I used to," Noland said.

"Get the one father made," Veronica said, turning to her bothers.

The twins took off down the beach for the house, racing each other, and pushing each other down onto the beach playfully. Noland smiled.

Yellaina was looking at him without seeing him. Noland glanced at Emile, who shrugged. Olivier stood up, and walked down to the water, rolling up his pants, and wetting his feet in the surf.

The twins returned with a guitar and a *djimbe*.

"You drum?" he asked Vidal, who was holding the djimbe.

"No, but she does," he said handing it to his sister.

"I'll follow you," Veronica said, meeting Noland's eye. He kept her eye as he started to play. He tried for something upbeat, and she followed him, skillfully filling out the tune. Noland began to sing, whatever praise and gratitude came to mind. His voice was hoarse from the smoke, and rasped. Veronica sang too, not in any words that made any sense to Noland, but her harmony was good. He smiled at her. Amelia joined, humming. Vito and Vidal started a sort of chant like accompaniment. Emile sang then, with Noland, following his heart, as much as his lead. Yellaina stood and followed Olivier to the sea.

As they played and sang, just whatever came to mind, Noland felt the tension ease in his shoulders. It was an exercise in faith. God has always provided and persevered. He would win in the end. He just had to trust Him, and Achaia. She was strong,

234

stubborn, and he had to believe that she would fight until the end. Shael was still off with Martinus, and hopefully when they came back, they would have a plan for how to get to her.

Noland let his final chord ring out, and their voices died down.

"You play well," Veronica said.

"So do you," Noland said nodding at the drum.

"My father went through a phase of making instruments. We learned to play just by experimenting. But, like my father, I like to create. That includes music."

"We didn't get that gift," Vito laughed.

"Our music sounds more like noise," Vidal agreed.

Noland and Emile laughed. Amelia smiled.

The water lapped up on Olivier's feet. It was warmer than he thought it would be. He felt the sand sift under his feet, out from underneath him, and back out to the sea. He looked out at the reflection of the moonlight on the water. It danced on the waves like it had its own prerogative.

He looked up, and realized he couldn't remember a time he'd been able to see so many stars. He thought they were a beautiful metaphor. God was clever. He had his own way of reminding them that there was always more going on than what they could see. It was always there though, behind the veil. Just because they forgot about them, didn't mean there weren't plans in the works.

"Hey," Yellaina said, coming up beside him.

He hadn't heard her approach over the music and the waves. "Hey," he said hesitantly.

"Are you angry with me?" Yellaina asked, sounding small and scared.

"No," Olivier said flatly. "I think if I'm honest, I must be hurt."

"Hurt?" Yellaina sounded surprised. "How did I hurt you?"

"You left. You chose Noland over me. You chose Emile and Amelia over me…" Olivier said gently.

Yellaina looked like each word caused her physical pain. "No."

Olivier smiled sympathetically, knowing that it was hard for her to hear. He knew that wasn't her exact thought process, but it was the effect of her decisions. "Yes."

"I chose right when the council was wrong. Then I chose purpose over.."

"Both of which left me in the dust," Olivier said not unkindly.

Yellaina looked like she was going to be sick. "When did we discover the power to hurt each other so acutely?"

"Isn't that what it is to love someone?" Olivier smiled weakly. "To hand them the power—"

"To hurt each other?" Yellaina looked incredulous.

"To care." Olivier took her hand. "What the other says, what they do, what they want…"

Yellaina looked down at their hands. "I never meant to

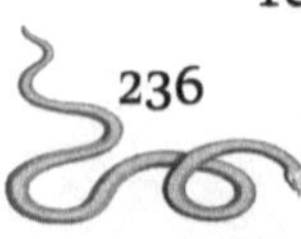

hurt you."

"I know." Olivier said. "Forgive me?"

Yellaina looked up at him surprised, "For what?"

"For going numb? For doubting you?"

Yellaina shook her head, tears filling up in her eyes, and then she was kissing him. "I missed you…" she repeated against his lips.

"Me too."

"The truth is a tyrant-
The only tyrant to whom
we can give our allegiance.
The servce of truth is a matter of heroism."
-John F Kennedy

Achaia had let Jude into her mind, and shared with him a little bit of what had happened with the shadows. The more she told him, the more he took off her chest, and bore in his own. He grew angrier than he had been because of her silence. The weight that left allowed her to breathe with a little less effort.

"I can't let him shape me, or the shadows take me," she said, desperate. "Hearing your voice, I knew I needed to fight and try to be strong for you. I couldn't leave you here by yourself."

Jude took her in his arms and squeezed. "You're not alone

either. We're going to get through this together."

Achaia squeezed him back and felt tears of relief burn her eyes. She was starting to feel more like herself. But she was still battling a feeling of worthlessness, and a dull voice in the back of her head that told her she wouldn't be much help to Jude, and that he was essentially already alone, even with her there.

Shael had come back late and found Noland sitting alone at what was left of a bonfire.

"Hey," Noland said as Shael got closer.

"Hey," Shael said taking a seat next to him on a log.

"So, what did Martinus say? When do we leave?" Noland sounded so hopeful.

Shael sighed.

"What?" Noland asked, looking concerned.

"We can't save her. She can only be saved by herself."

"What do you mean?" Noland asked.

"The only escape is hope. She has to feel hope."

Noland didn't look as upset and Shael felt.

"Well that's good isn't it?" Noland said, looking confused.

"How are we supposed to make her feel hope from here?" Shael said, as though it were obviously a hopeless cause.

"We don't," Noland said obviously. "She's already felt it once. She just didn't believe she was really free. Next time we just have to convince her it's real," Noland said.

"The longer she stays there, the more he…" Shael couldn't

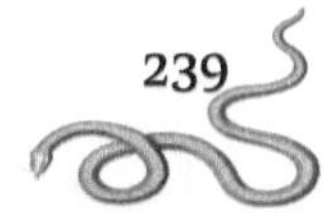

bring himself to talk of her being tortured, but he was sure it was happening, and it made him sick. "I don't think she's coming back again."

"Then we go to her," Noland said. "How do you get thrown in this prison? What brings more hope than a cavalry? We go in after her, and tell her how to get out."

"It's not that easy, son," Shael said, gently. "You can't just tell someone to feel happy, or to feel hope."

"No, but maybe you can help them remember a time when they did. If they remember that they've felt it before, that there was a time in life when things were good, it opens up the possibility in their mind that maybe there's a chance that could happen again."

Shael thought for a minute. Maybe Noland had a point.

"Have you ever thought that all hope was lost, only to be proved otherwise?" Noland asked, knowing the answer, because the boy knew his history.

Shael nodded, "When we surfaced after the Redemption, we were scattered to the wind. Only mates were kept together. We were stretched thin over the earth. In those days, there was no real way of finding each other, or communicating. It was His way of ensuring we behaved ourselves. If we couldn't organize, we couldn't mutiny again. I surfaced in a city called Achaia. I can't even tell you what it was like to feel the warmth of the sun, to take a breath that didn't stutter with the cold. To feel a warm breeze on my face… That was the first day I truly appreciated Heaven. As I looked out over that first sunset, I understood the grace in endings. I drank in the hope of a new beginning, a fresh

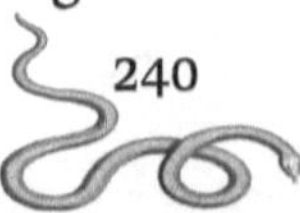

start.

"Of course, over the years, we were tracked down, or tracked each other down. Politics formed, and more mistakes and messes were made. Not Anna- I could never consider her a mistake. When we found out we were having a girl, I was filled with that same euphoria of grace and hope. I talked Anna into naming her Achaia. I told her it was a city I'd researched for one of my writing assignments and thought it sounded cool. But really, second to hearing my daughter's heartbeat for the first time, surfacing in Achaia after being in Hell, was the happiest I'd ever felt."

"Achaia has known despair," Noland said simply. Shael hadn't known what it was like for her after he was taken, and she was left with strangers, confused, and disoriented. "But she has witnessed the hope that comes from perseverance. She isn't the type to give up. If we can get to her, she'll consider that we are there to get her out, that there is a chance of escape. Maybe she will feel hope."

"What if it backfires?" Shael asked.

Noland looked at him quizzically.

"What if we show up there, and she thinks we're all imprisoned there with her, because of her? I know how this place works, and it makes it really hard to have a positive thought."

"We have to try, don't we?" Noland asked. "No matter the risk? I can't keep doing nothing."

Emile sat in the living room with his sister, Yellaina, Olivier, and Veronica. Martinus had come home looking weary beyond belief, and had gone straight to his room without talking to anyone. Emile couldn't make up his mind how he felt about Martinus. At times he felt like a normal father, with affection towards his children, but at the oddest times he would experience an anxiety that didn't fit the situation. The closer they got to these murder cases, the more he panicked. When Shael and Noland had arrived, it only added to the confusion. There was a strange mix of anxiety and relief around Shael, Emile had no clue what to make of. Noland seemed to particularly vex him. He didn't seem happy about Veronica befriending Noland, which might be explained by Noland being an exile. But when Veronica had told him she'd given him one of her swords, he seemed particularly anxious, and asked which one. He hadn't liked the answer either, but why? It wasn't taken from the council's order or inventory.

"What are you thinking about?" Veronica asked him.

Sometimes he thought her dark eyes were learning to pierce him. "Just thinking."

"He does that a lot," Amelia said as if it were one of his more annoying qualities.

The phone rang, and Veronica got up to answer it, running her hand across his shoulder as she passed it. It was strange how comfortable they had grown to be around each other, and how quickly.

"*Hola*?" She answered.

Emile felt his stomach drop, and turned around to see that Veronica had gone pale. He was on his feet in an instant.

"What is it?" He crossed the room to her in three steps, putting a hand on her shoulder, standing close enough behind her to hear the voice on the other end of the phone. Veronica responded in rapid soft spoken Chilean Spanish, which Emile struggled to understand.

She turned around and looked up in his eyes, then to the others, "There's been another murder."

"Who?"

"From the description, I think it was Eran. They want father to come down. They are trying to identify the body."

"Not the human police?"

"No, the Santiago safe house," Veronica said.

"Dead Nephilim? How?" Yellaina asked, standing.

"We already knew it was possible," Emile said bitterly.

"But not since—"

"That we know of," Emile said.

"Since who?" Veronica looked at them confused.

"Noland's parents."

Veronica's eyes were wide, and Emile could feel her surprise and sadness. "Oh."

"When? We did not hear of this here," Veronica asked.

"Six years ago, almost seven."

Veronica shook her head in disbelief. "I would have been young. Maybe my father just did not tell me."

"Sounds like we need to take a road trip," Amelia said.

Emile appreciated her low-key determination and resolve in such situations. Everyone else seemed despaired or stressed out. Amelia always just thought about the facts and what needed to be done.

Achaia was summoned by a demon and escorted to a wide foyer that reminded Achaia of Hell, where she'd found her father sitting on a sofa made of ice covered in furs. The foyer was decorated like a living room, with a mini bar, and chairs and sofas carved of ice. They were made to look more comfortable by pillows and blankets, but no amount of textiles could warm the room. Music was playing, a jazzy California kind of mix. Achaia recognized it as Saint Motel, *Just my Type*. She looked around and saw a gramophone record player. She was wondering where Luc was when he came around the corner moon walking, and singing into a bottle of bourbon. *He has slick moves*, Achaia had to admit. She'd never seen this laid-back side of him before. He danced halfway across the room before he saw her standing there.

He gestured for her to come and dance with him. Achaia cocked an eyebrow and shook her head. Luc danced over to her and grabbed her hands, wiggling her arms, and she could smell the alcohol on him. Luc made a pouty face and dropped her arms. "I've been experimenting," he slurred. "It takes an unholy about of alcohol to make a devil drunk." He offered her the bottle, "Want some?"

Achaia tried not to roll her eyes. "As much as that might make your presence more tolerable, no thanks." Achaia knew drunk people could be unpredictable. Luc being drunk set her

on edge, and her whole body seemed to tingle as if a low grade electric shock were racing through her limbs. She found herself clenching her jaw and shaken in a way she hated. She was hyper focused on everything, every expression on his face, every tone in his voice, ready to get back, duck or run at any moment if she should say or do something to set him off.

"You know whose fault it is your mom is dead?" Luc leveled her with a stare that made Achaia think he wasn't really looking at her.

"Mine," Achaia said numbly.

"Damn right!" Luc threw the bourbon bottle, and it shattered on a column of ice, sending a spray of liquor across Achaia's face. "But you blame me! And whose fault is it, that your father was with me last year?"

"His," Achaia said again, trying to stay calm, and even.

"He chose me!" Luc said quietly, nodding his head enthusiastically. "He chose me." He turned around wobbly, and stumbled over to a sofa. "So why won't you? I haven't ever done anything to you. Everything you hate about your life was your own making. I am offering you a way out!"

"I guess I'm just really screwed up."

Luc looked at her tenderly, "That's what I love about you, darling."

Achaia had to implement extraordinary effort to not roll her eyes. She kept repeating in her head *I know what is true. I know truth. You can't manipulate me.* "You want me to get back at my father," Achaia said, walking over to the bar and leaning against it, mocking a laid back posture. The shocks were still racing through her arms and legs. Her breathing was rapid and her heart was racing, but she carried herself like it was a lazy Saturday afternoon.

"No, I want you for you." Luc stood, insisting. The slur in his speech was already fading. He was sobering up quickly. "For your power, and your ability."

"Not for my personality." Achaia stepped away from him as he took up the bar next to her, a little too close to her face.

"Your stubbornness and fiestyrosity." Luc shook his head, trying to look at her like he was truly heartfelt, but just looking drunk "are what I love best of everything ever."

"Why did you call me here?" Achaia asked calmly, reminding him that he had probably had another reason.

"I just really love that song and I wanted to dance with my wife."

"I'm not your wife," Achaia said matter of factly.

"Not yet, but you're coming back to me day by day." Luc smiled.

Achaia lost her composure and rolled her eyes.

"There she is!" Luc smiled, running the back of his hand along her cheek bone. "My little firecracker."

"What if my human half keeps me from becoming like you and I never choose you?" Achaia asked, genuinely.

Lucs face fell. "You will be like me. It might just take longer."

"But if I don't ever choose you?" Achaia asked.

Luc's ice blue eyes turned to pure evil. "I'll take you anyway."

Achaia flinched away. Luc grabbed hold of her arm. "You listen to me." He squeezed so hard her arm already felt bruised. "You can't resist me. You're mine. I have you little darling, and there's not a damn thing you can do about it."

Achaia yanked her arm away, too full of rage to be afraid anymore. "Actually, from what I've read, I have free will. I am also made in the image of God himself. You can torture me, you can torment me, you can hold me here. But you can't have me. I am His and I will never choose you. He is everywhere, always, and if He can hear me, *I am His*."

Luc roared with rage, and back-handed her hard. "Take it back!" He hit her again. Achaia was stunned for only a second before she stood back up straight, and blocked his next blow. He stumbled back, unsteady on his feet.

"I will never choose you, especially now. You are desperate and *unlovable*." He charged her, and she side stepped and pushed him over. Luc sat slumped on the floor. "If you so much as raise a hand to me again, I will find a way to kill you." Achaia could feel her eyes were red. In that moment she felt more herself than she had since she had woken up surrounded by ice. She was rage, she was the angel of death, and if she could bring it to Lucifer, she would. If anyone could, it had to be her.

Luc curled in on himself sobbing. Achaia turned away disgusted.

As she walked herself back to her cell, she thought she felt a new power coursing through her. She had pledged allegiance to God. She didn't know what was necessary to make it official, but she had made her decision. It felt as natural as breathing, and she wondered if it was His power she felt, or if it was just the confidence of knowing she wasn't fighting for herself anymore, but something greater. She had chosen a side, a side with misguided council members, and Nephilim who hated her, sure. But they weren't God and He was the only one that mattered. She would get to know Him better. She would fight for Him because she couldn't stand with Luc, and when you boil it down, in the spiritual world, those really were your only two options. She couldn't choose herself. She must become less, and He must become greater.

Dina called while they were driving to Santiago. Olivier hadn't answered. He couldn't talk to her in a van full of people. Shael and Noland had had to stay behind, because, obviously they were exiled and weren't supposed to be in contact with any other Nephilim.

When they got to the safe house in Santiago they were led into the basement, which held a sort of morgue. "Do all safe houses have these?" Olivier asked.

"Only a handful," Martinus answered.

The healer who had called stood next to a body covered by a white sheet. "He is being removed to the valley of bones this evening."

Martinus nodded. The healer pulled back the sheet. The face was unfamiliar to Olivier, but his siblings, Yellaina and Veronica, all gasped and looked at each other fearfully. Yellaina

had tears in her eyes. Olivier wrapped a strong arm around her shoulders and she laid her head on him.

"So it's Eran then?" Olivier asked.

"*Si*," Veronica said.

"His charge was killed with her family recently, yes?" The healer asked.

"Yes, in our village. We are still investigating," Martinus said.

"Demonic?" The healer asked.

"We aren't sure," Martinus said. Olivier tensed. He thought they were sure. Yellaina stood up straight at that.

He looked at his sister, who looked livid.

"We are fairly certain it was demonic," she said defiantly, leveling Martinus with a glare. Olivier smiled. Amelia didn't take crap from anyone, even the original generation.

"We, however, don't have any solid proof," Martinus said.

The healer looked back and forth between them, nodded, and covered the Nephilim's face.

"Cause of death?" Emile asked.

The healer grimaced, and pulled the sheet back down to his abdomen. "This."

Eran had nearly been sliced in half, and along the edges of the laceration his skin was black with some sort of infection.

"I've never seen anything like it," Yellaina said stepping forward, and looking more closely. "What could have caused this?" She ran her fingers above the black bits of skin, without touching him.

"We've only seen it once before, but it was just about

exact. The Amsels were killed in a similar fashion. The infection around the wounds looked the same. We studied them, but never found the cause."

Emile flinched visibly. Amelia's eyes shot up to meet the healers, and Yellaina's hand froze where it hovered. She looked up at the healer. "What kind of weapon could kill a Nephilim?"

The healer shrugged. "We have speculated. Diemerillium wouldn't. Regular human weapons cannot. It has to be something new. Perhaps with another element? An unholy gem? We don't know."

Everyone else was looking at the healer, but Olivier was looking at Veronica, who had gone stiff and pale. She swallowed when she met his eyes and realized she was being watched. Olivier stared into her eyes, and wished he had his brother's gift.

Noland had felt sick since the others had been called to Santiago to identify a dead Nephilim. He remembered the day someone had told him his parents were dead. There had been so many phases of denial before he had come to acceptance. How could he have easily accepted something so, difficult, yes, but something so *impossible*? It had never happened. And now it was happening again. Why? His mind was racing with possibilities. Were there any connections, similarities? He wished he weren't exiled so he could have gone with them, seen the body, asked questions.

He fought against the feeling of hopelessness.

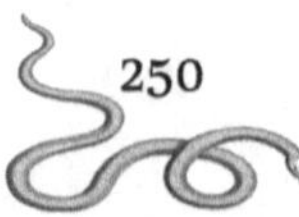

"What's going on in your brain?" Shael asked, coming out of their shack.

"How have you done it all this time?" Noland asked. "I feel so small and insignificant. What can I do, just me on my own, without the council, without help?"

"First of all, you're not insignificant." Shael looked awkward. Noland knew comforting people wasn't his forte. "Secondly, you're not in that bad of a position. We're never truly alone. Your friends haven't abandoned you. We have resources outside of the council that are more powerful than the council. Bale, Naphtali… We just have to make the most of what we've got, and not allow ourselves to be mistaken. We are not hopeless. We are powerful in our own right, and we are not alone. Our enemies will underestimate us, and that, too, is to our advantage."

Noland smiled weakly. "Cheering for the underdogs?"

"Every time," Shael said smiling. "You know why?"

Noland shook his head.

"We have something they don't."

"Odds stacked against us?" Noland huffed.

"Incentive."

Noland cocked an eyebrow.

"They are comfortable, thinking they are untouchable. We have a greater motivation, thinking we have to overcome, but also, look at what we are after. They want what? More power? Who knows? What do we want? To save the life of someone we love. Who will go to the furthest lengths?" Shael smiled almost mischievously. "I haven't made it this long believing I'm already defeated."

"What do you believe instead?" Noland asked, feeling something in his chest open up to receive something like hope.

"That I am a force to be reckoned with. They wouldn't hate me or fear me so much if I wasn't." Shael put a hand on his shoulder and gripped it tightly. "For someone as young as you to be exiled without so much as a trial, they must be truly afraid of the man you are becoming. Maybe you don't see it yet, but they sure do. Use that. I wanted them to forget about me. Don't let them forget about you. Don't let them rest."

Noland smiled, and looked out over the ocean. "What good is it being an exiled angel if you don't raise a little Hell?"

"My thoughts exactly." Shael clapped him on this back, like a proud father.

"Is it crazy or egotistical for me to think this is all somehow related? The exile, Eran being killed, the World War…"

"Not crazy, and only egotistical if you think it is revolving around you," Shael laughed. "This is the beginning of the end. It is more important than ever for us to know where we stand."

Noland felt a stone drop in his stomach. "Are you worried Achaia won't pledge allegiance in time?"

Shael's face fell flat.

"I worry," Noland admitted.

"Me too. And I only have myself to blame."

"I blame the council. They met her with so much suspicion and judgement, I am afraid they turned her away from God."

"They serve themselves under the pretext of allegiance to God. Achaia is smart enough to know that isn't a real depiction of God. I just hope she comes to know Him on her own, somehow,

and sees He is so much more than his representation. I hope she has, instead, seen Him through you, and your friends." Shael smiled. "The faithful few."

Noland nodded, not sure he was really any kind of good example to follow. Look at how his life had unraveled. "Where do we focus? What do we do? I've been so singly focused on Achaia, but there is so much going on in the world. This war, it isn't just human."

"No, it's not. But I think we are right. Bale predicted Achaia is the angel of death. We are going to need her in these end days. We have to get her away from Luc."

"You think her human nature will save her from demonic influence?" Noland asked. "Will it be enough?"

"If anything, I think it will help. Do the math, half human, and at this point probably about a quarter angel and quarter demon. If anything, maybe we should be worried about Luc. If I had to guess, Achaia is probably coming into her own right about now. At least, I hope she is." Shael took a deep breath and let it out slowly.

"Feels a bit like the calm before the storm, doesn't it?" Noland said listening to the waves crash against the beach.

"I much prefer the fighting," Shael smiled.

"Me too," Noland agreed.

As they were leaving, Olivier pulled Veronica aside. "What was that?" he asked her not unkindly.

"What?" Veronica asked.

Olivier cocked his head, and leveled her with a look.

Veronica sighed. "I've been experimenting with blades," she said softly. "But I don't know if they are capable of this." She looked truly upset, and Olivier was comforted in that, even if she had created the murder weapon, she hadn't meant to.

"When we get back, you have to show us everything you've made," Olivier said sincerely.

Veronica nodded. "I never meant for anyone to get hurt. My father told me I should let my creativity lead me."

"Veronica, this happened once before, long before you were forging." Olivier felt bad, he hadn't meant to make her feel responsible, if she wasn't.

"But not so close to home. No, I am sure this was one of my blades."

"We will take a look when we get back, but don't beat yourself up. You might have made the blade, but you didn't wield it."

Veronica nodded, but didn't look truly comforted as she climbed into the van and sat next to Emile. Without a word, Emile wrapped an arm around her, and looked at Olivier inquiringly. Olivier shot an eye at Martinus, and gave in to his feelings of unease and suspicion. Emile followed his eye, and Olivier knew he could feel what he was feeling. Emile nodded in agreement.

Olivier took his seat in the front row without a word. Amelia sat next to him, and nudged him with her shoulder in a would be annoying sisterly way. Olivier looked at her and smiled. "I've missed you, too."

254

The ride back was pretty silent. Everyone seemed lost in thought. As soon as the van was parked in the driveway, they were unloading and Olivier was leading the way down the beach to the forge. Martinus made some excuse about having to go to work at his human job, leaving Emile, Amelia, Yellaina and Olivier alone to talk to Veronica. The twins were training and doing their studies.

Noland met them as they got to his end of the beach. "What's the word?"

Emile answered, "Dead Nephilim, gutted with some sort of unholy blade. We're here to see if anything Veronica's been making could have done this."

Noland looked at Veronica in surprised disbelief.

Veronica was on the verge of tears when she said, "I swear I didn't mean to." Her voice was quiet and coated in misery.

They walked into the forge which was organized, with weapons hung on the walls, and tools put away in their place. There was a rustic work table that took up most of the center of the shack.

"Which ones are experiments?" Olivier asked. Veronica walked around, taking certain weapons off the walls and laying them out on the table.

Olivier couldn't help being impressed. They were among the nicest weapons he'd ever seen. The craftsmanship was par none. "These are…"

Veronica shook her head for him to stop talking; tears were pouring over her eyelashes.

Olivier stopped. He picked up an axe that looked almost

golden. "What stone is this?"

"Citrine," Veronica answered, "for a clear mind, a soul stirred to action, and life-giving comfort."

"Doesn't sound like a blade to kill an angel," Olivier said putting it back down.

"What is this one?" Emile said picking up a mace. It shone a limier green than Diemerilium.

"Prehnite, to illuminate fear, unconditional love, and to heal the healer."

"Again, not an angel killer." Emile put the mace down.

"What about the Pyrite?" Noland said, picking up a katana, not from her passion projects, but from the council's order over on her workbench.

"Protects the user, luck, and manifestation," Veronica said quietly.

"Sounds good at first, but in the wrong hands…" Noland cocked an eyebrow.

"But the council isn't the wrong hands," Veronica said with wide eyes.

"I'm not so sure," Noland said sounding regretful. "The more I learn about them, the less I trust them."

"But for them to kill their own?" Veronica sounded terrified and indignant.

"That might be the price of silence," Olivier said, agreeing with Noland. "Honestly, that doesn't surprise me at all."

"But you work for them." Veronica looked at Olivier confused.

"Eyes and ears, dear girl, eyes and ears…"

"What about the blade you gave me?" Noland asked, "What does onyx do?"

"Powerful protection, absorbs negative energy, prevents your energy from being depleted, and provides emotional and physical stamina, heightened in times of stress or grief. Perfect for battle, no?" Veronica seemed deeply disturbed.

Noland smiled. "You create beautiful weapons Veronica. The council, or whoever wields it has the option to use that to an evil purpose. That does not mean that you are responsible for any of this."

"Look on the bright side," Olivier said, stepping forward. "You haven't fulfilled the order yet. Just don't send them these weapons. Send them something else instead. Send them something that can't kill Nephilim."

Veronica shook her head. "They will know."

"Will they?" Noland asked.

"Isn't there another stone that will look like Pyrite?"

"I've already sent them the prototype. They will be able to tell the difference. They will know I switched them."

"Is the fear of retribution worth furnishing them with weapons that can kill those who are trying to serve God?" Noland sounded almost angry. "It should be a no brainer. You can't send these to the council."

"We don't know for a fact it was them!" Veronica's voice was raised defensively.

Emile walked over to her and put a hand on her forearm. "Ronnie, I'm afraid to tell you, the council isn't pure. They *are* corrupt. You weren't responsible for Eran dying. But, if you furnish the council with an armory of blades that can kill us, you will be responsible for the angels that die on them."

Veronica collapsed, and looked like she was going to be sick. Emile knelt next to her. Olivier slipped outside as the others continued their discussion.

Once he was far enough from the shack he dialed Dina's number. The sun was setting and creating what looked like fire on water.

"Olivier, thank God!" Dina answered the phone. "What have you got?"

"Dina, the blades the council ordered, they can kill Nephilim."

Dina was silent for a long moment on the other end. "What are they made of? How is this possible? Are you sure?"

"I'm reasonably sure. Eran was murdered."

"Eran?" Dina asked.

"We just went to identify the body. He was gutted by an unholy blade."

"What could do that?"

"We think it was the prototype Veronica sent to the council. She has been experimenting with different stones. They ordered blades with pyrite."

"And it worked?"

"She is extraordinarily talented. That is why it is taking so long to fill the order though. It takes her longer to create these blades, and she doesn't have heavenly fire. Except…"

"What?" Dina asked, sounding expectant.

"Noland is here, now, so she kind of does," Olivier said.

"Olivier, you can't let her fill that order." Dina sounded desperate. "Can the blades be destroyed?"

"We'll figure it out."

"Do." Dina sounded nervous. "For the love of all things holy, I hope you do."

Day Ten

"Do not be afraid of what you are about to suffer. I tell
you, the devil will put some of you in prison to test you,
and you will suffer persecution for ten days. Be faithful,
even to the point of death, and I will give you life as
your victor's crown."
-Revelation 2:10

They spent the night brainstorming methods to dispose of the weapons. Olivier had pitched the idea of taking a boat out to sea and dumping them. But they could be retrieved, if the council discovered where they were dumped.

Noland had known the only way was for them to be unmade. "We have to melt them down, and completely destroy them," he had said. He was the only one on earth who could produce a fire hot enough. There were enough weapons that the fire would have to be large. They would have to transport them out to the middle of nowhere, and he would have to do it alone. No one could be near a fire that hot without being consumed. They had made the plan. Veronica knew the place, and would take Noland in the morning. He woke up early, and had gone to the forge to start packing up the weapons, but he stood in the doorway looking at the empty forge, with nothing to do.

"I've got Vito and Vidal coming to help load the van," Veronica said coming up behind him.

"With what?" Noland asked. "They're gone."

"What?" Veronica pushed passed him into the forge. "How? Where?"

Veronica checked under the table and workbench as if the weapons could be hiding. Without another word, Veronica took off toward the house, and Noland followed her at a jog.

"Papa!" Veronica called as she reached the floor that held the living room.

"*Mija?*"

"Papa, do you know what happened to my weapons order for the council? It is all gone!"

"Don't worry *Mija*," Martinus smiled and patted her shoulder comfortingly. "They've been impatient, so I sent them what we have and told them the rest would follow soon. You really need to focus on finishing your job *Mija*. They aren't to be kept waiting."

Veronica stood frozen, and Noland felt a rage burn up inside of him. "You sent them the weapons?" Veronica asked in disbelief.

"Of course I did," Martinus said, losing patience. "That is

our job. We fill weapons orders."

"What are they going to use them for?" Veronica asked. "Why pyrite?"

"That is up to them. We just fill the orders, you understand. And you had better finish it." Martinus sounded like he was on the verge of becoming angry.

"Those weapons—" Noland started, but he was cut off.

"What are you even doing here?" Martinus shot him a glare. "This is a discussion about family business. This does not concern you."

"It concerns me very much," Noland said, raising his voice. "Those weapons can kill Nephilim, and I'm sure you remember how it was my parents were killed."

"What is going on out here?" Vito asked as he and his brother came into the room rubbing the sleep from their eyes.

"Papa shipped the weapons to the council," Veronica almost yelled.

"What's going on?" Emile asked, coming up the stairs from the training room with Olivier and Amelia. Yellaina joined them a moment later coming from the bedroom she and Amelia shared.

"Martinus has handed the pyrite weapons over to the council."

Emile looked at Martinus in disbelief. "Did you not know those can kill us?"

Martinus did not answer; he just stared at Emile insolent. "I answer to the council, not to children. I have done exactly what the council has asked."

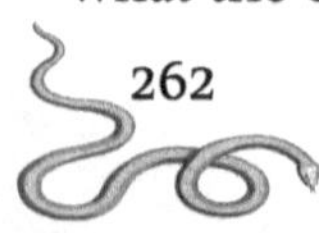

"The council is corrupt," Noland said flatly. "How many blades were there?" he asked, looking to Veronica.

"In total, two thousand, maybe more."

"How many did they order?" Noland asked.

"Ten thousand."

Noland looked dumstruck. "Ten thousand?"

"They said they were refitting all of the armories in all of the safe houses with the new blades, that they were supposed to be better than Diemerillium."

"Sounds more like they are going to outfit an army," Emile said, coming fully into the room to stand with Noland.

"But an army to march on who?"

"Whom," Yellaina said, before blushing. "Sorry, I hyper focus on grammar when I'm stressed."

Martinus rolled his eyes. "This is ridiculous. You are all stressing out over nothing. The council isn't going to attack itself. If anyone is going to be in possession of weapons that can kill Nephilim, shouldn't it be Nephilim? That is the safest place for these weapons."

"Can you, with confidence, make the same statement for humans?" Yellaina asked him, boldly. Noland was impressed. "We are more like them than you care to admit."

Achaia was sick to her stomach. Luc was angry with her. Really angry with her, and he was taking it out on Jude. She knew it. He had taken him hours ago, and he hadn't come back yet. Achaia didn't know what he was doing to him. She should have kept her mouth shut. She should have known better than to argue with a drunk devil. Her brain taunted her by repeating the word *rash*.

Achaia didn't know what else to do, so she'd tried her hand at praying. She wasn't really sure what she was doing, so she just pretended like God was sitting across from her, sitting cross legged like her. She just talked. She talked about everything: how stressed she was, how angry, how scared, what she wanted to happen, what she hoped wasn't going to happen. Then she started asking things- asking where God was in all of this, if He could protect Jude, if He could save them, if He could hear her. She promised that if He got her and Jude both out safely, she would give her life to Him, whatever that meant, whatever that took; she'd give Him anything, to get out.

After a few hours of this, she found herself talking about things she hadn't planned on. She told Him about the visions the shadows had shown her, and asked if they were true. She asked if He wanted her, or if she really was an abomination. She talked about her father and asked God to forgive him.

Slowly but surely, she felt an unexplainable peace washing over her. It made no sense, under the circumstances. The only thing she could think to explain it was that He could hear her, and that He was there to comfort her.

Achaia heard commotion, and thought the guards were bringing Jude back, but the door didn't open. She heard a clamor near by, and felt the room shake, and the ice wall she was facing cracked.

"Achaia?" She heard a voice calling, muffled by the ice.

"Jude?" Achaia called back, throwing herself against the wall. "Jude I'm here."

"They separated us," he called back.

Achaia slumped against the wall. There was no way for them to speak without yelling and all the demons being able to hear. "What did he do to you? Are you okay?" Achaia called out.

"Achaia, you can't care about me okay. You have to stop. He can only use it against us. And, I can't care about you." Jude's voice sounded rough.

Achaia felt like she'd been punched in the chest. "What happened to being in this together?" she yelled back.

"That only gives us more to lose, and something for him to use against us." Jude called back, choking on his words.

"Jude," Achaia called. She leaned against the ice, trying to see through the wall, to see if she could make out his form. She could see a shadowed outline of someone, but he didn't respond. "This is all my fault." Achaia couldn't keep back the flood of tears. They burned her eyes and choked her breath. She felt like she had to throw up, but there was nothing in her stomach, so she heaved dryly.

"God, don't leave me here alone. Don't leave me. Don't leave me." Achaia muttered until out of complete and total exhaustion she passed out.

Olivier had called Dina and told her that the weapons

had shipped. "Is there any way they can be intercepted?" he asked hopefully.

"Would that we could. We don't have the numbers or manpower without being discovered." Dina said sounding stressed. "Please tell me she isn't going to fill the rest of the order."

"No, but her dad might." Olivier sighed.

"This isn't good," Dina said breathing hard.

"Are you pacing?" Olivier asked.

"How did you know?" Dina asked.

"Stop it, you're freaking me out," Olivier said, trying to make her laugh.

"Weirdo." He could hear the smile in her voice. "Is Yellaina there?"

"Yeah," Olivier said. "We're alone. I'm going to put you on speaker okay?"

"Yellaina?" Dina asked.

"I'm here," Yellaina said sitting next to Olivier on a log by the firepit.

"I think it's time." Yellaina's face went white.

"Time for what?" Olivier asked nervously.

"Time for the council members to know what the council is up to, and to get on the same page," Dina said. "Time for Yellaina to come back to Rome."

"But I haven't rallied the troops. I thought I had more time. I was going to find more Nephilim."

"Let's hope there's enough holding seats," Dina said. "You can find more after, with hopefully more help."

"Are you sure? Once we play this card, it can't be undone,"

Yellaina said sounding sick.

"Yellaina, those weapons are on their way here. They might beat you here. The council needs to know what those weapons can do. If there is a chance of them being stopped or destroyed, this is the only way."

"How am I supposed to get back? Airports are still shut down."

"I'm sending you a jet. Olivier, make sure you're *not* on it." Dina sounded strict.

"What?" Olivier sounded shocked.

"You can't blow your cover. Yellaina is already known as a rebel. You are there on council orders to get these weapons rushed. Martinus sending these weapons works in your favor. It looks like you're doing your job. Stay." Olivier sighed.

"I guess you better rant about me a lot when you get back, so the council thinks we're in a fight." Olivier smiled at Yellaina.

"That should be easy enough," she laughed.

Emile sat with Noland on the steps leading down to the beach. Looking around, it looked like paradise, but since he'd come to this place, he'd been more afraid than he'd ever been in his life. He had more than ever to lose, and the possibility of losing everything was more real than ever. "I think if we are going to entertain the theory of the council being corrupt, we have to consider how deep that corruption goes. I've been thinking," he started.

"Yeah?" Noland prompted him on.

"What if the weapons the council ordered aren't for Nephilim? What if they ordered them for someone else?"

"Luc?"

"I mean would it be so hard to believe that Joash and Luc were working together? I mean, I'm just spit-balling worst case scenario—"

Noland didn't feel as surprised or off-put as Emile had been expecting. To him, this had been a crazy, way-out-there theory, but Noland just nodded, like it made perfect sense.

"Tell me I'm crazy. Tell me I'm wrong," Emile begged.

"I'm sorry, I can't," Noland said. "It isn't beyond the realm of possibility. The question I have, would be why?"

Emile sat in silence for a moment. "I don't know. He hates him."

"Okay, so it can't be out of a sense of camaraderie. It would have to be a mutual goal to bring enemies together. So, the question is, what would it accomplish for them to join forces and take out guardians?" Noland asked. Emile could tell he was methodically trying to focus on only the important details in his head. This is what made Noland a great leader, and a threat to Joash. He thought outside the box. He also could, and would, challenge him.

"The end times." A voice came from the brush. "You really should be more careful where you choose to have treasonous conversations. Martinus stepped out from behind the foliage.

Yellaina sat on the jet, with butterflies in her stomach. She was so nervous that her hands were shaking. What was she supposed to say? "I can't do this, God," she whispered. "I need you to speak through me." She looked out her window and prayed without ceasing the whole way back to Rome.

Naphtali once more pushed through the gates of Heaven. This time he ran through its streets, pushing past angels who grunted in annoyance or protest. When he reached Lailah's door, he pounded on it. No one answered. *Where would she be?*

Naphtali turned and ran back through the courtyard and toward the throne room, passing buildings of gold, reflecting the very radiance of God. The closer he got, the more he slowed, considering. Was this God's will? Was this on his list of top priorities right now? So much was happening below. What was God's plan in all this?

As Naphtali climbed the golden steps, and ascended into a wall of cloud, he felt the electricity of anticipation. He felt the presence of other angels, and heard their voices like a roll of thunder.

"Naphtali?" Her voice called out to him through the haze of vapor like a ringing bell.

"Lailah." Her hand slid into his, and he was being pulled back out of the throne room, but not before he felt a strong sense of approval. *My Lord, what are you approving?*

"Naphtali," Lailah threw her arms around him as soon

as they were outside the doors. "Terrible things…" Lailah's eyes were brimming with tears.

Naphtali pulled her back to his chest. "It's not so very bad."

Lailah slapped his shoulder. "Don't you dare lie, in Heaven."

Naphtali grinned, "I'm not." He pulled away from her and held her by the shoulders. "The end isn't going to be pretty, but it will be victorious."

Lailah looked like she believed that was true, but she never imagined it would happen like this.

"Achaia needs help," Naphtali said.

Lailah sighed, "She takes after her father, in that sense."

Naphtali cocked his head in admittance. "Lucifer has her. She is half human, with more free will than Luc is used to, and more than double the amount of stubbornness. I fear for her."

"Maybe this is good?" Lailah said looking like she had an idea, albeit one she didn't seem to like very much. She shook her head before saying, "But, I can't help her from here." She frowned. "I need them *all* brought to me, that I might bless them."

Naphtali's stomach dropped. "Lailah, do you really think that will work?"

"If I'm wrong, this could ruin everything. But if I'm right, this could end the war. I will ask Father for guidance, if He will aid us, if we have His blessing—"

Naphtali studied her porcelain face and wondered, not for the first time, how Shael ever could have left her. His hands slid down her bare arms, until his fingers were lacing through

hers. "Thank you Lailah. *Thank you.*"

"You have to go, don't you?" Her fingers tightened around his.

"Watch over me?" Naphtali raised her hands to his lips and kissed them.

"Always," Lailah said softly, just as he turned to leave.

Achaia sat in the stands, as the demons talked excitedly about the match. Luc was in the cage preparing for a dual, and a small angel was dragged in, looking terrified. Achaia sat up straight. He looked young, like, her generation young. "No," Achaia called out.

The young Nephilim looked up at her in surprise. There was a look in his eyes, like hope. Like he thought she could help him. Achaia, again, felt sick with despair. She couldn't watch this. But there wasn't anything she could do to help him, was there? Could she live with herself if she didn't at least try? She was unarmed… She weighed all the options and outcomes in her mind, then, against them all she jumped over the demon sitting in front of her, and started fighting her way down the bleachers.

"Achaia, no!" Achaia stopped and look up. Jude was across the room, on the stands. He was covered in bruises and dried blood. The look on his face told her he regretted calling out to her. It had shown concern. That comforted her. He did care, even though he knew he shouldn't.

Achaia steadied herself, and continued fighting forward.

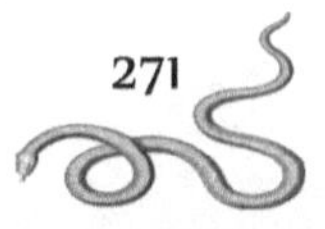

The young Nephilim took her lead, and fought back against the two demons that held him.

"No!" Achaia yelled, as she saw Luc rise up behind the young Nephilim with a sword in hand. The boy never saw it coming. He was fighting his demons when Luc swung his sword and stabbed the boy through his back. Achaia could see the tip of the sword peeking out through the boy's chest. The boy lived long enough to look down at the blade sticking out of his sternum, and register the surprise and disbelief of it all. Achaia saw it all written on his face. Luc pulled the blade free, and wiped it off. The demons booed, their show ruined.

Achaia reached the boy as he fell to his knees, struggling to breathe as his lungs filled with blood.

"I'm here," she whispered in his ear. "You're not alone. God be with you." She laid her hand across the bleeding wound on his chest. The boy looked up into her eyes, spit up blood, and was gone. The emptiness on his face told her his body remained, but his soul was gone. She wondered where it had gone.

"That, Love," Luc said, standing over them, "was your fault. If you hadn't intervened he would have had the chance to fight me one on one, a fairer fight."

"This, *Love*," Achaia spat with disdain, holding the boy's body still in her arms, his blood freezing on her worn out clothes, "is and always will be your doing. You made a choice. You swung the blade. Just like you manipulated Eve, you started a war. You," Achaia laid the boy down and stood, "are responsible for your own misery. You had *everything* in heaven, and it wasn't good enough for you. You wanted to be God, but you're incapable, so

in your misery you try to destroy everyone around you so they can't gain what you forfeited. You're pathetic."

Luc raised his hand, and Achaia caught him by the wrist. "You want a fair fight?" she said, throwing his arm away from her. Her eyes were burning, and she saw the red of them reflected in Luc's eyes. "I challenge you."

The auditorium fell silent.

"I challenge you, Lucifer Ben Yahweh, to a duel."

Dina met Yellaina at the seemingly abandoned airport. "You nervous?" she asked.

"That's an understatement. I want to throw up my feet, the nausea runs so deep."

Dina laughed.

"You're coming back to my place. The next full council meeting isn't until tomorrow, so you'll drink some tea, get some rest, and then tomorrow you'll start a revolution."

"Just a typical Thursday," Yellaina laughed nervously.

Yellaina liked Dina's apartment. She had a soothing space, in neutral colors. Dina did what she could to try and calm Yellaina's nerves. She lit a candle, plied her with lavender chamomile tea, and told her that more Nephilim than she realized would be shocked to discover the council's transgressions. They had every reason to hope for a majority.

Yellaina wasn't sure if that were necessarily true or just

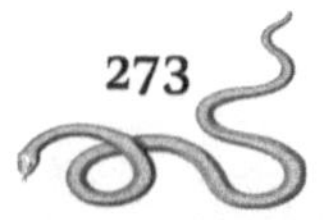

wishful thinking, but she tried to believe it. "What am I supposed to say? I can't get up there and just air out all the council's dirty laundry."

"No," Dina agreed. "This isn't so much about making the council look bad or evil as it is a call to action for the Nephilim to rise up and be who they were made to be. Part of the body has been shooting the rest of the body in the foot. That part must be pruned, but we have to believe that these Nephilim repented once, and they meant it. They have since maybe, just been led astray again. They mean well. They just need a wake up call."

"A wake up call- like, 'Hello, your leader is evil.'" Yellaina laughed.

"I might start with 'good morning.'" Dina smiled. "I'm going to draw you a lavender bath. You really need to get some rest."

Yellaina curled up and wrapped an arm around her legs. She finished her tea, and took the bath that Dina had filled with lavender oil and sprigs of dried flowers. She breathed deep the scent. When she came out of the bathroom, dewing with steam, and her head full of lavender, she found the couch made up into a bed, and laid down, falling asleep almost immediately.

Noland stood reflexively. "Who's side are you on?" he asked point blank.

Martinus laughed. "Mine."

"What does that even mean?" Emile asked. "What do you

want?"

"To protect my family and to survive," Martinus said simply. "Surely you can't begrudge me wanting what is best for my daughter," he said leveling Emile with a look.

"But that doesn't really answer the question," Noland said. "To what purpose?"

"Survival, I already told you. I just want to take care of my family."

"Then, by what means?" Noland asked, growing impatient. "Did you know the council was corrupt and potentially using these weapons against their own Guardians?"

"They can do whatever they want with them. I just fill orders."

"And you don't care if innocent Nephilim are being killed?" Noland was outraged.

Martinus laughed. "Innocent *Guardians*." He laughed harder. "We wouldn't be here," he gestured to the world around them, "if we were *innocent*. Who's to say we don't deserve death for our transgressions? Maybe *that* is our due penance."

"God decided otherwise. You can't believe that," Emile said, his face white.

"Why not?" Martinus shot back at him angrily. "I was there. I saw what we did. I know who we are. You can't fix that level of broken. God is abundant in mercy, but maybe He just doesn't know when to give up on a cause that's lost."

"No cause that breathes is ever lost," Shael said coming up the steps.

"You would know!" Martinus spat at him.

"Martinus, what have you done?" Shael asked.

Noland looked back and forth between the two men. They couldn't be more different. Shael, fallen, broken, disgraced, still filled with hope and purpose. Martinus, a safe house keeper, forger of weapons for the council itself, full of despair and guilt.

"I've done what we do," Martinus answered.

"Martinus?" Shael said cooly.

"I've sinned."

"How?" Noland asked.

"Emile?" Veronica was coming down the steps with a bowl of something to eat. She stopped short, and slowed the rest of her decent. "What is going on here? Papa?"

"I knew what the weapons could do. I didn't care. They wanted them and I didn't care."

"Who exactly is they?" Noland asked, losing patience again.

"Shall I start from the beginning?" Martinus said, taking a seat on the step above Noland and Emile. They gathered around him, to hear as he lowered his voice.

"Eight years ago, the council came to me and asked if another heavenly metal could be formed, one stronger than Diemerillium. I began experimenting. It was difficult. The elements would only bond over extreme heat."

"Heavenly fire," Noland nodded. "Or as close as you could get to it."

Martinus nodded. "It took me a year, but I found that I could manipulate pyrite. I delivered the prototype, and it was issued to Nathaniel ben Yahweh."

Noland felt his stomach drop. "You're saying, my father was killed with his own sword?"

"And your mother, after." Martinus swallowed. "I felt terrible."

Noland wanted to punch him in the throat.

"Unfortunately," Martinus went on, looking like he was going to throw up. "I had by that time filled many orders, for the same weapon. I didn't know what it could do." He said looking at Noland. "I didn't know."

"But you know, now. Why would you agree to fill this order for the council knowing what you know?" Veronica asked bewildered and outraged. "You had *me* make them." She sounded betrayed.

"Because," Martinus went on really looking nauseous. "Those orders I filled all those years ago…"

Everyone was waiting on bated breath.

"I believed these were lesser weapons, unequal to Diemerillium. I didn't realize."

"What about the orders," Shael asked.

"They weren't for the council." Martinus looked up at Shael, with eyes full of guilt. "They were for Luc."

"What!" more than one of them yelled.

"You made weapons for Lucifer, knowingly?" Veronica looked totally betrayed, and Noland couldn't imagine how she must feel. Indeed, he would rather have dead parents than Martinus for a father.

"The council had gone silent. They had stopped sending me orders. They shut me out of the council meetings. I thought

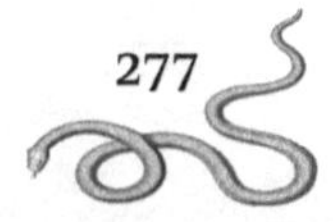

they had abandoned me, and that the weapon was a failure. I feared I had lost my gift. Lucifer was willing to pay, and I thought that the weapons were worthless. I didn't realize!" Martinus looked at his daughter with desperation.

Veronica looked disgusted and heartbroken.

"What does that have to do with these murders?" Emile asked.

Noland felt a little whiplash. He wasn't sure how they were related at all.

"I just want this to be over," Martinus said frantically.

"Well, too bad. We're having this conversation, so out with it," Emile said.

"Not this conversation, you ignorant boy, this world, this penance," Martinus spat.

"Martinus, what have you done?" Shael asked in a low voice.

"I want it to end. All of it." He looked at Shael with eyes that were pleading for Shael to understand.

"You started this ball rolling didn't you, when you realized what the weapons could do?" Shael asked, seeing something in Martinus' eyes that Noland didn't.

"I saw a way out. We could die. We could be done. We could be free." Martinus said, still looking at Shael.

"So you sold weapons to both sides, hoping for the ultimate war, the end times," Shael said looking disgusted.

"It's coming," Martinus said smiling. "Now, your friend has gone off to tell the council. There will be a civil war between the angels, demons will roam rampant, unchecked, and the

faithful few will be divided fighting a war on two fronts. They won't last long. The world is going to end. It's going to be over." Martinus smiled, as if this were good news.

"We have to call Yellaina," Noland said, looking at Emile. "Where is Olivier?"

"With Amelia in the training room," Veronica offered.

Emile took off after Olivier. Noland looked at Shael and saw his fear mirrored there, "Luc has weapons that can kill Nephilim."

"We have to get to Achaia, now," Shael said grabbing Martinus by the neck. "You tell me, right now, how to get to my daughter, or I swear to God, I will keep you alive for an eternity of misery."

Yellaina sat in her seat shaking, waiting for the council to open up the floor for comment. It had been a mind numbingly long meeting. Everyone looked tired and like they'd checked out, when Joash finally announced the floor was open for anyone with an item to bring forward.

Yellaina stood, and felt like her legs could barely hold her. Her heart was hammering in her chest. And she heard her voice as if it were someone else, weak and quiet, but it echoed in the cavernous room. "I do."

Everyone turned to look at her. "Yellaina Rosenov, I thought we'd seen the last of you," Joash said with thinly veiled anger.

Looking at him gave her the hateful motivation to speak up and step forward. Her feet carried her down to the floor without much prompting from her brain. She saw Dina on the dais behind Joash. She nodded at her to proceed.

"Brothers and sisters, greetings. Peace be with you, in our Lord God Almighty, who in His righteousness granted us mercy and favor." The traditional greeting the Nephilim gave before addressing large numbers of Nephilim at once out of the way, Yellaina went on, "I am here today to bring you tidings from your brothers and sisters in Chile. One of our own has fallen. Eran ben Yahweh was murdered."

A gasp ran through the crowd. Apparently this news had been kept quiet.

"How?" "When?" Questions ran through the crowd.

"We are still investigating—" Joash started, trying to silence the crowd.

"I believe I have the floor, brother Joash." Yellaina fixed him with a pointed glare.

"She does," some council members murmured.

"This is not the first Nephilim casualty, but we have discovered how it is our brothers and sister were killed," Yellaina said boldly.

Silence hung like a heavy night sky in the room. Yellaina felt her phone vibrate in her back pocket, momentarily distracting her. She turned her phone off with one hand, reaching behind her, before going on. "It appears that a weapon has been created that has the power to vanquish angelic life."

More murmurs…

"Now that we know these weapons are out there, we must unite. We must stand strong together as one body."

The council members cheered in agreement. Joash looked momentarily relaxed.

"I motion that we track down those Guardians who have gone silent. There may have been more deaths than we realized."

Grunts of agreement rang through the crowd.

"But I motion that we also have a time of introspection, that we take a close look at ourselves as individual Nephilim, and as a body. Part of our body is corrupt. I ask that you join me in hunting down that which is tainted, and prune it." The council members sat silent and stunned in their seat, staring around the room at each other.

"How do you know there is corruption?" Someone called out from the back, a tall dark man, in a turban.

"Because these weapons that are able to kill us, were commissioned by us," Yellaina said, bracing herself for impact. Outrage ran through the crowd.

"Who ordered the weapons?"

"How do you know?"

"Where is the proof?"

Yellaina held up her hands. "Suffice it to say, there is proof, or I would not place myself here before you. In time we will provide proof. But I need your help finding who is responsible."

"These are serious allegations, young lady." Joash stood up looking livid.

"Because they are against *you*?" Yellaina asked defiantly. Joash took a deep breath to respond but before he could, Yellaina

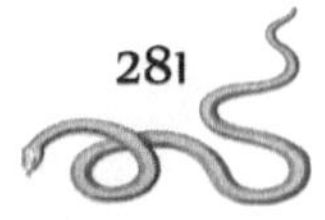

bellowed over the crowd, "I motion that pending an investigation, Joash ben Yahweh be removed from office and leadership until he can be proved innocent, or," she added as the crowd fell silent once more, meeting his glare, "guilty."

The crowd seemed to be divided.

Dina stood up and put a comforting hand on Joash's shoulder. He looked at her and took her cue to sit. "It seems the only way forward is to put it to a vote." Dina spoke with steady confidence over the crowd until there was silence.

"All in favor of the first motion, to track down our MIA guardians?" A unanimous amount of hands were in the air.

"Passed," Dina said. "Now, all in favor of the second motion to initiate an internal investigation to find any and all traitors, and exile them?"

There was an obvious majority, but a noticeable amount of hands not in the air.

"Passed." Dina said. "Now, who is in favor of the third motion to place Joash ben Yahweh on probation, pending investigation?" The amount of hands was so close to being half, that they had to actually place written votes, and count. One vote made the decision.

Dina frowned after she was done counting the votes in front of all of them. "By one vote, the motion is not passed."

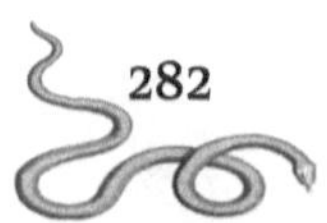

"She wears strength and darkness equally well,
the girl has always been half goddess, half hell."
-Nikita Gill

Yellaina saw that the call she missed was from Olivier, and locked the bathroom door to call him back. She could hear the debate raging on in the meeting room. A plan was being formed, and committees for each passed motion. Yellaina had stepped out for a moment to breathe.

"Hey," Yellaina said when Olivier answered.

"Tell me you haven't already done it," Olivier said sounding frantic.

"Of course I have," Yellaina said confused.

Olivier sighed.

"What?" Yellaina asked, pacing.

"It was all a part of Martinus' plan. The man is insane. He wants to start a civil war in the Nephilim so they are distracted and Lucifer can finally start the final battle. He is trying to bring about the end times."

"What?" Yellaina asked more out of disbelief than for clarification.

"Well, some good luck on that front then. I didn't think it was, but I lost by one vote, to remove Joash from leadership. The council isn't divided."

"If what you say is true, and that motion was saved by one vote, the council has never been more divided, and now they know their numbers. And they are evenly matched." Olivier sounded bleak. And he was right. What had she done?

"What do we do?" she asked.

"What we can. We track down those missing Guardians, and we make our numbers greater. We recruit. But," Olivier paused. Yellaina didn't like the shift in his tone.

"What?" Yellaina asked, her voice full of dread.

"There's one of our number that we're really going to need if this is the end, and we can't waste any more time in going to rescue her," Olivier said.

"Olivier, you can't. You can't go." Yellaina felt her knees give way, and she fell into a crouch on the floor.

"Yellaina she is my best friend, and they are going to need all the help they can get."

"But you barely made it out last time," Yellaina said, her

throat sore from choking back tears. "Take me with you. Wait for me to get back and take me with you."

"I can't," Olivier said sounding choked himself. "I can't wait, and I won't take you with me. You're not trained Yellaina. You're needed here with the recruitment and council proceedings. I wouldn't be able to fight my best if I was making sure you were safe, too." It was harsh, but it was true, and Yellaina knew it.

"I didn't even really say goodbye to you," Yellaina sobbed.

"Shhh, this isn't goodbye. It's I'll talk to you soon," Olivier said, and she could feel him smiling on the other end.

"I hate this," Yellaina said, kicking out at the wall.

"I know. But with any luck, and some help from God, we'll be back in no time with Achaia. You know we need her."

"I know," Yellaina mumbled like a pouting child.

"Yellaina, when I get back, I'm going to marry you."

Yellaina laughed and smiled. "You do that."

Dina stood on the Dais next to Joash as they formed search parties for the missing Guardians, and voted on the committee members for the internal investigation. They were talking about what process to use. They'd never had to perform an internal investigation of this magnitude, and it was crucial that the most trustworthy were in charge. The DuBois were an obvious choice. Their loyalty was renown. They had been hesitant at best to join with Lucifer for the war, and the first to repent when Shael had entreated them. Their pride was for God, not themselves.

"Dina," a voice said from the crowd below her, "I would like to make another motion."

Dina looked down and saw a small group of council members. Dina looked to Joash, feeling a little awkward; he, after all, was still their leader. Apparently, this group had voted otherwise and wanted it known.

"What is that?" Joash asked.

"We want to send a delegation to retrieve this weapons maker. We believe punishment is required if he knew what these weapons could do. We want to bring him in for a trial."

"Passed," Joash said. "Bring him in and I will interrogate him myself."

Dina looked sideways at him. "Is that wise?" she asked him under her breath.

Joash looked at her quizzically.

"If nearly half of our population wanted to investigate you, don't you think interrogating the weapons manufacturer yourself might make you look like you're trying to hide something?" Dina tried to sound merely rational. But really, she wanted him to know that his sins were soon to come into the light. She wanted him to be afraid.

"Don't worry my dear." Joash put a comforting hand on hers. "I have nothing to hide." And just like that, he lied to her face.

Everyone was bustling around the house. Emile and

his siblings were preparing with Noland and Shael to go after Achaia. Veronica had offered them whatever they wanted from her passion project weapons. They were down at the forge, and she was on her way to bring them sacks of food she had packed for them, not knowing how long they would be gone.

"*Mija*," her father called out, as she struggled to open the door with her hands full.

Veronica stopped. Her father opened the door for her and followed her outside.

"*Mija*, I must ask something terrible of you."

"What is it Papa?" Veronica stopped in her tracks. Her father's face was grave, and it made a knot form in her stomach. She had begun to understand she had underestimated what he was capable of. She had only ever seen him as her father, not as a fallen angel who fit into a much bigger picture. She didn't like the part he had chosen to play in it, either.

"*Mija*, I need you to understand our situation."

"I understand it," Veronica said, clenching the sacks in her hand. She was afraid and angry. Her father had brought this upon them all, on everyone. But, he was still her papa.

"The council will be wanting a scapegoat for the creation of these weapons. We need them to believe I made them. They will come; very soon they will come. And when they do, it will be for me."

Veronica's breath seemed forced out of her. She hadn't thought about that.

"When they do, I will need your help." Her father looked desperate. "You mustn't let them take me. It will be under pretense of trial, but Joash would never allow for that. I know too much. They will torture me, and hide me away. It will be a fate worse than death. You must help me escape."

Veronica looked up at her father, unable to hide the shock. "Papa— you mean to run away?"

"You don't understand *Mija*. They will torture me; I need you to help me *escape*."

Olivier picked up a dagger with a golden handle. The filigree laid into the handle was bronze.

"That reminds me of a dagger I used to have," Shael said taking it from him and looking it over. "You don't usually see them like this anymore." He handed it back to Olivier. "That is a good weapon."

Veronica came in carrying lunch sacks for them.

"Thanks mom," Olivier said smiling. Veronica ruffled his hair just like a big sister.

"Hey, what is this one?" Olivier asked.

"Citrine," Veronica smiled, "for manifestation of personal will, and the life-giving power of the sun."

"Hell could use a little taste of that," Olivier said, tucking it into his belt.

"I like this one," Amelia said picking up a rapier, her weapon of choice. Very French of her, Olivier always thought. It was brighter than diemerilium, more of a lime green under the water-like diamond.

"That is Prehnite, for unconditional love. Healer of the healer." Veronica smiled.

Amelia slashed it through the air. "You do great work," she said admiring the blade.

"Thank you." Veronica smiled, but it didn't quite reach her eyes. She looked worried. Olivier could only imagine. "What will you take?" Veronica asked turning to Emile.

"I'm set," Emile said holding his trusty bow in one hand." When in close combat, the bow could be drawn in two, and unsheathed two blades, that Emile wielded expertly.

"Then take these," Veronica said, opening up a trunk under the window. She pulled out a quiver of arrows tipped in vibrant blue. "The arrowheads are bound with lapis lazuli." Veronica bent back down into the trunk. "Take these too." She stood back up handing Emile a handful of throwing stars, the same shade of blue. "Can I come with you?" she asked under her breath to Emile.

Olivier felt like he was intruding, but they were blocking the door and none of the rest of them could get out. Amelia made a show of studying her new blade, Noland and Shael were whispering to each other, and Olivier stood there alone, awkwardly shuffling his feet in the dirt.

"You belong here. I'll be back for you," Emile said cupping her cheek in his hand.

Shael cleared his throat.

"Oh, thank God," Olivier said not as quietly as he had intended. He shot Emile an apologetic look. Emile rolled his eyes.

"We really need to get this show on the road," Shael said, gesturing for them to file out of the forge. "Where is your father?" he asked Veronica as he caught up to her.

"In the training room," Veronica said, sounding not like herself.

Olivier suspected, not far beneath her surface, troubled emotional waters. This is what Nephilim did, though; they went on missions. Granted this wasn't the average mission. Maybe she just wasn't used to it since the council had ghosted them. Her family didn't act until people were already dead. Maybe this primitiveness was just new for her. She didn't understand the *Nephilim normal*.

They gathered in the training room where Martinus was indeed waiting for them. They stood huddled together. The room was a little cramped.

"Maybe we had better move this out on the beach?" Shael suggested.

Martinus swallowed. He looked nervous. Olivier looked at Emile, who looked distrustful, and curious. But, Martinus complied and followed them out, grabbing a sword off the wall on the way. Olivier thought that was strange. He wasn't coming with them. What did he need a sword for?

Shael was giving Martinus a side eye, too. Olivier felt uneasy. He didn't trust Martinus, and hated that this man was their only way to get to Achaia.

They lined up on the beach, and Martinus paced the surf in front of them. "You must feel despair like you have never known. You must lose all hope, and believe that your mission is

doomed before it even begins, but you must go anyway."

"How exactly are we supposed to manage that?" Amelia asked sounding annoyed.

Shael grinned. Olivier did, too. He loved when his sister's sassy side came out, as long as it wasn't directed at him.

"Put away your weapons, and get on your knees in a posture of surrender. Physically you need to take on the posture of your fight being over, and you being helpless."

Rolling their eyes and grumbling, they complied.

"Close your eyes and let yourselves give in fully to the images I am going to try to inspire in you. Try your hardest to believe them."

Olivier heard some of the others sigh or grunt.

"You won't succeed," Martinus started. "Veronica, back away from Emile please. You can't comfort him right now."

Olivier peeked to see Emile releasing Veronica's hand, and she stepped back away from him, looking distressed.

"You will probably die, or remain stuck in your own personal form of Hell. Achaia is probably already dead. Lucifer had his way with her, torturing her ruthlessly. It was a slow and miserable death, and you waited too long to do anything to help her. Your selfish delay is the reason she is dead. She probably cried out for you before she died, wondering why she didn't mean enough to you for you to at least try and rescue her before now; what took you so long… Her hope had fled her when she realized you didn't care, that you weren't coming. You aren't enough to rescue her."

Olivier's breath became shallow and harder to come by,

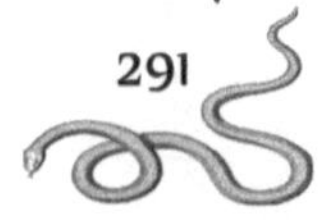

mostly because he had already been harboring these thoughts.

"She hated you toward the end, for lying to her, for making her believe you cared, when you obviously didn't. Her *fate* is your *fault*."

Olivier knew in the back of his mind that this was an exercise, but he couldn't help but feel like it was true. Why had they waited so long? So many things had come up and felt important, but were they really more important than Achaia's life, her suffering? Was she even still alive? How did they know? What were they even going to do once they got there to get her out? Could they really succeed? Olivier felt the guilt settle in his stomach like a stone, dragging him under the surface of some thick black surface.

"Papa!" Veronica cried out suddenly.

Olivier opened his eyes. Down the beach coming toward them was a hoard of council members, marching toward them like they were on a mission. Olivier felt hope leave him. If they were interrupted now, they would never get to Achaia. It was enough. Olivier felt the thick darkness overtake him.

Emile felt the fear. Veronica was terrified. Olivier vanished. His little brother was gone. Noland was watching the oncoming council members with something like regret, and then he vanished. When Emile turned to look, Shael was already gone. He looked at Amelia, and she looked back at him, confused. The hoard was coming toward Martinus, and Martinus was shouting

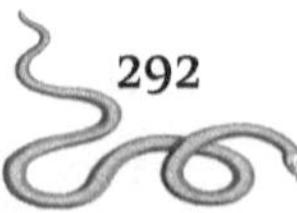

something at Veronica. Emile rose to his feet.

"NO!!!!!" Vito and Vidal were running from the house with swords in hand. A couple of the council members turned to hold them off. It wasn't difficult. They were young in their training. What was happening? He drew out his bow, but he couldn't fire on anyone. They were all on the same side, weren't they? Amelia had drawn her rapier, and was also on her feet, but she seemed to be having the same problem. Martinus drew his sword and fought back against the council members. If they had come to arrest him, he wasn't going down without a fight. Then it occurred to Emile, what if they knew Veronica had made the weapons? What if they had really come for her? The scene went fuzzy. Emile fought to stay present, but he was horrified to see the blood speckled on the beach. Nephilim against Nephilim. This really was the end. Angels warring angels, while humanity was at its most desperate time of need. They were neglecting their call, failing God, and aborting their mission, in favor of their own selfishness.

Veronica stood frozen. She couldn't believe it. They had come so soon. She never imagined they would come so soon. They must have deployed Nephilim already in the area. She ran to her brothers, where she could see they were wounded and bleeding. She couldn't believe Nephilim would hurt children. They were more than fending them off. But her brothers fought relentlessly.

"Stop it!" she screamed. "Put down your swords." She knew they were hot headed enough to go too far without even thinking. "Leave them alone. They are only children!" Veronica ran until she was between her brothers and their opponents. They would not attack her, without her being equally armed. Instead, the council members left them, and ran to aid those attacking her father.

Veronica remembered what her father had said, that they would torture him. They were cutting him down to the ground. Without second thought, or allowing herself to reconsider, she remembered her promise to help him escape, and grabbed Vidal's sword out of his hand. "Go back to the house," she told her brothers. Then she turned and ran back down the beach toward her father. She cursed the sand, and the way her feet sunk into it, slowing her down. Every blow her father received, she felt in her heart.

"STOP!" she screamed, feeling as if she were running in slow motion for the time it took to close the distance. Her father was outnumbered, five to one.

"*Mija*! NOW!" Martinus yelled, as they cut him down to his knees. He hit the surf with a splash, just before the waves were recalled to the sea. She saw in the waters thick cords of red, turning the foam pink.

She charged and placed herself between the council members and her father. She held up her blade and for the first time noticed it. It was one of the Pyrite weapons. Her father had kept one for *them*. Then she *realized...*

If I can't escape on my own, I need you to help me, he had

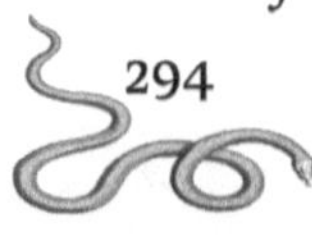

told her.

The council members stood back on edge, watching to see what she meant to do.

"*Mija*," her father whispered. "Now."

Veronica turned, not giving herself time to hesitate, and drove the sword through her father's chest. His eyes went wide in surprise. Veronica immediately fell to her knees. "Papa, I'm sorry. I'm sorry, Papa. I'm sorry." Her father slumped forward onto her. "Papa," she wept, squeezing him.

"NOOOOOOO!" Vito and Vidal ran to them. Veronica lifted her father's face and saw that he was gone. She laid him down on the beach.

The council members stood all around them, staring in baffled silence.

The surf lapped up on the beach turning the sand around them pink.

"What have you done?" Vidal yelled at her. "What have you done?" His voice was hoarse, as he and Vito sobbed over their father. Vernoica stood stunned, and dropped the sword that was still in her hand. She stared at them, and backed away slowly, the dawn of what she'd done settling in. Then she fled. Covered in her father's blood, she ran.

Noland looked around them. Everywhere was ice. "Looks like Hell, but it's not?" Shael had settled next to him. "Where are the others?"

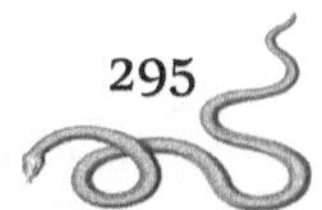

"I don't know," Shael said. "I guess they surfaced somewhere else."

"I guess we just start looking around?" Noland asked, stepping forward.

Shael nodded. They walked silently, slowly, down the halls. It was eerily quiet.

"Where is everyone? I thought there would be guards, demons, something…" Noland said stopping at an intersection of halls.

"Shh." Shael put up a hand as he looked down each hall. There was something in the distance, some faint noise. What it was Noland couldn't tell, perhaps a hum of some sort of machinery?

"What is that?" Noland asked.

"A multitude," Shael said, "demons."

"What?" Noland asked stunned. "Guards? Why would they be all in one place?"

"Blood battles," Shael said, going pale. "Duals."

Noland followed as they started toward the sound.

Olivier surfaced in a hallway next to an open door to an empty room.

"Come on," a gruff voice said. Olivier tucked himself away behind the door and watched as a demon manhandled a boy a year or two older than him. He had dark skin, and long dreaded hair. The boy looked over at the demon shooting him a

death glare, and saw Olivier peeking out from behind the door. Olivier met his bright blue eyes and held a finger up to his lips. The boy took heed and looked away from him quickly.

Who is that? Olivier wondered. He kept his distance but followed them down the hall.

Emile and Amelia surfaced together in an empty room. Emile glanced around taking in their surroundings. He felt an odd amount of shock coming from Amelia, considering this wasn't far from what he had expected.

"Are you okay?" Emile asked.

"Are you?" Amelia looked at him in surprise.

"I'm alright," Emile confirmed.

"Did you not just see that?" Amelia asked.

"The council come?" Emile shook his head in disbelief.

"I was referring to Veronica."

Emile looked at Amelia puzzled, and felt her dread.

"She just killed her own father," Amelia said gently.

"What?" Emile stood stunned.

"She stabbed him through the chest with her brother's sword, one of the pyrite blades."

Emile felt a deeper despair than he had ever imagined. "I didn't see—"

"Why would she do it?" Amelia asked, stunned.

Emile shook his head. If it was something she had been planning, he didn't know about it. He had never felt her feel anything but love and loyalty toward her father. This made no sense. What was she feeling now? What could have made her do it?

Amelia closed the space between them and hugged him. "Let's find Achaia and get out of here. My guess is Veronica needs you. Where are the others?" She looked around.

"I don't know," Emile said shaking.

Achaia had been shown to a luxurious room to prepare for the dual. Luc had fitted it out with fresh gear, and whatever she could have wanted, save for warmth.

Achaia dressed in the clean clothes- black leather fighting pants and a long-sleeved black shirt. She pulled her hair back and braided it down to the tips. Achaia looked at her reflection in the ice on the wall and hardly recognized herself. She remembered seeing herself for the first time in Paris after their stint of being snowed in at a hunting lodge in the Alps. She hadn't recognized herself then, either. *How many times can a person change in the course of a year, let alone a life?* She wondered. Was anything constant? *Are you?* She asked God. Achaia took a deep bracing breath, and opened the door to walk to the arena. "God, I hope you're with me in this."

"Achaia?"

Achaia stood stunned. "Noland?" Her father came into view, too. "Dad!"

Achaia pulled them into the room and closed the door

back tight.

"Achaia!" They hugged her and kissed her head.

"What are you doing here? How are you here?" Achaia asked.

"We're here to tell you how to get out."

"There's a way out?" Achaia asked.

"Yes," Noland said sounding relieved and looking so happy to see her.

"I have to get Jude. I can't leave him here," Achaia said before asking anymore questions.

"Who is Jude?" Noland asked looking confused.

"He's another prisoner. He's like me," Achaia said looking at her father. "He's half human, too." For some reason, she held back the part about his Angelic half being from Lucifer.

Noland and Shael exchanged shocked glances. "Another *hybrid*?" Her father looked pensive.

"We don't have time for that now. Where is he?" Noland asked.

"I don't know. He will probably be in the arena for the duel."

"So, he is hosting duels here—" Shael nodded, as if he had expected this.

"Actually," Achaia swallowed. "This one is—"

"What?" Noland asked, grabbing hold of her hand, and sending warmth through her whole body.

Achaia relaxed, and breathed deeply. "*I* challenged *him* to a duel. If I win, Jude and I get to leave. If I lose—"

"What?" her father asked sounding skeptical.

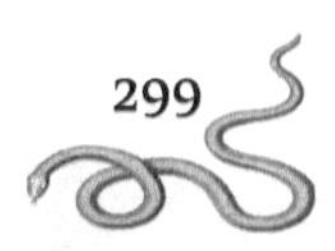

"He wants me to marry him, dad," Achaia said unable to hide her fear.

"He WHAT?" Shael fumed. He turned to march out of the room and hunt Luc down, right then and there.

"I'll kill him," Noland said burning to the point that for the first time in God-knew-how-long Achaia was hot. Noland followed Shael, on his heels.

"Stop that!" Achaia said, swatting at them both. "I can fight my own battles. Thank you very much, and besides, you can't kill him."

"Actually, we probably could," Noland said, factually.

"I get it, you're mad." Achaia nodded.

"No, I mean, there're weapons that can kill Nephilim out there, now."

"Haven't there always been?" Achaia asked.

"No," Shael answered. "We were meant to be truly immortal. That's why, until Nathaniel," he looked apologetically at Noland, "Nephilim had never been killed before."

"Luc kills them all the time down here. That's why I challenged him. He—" Achaia remembered the look on the young boy's face, like he'd really believed he'd had more time.

"A lot of Nephilim have gone missing. We were afraid of something like this." Noland looked at Shael.

Achaia shook her head, coming back to the present moment. "I have to go. They are expecting me," Achaia said, leveling them both with a look. "Though I'm not confident I can win, I have to do this."

"Wait," Noland took her hand back and pulled her toward

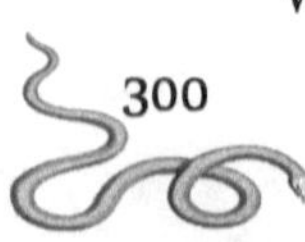

him. "Once Nephilim are married, they become one flesh." Noland looked at her father, as if begging Shael not to punch him, but to follow his train of thought.

Shael cocked an eyebrow. "I don't think we have enough time for you to marry my daughter right now."

Noland blushed. "No, but we are mates. Is there any way I can lend her some of my ability, just temporarily? My strength, my fire?" Noland asked.

"Yes, but I can't watch this," Shael said walking toward the door, and turning his back to them.

"Is there a way?" Achaia asked turning back to Noland. In answer, his hand was on her cheek lifting her face to his, and he was kissing her. His lips were soft, and really warm. His hand was large enough to cup her cheek and the back of her neck all at once, as he pulled her deeper into the kiss. He tasted like sea salt. His lips grew hotter. And she felt like fire was pouring into her, but it wasn't painful. She stood on tippy toes, allowing her fingers to explore his hair, getting tangled in his soft curls. His other arm wrapped around her waist. Achaia felt power surge through her, too. She felt like Noland was giving her spiritual CPR. *So, this is kissing?* Achaia thought, just before Noland pulled away. Achaia could have stayed there forever, she thought. Noland studied her face.

Achaia tried really hard not to blush. "How do we know if that worked?" Achaia asked.

"It worked." Noland smiled. "Your eyes are flames like mine, but red."

"*Oh gawd,*" Shael choked, still facing the wall.

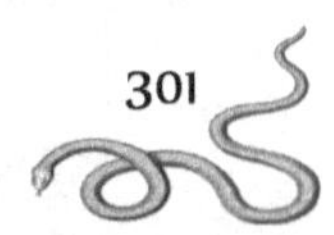

Achaia stood up on her tippy toes and kissed Noland again. "I have to go. I can't believe you're here." She smiled, gripping his hand tightly.

"It worked!" Noland told Shael excitedly, as they filed out of the room.

"Shhh—" Shael waved his hands in the air to silence them, like he was swatting invisible flies. "I don't want to know."

Achaia smiled and gripped Noland's hand tighter. "You should hide," Achaia said quietly to them both.

"We will be discovered eventually. We might as well walk out and face them with confidence. I won't be discovered hiding," Shael said defiantly.

"You're sure?" Achaia asked.

"The easiest way for us to find the others will be for them to easily be able to find us." Noland agreed.

"Who all is here?" Achaia asked.

"Olivier, Emile and Amelia are around here somewhere, hopefully…" Noland answered.

Achaia took a deep breath. That was a lot more riding on her duel. More reasons she had to win. She stopped. Her father and Noland turned back and looked at her.

"Do you think I can do it?" Achaia asked, her brow furrowed with worry. "Can I win this?"

Noland looked at her silently, anxiety clear on his face.

Her father on the other hand looked at her like they were talking about her finishing her homework. "Well, you have to, don't you?" he said, as if this were any other day, any other training session. "Don't consider that there is another alternative.

There isn't. Losing isn't an option. Victory is the only outcome. You just have to figure out what it is going to look like to get there."

Noland looked at him, as if he wished it were that simple. Achaia realized that if she was going to win, the only chance she had was to trick herself into believing there was no other option, that victory was already hers.

Her father closed the distance between them and hugged her tightly. "You are the angel of death, Achaia. Speculation is true, Bale was right." He released her and looked her in the eye, like he was willing her to hear every word he was about to say. "If anyone can defeat the father of lies, it is that truth. You are Achaia bat Shael, daughter of destruction itself." Her father smirked. "You can end him. The sweetest part is that he won't even see it coming," Shael said in a low voice.

"But he is more powerful than me. He draws it from the demons around him," Achaia said, not wanting to underestimate her opponent.

"You'll have friends there, praying, that you can draw from, too. We'll be there," Noland said, squeezing her shoulder. "You're never in this alone. One angel is more powerful than a thousand demons, and you've got several of us backing you."

Achaia nodded, and they walked forward once again.

Emile and Amelia stalked the hallow halls until they heard commotion, and followed the sounds to an arena of sorts.

Demons filled the stands, and Emile could feel the excited energy like a vibration through his chest.

Amelia grabbed his sleeve and pulled him into an alcove where they were less visible, but they could watch from there. A demon entered the room dragging a Nephilim boy Emile had never seen before, which was odd, considering he looked to be in their generation.

Amelia stared at him. "Who is that?"

"I don't know."

A moment later, Olivier appeared for a brief second, as a flash, as he ran to an alcove halfway between them. "Olivier," Emile pointed to where their brother was hiding.

Just then a hush and a murmur ran through the crowd of demons, then a gasp. Emile felt their surprise. He redirected his attention and saw Achaia, with her bright red hair braided back out of her face, enter the arena. She wasn't alone. Flanking her were Noland and Shael.

"What is this?" Luc shouted sounding outraged.

"You didn't think I'd miss my daughter's first real duel, did you?" Shael said sounding casual. "From what I hear you've reached an understanding. However, given the change of circumstance, I think we should take a second to renegotiate the terms," Shael said.

"The terms are fine. They stand," Luc spat. "You think because you show up with this," Luc gestured to Noland, "child, that you can challenge me?" Luc laughed. It was a bitter sound.

"The three of you cannot hope to escape here alone."

"They aren't alone," Emile found himself saying aloud. On

cue, Olivier came out from his hiding place and walked forward with them. Amelia followed him faithfully, and they circled the arena until they reached Noland, Shael, and Achaia.

Luc laughed again, but didn't look pleased. "Still, six, against my numbers, hardly bodes well for you." Luc smirked.

"Seven," Achaia said looking across the room at the captive boy. "And, as I recall, we fared pretty well against them last time, with less."

"Demons are no company for a Prince," Shael smiled. "They know who holds the victory, and that their fight is in vain. The difference is that of motivation, Lucifer. Surely you have not forgotten the importance of motive."

Luc glared at Shael. It was a look that chilled Emile to the bone, but Shael bore it well, nearly unphased.

"New terms," Shael said, resting his hand casually on the hilt of his sword.

"Just out of curiosity, what would they be?" Luc sneered.

Achaia stepped forward.

"If I win, me and mine walk out of here, free to go, including Jude."

"If I win?" Luc's eye contact with Achaia was intense. It was unsettling to Emile, and he could feel something shift in Achaia. The familiarity between them made Emile severely uncomfortable.

"I'll marry you," Achaia said, disgustedly.

"What?" Amelia let out, disgusted.

"And your mate will be our slave," Luc added. "Your father and friends will remain here, and Jude," Luc smiled sadistically, "dies."

Emile felt Achaia's shock. Her face went white, and her eyes filled with loathing and disgust. "He's your *son*."

Emile tensed. It wasn't known that Lucifer had a son. His mate hadn't been heard from in centuries. But surely the council would have heard word that he had a son. Emile's heart was beating hard. Everyone around him was on edge, demon and Nephilim alike.

"He's a bastard." Luc waved a hand dismissively. "You will bear me a real heir."

Achaia looked up at the boy in the stands being held by the arms by two demons. The boy nodded. Emile could feel his resolve, and Achaia's disgust. The boy clearly trusted Achaia. They had grown close here. Noland whispered something in Achaia's ear.

Achaia took a deep breath. "Deal."

Everyone watched in silence as Achaia and Lucifer shook on it. Emile felt increasingly uneasy. He really didn't see this ending well. Even if Achaia did win, which wasn't likely, he didn't expect that Lucifer would be true to his word. He was, after all, the father of lies. But, now that they knew how to escape, maybe they could teach Achaia and the boy how to leave anyway, before Achaia could marry Lucifer. Noland had to have a backup plan…

The group of them were led to seats on the front row. "I want you to be able to see her bleed," Luc said in a low voice to Shael. Emile felt his rage, but Shael's face remained calm, and he smiled.

"If she gives you the chance. I trained her myself," Shael

306

said, his voice lower and gruffer than Lucifer's. "Who trained you?"

Luc glared, and Emile got the feeling that Shael had maybe trained Luc, and he knew from the histories that Shael had always been the more gifted fighter.

They took their seats and waited- Noland feeling exceedingly anxious, Olivier in disbelief and shock, Amelia with an angry sort of resolve, Shael with some level of anxious expectation. Emile hardly knew what he himself felt. Whatever it was, it definitely wasn't optimism.

"And I will be to her a wall of fire all around, declares
the Lord,
and I will be the glory in her midst."
-Zechariah 2:5

A trunk was brought forth, holding a plethora of weapons. "Make your choice." The demon holding it between his thick arms shook the trunk so they rattled.

Once again, there was something marred about the metal. The crisp clear of the diemerilium was smoky and smudged. "What are these?" Achaia asked looking at Lucifer.

"Unlike anything you've ever held." Luc grinned in a way that made Achaia wonder if the blades were poisoned.

"Wait!" Noland was running over to them from the

stands. "Achaia has her choice of *any* two weapons," he said, reaching them.

"Did you really think I forgot the rules of the blood games?" Lucifer looked annoyed.

"No," Noland said tilting his head and cocking his eyebrows. "Just reminding you why you can't deny her the use of her own weapon." Noland reached out his hand and Akakios, her diemerilium snake whip, slithered down his wrist toward her outreached fingers.

"Hello dear friend," Achaia whispered raising the snake up to her lips. It nuzzled against her face affectionately.

Luc scowled. "That's one."

Achaia smiled at Noland, in way of thanks. Noland nodded knowingly and left them.

"What will your second choice be?" Luc asked, almost seductively.

"What is your first?"

Luc reached down and pulled out the sword she had seen him claim so many times before. The blade was broad and curved and made her think of an Arabian knight.

Achaia studied the contents of the case, and found a dagger buried under the bulk.

"You travel light," Luc noted. "You are your father's daughter, but I find it amusing that you have chosen the symbol of serpent, like me."

"Who knows. Maybe it takes one to kill one." Achaia wrapped the dagger sheath around her thigh and secured it.

"Or maybe you're more like me than you care to admit."

Achaia's eyes wandered up Luc. "Wishful thinking looks pathetic on you."

Luc clenched his jaw with contempt and sneered. "You speak to me as if you're somehow better than me. But look around Love, it's a lovely bed you're making for yourself. And you're going to lie with me in it."

Achaia swallowed back bile and tried to remind herself to believe she had already won. Victory was the only option. Thinking about what it would cost, not only her, but her friends if she lost was a path she couldn't wander down right now. "And I'll sleep in it. But you don't, do you?"

"Don't what?" Luc spat. He was standing close enough that she could feel his cold breath on her face. All he had to do was lean forward and he'd be kissing her. She didn't back down. She kept his eye, and answered, "sleep. Your waking hours are more of a nightmare than anything you could ever dream, grappling for control you can never have, and the truth you can't escape."

"What truth?" Luc leaned closer; his nose nudged hers.

Achaia leaned in now, her lips brushing his ear, "That you've already lost."

Luc pushed her away from him. "The fighting's not done yet," he spat, pushing her toward the door of the cage. "Ladies first."

Achaia stumbled slightly, but laughed, and she turned to look at him before stepping into the cage. "What's the matter? *Did I get in your head?*" She clenched her teeth as she spoke and spat the words at him like they were poison, willing them to cut him. "You know that no matter what happens next, I'll never

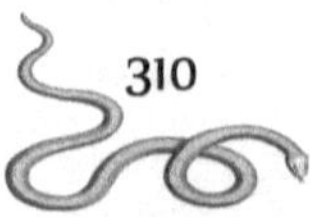

truly be yours. I am *His*."

"Loyal saints don't make deals with the devil, sweet pea." Luc smiled.

Dina was sitting in her office trying Olivier's phone for the thirtieth time. Yellaina was sitting across the desk looking positively miserable.

"I can't reach him." She set the phone down, admitting defeat.

"He's already gone," Yellaina said, with a dead look in her eyes.

"He'll come back," Dina said, though she wasn't any more confident than she sounded.

The phone on her desk beeped and a voice paged her. "Dina?"

Dina placed a silencing finger over her lips, and Yellaina nodded.

"Yes?"

It was Joash. "There's been an unfortunate new development," he said though not sounding terribly upset about it.

"What's that?" Dina asked.

"The weapons dealer was slain before he could be questioned."

Yellaina's eyes flew wide open in surprise.

"How is this possible? The council members were given

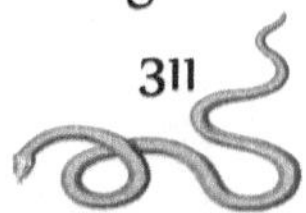

strict orders to bring him in civilly for questioning." Dina was livid.

Yellaina was shaking her head in disbelief.

"We didn't do it," Joash said smugly. "His own daughter did."

Yellaina looked up sharply at that.

"What?" Dina said shocked. "Where is she now?"

"She escaped. She would have been exiled for her crimes as it is. Serves her right. She won't make it long on her own."

"No," Dina agreed. "She won't." She looked up across her desk at Yellaina.

"Be in my office in twenty minutes." Joash said sounding more pleased than ever. "We have new plans to discuss."

"Yes, sir," Dina said, and waited for the red light on her phone to disappear before she risked speaking.

"You have to go. You have to find her."

Yellaina was already on her feet, and nodded. "I don't know how. But I'm just going to grab a few things from your place. Can you get a plane for me?"

"It'll be done. I'll send numbers with you, under the cover of the search and rescue initiative. There are a few people I trust."

"Thank you." Yellaina had her bag slung over her shoulder and was already halfway out of the door.

"Yellaina," Dina called out.

"Yeah?" she paused and turned around.

"Be careful."

Yellaina nodded.

Veronica had no clue how she was going to get there, but she knew where she was headed. After all her talks with Emile and the others she thought of only one place that might be safe for her now. She had no bags, no money, nothing to slow her down, but nothing to aid her. However, she was nothing if not creative. She would get there some way, somehow. Her father had taught her to be resourceful. Her father… *Dios…Don't think, just move.*

She had made it to a main road after scaling the cliff. She was covered in dust and dirt, but had caught a ride. She had told them her car had broken down and gotten them to drop her off in town. From there, she walked to the bus station, and waited. If they were tracking her, she wouldn't make it easy.

She watched the man storing people's bags in the undercarriage. When he was called away, she ran and rolled into the chamber, and pulled bags in front of her, and laid still, hardly breathing. The door was shut, and she took the first real breath since leaving her father lying in the surf.

It was a bumpy and uncomfortable ride to Santiago. But it was one leg of the journey behind her. She only knew she had to keep moving forward. She shook away the memory and picture of her father's eyes meeting hers, of the red mixing with the white foam of the waves.

She needed an impossible mission right now. Getting to Moscow was just that.

Luc followed Achaia into the cage after grabbing a morning star.

Fitting, Achaia thought. She turned and paced backwards until she reached her corner. She focused on her breathing, slow and calculated. *I am in control of my breath; I am in control.* She thought through all of Luc's tricks. She had taken detailed mental notes while she studied his fighting style. She pushed that knowledge to the back of her mind, lest she rely too heavily on it. She needed to get out of her head, to know what she knew but rely on her instincts. Her body would tell her what to anticipate, with little cues like the hair on the back of her neck raising, or a heaviness in her gut. She would rely more on those than anything she *thought* she knew.

"Be here now," Achaia whispered under her breath. "If you're for me, don't let him defeat me." Achaia raised her eyes to meet Luc's. His would have been beautiful if they weren't so full of hate- the bluest eyes she'd ever seen, crisp, clear, the definition of blue, and colder than the ice surrounding them. Time seemed to slow. Everything outside of the cage was gone. Achaia took another deep steadying breath and tried to clear her mind. Luc stepped forward. Achaia moved. Every move mirrored by the other, they danced around the cage, neither one striking first. Every passing second added to the tension in the air, bringing them closer to the moment of first blood.

Luc struck out first, but Achaia dodged, faster than he anticipated. Her feet thought for her. Achaia lunged forward, but Luc side stepped and grabbed her from behind. Achaia used every ounce of borrowed strength to flip him over her head, and

onto the floor. Once there, she kicked down hard, and his lip shown bright red with blood.

He got to his feet quicker than humanly possible, and spit the blood from his mouth. But as Achaia looked down, she noticed that she too was bleeding. His sword has slashed her arm. She hadn't felt it. Then it struck her, *she* hadn't felt it. Out of the corner of her eye she looked over to see Amelia coyly holding her arm tightly, but her face was a study in focus. She wouldn't show the pain she now felt on Achaia's behalf.

Achaia took another steadying breath and the dance continued. With her borrowed strength from Noland, and Amelia taking her blows, Achaia felt like she wasn't in the cage alone with Luc; she had an army behind her. Luc vanished before her eyes, but she was ready for his tricks, and turned stabbing into the nothingness behind her just in time to catch him in the gut.

His eyes were wide in surprise, more than anything else. "Two." Achaia said pushing him back, off her dagger. She kept eye contact with Luc, and she watched as he struggled to process what had just happened. "You let me in. You didn't mean to, but you did. And in those moments, I got to *know* you," she said quietly so that only he could hear her.

Luc stumbled, fear, realization and a flash of vulnerability filling his eyes. For a split-second Achaia felt guilty, and sad for the Luc she had seen in the projection room, but she shook it off. Distantly, she could hear the demons booing her. She tried again to focus her mind.

Luc's gaze deepened and shifted until it was full of rage,

and he attacked, savagely. It took every ounce of Achaia's skill to deflect his blows with her dagger. She lashed out with her whip and took his feet out from underneath him, and retreated, to regain her composure. Luc got up to his feet looking absolutely wild, more demon than angel.

Achaia felt fear fight for purchase in her very soul. She knelt down, and sought out the fire within her, knowing it was now or never. A wall of flames shot up surrounding her. She heard the awed gasp from the demons, some of whom may never have seen fire or felt warmth. She unleashed her wings and her whip at the same moment and launched herself into the air. Fire burst forth from her chest, engulfing her. It traveled down her whip as it wrapped around Luc's throat. He was lifted into the air, her whip like a noose around his neck, burning him. But there was no sign of blood from the wound.

Cries of surprise and outrage came from the demons around them, and she was distracted for a moment by the extent of her own fire.

That moment was all it took. Luc grabbed the length of whip between them, gasping for breath, and yanked her down.

"Achaia!" Noland yelled. He was on his feet.

As Achaia was jerked down, Luc thrust his sword up. The only thing Achaia had time to feel was surprise. But pain was written on Noland's face.

"NO!" Her father was at the cage side. "Achaia!" Demons were pulling him back.

Achaia's vision blurred through warm tears.

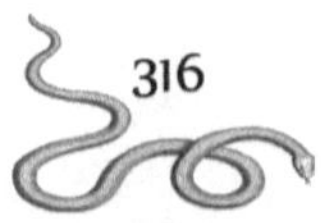

Yellaina reached the airport and boarded the jet. There were already three other Nephilim on board. Olivier's parents were two of them. The third was a young Nephilim maybe her age.

"*Bonjour* Yellaina," Olivier's mother grabbed her in a hug and kissed the top of her head.

"You're coming with me?" Yellaina pulled away and felt tears of relief pour from her eyes.

"You are as good as my daughter, and this Veronica is, too, now."

"We trust Dina," Mr. DuBois said simply. "There is more at work here than Joash is telling us."

"Who is this?" Yellaina asked turning to the young boy with them.

"This is Adisa ben Abdoulaye, from the Cameroon safe house."

"It is a pleasure. My spiritual gift is for tracking. I thought I could be of service in this initiative," Adisa said in a thick accent.

Yellaina smiled at him and they took their seats to buckle up for take off. Yellaina felt a peace and safety around Olivier's parents that she didn't around her own. She hadn't seen or spoken to her mother in years, and her father wanted her to be something she wasn't. The DuBois had always treated her like one of their own whenever they came to visit, even before they knew she and Olivier had been matched. Their presence alone gave her a refreshed sense of hope.

"So how do we go about finding her?" Yellaina turned and asked Mr. DuBois as the plane took off.

"We go back and see if her family knows anything, and we try to track her from there. She can't have made it far with all flights canceled. She'll still be in Chile."

Yellaina nodded. She couldn't think of another way to track her better. On the long quiet flight, Yellaina had plenty of time to put herself in Veronica's shoes. Yellaina wasn't the hugest fan of her father, but she could never imagine killing him. Veronica was so close to hers. What on Earth could have prompted her? Then the thought about how she must be feeling. She was glad she didn't have Emile's gift at that moment. When she did find Veronica, she didn't want to know.

Emile's body was completely numb. The rest of him, however, was on fire. Every nerve in his body had his hair standing on end. The demons were chanting something low and booming. His Demonic was a little rusty, so he didn't know what they were saying, but he was pretty sure it could be loosely translated as "We are horrible, awful, smelly, and creepy. Hear us roar!" Or maybe just "Satan! Satan! Satan!" Either way, Emile didn't care. It wasn't what they were chanting that mattered. What mattered was that his brothers and sisters felt afraid, and angry, and anxious at the sound of it.

Then, it had happened so fast. Luc had yanked Achaia's whip, pulling her down from the air, as he thrusted his sword

up, piercing her abdomen. Emile could see the tip of the sword protruding from her back.

The shock rang through Emile's chest like the chime of a gong. He was frozen, stunned.

"ACHAIA!" Olivier screamed.

Achaia's eyes looked up at Luc wide in surprise, then down at the sword that had skewered her. Her feet hit the floor unsteadily, and she fell to her knees. Luc smiled down at her with an arrogance that seeped through every pore. She breathed out, and Emile felt his own heart stop. When it beat again, it felt like only half of its former self. A dead weight had taken up the other half, tugging it down. Down. Down.

Emile stared at Achaia's face, her chest, waiting, watching to see if she was still breathing. The stadium was silent. Everyone was holding their breath. Then, with the sound like a whispered breeze, Achaia breathed. She took the hilt of the sword that was in her and pulled it out, and in one fluid motion, spun it around in an arc across Luc's chest. A deep gash dripping dark crimson spread across his tunic. Third blood. She'd won.

Emile found himself standing. Noland and Shael had already been on their feet, and Olivier stood with him. They stared.

Against the laws of biology, and everything human, Achaia stood. Luc's face held all of the shock in the world as he grasped at his bleeding chest, but Achaia wasn't looking at him. She was looking at them. No. Not them. *Her*.

With a knot in his stomach, realization dawned on him. How could he have forgotten? Emile turned and saw Amelia, his twin, his heart, lying on the floor, dead.

Emile was in a haze. Seconds passed like hours. He couldn't stop thinking that this was all just a horrible nightmare, that any moment he was going to wake up. If there was a way to rewind time, there had to be—She had just been with them a moment before. They could still undo this, right? She wasn't really gone. She had just been there. She was right here. She was. It had just happened. It wasn't too late...

He pleaded with God, *take it back, undo it. You can fix this…* But Emile already knew, He wouldn't. She was gone.

Olivier felt his heart stop as he watched Luc pull Achaia down and thrust his blade upward as they both fell to the ground. Jude beside him yelled "NO!" and stood to his feet rushing to the cage. Noland's face went white, and he and Olivier looked at each other for a split second of dread. Olivier heard Emile choke a sob and turned to see him hunched down over their sister.

"Amelia?" Olivier whispered, stumbling over and crouching down. He grabbed her face in his hands.
Noland, who had been by his side, looked up to Achaia. Olivier followed his gaze. He couldn't lose them both.

Achaia looked down at the hole in her abdomen, and up at them, her fingers smearing the blood across her shirt, but a spark of flame appeared sealing the wound; the gash had cauterized.

Luc was watching them, Olivier realized, with a grin on

his face. He stepped over to Achaia and grabbed her hand raising her arm as the winner.

The demons gave a halfhearted cheer, but Olivier turned his attention back to his sister. "Come on Amelia wake up!" Emile was on his knees with Amelia's head in his lap.

Noland was pressing on the wound that had appeared in her stomach, burning the flesh back together to stop the bleeding. Shael was watching Achaia, and Jude was running around to meet Achaia at the door of the cage, completely unaware that Amelia was the one really paying the price.

Amelia wasn't waking up. Olivier felt the hot tears pouring down his face. He pounded on her chest, but she didn't move.

"Olivier stop!" Emile pleaded. "She's gone. She's gone. I can feel it." He heard Emile's voice as if from a great distance. Noland took Olivier by his hands grabbing him into a sort of bear hug, Olivier struggled to break free, to wake her up, but Noland was too strong for him. Olivier cried out in anguish. He felt the strain of it in his throat all the way through his chest and into his diaphragm.

Achaia rushed over and fell to her knees sobbing when she saw, what Olivier guessed, she was most afraid of. He couldn't hear anyone else's cries anymore. He couldn't hear their yells, or the demons' sneers. Everything seemed like it was in slow motion, which made it hurt all the worse for someone who was made for speed, to blast through things as quickly as possible. Olivier collapsed in Noland's arms. Noland bore his weight, gracefully. Olivier couldn't feel his legs. All he could feel was a raw burn in his throat, and the urge to be near his sister.

As if sensing this Noland released him, and Oliver fell forward onto his sister. He could smell her perfume, her shampoo, that sisterly scent he had always associated with safety, love, support, frustration, and arguing. "You can't leave me," Olivier sobbed. "How could you leave me?"

Veronica wandered the streets of Santiago until a little after midnight when she found herself hiking up the stone steps to the Castillo Hidalgo gates. The iron gates would have seemed impenetrable or at the very least daunting to an average person, but Veronica with her Nephilim strength, and years of parkour training with her younger brothers had no problem getting up and over them. She could have easily flown, but she didn't want to risk the unwanted attention a pair of bright white wings could possibly attract.

She kept climbing, thinking she would find a nook to hide in to sleep. She found a crevice between two boulders and slipped inside. She stared up at the silhouette of the small cathedral next to her hiding spot and prayed for God to forgive her, to shield and protect her, and to help her forgive herself. Finally, in the quiet and stillness, reality caught up to her, and she wept until she fell asleep.

"It is impossible to go on as you were before,
so you must go on as you never have."
-Cheryl Strayed

Achaia couldn't see Amelia for the crowd that had gathered around her. She yanked her arm out of Luc's grasp to run to her. They were both covered in blood so she slipped out of his grasp easily. Luc grabbed her arm, again, and pulled her toward him. "An admirable use of your resources," he laughed, glancing over toward Amelia.

Achaia yanked her arm back again, disgusted and ran toward the door of the cage. Her father and Jude were there.

"Achaia!" She wasn't sure who had spoken. Both of them

were checking her over, confused and amazed, that though she was covered in blood, her wounds were healed and closed.

"What?" Jude mumbled, checking her abdomen that should have been torn apart.

"Move!" Achaia said, pulling away from them to run to Amelia. They followed her, stunned. Noland knelt behind Olivier who was slumped, and sobbing. Emile looked like a ghost, staring down, all the color gone from his face. Achaia made her way forward tentatively. She had to step around them before she could see Amelia, lying, lifeless on the ice floor.

Achaia fell to her knees. She couldn't bring herself to speak. She looked again at the faces of her friends. Their pain, their agony, was her fault. She had caused this.

"Come," her father said behind them. "It's time to go. We cannot linger. Grab her. Let's go."

"He's right," Emile said, taking Amelia by the shoulders and hefting her over his own.

Olivier struggled to breathe, and he wiped his face and tried to stand. He was off balance. Noland clapped a supportive hand on his shoulder, and Olivier grabbed it in thanks.

"Oh, I don't think so," Luc said strolling over.

Achaia stood glaring at him. "What?"

"Honey, you cheated," he said casually. "See, that should be you, I would have won. Therefore, you forfeit, and I win. Cheaters never prosper."

"Which is why you've done so well for yourself," she retorted, bitingly.

Her father stiffened next to her. "She didn't cheat. She

didn't use any abilities in addition to her own, and she drew the third blood first. She won. Amelia's gift was her own doing, not Achaia's."

Achaia felt like she'd been punched in the stomach. Though her father was saying that Amelia's death was her own doing, Achaia knew the truth, she felt it in her bones; Amelia's death was her fault.

"We could take a vote and see who wins? You live in America now, right? Isn't that how democracy works?"

Shael stiffened. "You know she won."

"I know that if that little bitch wasn't sitting in the stands, I would have. It wasn't her duel. It was ours, and she paid her price for interfering. But I won." Luc's voice was knife sharp.

"Did you just call my sister a bitch?" Olivier said stepping forward. And before anyone could have seen him, let alone stopped him, he decked Lucifer across the face so hard it knocked him off his feet.

The shouts and roars shook Achaia's chest like thunder, and the demons broke on them like a typhoon.

"Go!" Her dad yelled, gesturing for them to make for the tunnel.

Achaia lost track of Luc in the throng, but she turned and ran for the nearest tunnel. Emile was ahead of her carrying Amelia over his left arm as he struggled to fight with his right. Noland was at his side, defending his blind spot. Olivier was right behind her, cussing under his breath. Jude came up next to her, and yelled at the group, "This way!" Noland and Emile turned to follow him down a small service tunnel. Achaia turned to find her father, but he hadn't followed. He had hung back to fight the horde and give them a running start. "Dad!" she called.

Shael turned and met her eyes, and in that moment of distraction, was run through with a spear.

Emile felt a stab in his chest and heard the blood curling scream before he turned to look and see what had happened.

Noland was a step ahead of him, already running toward Achaia, who was charging the demons pursuing them.

Then he saw him, Shael. His face was drained of blood, and his eyes were glued to Achaia, a sort of apology in them, and Emile could feel Shael's *realization.* Emile wanted to throw up. He was filled with the knowledge that Shael was never going to see his daughter get married, or meet his grandchildren. He was filled with fear that she wasn't going to make it out, and guilt and anger that he wasn't going to be able to help her escape. He felt humiliated and stupid for allowing himself to be distracted. Then he felt tired. Tired of fighting a war that never ended. Tired of trying to choose a side, when neither side wanted him…

Noland's arms encircled Achaia and lifted her back off her feet. She kicked and screamed "DAD!" but Noland dragged her back toward the tunnel.

"We have to go. I'm so sorry," Noland was saying.

Emile's eyes were glued on Shael's. He felt peace, knowing that Achaia was in good hands. He had confidence in Noland, and it gave him peace that he was going to watch over his daughter.

Then, slowly, as though his last fight was to keep his eyes open to see his daughter to safety, they closed, and he fell.

"DADDY!" Achaia's cries rang through Emile's chest, the sound itself sounding like it was tearing her throat to shreds.

Emile turned and followed as Noland carried Achaia after Jude. Olivier took up the rear, covering them. The tunnel was too narrow for a mass pursuit, and they made it to a room. They hurried inside, and Jude slammed the door shut behind them. Jude and Olivier threw themselves against it to keep it closed against the onslaught of demons.

"How do we get out of here?" Jude yelled.

Emile felt the exhaustion wash over him like a thick fog. "We have hope."

Jude looked around the room at them all as if nothing more impossible had ever been suggested.

"And how do we do that?" Olivier asked, his voice dead.

Noland set Achaia back on her feet, and held her face against his chest while she punched at him, and sobbed.

He looked over her head at the rest of the group. Olivier and Emile both looked like parts of their own souls had died. Jude looked panicked and confused. Amelia…

"Amelia would be super annoyed with you for even asking that," Noland dared to say, looking at Olivier. "Sheer force of will and determination, that's how." Noland hugged Achaia to his chest as she stopped pounding on him, and just wept.

"The knowledge that this doesn't end here, now, like this. The knowledge that ours is the victory, somehow, someday. Every moment and every breath moves us closer to that hour. *This* is not the end. This is the bloody middle, but a day of victory is coming when there will be no more bloodshed, no more death, no more pain," Noland looked down at Achaia's face, "no more tears." He wiped her cheek with his finger. "That day is the Lord's, and we are his vessels. We are His hands, His sword. We will fight again, and we will win. Those demons," he pointed to the door, his hand wet with Achaia's tears, "will cower in our midst. Today, we just need to keep going."

"Where do we even go?" Olivier asked, looking a little bit more on board.

Noland only thought for a moment. "Bale's. we need medical attention and protection from the council. He can give us both."

Emile nodded. "We are with you."

Jude nodded like he had no clue what was going on, but anything was better than this. "What's Bale's?"

Achaia was silent against his chest.

Olivier grabbed hold of Jude's shoulder to try and lead him. He nodded at Noland that he was ready to try.

"We are free from this place, and the dark holds no power over us," Noland said, and the room faded away.

It was early morning when Yellaina and the others landed

in Santiago. They hired a car to take them to the safe house. Yellaina stood before the door for a moment to brace herself before knocking. She wasn't really sure what to expect inside. It was Vito who answered the door.

"You're back." His voice was deadpan. Yellaina had never heard him speak with so little animation. She wasn't sure if he was happy she was there, or if he wanted her to leave immediately.

Yellaina asked if it was alright for them to come inside, in Chilean Spanish, which she hoped would be perceived as comforting. Vito just shrugged. His brother was sitting on the sofa with their mother, Alexandra. Vito joined them, sitting on his mother's right to flank her. She held each of her son's hands, and looked so stricken, Yellaina felt guilty for intruding; this woman had shown her nothing but kindness.

"I am so sorry to have to come at such a time." She nodded solemnly as she sat across from them. Adisa joined her, but the DuBois remained standing just inside the room. "But I have to ask, do you know why Veronica would slay her father?"

Vidal stood and made an angry wave of his arm, and mumbled some rapid insults toward his sister and left the room.

"Forgive him, he is hurting," Alexandra said, sounding exhausted. She had dark circles under her eyes, and her skin had lost some of its former radiance.

Yellaina nodded, "I—" she was about to say that she could understand, but could she really? She didn't want to sound pompous or disrespectful. The truth was, she couldn't even begin to imagine what they were going through, let alone understand it. She decided not to finish and gave an apologetic smile instead that she hoped conveyed that she didn't take offense.

"I don't know how much we can help you. I would say that Ronnie would never do such a thing, but she has. Her brothers saw her do it. I can't—" Alexandra choked, trying to hold back a sob. Vito clung to her hand, and whispered in her ear. She gave him a small smile and squeezed his hand back. "Martinus has—" she took a deep steadying breath, "had his shortcomings. It was his idea to join Shael and Lucifer in the rebellion… But I honestly don't know why the council came after him. They won't tell me anything." She directed a sharp look at the DuBois standing on the periphery of the room.

Yellaina went on, "Do you know where Veronica would have gone? Did she have a place she was fond of?"

Alexandra thought for only a moment, then shook her head in frustration. "No. She lived in her forge. That was her refuge. If she wasn't there, she was here or on the beach. She never went anywhere else." Tears began to overflow and roll down her cheeks. "She left her tools—" Alexandra sobbed.

Vito looked like he didn't quite know what to make of this. Yellaina supposed he was still in shock. While his brother had moved on to anger in the grieving process, Yellaina suspected that Vito still hadn't processed that his father was actually dead, and his sister was gone, perhaps forever. "She'll be back. She wouldn't leave without her tools, right?"

Alexandra gripped his hand tighter, and Yellaina looked at him with all the pity she possessed. When it finally hit him, it would hit him hard, she knew.

"*Estúpido*," Vidal said coming back into the room. "She

isn't coming back. She knows better. If she shows her face here, I'll—"

"*Silencio!*" Alexandra said looking devastated and exhausted. "Go." She waved at the boys.

Vidal huffed and went back down the stairs, but Vito looked around the room at each of them, and decided to stay.

"They are handling this so differently, and I am too..." Alexandra sighed. "The truth is, I don't know what my husband was up to. As far as I knew he and Veronica made the weapons for the council and the council would distribute them to safe houses. We worked with and for the council..." She shrugged, obviously at a complete loss. "And I have no idea what would make Ronnie... why she would... I just can't believe it." Alexandria shook her head. "They took his body for cremation at the valley of martyrs. So, he is still getting an honorable burial. The council says they just wanted to talk to him, and question him about something, but I don't know what." She looked up at the DuBois. "Do you? Can you tell me why this awful thing has happened to my family?"

It was Mrs. DuBois who finally stepped into the room. Her accent was thickly French as she knelt in front of Alexandra, "As a wife, and as a mother I grieve for you. I wish I could give you answers and tell you why, but I don't have answers for your true questions. All I have is a heart that breaks for yours."

Alexandra sat in silence, and for a moment that felt like forever to Yellaina. The two women just stared at each other.

"I am sorry to ask this, but do you have anything of Veronica's that we could take to try and track her?"

"I will get her tools! She will want them when you find her," Vito said, happy to have a purpose, a job. He got up hastily and left.

"If you find her," Alexandra said, still staring at Mrs. DuBois. "You tell her a mother always loves. *Always.*"

Mrs. DuBois nodded, and grasped Alexandra's hands and gave them a slight squeeze. "It will be done."

"And if she will not come home to me," Alexandra took a shaky breath, fighting back more tears, "you love her for me."

Tears filled Mrs. DuBois eyes now, "It will be done."

18

Beautiful Ends

"Her absence is like the sky,
spread over everything."
-C.S. Lewis

Achaia looked up from Noland's chest and found that they were in the library in the Russian Safe House. Bale looked up from his chair before the fireplace, and dropped his book.

"You did it!" His eyes found Amelia slumped over Emile's shoulder. Then his eyes met Emile's, red rimmed, and dry from crying. Achaia watched the dawn of realization on his face, and then acceptance. He swallowed hard, once. "May I?" he asked, opening his arms to Emile. Emile hesitated before slowly lowering his sister's body into Bale's strong arms. The moment he was no longer touching her, he collapsed into wailing sobs. Achaia ran out of the room into the hall and vomited.

Bale stopped at the door, looked down at the puddle of puke on the priceless rug lining the hallway, then back up at Achaia. "Healer, now," he said gently.

Achaia nodded and stood. She remembered her way, and walked in, looking for the strict old lady who had tended to her wounds after she had leapt out of the window and trudged headfirst into the bombings on the city. Noland had been blown up to save her that day. Achaia was sensing a theme. Where she was concerned, people were hurt, if not killed. She was the angel of death, and she took it everywhere she went, to her enemies and loved ones alike. Noland had only almost died. Had he not been gifted with fire, he would have been reduced to ashes. Amelia was dead, her father—Achaia stopped. She couldn't breathe.

"You again," the old woman said in a thick Russian accent, looking as displeased with her as Achaia was with herself.

Achaia looked at her apologetically, as if she owed her a personal apology for existing. Achaia tried to remember her name- Inessa. The old woman, always hard, always stern, softened. Her eyes gave her a once over, but settled on her face. "I can't fix this," Inessa said gesturing to her own heart, "but I fix this." She gestured to Achaia's person. "First a hot bath. You go undress. I'll get you tea."

Achaia didn't have it in her to tell her she didn't really like tea. She didn't deserve to get what she liked. She would take what she was given. She followed her directions and stripped in one of the small bathrooms off of the healer's main room. She ran the

334

water as hot as she could stand it, and sank in. Her skin burned where it was split with cold. She absorbed the pain, a reminder that she was alive, whereas her father—Achaia stopped herself. She couldn't think. She could only deal with right now. Inessa came in with a tea tray, full of pastries and Russian tea, and set it on a small table next to the tub.

Achaia grabbed the tea cup and sipped, then started tearing apart a sort of twisted knot of a pastry with maybe cinnamon in it? She ate and drank without tasting as the healer added all manner of oils and dried herbs and flowers to her bath water.

"I want you to eat all of it," Inessa said, regaining her stern tone, "and then breakfast, lunch and dinner too. You are half gone. A skeleton girl." Her voice was hard, but there was a gentleness behind her eyes that scared Achaia. She had been bad off before without a lick of sympathy from this woman. To have her baby her now couldn't be a good sign. Achaia knew she didn't deserve pity. It should be saved for anyone who found themselves near her. She was cursed.

Inessa left the room, leaving a fluffy white towel on the chest by the door. Once she was gone, and Achaia knew she was alone, something in her snapped. It was like the floodgates of her lungs and eyes opened at the same time and she wailed into her hands, hardly able to keep breathing. She wept until she ran out of tears and it became more of a hyperventilating rather than crying, until she was totally exhausted, and the bath water turned cold.

She curled in on herself, tucking her knees up to her face,

and she didn't care that she drooled on them, or that her nose was running and she didn't have a tissue. She couldn't sob hard enough to expel her demons. They were a part of her now.

Noland looked at Jude. He was worse for wear. He wasn't sure if it was from being held in such absolute cold for so long, or if he had been tortured, but he definitely needed to see a healer. They all did. Emile and Olivier had followed Bale back to his office after they had deposited Amelia's body into her old bed.

Bale was going to call Emile's parents and tell them the news, and he thought it would be good for the boys to be available for their parents to speak with after.

"Follow me," Noland said, and Jude did. After a moment, Noland tried for some conversation, "So, you're Luc's son?"

Jude rolled his eyes, "I'd rather not own up to that at the moment."

Noland nodded, but took it as a confirmation.

"And you're," Jude paused, looking awkward, "Achaia's—"

"Mate, boyfriend, all of the above."

"Oh," Jude nodded.

They walked on in silence, Noland feeling a little bugged. "She didn't mention me?"

"It just never really came up what with all the torture and trying to survive and stuff, you know… I'm sure she didn't mean anything by it," Jude said half encouragingly, but in a way that still made it feel like a jab.

"I can imagine," Noland said, not taking the bait. "So, what about you? Did he torture you? Are you okay?"

Jude stopped, and looked at him stunned. "You care?" he asked a little hopeful, a little sarcastic.

"Yeah, I do. That's why I am taking you to be looked over by a healer," Noland said as though it were the most simple and obvious thing in the world. "Why wouldn't I?"

"Sorry," Jude said, looking like he thought about meaning it. "I've just never really gotten that impression from Nephilim."

"Achaia is a Nephilim--"

"Yeah, but she's like me, half human. We're different."

Noland tried not to feel irked, but he failed. "This is it," he said, opening the door.

"Ah, finally," the healer said ushering them into the room. "Strip in there, and take baths," she said gesturing to two small rooms to their right. "Your baths are ready." She turned to Noland as Jude left. "Where are the other four?"

"Four?" Noland asked, before it dawned on him. "Oh, Yellaina isn't with us, Emile and Olivier are with Bale and Amelia is—" Noland choked. He couldn't bring himself to say it out loud, not yet. The healer nodded in understanding and tried her best to mask her surprise. Nephilim didn't die every day. Noland knew that better than most.

"And Shael ben Yahweh?" she asked, trying to mask her contempt, like so many other Nephilim who despised or mistrusted him.

"He... He's," Noland felt a hard lump form in his throat, and his eyes burned as they blurred with tears. It was only slightly less painful than when he had lost his own father. Noland had thought he'd get to have a dad again, in a way- a father in law. But it looked as if Achaia and Noland were matched in more ways than one now.

She nodded again in shock and understanding. "Today has been a dark day."

Noland nodded, a tear escaping down his cheek.

"Baths help," she said pointing him sternly toward the bathroom.

Bale sat at his desk, feeling heavy. He looked at the two boys sitting across from him, as if the universe were pressing on their shoulders, pushing them down. Down. Down. He hit the button to use the speaker on the phone and dialed their father's number.

He picked up after the fourth ring, "Hello?"

"Dad?" Emile said, with all the voice he could muster.

"Emile? What's wrong?" His father sounded worried. Bale swallowed, and gestured to Emile that he needed say the words.

"Mr. DuBois, this is Bale ben Yahweh. Emile and Olivier are here, safe with me. However, I am so sorry. Amelia was slain in battle on a rescue mission."

"What rescue mission? She wasn't assigned a rescue mission. She's too young to go on a rescue mission. She was assigned to be here in Chile."

"You're in Chile?" Emile asked.

"Where's my daughter?" He spoke over Emile.

Bale took a deep breath. "The rescue mission wasn't council sanctioned. Amelia's body is here with us, at the Russian safe house. We will bring her to the valley of martyrs as soon as you pick a date, to be sent off."

"Is that what we do when Nephilim die? Is that what they did with Noland's parents?" Olivier asked, curiously.

Their mother was talking in the background asking what had happened. Bale assumed their father was putting the phone on speaker, but he knew the moment he conveyed the message, because he heard her sobs.

"My Amelia!"

"Mom!" Olivier shouted.

"Olivier? *Mon petit chu*?" Her voice was shaky, but clear.

"Mom," Olivier apparently had nothing else to say, but his voice seemed to soothe the woman on the other end of the phone.

"Olivier, Emile, you are alright?" she asked.

"*Oui, c'est vrai*," Emile said, leaning forward.

"Would you like to speak with your husband and pick a date for the burial and call me back? We will meet you in the valley."

She sniffed. "Yes, I will speak with him. He has gone off to walk. But I will call you back. Take care of my boys."

"It will be done," Bale said, nodding though she couldn't see him.

She hung up the phone, and Bale looked across at Emile

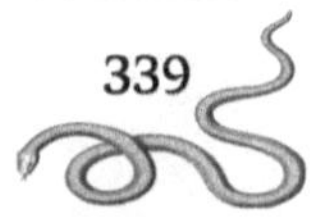

and Olivier. "You both should go to the healer to be looked over."

"Why?" Olivier asked. "It's not like she can fix what we need her to…"

Emile elbowed him lightly in the arm, and gestured for him to come along.

"Emile," Bale said, standing. Emile paused in the doorway. "There's something I have to do. The staff will alert you if your mother calls back." Emile nodded knowingly and left.

Yellaina sat inside with Alexandra as Mr. DuBois took his phone call outside. A moment later they all heard his raised angry voice, and Mrs. DuBois went outside to check on him. Yellaina felt emotionally exhausted from the last couple of days and waited anxiously to know what was going on. She wondered if Joash had found out what they were really doing here. But she couldn't imagine Dina giving anything away.

Mrs. DuBois came back in alone, holding Mr. DuBois' phone in a limp hand. Her eyes immediately sought out Yellaina's and she let out a sob. Panic filled Yellaina's chest, and she stood abruptly to her feet, staring into Mrs. DuBois' stricken face. "Olivier?"

Mrs. DuBois shook her head, and tried to suck in a breath. "My Amelia is dead." Yellaina felt her legs go numb as they stopped bearing her weight, and she began to fall. Alexandra caught her and guided her back down next to her on the sofa. Then she stood and crossed the room quickly to wrap Mrs.

DuBois in a tight embrace.

Yellaina's head was spinning. How was this possible? When? What had happened? She needed to know more information. She needed answers… Yellaina stood, slowly, and went outside taking out her own phone.

It rang and rang until it went to voicemail, "Noland? Please call me back as soon as you get this. What happened? It can't—It can't be true…"

Yellaina hung up the phone when Mr. DuBois rounded the tree line, coming back to the house.

"Yellaina," he said sympathetically, rushing up to her and wrapping her in a fatherly embrace.

"I'm so sorry," Yellaina mumbled into his chest. "I wish there was something I could do." Saying the words aloud made Yellaina feel the weight of helplessness to *do* anything.

"There's something we can do," he said, and as she stood back she saw the determination in his face.

"What's that?" Yellaina asked, puzzled.

"I may have lost my daughter, but we are going to find Alexandra's."

Bale stood in a room of white, surrounded by vapor and light. He rocked back and forth on his heels, waiting. Then, the clouds before him parted, and there, porcelain skin, and the bluest eyes in Heaven with hair as black as a raven's wings, she stood. Bale smiled, and ran forward, taking her face in his hands.

"Welcome home, Amelia. Welcome home."

Veronia had cleaned herself up to almost presentable in the bar bathroom. The place was crawling with servicemen. Her goal was to find and flirt with one who could maybe sneak her onto the base, for a romantic evening tour, at which point she would disappear and sneak into the cargo bay of a plane to take her anywhere but here, but hopefully closer to Moscow. She just needed to get onto the right continent, if possible. She could figure out the rest from there.

She emerged from the bathroom trying to look more confident than she felt, and slid into a seat at the bar, next to a group of guys who looked a little older than her. They looked at each other and smiled. She smiled back.

"Veronica?"

Veronica froze at the sound of her name, and braced herself before she turned around. Yellaina stood, with three others, looking drawn and tired.

"Yellaina?" Veronica was stunned. "How did you find me?"

"This is Adisa. He's a tracker," Yellaina said flatly. "And these are Emile's parents."

Veronica instantly felt like she wanted to vomit. When she had imagined meeting her mate's parents, it hadn't included her flirting with a bar-full of other men. She straightened herself up, none the less, and met the situation head on just like her

342

father had taught her—she pushed back the rest of the thought.

"Not how I imagined meeting you. I apologize." She stepped forward offering them each her hand. They looked grave. Apparently her first impression was as bad as she feared.

"Veronica, will you please come with us outside. There is something we need to tell you."

Veronica stiffened. For a second it occurred to her that this could be a trap. If she took the bait would there be a patrol of council members waiting outside? Emile's parents were council members, but she didn't think Yellaina would do that to her. But after what she'd done…

"Sure," she said hesitantly, and followed them out of the bar. It was much quieter outside.

"Veronica, several terrible things have happened."

"I know," Veronica said dropping her eyes to her feet.

"You don't, though," Yellaina said gently. "I am sorry about your father, and we would love to hear your side of that story, but something else has happened as well."

Veronica looked up, worried. Emile's parents were here, but not Emile… "Not Emile—"

"No." It was his mother who spoke, looking at her with compassion. She hoped she could tell that Veronica truly and deeply cared about her son, not the men at the bar.

"It's Amelia," Yellaina said, fighting for her full strength of voice. "She's gone."

"Gone?" Veronica said, unable to understand, gone from Chile? From the council?

"She died trying to rescue Achaia." Yellaina sniffed her

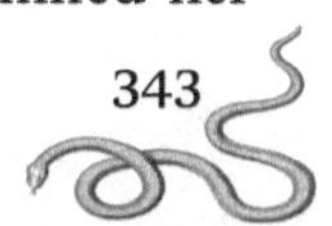

nose, and only then did Veronica realize that three of the four of them had been crying.

"Emile must be devastated. And you must be also," she said looking to each of them in turn. "Where is Emile? Is he alright?"

"He is as well as the circumstances will allow," his father stated.

"We have set a date for her cremation in the valley of martyrs. She will go up with your father," Emile's mother said.

Veronica gulped back tears at the thought of her father's ashes rising to the heavens, because of her. "The council isn't looking for you. They have other concerns weighing on their minds. Will you please come with us?" Yellaina's eyes were pleading.

"Where? I can't go home." Veronica shook her head vehemently.

Yellaina nodded in understanding, "We are going to the Russian Safe House."

"That's where I was trying to go," Veronica admitted in way of accepting the offer.

"It's a long flight. I want to hear your side of the story." Yellaina offered her arm, and Veronica took it, laying her head on the girl's shoulder, and for the first time she thought, this is what it would be like to have a sister. Then it hit her, hard. The only sister she would ever possibly have had, just died.

Emile sat on the roof of the safe house, looking over Moscow. The sun was out and warm on his skin. He found himself seeking solitude, in an attempt to process through his own feelings, instead of having to mourn for everyone else, and himself, all at once. It was practical, but it was lonely having to isolate himself just to be able to control the flood of grief. He just wanted the option of being numb.

The hum and bustle of the city was a surprisingly comforting white noise, a reminder that life was going on, moving forward. Toward what, he didn't know. He heard the creak of the metal roof door opening, and turned to see who had found his hiding spot.

"Noland said I would find you up here," Veronica said, her honey golden skin catching the sun, and doing it justice.

"You're here!" Emile stood and closed the distance between them, hugging her tightly.

He could feel her relief, comfort, worry, guilt, sorrow… He didn't have to ask how she was. He already knew.

"I'm so sorry about Amelia," she said into his shoulder. She squeezed him harder, trying to comfort him.

"I'm sorry about your father," Emile said kissing the top of her head.

Veronica nodded against him before lifting her head to look at him. He could see that familiar red rim around her eyes, that all his friends sported these days. Everyone was dealing with the losses in their own way, but all of them cried, and all of them lost sleep. While some wanted solitude, others craved companionship.

"How did you get here?" Emile asked, leading her over to where he had sat on the edge of the building. The sun was sinking in the sky, and it would set soon. The late afternoon golden glow sparked off of Veronica's piercings and the beads she wore in her hair.

"Yellaina and your parents tracked me down, and brought me here. I think they are starting to compile forces."

"Forces?" Emile racked his brain trying to remember if he should know something about this, but came up empty.

"Yellaina said that she has an ally in the council who has advised her to unify the outliers. They are forming a sort of recruitment committee."

"So, you've been recruited?"

"Well, I definitely can't go home." Emile felt his own stomach sink. "And I figured you'd be here, so I—"

"Where you go, I will go, and where you stay, I will stay." Emile smiled.

"Your people will be my people and your God my God. Where you die I will die, and there will I be buried. May the LORD deal with me, be it ever so severely if even death separates you and me." Veronica leaned against his shoulder.

"You've read the human scriptures?" he asked, impressed.

"There's something beautiful in how they struggle and fail, and find one another; and how they choose Him over and over again." Her voice became distant and a little scared.

"What is it?" Emile asked, worried.

"Where was He?" Veronica asked.

Emile let the question sit between them. The silence

lingered as the sun lowered into a blistered orange. "I can understand it, you know. Why my father did what he did. Not that I would have done the same, but I can see where he was coming from…"

Emile nodded, and took her hand in his.

"He was afraid they would torture him. He wanted to die quickly and mercifully. He begged me, and so I promised, but I didn't think the day would actually come," Veronica swallowed, choking back tears, "not so soon."

Emile rubbed his thumb back and forth along her hand, but didn't interrupt. She needed to get this all off her chest. All of it.

"I am angry at him for making me promise. I am angry at God for not intervening. Where was He when I needed Him? Where is He now?"

Emile sighed, not only understanding from his own experience, but able to feel the exact depth of her despair. There was a beauty in that moment that he hadn't really anticipated.

"Maybe God was there, in that moment before you," Emile said in an almost whisper.

"What do you mean?" Veronica looked up at him, not in anger but curiosity.

"He knew what was coming. And maybe for whatever reason, it needed to happen. But, He knew you were going to walk this path." Emile smiled. "You know at first glance, we don't make much sense. You and Noland look like a better match. But God knows everything, and He knew what was going to happen. He knew you were going to have to walk through this hard thing.

Maybe He wanted you to have someone who would know *exactly* how it feels and who would be able to truly understand you. He didn't want you to feel alone. He is still taking care of you, even now. He's always been planning on taking care of you."

Veronica looked into Emile's eyes as if she was looking through him to God himself, and understanding for the first time, how great and unfathomable His love was. Through the pain, through the tears, through the guilt and through the anger, He was never going to leave. He had been there all the while...

"I don't want to try to explain it to people. I don't want to have to explain it to myself." Veronica's eyes were swimming with tears.

Emile let go of her hand and cupped her cheek. The tears ran down her face like tiny rivers, and he let them. There was something cleansing about letting them flow. He knew better than anyone the release that could be found in a good cry. Slowly, gently, he leaned closer. Then Veronica met him, tenderly meeting his lips with hers. It wasn't the deep passionate kind of kiss many people dreamed of, but the determined trusting kind of companionship Emile always had.

19

The Valley of Martyrs

"The smoke of the incense,
together with the prayers of the saints,
went up before God from the angels hand."
-Revelation 8:4

Achaia stood on the precipice, looking down into the valley of martyrs. There were two pyres set up, one for Martinus, and one for Amelia.

From what Noland had told her, Achaia owed her escape from Luc to both of them. Martinus wasn't perfect. He had designed her prison, and betrayed the council, but at the same time, he had helped her father rescue her. He was a loving father. Achaia realized just how muddy grey could be, and that things were never really black and white. When push came to shove, she had chosen God over Lucifer… But, could God want her? Abomination that she was… Still, she had made Him a promise. *She* had made it out alive.

Achaia watched the pyres catch fire and burn, the smoke rising to heaven in billows. After the last few days, Noland didn't question Achaia when she said she hadn't wanted to go down to the service, that she would rather watch from a distance. They hadn't ever gotten the chance to talk about what all Achaia had experienced, what all she had thought; about herself, about Luc- how turned around and confused she had gotten, and how quickly it had happened. Achaia had always hoped her mind was stronger than that, that she was smarter than that. She knew better than to fall for Luc's tricks. And yet, she had taken one look into his vulnerability and questioned whether or not she'd been wrong about him all along.

She wasn't as strong as she thought. She wasn't as smart as she hoped, and she wasn't as ready as she needed to be.

"Hey," a low comforting voice said coming up behind her.

"Hey," Achaia said without turning around, still staring at the twin flames.

"Don't beat yourself up." Jude said, nudging her gently with his elbow. "My dad's a douche."

"I just feel like, I—"

"Older, wiser, and—well, maybe not mightier, than you, have been defeated by him before. He's really good at being bad."

Achaia nodded silently, hearing the truth in his words, without it really hitting home.

"You ready?"

Achaia finally looked over at Jude and saw that he had his bag slung over his shoulder, and hers in his hand. He held it out to her. Achaia looked back down at the crowd of people mourning below. Somewhere among them, Noland was comforting people who let him, thinking that she would be waiting for him when he came back. Would he hate her when she wasn't? Would he be angry? Scared? Hurt? She didn't want to hurt him. But she didn't want to hurt anymore, either. And, that's what it would be to stay.

It killed her every time she saw the red outline around Olivier and Emile's eyes. She couldn't face their parents. She wouldn't blame Yellaina if she hated her for taking away her best friend. Noland would be loyal to her because he had to be. He didn't have a choice. But if she removed herself, and that burden, he'd be free.

She was a plague to them. Leaving was the best thing she could do. So what, if they were angry at her… Anger was better than dead. "Yeah, I'm ready." She took her bag out of his grip and slung it over her shoulder.

"So, where to?" he asked, as they started walking away from the cliff, the ascending smoke following them.

"Nowhere cold," Achaia said, a shiver going down her spine.

"Then, let's chase the sun, shall we?"

Book Discussion Questions

1. The Nephilim have no idea what happens to them if they should die. What do you think happens when this life is over? Do you think how we spend this life makes a difference after? Why or why not?

2. Dina reveals that the whole council isn't currupt, only some of its most prominent figures. Why do you think this makes the whole council look bad? What do you think they should do about it?

3. Yellaina almost follows Noland into exile out of loyalty, before Dina stops her. Do you think this have been a mistake on her part? Explain.

4. Olivier feels isolated and unimportant when he hand his friends are separated. Why do you think the isolation affected him that way?

5. Noland was torn between being worried about Achaia and trusting that she was strong enough to fight for herself. Would you have been more worried, or more trusting if you were in his shoes? Why?

6. Dina explains to Yellaina that wars aren't only won by warriors. Why do you think making good use of our words might be more important than combat when handling conflicts?

7. Martinus would rather take his chances perishing than face the consequences of his actions. How do you think this affected those who cared about him? How do you think this decision will affect Veronica in the future? What about Vito and Vidal?

8. Shael is afraid he wasted time he could have been training Achaia by lying to her. Do you think it was right for Shael to keep the spiritual world a secret from her? Why or why not?

9. Emile speculates that he and Veronica were matched so that she would have the support she needed as she processes her guilt and grief. Have you ever felt like you met the right person at just the right time in your life? Who was it, and what did they provide?

10. Achaia finds herself questioning whether Luc is really all that evil, or simply misunderstood. Have you ever been drawn to someone you weren't sure was good for you? Why do you think it is sometimes hard to tell?

Brace Yourselves!
The story continues in

For a bonus short story that takes place immediately following Penance

Visit https://mailchi.mp/332c65b56284/pqu2c3r8f4

About the Author

PHOTO CREDIT C LEIGH PHOTOGRAPHY

Brandy Ange is the YA author of The Kingdom Come Series. With a BA in Bible, her fiction explores age old mysteries of the spiritual world, and mortal world alike. She currently resides on the barrier islands of North Carolina where she mentors at risk youth. For more information or to contact the author you can visit her website brandyange.me

Instagram: @vagabee

Twitter: @vagabee

Facebook:https://www.facebook.com/TheKingdomComeSeries/

YouTube: Brandy Ange

Goodreads: Author Brandy Ange

To interact with the series in a unique way and get access to all the bonus content available become a patron.

Patreon: https://www.patreon.com/brandyange

If you Liked the Book:

Please consider leaving a review on Amazon and Goodreads!

Thank you!

Notes from the Author

The Brooklyn Farmacy and Soda Fountain is a real place! It is one of my favorite spots in Brooklyn and I highly suggest you all try it out if you're ever in the neighborhood.

Brooklyn Farmacy
513 Henry Street
Brooklyn New York 11231

http://www.brooklynfarmacyandsodafountain.com/

Rapha House is an organization that I have admired and supported for years. They serve an important purpose in our world today, helping those who often cannot help themselves. For more details, and to see where a portion of the proceeds of this book have gone, visit their website.

https://rapha.org/